Awkward pauses

There was a bit of interference, and a short exchange, as the receiver was handed over. Then Eli said, "You are missing out on some *serious* apple crumble right now."

"I got dragged to a hot-dog party," I said.

A pause. "Really."

"Yeah." I turned around, shutting the phone book. "Apparently, they are a very important rite of passage. So I figured I should check it out, for my quest and all."

"Right," he said.

For a moment, neither of us said anything, and I realized that it was the first time in a long while that I'd felt nervous or uncomfortable around Eli. All those crazy nights, doing so many crazy things. And yet this, a simple phone conversation, was hard.

along *for the* ride

a novel by

Sarah Dessen

speak
An Imprint of Penguin Group (USA) Inc.

SPEAK
Published by the Penguin Group
Penguin Group (USA) Inc., 345 Hudson Street, New York, New York 10014, U.S.A.
Penguin Group (Canada), 90 Eglinton Avenue East, Suite 700, Toronto, Ontario, Canada M4P 2Y3
(a division of Pearson Penguin Canada Inc.)
Penguin Books Ltd, 80 Strand, London WC2R 0RL, England
Penguin Ireland, 25 St Stephen's Green, Dublin 2, Ireland (a division of Penguin Books Ltd)
Penguin Group (Australia), 250 Camberwell Road, Camberwell, Victoria 3124, Australia
(a division of Pearson Australia Group Pty Ltd)
Penguin Books India Pvt Ltd, 11 Community Centre, Panchsheel Park, New Delhi - 110 017, India
Penguin Group (NZ), 67 Apollo Drive, Rosedale, North Shore 0632, New Zealand
(a division of Pearson New Zealand Ltd.)
Penguin Books (South Africa) (Pty) Ltd, 24 Sturdee Avenue,
Rosebank, Johannesburg 2196, South Africa

Registered Offices: Penguin Books Ltd, 80 Strand, London WC2R 0RL, England

First published in the United States of America by Viking,
a member of Penguin Group (USA) Inc., 2009
Published by Speak, an imprint of Penguin Group (USA) Inc., 2011

1 3 5 7 9 10 8 6 4 2

LIBRARY OF CONGRESS CATALOGING-IN-PUBLICATION DATA IS AVAILABLE

Speak ISBN 978-0-14-241556-6

This is a work of fiction. Names, characters, places, and incidents either are the product
of the author's imagination or are used fictitiously, and any resemblance to actual persons,
living or dead, businesses, companies, events, or locales is entirely coincidental.

Printed in the United States of America
Set in Berling
Book design by Nancy Brennan

For my mother, Cynthia Dessen, for helping me to learn almost everything I know about being a girl

and my daughter, Sasha Clementine, who is teaching me the rest

WRITING A BOOK is never easy, and sometimes you need a little help. For this novel and so many others, I am incredibly lucky to have had the wisdom and guidance of Leigh Feldman and Regina Hayes. Barbara Sheldon, Janet Marks, and my parents, Alan and Cynthia Dessen, provided the moral support any crazy writer needs, especially postpartum. And, as always, I am thankful for my husband, Jay, for making me laugh, helping me remember, and teaching me more than I ever needed to know about bicycles.

Finally, I'd like to recognize my own world of girls, my babysitters, without whom I would never have had the time to write this book: Aleksandra Marcotte, Claudia Shapiro, Virginia Melvin, Ida Donner, Krysta Lindley, and Lauren Caccese. Thank you for taking such good care of us.

along *for the* ride

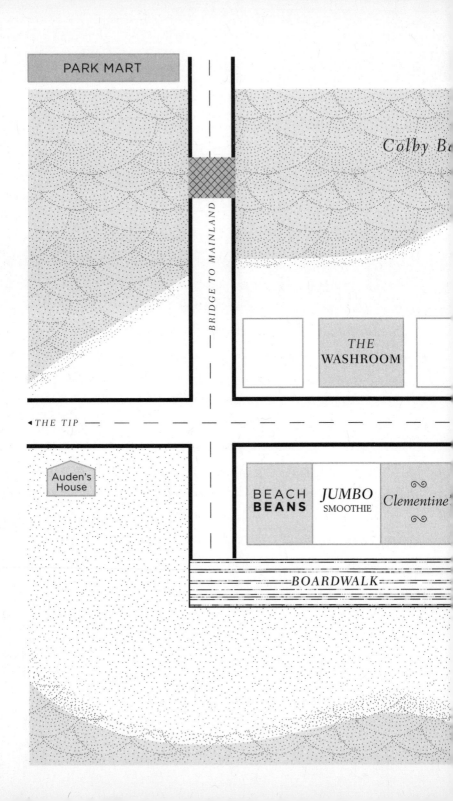

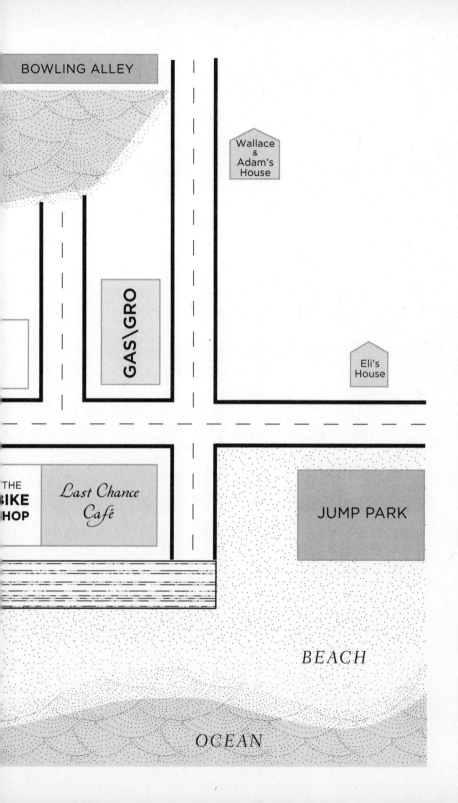

one

THE E-MAILS ALWAYS began the same way.

Hi Auden!!

It was the extra exclamation point that got me. My mother would call it extraneous, overblown, exuberant. To me, it was simply annoying, just like everything else about my stepmother, Heidi.

I hope you're having a great last few weeks of classes. We are all good here! Just finishing things up before your sister-to-be arrives. She's been kicking like crazy lately. It's like she's doing the karate moves in there! I've been busy minding the store (so to speak) and putting the final touches on the nursery. I've done it all in pink and brown; it's gorgeous. I'll attach a picture so you can see it.

Your dad is busy as always, working on his book. I figure I'll see more of him burning the midnight oil when I'm up with the baby!

I really hope you'll consider coming to visit us once

you're done with school. It would be so much fun, and
make this summer that much more special for all of us.
Just come anytime. We'd love to see you!

Love,
Heidi (and your dad, and the baby-to-be!)

Just reading these missives exhausted me. Partially it
was the excited grammar—which was like someone yelling
in your ear—but also just Heidi herself. She was just so . . .
extraneous, overblown, exuberant. And annoying. All the
things she'd been to me, and more, since she and my dad got
involved, pregnant, and married in the last year.

My mother claimed not to be surprised. Ever since the
divorce, she'd been predicting it would not be long before
my dad, as she put it, "shacked up with some coed." At
twenty-six, Heidi was the same age my mother had been
when she had my brother, Hollis, followed by me two years
later, although they could not be more different. Where
my mother was an academic scholar with a smart, sharp
wit and a nationwide reputation as an expert on women's
roles in Renaissance literature, Heidi was . . . well, Heidi.
The kind of woman whose strengths were her constant
self-maintenance (pedicures, manicures, hair highlights),
knowing everything you never wanted to about hemlines
and shoes, and sending entirely too chatty e-mails to people
who couldn't care less.

Their courtship was quick, the implantation (as my
mother christened it) happening within a couple of months.
Just like that, my father went from what he'd been for

years—husband of Dr. Victoria West and author of one well-received novel, now more known for his interdepartmental feuds than his long-in-progress follow-up—to a new husband and father-to-be. Add all this to his also-new position as head of the creative writing department at Weymar College, a small school in a beachfront town, and it was like my dad had a whole new life. And even though they were always inviting me to come, I wasn't sure I wanted to find out if there was still a place for me in it.

Now, from the other room, I heard a sudden burst of laughter, followed by some clinking of glasses. My mother was hosting another of her graduate student get-togethers, which always began as formal dinners ("Culture is so lacking in this culture!" she said) before inevitably deteriorating into loud, drunken debates about literature and theory. I glanced at the clock—ten thirty—then eased my bedroom door open with my toe, glancing down the long hallway to the kitchen. Sure enough, I could see my mom sitting at the head of our big butcher-block kitchen table, a glass of red wine in one hand. Gathered around her, as usual, were a bunch of male graduate students, looking on adoringly as she went on about, from the little bit I could gather, Marlowe and the culture of women.

This was yet another of the many fascinating contradictions about my mom. She was an expert on women in literature but didn't much like them in practice. Partly, it was because so many of them were jealous: of her intelligence (practically Mensa level), her scholarship (four books, countless articles, one endowed chair), or her looks (tall and curvy with very long jet-black hair she usually wore loose and wild, the only out-of-control thing about her). For these reasons, and others, female students seldom came to these gatherings, and if they did, they rarely returned.

"Dr. West," one of the students—typically scruffy, in a cheap-looking blazer, shaggy hair, and hip-nerdy black eyeglasses—said now, "you should really consider developing that idea into an article. It's fascinating."

I watched my mother take a sip of her wine, pushing her hair back smoothly with one hand. "Oh, God no," she said, in her deep, raspy voice (she sounded like a smoker, although she'd never taken a drag in her life). "I barely even have time to write my book right now, and that, at least, I'm getting paid for. If you can call it payment."

More complimentary laughter. My mother loved to complain about how little she got paid for her books—all academic, published by university presses—while what she termed "inane housewife stories" pulled in big bucks. In my mother's world, everyone would tote the collected works of Shakespeare to the beach, with maybe a couple of epic poems thrown in on the side.

"Still," Nerdy Eyeglasses said, pushing on, "it's a brilliant idea. I could, um, coauthor it with you, if you like."

My mother lifted her head and her glass, narrowing her eyes at him as a silence fell. "Oh, my," she said, "how very sweet of you. But I don't do coauthorship, for the same reason I don't do office mates or relationships. I'm just too selfish."

I could see Nerdy Eyeglasses gulp, even from my long vantage point, his face flushing as he reached for the wine bottle, trying to cover. Idiot, I thought, nudging the door back shut. As if it was that easy to align yourself with my mom, form some quick and tight bond that would last. I would know.

Ten minutes later, I was slipping out the side door, my shoes tucked under my arm, and getting into my car. I drove down the mostly empty streets, past quiet neighbor-hoods and dark storefronts, until the lights of Ray's Diner appeared in the distance. Small, with entirely too much neon, and tables that were always a bit sticky, Ray's was the only place in town open twenty-four hours, 365 days a year. Since I hadn't been sleeping, I'd spent more nights than not in a booth there, reading or studying, tipping a buck every hour on whatever I ordered until the sun came up.

The insomnia started when my parents' marriage began to fall apart three years earlier. I shouldn't have been sur-prised: their union had been tumultuous for as long as I could remember, although they were usually arguing more about work than about each other.

They'd originally come to the U straight out of grad school, when my dad was offered an assistant professor-ship there. At the time, he'd just found a publisher for his first novel, *The Narwhal Horn*, while my mom was preg-nant with my brother and trying to finish her dissertation. Fast-forward four years, to my birth, and my dad, riding a wave of critical and commercial success—*NYT* best-seller list, National Book Award nominee—was heading up the creative writing program, while my mom was, as she liked to put it, "lost in a sea of diapers and self-doubt." When I entered kindergarten, though, my mom came back to aca-demia with a vengeance, scoring a visiting lectureship and a publisher for her dissertation. Over time, she became one of the most popular professors in the department, was hired on for a full-time position, and banged out a second, then a third book, all while my father looked on. He claimed to be proud, always making jokes about her being his meal ticket, the breadwinner of the family. But then my mother got her endowed chair, which was very prestigious, and he got dropped from his publisher, which wasn't, and things started to get ugly.

The fights always seemed to begin over dinner, with one of them making some small remark and the other taking offense. There would be a small dustup—sharp words, a banged pot lid—but then it would seem resolved . . . at least until about ten or eleven, when suddenly I'd hear them start in again about the same issue. After a while I figured out that this time lag occurred because they were waiting for me to fall asleep before really going at it. So I decided, one night, not to. I left my door open, my light on, took pointed, obvious trips to the bathroom, washing my hands as loudly as possible. And for a while, it worked. Until it didn't, and the fights started up again. But by then my body was used to staying up way late, which meant I was now awake for every single word.

I knew a lot of people whose parents had split up, and everyone seemed to handle it differently: complete surprise, crushing disappointment, total relief. The common denominator, though, was always that there was a lot of discussion about these feelings, either with both parents, or one on one separately, or with a shrink in group or individual therapy. My family, of course, had to be the exception. I did get the sit-down-we-have-to-tell-you-something moment. The news was delivered by my mother, across the kitchen table as my dad leaned against a nearby counter, fiddling with his hands and looking tired. "Your father and I are separating," she informed me, with the same flat, businesslike tone I'd so often heard her use with students as she critiqued their work. "I'm sure you'll agree this is the best thing for all of us."

Hearing this, I wasn't sure what I felt. Not relief, not crushing disappointment, and again, it wasn't a surprise. What struck me, as we sat there, the three of us, in that room, was how little I felt. Small, like a child. Which was the weirdest thing. Like it took this huge moment for a sudden wave of childhood to wash over me, long overdue.

I'd been a child, of course. But by the time I came along, my brother—the most colicky of babies, a hyperactive toddler, a "spirited" (read "impossible") kid—had worn my parents out. He was still exhausting them, albeit from another continent, wandering around Europe and sending only the occasional e-mail detailing yet another epiphany concerning what he should do with his life, followed by a request for more money to put it into action. At least his being abroad made all this seem more nomadic and artistic: now my parents could tell their friends Hollis was hanging out at the Eiffel Tower smoking cigarettes, instead of at the Quik Zip. It just sounded better.

If Hollis was a big kid, I was the little adult, the child who, at three, would sit at the table during grown-up discussions about literature and color my coloring books, not making a peep. Who learned to entertain myself at a very early age, who was obsessive about school and grades from kindergarten, because academia was the one thing that always got my parents' attention. "Oh, don't worry," my mother would say, when one of their guests would slip with the *F*-word or something equally grown-up in front of me. "Auden's very mature for her age." And I was, whether that age was two or four or seventeen. While Hollis required constant supervision, I was the one who got carted everywhere, constantly flowing in my mom's or dad's wake. They took me to the symphony, art shows, academic conferences, committee meetings, where I was expected to be seen and not heard. There was not a lot of time for playing or toys, although I never wanted for books, which were always in ample supply.

Because of this upbringing, I had kind of a hard time relating to other kids my age. I didn't understand their craziness, their energy, the rambunctious way they tossed around couch cushions, say, or rode their bikes wildly around culs-de-sac. It did look sort of fun, but at the same time, it was so different from what I was used to that I couldn't imagine how I would ever partake if given the chance. Which I wasn't, as the cushion-tossers and wild bike riders didn't usually attend the highly academic, grade-accelerated private schools my parents favored.

In the past four years, in fact, I'd switched schools three times. I'd lasted at Jackson High for only a couple of weeks before my mom, having spotted a misspelling *and* a grammatical error on my English syllabus, moved me to Perkins Day, a local private school. It was smaller and more academically rigorous, although not nearly as much as Kiffney-Brown, the charter school to which I transferred junior year.

Founded by several former local professors, it was elite—a hundred students, max—and emphasized very small classes and a strong connection to the local university, where you could take college-level courses for early credit. While I had a few friends at Kiffney-Brown, the ultracompetitive atmosphere, paired with so much of the curriculum being self-guided, made getting close to them somewhat difficult.

Not that I really cared. School was my solace, and studying let me escape, allowing me to live a thousand vicarious lives. The more my parents bemoaned Hollis's lack of initiative and terrible grades, the harder I worked. And while they were proud of me, my accomplishments never seemed to get me what I really wanted. I was such a smart kid, I should have figured out that the only way to really get my parents' attention was to disappoint them or fail. But by the time I finally realized that, succeeding was already a habit too ingrained to break.

My dad moved out at the beginning of my sophomore year, renting a furnished apartment right near campus in a complex mostly populated by students. I was supposed to spend every weekend there, but he was in such a funk—still struggling with his second book, his publication (or lack of it) called into question just as my mom's was getting so much attention—that it wasn't exactly enjoyable. Then again, my mom's house wasn't much better, as she was so busy celebrating her newfound single life and academic success that she had people over all the time, students coming and going, dinner parties every weekend. It seemed like there was no middle ground anywhere, except at Ray's Diner.

I'd driven past it a million times but had never thought of stopping until one night when I was heading back to my mom's around two A.M. My dad, like my mom, didn't really keep close tabs on me. Because of my school schedule—one night class, flexible daytime seminar hours, and several independent studies—I came and went as I pleased, with little or no questioning, so neither of them really noticed that I wasn't sleeping. That night, I glanced in at Ray's, and something about it just struck me. It looked warm, safe almost, populated by people who at least I had one thing in common with. So I pulled in, went inside, and ordered a cup of coffee and some apple pie. I stayed until sunrise.

The nice thing about Ray's was that even once I became a regular, I still got to be alone. Nobody was asking for more than I wanted to give, and all the interactions were short and sweet. If only all relationships could be so simple, with me always knowing my role exactly.

Back in the fall, one of the waitresses, a heavyset older woman whose name tag said JULIE, had peered down at the application I was working on as she refilled my coffee cup.

"Defriese University," she read out loud. Then she looked at me. "Pretty good school."

"One of the best," I agreed.

"Think you'll get in?"

I nodded. "Yeah. I do."

She smiled, like I was kind of cute, then patted my shoulder. "Ah, to be young and confident," she said, and then she was shuffling away.

I wanted to tell her that I wasn't confident, I just worked really hard. But she had already moved on to the next booth, chatting up the guy sitting there, and I knew she didn't really care anyway. There were worlds where all of this—grades, school, papers, class rank, early admission, weighted GPAs—mattered, and ones where they didn't. I'd spent my entire life squarely in the former, and even at Ray's, which was the latter, I still couldn't shake it.

Being so driven, and attending such an unorthodox school, meant that I'd missed out on making all those senior moments that my old friends from Perkins Day had spent this whole last year talking about. The only thing I'd even considered was prom, and then only because my main competition for highest GPA, Jason Talbot, had asked me as a sort of peace offering. In the end, though, even that hadn't happened, as he canceled last minute after getting invited to participate in some ecology conference. I told myself it didn't matter, that it was the equivalent of those couch cushions and cul-de-sac bike rides all those years ago, frivolous and unnecessary. But I still kind of wondered, that night and so many others, what I was missing.

I'd be sitting at Ray's, at two or three or four in the morning, and feel this weird twinge. When I looked up from my books to the people around me—truckers, people who'd come off the interstate for coffee to make another mile, the occasional crazy—I'd have that same feeling that I did the day my mother announced the separation. Like I didn't belong there, and should have been at home, asleep in my bed, like everyone else I'd see at school in a few hours. But just as quickly, it would pass, everything settling back into place around me. And when Julie came back around with her coffeepot, I'd push my cup to the edge of the table, saying without words what we both knew well—that I'd be staying for a while.

❊   ❊   ❊

My stepsister, Thisbe Caroline West, was born the day before my graduation, weighing in at six pounds, fifteen ounces. My father called the next morning, exhausted.

"I'm so sorry, Auden," he said, "I hate to miss your speech."

"It's all right," I told him as my mother came into the kitchen, in her robe, and headed for the coffeemaker. "How's Heidi?"

"Good," he replied. "Tired. It was a long haul, and she ended up having a caesarean, which she wasn't so happy about. But I'm sure she'll feel better after she gets some rest."

"Tell her I said congratulations," I told him.

"I will. And you go out there and give 'em hell, kid." This was typical: for my dad, who was famously combative, anything relating to academia was a battle. "I'll be thinking about you."

I smiled, thanked him, then hung up the phone as my mother poured milk into her coffee. She stirred her cup, the spoon clanking softly, for a moment before saying, "Let me guess. He's not coming."

"Heidi had the baby," I said. "They named her Thisbe."

My mother snorted. "Oh, good Lord," she said. "All the names from Shakespeare to choose from, and your father picks *that* one? The poor girl. She'll be having to explain herself her entire life."

My mom didn't really have room to talk, considering

she'd let my dad name me and my brother: Detram Hollis was a professor my dad greatly admired, while W. H. Auden was his favorite poet. I'd spent some time as a kid wishing my name were Ashley or Katherine, if only because it would have made life simpler, but my mom liked to tell me that my name was actually a kind of litmus test. Auden wasn't like Frost, she'd say, or Whitman. He was a bit more obscure, and if someone knew of him, then I could be at least somewhat sure they were worth my time and energy, capable of being my intellectual equal. I figured this might be even more true for Thisbe, but instead of saying so I just sat down with my speech notes, flipping through them again. After a moment, she pulled out a chair, joining me.

"So Heidi survived the childbirth, I assume?" she asked, taking a sip off her coffee.

"She had to have a caesarean."

"She's lucky," my mom said. "Hollis was eleven pounds, and the epidural didn't take. He almost killed me."

I flipped through another couple of cards, waiting for one of the stories that inevitably followed this one. There was how Hollis was a ravenous child, sucking my mother's milk supply dry. The craziness that was his colic, how he had to be walked constantly and, even then, screamed for hours on end. Or there was the one about my dad, and how he . . .

"I just hope she's not expecting your father to be of much help," she said, reaching over for a couple of my cards and scanning them, her eyes narrowed. "I was lucky if he changed a diaper every once in a while. And forget about him getting up for night feedings. He claimed that he had sleep issues and had to get his nine hours in order to teach. Awfully convenient, that."

She was still reading my cards as she said this, and I felt the familiar twinge I always experienced whenever anything I did was suddenly under her scrutiny. A moment later, though, she put them aside without comment.

"Well," I said as she took another sip of coffee, "that was a long time ago. Maybe he's changed."

"People don't change. If anything, you get more set in your ways as you get older, not less." She shook her head. "I remember I used to sit in our bedroom, with Hollis screaming, and just wish that once the door would open, and your father would come in and say 'Here, give him to me. You go rest.' Eventually, it wasn't even your dad I wanted, just anybody. Anybody at all."

She was looking out the window as she said this, her fingers wrapped around her mug, which was not on the table or at her lips but instead hovering just between. I picked up my cards, carefully arranging them back in order. "I should go get ready," I said, pushing my chair back.

My mother didn't move as I got up and walked behind her. It was like she was frozen, still back in that old bedroom, still waiting, at least until I got down the hallway. Then, suddenly, she spoke.

"You should rethink that Faulkner quote," she said. "It's too much for an opening. You'll sound pretentious."

I looked down at my top card, where the words "The past isn't dead. It isn't even past" were written in my neat block print. "Okay," I said. She was right, of course. She always was. "Thanks."

＊　＊　＊

I'd been so focused on my last year of high school and beginning college that I hadn't really thought about the time in between. Suddenly, though, it was summer, and there was nothing to do but wait for my real life to begin again.

I spent a couple of weeks getting all the stuff I needed for Defriese, and tried to pick up a few shifts at my tutoring job at Huntsinger Test Prep, although it was pretty slow. I seemed to be the only one thinking about school, a fact made more obvious by the various invitations I received from my old friends at Perkins to dinners or trips to the lake. I wanted to see everyone, but whenever we did get together, I felt like the odd person out. I'd only been at Kiffney-Brown for two years, but it was so different, so entirely academic, that I found I couldn't really relate to their talk about summer jobs and boyfriends. After a few awkward outings, I began to beg off, saying I was busy, and after a while, they got the message.

Home was kind of weird as well, as my mom had gotten some research grant and was working all the time, and when she wasn't, her graduate assistants were always showing up for impromtu dinners and cocktail hours. When they got too noisy and the house too crowded, I'd head out to the front porch with a book and read until it was dark enough to go to Ray's.

One night, I was deeply into a book about Buddhism

when I saw a green Mercedes coming down our street. It slowed as it neared our mailbox, then slid to a stop by the curb. After a moment, a very pretty blonde girl wearing low-slung jeans, a red tank top, and wedge sandals got out, a package in one hand. She peered at the house, then down at it, then back at the house again before starting up the driveway. She was almost to the front steps when she saw me.

"Hi!" she called out, entirely friendly, which sort of alarming. I barely had time to respond before she was heading right to me, a big smile on her face. "You must be Auden."

"Yes," I said slowly.

"I'm Tara!" Clearly, this name was supposed to be familiar to me. When it became obvious it wasn't, she added, "Hollis's girlfriend?"

Oh, dear, I thought. Out loud I said, "Oh, right. Of course."

"It's so nice to meet you!" she said, moving closer and putting her arms around me. She smelled like gardenias and dryer sheets. "Hollis knew I'd be passing through on my way home, and he asked me to bring you this. Straight from Greece!"

She handed over the package, which in a plain brown wrapper, my name and address written across the front in my brother's slanted, sloppy hand. There was an awkward moment, during which I realized she was waiting for me to open the package, so I did. It was a small glass picture frame, dotted with colorful stones: along the bottom were etched the words THE BEST OF TIMES. Inside was a picture of Hollis standing in front of the Taj Mahal. He was smiling one of his lazy smiles, in cargo shorts and a T-shirt, a backpack over one shoulder.

"It's great, right?" Tara said. "We got it at a flea market in Athens."

Since I couldn't say what I really felt, which was that you had to be a pretty serious narcissist to give a picture of yourself as a gift, I told her, "It's beautiful."

"I knew you'd like it!" She clapped her hands. "I told him, everyone needs picture frames. They make a memory even more special, you know?"

I looked down at the frame again, the pretty stones, my brother's easy expression. THE BEST OF TIMES, indeed. "Yeah," I said. "Absolutely."

Tara shot me another million-watt smile, then peered through the window behind me. "So is your mom around? I would love to meet her. Hollis adores her, talks about her all the time."

"It's mutual," I said. She glanced at me, and I smiled. "She's in the kitchen. Long black hair, in the green dress. You can't miss her."

"Great!" Too quick to prevent, she was hugging me again. "Thanks so much."

I nodded. This confidence was a hallmark of all my brother's girlfriends, at least while they still considered themselves as such. It was only later, when the e-mails and calls stopped, when he seemingly vanished off the face of the earth, that we saw the other side: the red eyes, the weepy messages on our answering machine, the occasional angry peel-out on the road outside our house. Tara didn't seem like the angry drive-by type. But you never knew.

By eleven, my mother's admirers were still hanging around, their voices loud as always. I sat in my room, idly checking my Ume.com page (no messages, not that I'd expected any) and e-mail (just one from my dad, asking how everything was going). I thought about calling one of my friends to see if anything was going on, but after remembering the awkwardness of my last few social outings, I sat down on my bed instead. Hollis's picture frame was on the bedside table, and I picked it up, looking over the tacky blue stones. THE BEST OF TIMES. Something in these words, and his easy, smiling face, reminded me of the chatter of my old friends as they traded stories from the school year. Not about classes, or GPAs, but other stuff, things that were as foreign to me as the Taj Mahal itself, gossip and boys and getting your heart broken. They probably had a million pictures that belonged in this frame, but I didn't have a single one.

I looked at my brother again, backpack over his shoulder. Travel certainly did provide some kind of opportunity, as well as a change of scenery. Maybe I couldn't take off to Greece or India. But I could still go somewhere.

I went over to my laptop, opening my e-mail account, then scrolled down to my dad's message. Without letting myself think too much, I typed a quick reply, as well as a question. Within a half hour, he had written me back.

Absolutely you should come! Stay as long as you like. We'd love the company!

And just like that, my summer changed.

❋ ❋ ❋

The next morning, I packed my car with a small duffel bag of clothes, my laptop, and a big suitcase of books. Earlier in the summer, I'd found the syllabi to a couple of the courses I was taking at Defriese in the fall, and I'd hunted down a few of the texts at the U bookstore, figuring it couldn't hurt to acquaint myself with the material. Not exactly how Hollis would pack, but it wasn't like there'd be much else to do there anyway, other than go to the beach and hang out with Heidi, neither of which was very appealing.

I'd said good-bye to my mom the night before, figuring she'd be asleep when I left. But as I came into the kitchen, I found her clearing the table of a bevy of wineglasses and crumpled napkins, a tired look on her face.

"Late night?" I asked, although I knew from my own nocturnal habits that it had been. The last car had pulled out of the driveway around one thirty.

"Not really," she said, running some water into the sink. She looked over her shoulder at my bags, piled by the garage door. "You're getting an early start. Are you that eager to get away from me?"

"No," I said. "Just want to beat traffic."

In truth, I hadn't expected my mom to care whether I was around for the summer or not. And maybe she wouldn't have, if I'd been going anywhere else. Factor my dad into the equation, though, and things changed. They always did.

"I can only imagine what kind of situation you're about to walk into," she said, smiling. "Your father with a newborn! At his age! It's comic."

"I'll let you know," I told her.

"Oh, you must. I will require regular updates."

I watched as she stuck her hands into the water, soaping up a glass. "So," I said, "what did you think of Hollis's girl-friend?"

My mother sighed wearily. "What was she doing here, again?"

"Hollis sent her back with a gift for me."

"Really," she said, depositing a couple of glasses into the dish rack. "What was it?"

"A picture frame. From Greece. With a picture of Hollis in it."

"Ah." She turned off the water, using the back of her wrist to brush her hair from her face. "Did you tell her she should have kept it for herself, since it's probably the only way she'll ever see him again?"

Even though I'd had this exact same thought, after hearing my mom say it aloud I felt sorry for Tara, with her open, friendly face, the confident way she'd headed into the house, so secure in her standing as Hollis's one and only. "You never know," I said. "Maybe Hollis has changed, and they'll get engaged."

My mom turned around and narrowed her eyes at me. "Now, Auden," she said. "What have I told you about people changing?"

"That they don't?"

"Exactly."

She directed her attention back to the sink, dunking a plate, and as she did I caught sight of the pair of black, hip-nerdy eyeglasses sitting on the counter by the door.

Suddenly, it all made sense: the voices I'd heard so late, her being up early, uncharacteristically eager to clean out everything from the night before. I considered picking the glasses up, making sure she saw me, just to make a point of my own. But instead, I ignored them as we said our good-byes, her pulling me in for a tight hug—she always held you close, like she'd never let you go—before doing just that and sending me on my way.

two

MY DAD AND Heidi's house was just what I expected. Cute, painted white with green shutters, it had a wide front porch dotted with rocking chairs and potted flowers and a friendly yellow ceramic pineapple hanging from the door, that said WELCOME! All that was missing was a white picket fence.

I pulled in, spotting my dad's beat-up Volvo in the open garage, with a newer-looking Prius parked beside it. As soon as I cut my engine I could hear the ocean, loud enough that it had to be very close. Sure enough, as I peered around the side of the house, all I could see was beach grass and a wide swath of blue, stretching all the way to the horizon.

The view aside, I had my doubts. I was never one for spontaneity, and the farther I got from my mom's house, the more I started to consider the reality of a full summer of Heidi. Would there be group manicures for me, her, and the baby? Or maybe she'd insist I go tanning with her, sporting matching retro I LOVE UNICORNS tees? But I kept thinking of Hollis in front of the Taj Mahal, and how I'd found myself so bored all alone at home. Plus, I'd hardly seen my dad since he got married, and this—eight full weeks when he wasn't teaching, and I wasn't in school—seemed like my last chance to catch up with him before college, and real life, began.

I took a deep breath, then got out. As I started up to the front porch, I told myself that no matter what Heidi said or did, I would just smile and roll with it. At least until I could get to whatever room I'd be staying in and shut the door behind me.

I rang the doorbell, then stepped back, arranging my face into an appropriately friendly expression. There was no response from inside, so I rang it again, then leaned in closer, listening for the inevitable sound of clattering heels, Heidi's happy voice calling out, "Just a minute!" But again, nothing.

Reaching down, I tried the knob: it turned easily, the door opening, and I leaned my head inside. "Hello?" I called out, my voice bouncing down a nearby empty hallway painted yellow and dotted with framed prints. "Anyone here?"

Silence. I stepped inside, shutting the door behind me. It was only then that I heard it: the sound of the ocean again, although it sounded a little different, and much closer by, like just around the corner. I followed it down the hallway, as it got louder and louder, expecting to see an open window or back door. Instead, I found myself in the living room, where the noise was deafening, and Heidi was sitting on the couch, holding the baby in her arms.

At least, I *thought* it was Heidi. It was hard to say for sure, as she looked nothing like the last time I'd seen her.

Her hair was pulled up into a messy, lopsided ponytail, with some strands stuck to her face, and she had on a ratty pair of sweatpants and an oversize U T-shirt, which had some kind of damp stain on one shoulder. Her eyes were closed, her head tipped back slightly. In fact, I thought she was asleep until, without even moving her lips, she hissed, "If you wake her up, I will *kill* you."

I froze, alarmed, then took a careful step backward. "Sorry," I said. "I just—"

Her eyes snapped open, and she whipped her head around, her eyes narrowing into little slits. When she spotted me, though, her expression changed to surprise. And then, just like that, she was crying.

"Oh, God, Auden," she said, her voice tight, "I am so, so sorry. I forgot you were . . . and then I thought . . . but it's no excuse. . . ." She trailed off, her shoulders heaving as, in her arms, the baby—who was tiny, so small she looked too delicate to even exist—slept on, completely unaware.

I took a panicked look around the room, wondering where my dad was. Only then did I realize that the incredibly loud ocean sound I was hearing was not coming from outside but instead from a small white noise-machine sitting on the coffee table. Who listens to a fake ocean when the real one is in earshot? It was one of many things that, at that moment, made absolutely no sense.

"Um," I said as Heidi continued to cry, her sobs punctuated by an occasional loud sniffle, as well as the fake pounding waves, "can I . . . do you need some help, or something?"

She drew in a shaky breath, then looked up at me. Her eyes were rimmed with dark circles: there was a pimply red rash on her chin. "No," she said as fresh tears filled her eyes. "I'm okay. It's just . . . I'm fine."

This seemed highly unlikely, even to my untrained eye. Not that I had time to dispute it, as right then my dad walked in, carrying a tray of coffees and a small brown paper bag. He was in his typical outfit of rumpled khakis and an untucked button-down, his glasses sort of askew on his face. When he taught, he usually added a tie and tweedy sport jacket. His sneakers, though, were a constant, no matter what else he was wearing.

"There she is!" he said when he spotted me, then headed over to give me a hug. As he pulled me close, I looked over his shoulder at Heidi, who was biting her lip, staring out the window at the ocean. "How was the trip?"

"Good," I said slowly as he pulled back and took a coffee out of the carrier, offering it to me. I took it, then watched as he helped himself to one before sticking the last on the table in front of Heidi, who just stared at it like she didn't know what it was.

"Did you meet your sister?"

"Uh, no," I said. "Not yet."

"Oh, well!" He put down the paper bag, then reached over Heidi—who stiffened, not that he seemed to notice—taking the baby from her arms. "Here she is. This is Thisbe."

I looked down at the baby's face, which was so small and delicate it didn't even seem real. Her eyes were shut, and she had tiny, spiky eyelashes. One of her hands was sticking out of her blanket, and the fingers were so little, curled slightly around one another. "She's beautiful," I said, because that is what you say.

"Isn't she?" My dad grinned, bouncing her slightly in his arms, and her eyes slid open. She looked up at us, blink-ed, and then, just like her mom, suddenly began to cry. "Whoops," he said, jiggling her a bit. Thisbe cried a little louder. "Honey?" my dad said, turning back to Heidi, who was still sitting in the exact same place and position, her arms now limp at her sides. "I think she's hungry."

Heidi swallowed, then turned to him wordlessly. When my father handed Thisbe over, she swiveled back to the windows, almost robotlike as the crying grew louder, then louder still.

"Let's step outside," my dad suggested, grabbing the pa-per bag off the end table and gesturing for me to follow him as he walked to a pair of sliding glass doors, opening one and leading me outside to the deck. Normally, the view would have left me momentarily speechless—the house was right on the beach, a walkway leading directly to the sand—but instead I found myself looking back at Heidi, only to real-ize she'd disappeared, leaving her coffee untouched on the table.

"Is she all right?" I asked.

He opened the paper bag, pulling out a muffin, then offering it to me. I shook my head. "She's tired," he said, tak-ing a bite, a few crumbs falling onto his shirt. He brushed them off with one hand, then kept eating. "The baby's up a lot at night, you know, and I'm not much help because I have this sleep condition and have to get my nine hours, or else. I keep trying to convince her to get in some help, but she won't do it."

"Why not?"

"Oh, you know Heidi," he said as if I did. "She's got to do everything herself, and do it perfectly. But don't worry, she'll be fine. The first couple of months are just hard. I remember with Hollis, your mom was just about to go out of her mind. Of course, he was incredibly colicky. We used to walk him all night long, and he'd still scream. And his appetite! Good Lord. He'd suck your mom dry and still be ravenous. . . . "

He kept talking, but I'd heard this song before, knew all the words, so I just sipped my coffee. Looking left, I could see a few more houses, then what appeared to be some sort of boardwalk lined with businesses, as well as a public beach, already crowded with umbrellas and sunbathers.

"Anyway," my father was saying now as he crumpled up his muffin wrapper, tossing it back in the bag, "I've got to get back to work, so let me show you your room. We can catch up over dinner, later. That sound good?"

"Sure," I said as we headed back inside, where the sound machine was still blasting. My dad shook his head, then reached down, turning it off with a click: the sudden silence was jarring. "So you're writing?"

"Oh, yeah. I'm on a real roll, definitely going to finish the book soon," he replied. "It's just a matter of organizing, really, getting the last little bits down on the page." We went back to the foyer, then went up the staircase. As we walked down the hallway, we passed an open door, through which I could see a pink wall with a brown polka-dot border. Inside, it was silent, no crying, at least that I could hear.

My dad pushed open the next door down, then waved me in with one hand. "Sorry for the small quarters," he said as I stepped over the threshold. "But you have the best view."

He wasn't kidding. Though the room was tiny, with a twin bed, a bureau, and not much room for anything else, the lone window looked out over an undeveloped area of land, nothing but sea grass and sand and water. "This is great," I said.

"Isn't it? It was originally my office. But then we had to put the baby's room next door, so I moved to the other side of the house. I didn't want to keep her up, you know, with the noises of my creative process." He chuckled, like this was a joke I was supposed to get. "Speaking of which, I'd better get to it. The mornings have been really productive for me lately. I'll catch up with you at dinner, all right?"

"Oh," I said, glancing at my watch. It was 11:05. "Sure."

"Great." He squeezed my arm, then started down the hallway, humming to himself, as I watched him go. A moment after he passed the door to the pink-and-brown room, I heard the door click shut.

❄   ❄   ❄

I woke up at six thirty that evening to the sound of a baby crying.

Crying, actually, was too tepid a word. Thisbe was *screaming,* her lungs clearly getting a serious workout. And while it was merely audible in my room, with just a thin wall

between us, when I went out in the hallway in search of a
bathroom to brush my teeth, the noise was deafening.

I stood for a second in the dimness outside the door
to the pink room, listening to the cries as they rose, rose,
rose, then fell sharply, only to spike again, even louder. I was
wondering if I was the only one aware of it until, during a
rare and short moment of silence, I heard someone saying,
"Shh, shh," before quickly being drowned out again.

There was something so familiar about this, it was
like a tug on my subconscious. When my parents had first
started to fight at night, this had been part of what I'd
repeated—*shh, shh, everything's all right*—to myself, again
and again, as I tried to ignore them and fall asleep. Hearing
it now, though, felt strange, as I was used to the sound
being private, only in my head and the dark around me, so
I moved on.

"Dad?"

My father, sitting in front of his laptop at a desk facing
the wall, didn't move as he said, "Hmmm?"

I looked back down the hallway to the pink room, then
at him again. He wasn't typing, just studying the screen, a
yellow legal pad with some scribblings on the desk beside
him. I wondered if he'd been there the whole time I'd been
sleeping, over seven hours. "Should I," I said, "um, start dinner, or something?"

"Isn't Heidi doing that?" he asked, still facing the screen.

"I think she's with the baby," I said.

"Oh." Now, he turned his head, looking at me. "Well, if
you're hungry, there's a great burger place just a block away.
Their onion rings are legendary."

I smiled. "Sounds great," I said. "Should I find out if Heidi wants anything?"

"Absolutely. And get me a cheeseburger and some of those onion rings." He reached into his back pocket, pulling out a couple of bills and handing them to me. "Thanks a lot, Auden. I really appreciate it."

I took the bills, feeling like an idiot. Of course he couldn't go out with me: he had a new baby at home, a wife to take care of. "No problem," I said, even though he was already turning back to his screen, not really listening. "I'll just be back in a little bit."

I walked back to the pink room, where Thisbe was still going full blast. Figuring at least this time I didn't have to worry about waking her up, I knocked twice. After a second, it opened a crack, and Heidi looked out at me.

She looked more haggard than before, if that was even possible: the ponytail was gone, her hair now hanging limp in her face. "Hi," I said, or rather shouted, over the screaming. "I'm going to get dinner. What would you like?"

"Dinner?" she repeated, her voice also raised. I nodded. "Is it dinnertime already?"

I looked at my watch, as if I needed to confirm this. "It's about quarter to seven."

"Oh, dear God." She closed her eyes. "I was going to fix a big welcome dinner for you. I had it all planned, chicken and vegetables, and everything. But the baby's been so fussy, and . . ."

"It's fine," I said. "I'm going to get burgers. Dad says there's a good place right down the street."

"Your father is here?" she asked, shifting Thisbe in her arms and peering over my shoulder, down the hallway. "I thought he went down to campus."

"He's working in his office," I said. She leaned closer, clearly not having heard this. "He's writing," I repeated, more loudly. "So I'm going. What would you like?"

Heidi just stood there, the baby screaming between us, looking down the hallway at the light spilling out from my dad's barely open office door. She started to speak, then stopped herself, taking a deep breath. "Whatever you're having is fine," she said after a moment. "Thank you."

I nodded, then stepped back as she pushed the door back shut between us. The last thing I saw was the baby's red face, still howling.

Thankfully, outside the house it was much quieter. I could hear only the ocean and various neighborhood sounds—kids yelling, an occasional car radio, someone's TV blaring out a back door—as I walked down the street to where the neighborhood ended and the business district began.

There was a narrow boardwalk, lined with various shops: a smoothie place, one of those beach-crap joints that sell cheap towels and shell clocks, a pizzeria. About halfway down, I passed a small boutique called Clementine's, which had a bright orange awning. Taped to the front door was a piece of paper that read, in big block print, IT'S A GIRL! THISBE CAROLINE WEST, BORN JUNE 1, 6 LBS, 15 OZ. So this was Heidi's store, I thought. There were racks of T-shirts and jeans, a makeup and body lotion section, and a dark-haired girl in a pink dress examining her fingernails behind the register, a cell phone clamped to her ear.

Up ahead, I could see what had to be the burger joint my dad mentioned—LAST CHANCE CAFÉ, BEST O RINGS ON THE BEACH! said the sign. Just before it, there was one last store, a bike shop. A bunch of guys around my age were gathered on a battered wooden bench outside, talking and watching people pass by.

"The thing is," one of them, who was stocky and sporting shorts and a chain wallet, said, "the name has to have punch. Energy, you know?"

"It's more important that it be clever," another, who was taller and thinner with curly hair, a little dorky-looking, said. "Which is why you should go with my choice, the Crankshaft. It's perfect."

"It sounds like a car shop, not a bike place," the short guy told him.

"Bikes have cranks," his friend pointed out.

"And cars have shafts."

"So do mines," the skinny guy said.

"You want to call it the Mine Shaft now?"

"No," his friend said as the other two laughed. "I'm just making the point that the context doesn't have to be exclusive."

"Who cares about context?" The short guy sighed. "What we need is a name that jumps out and sells product. Like, say, Zoom Bikes. Or Overdrive Bikes."

"How do you go into overdrive on a bike?" another guy, who had his back to me, asked. "That's stupid."

"It is not," the guy with the wallet muttered. "Besides, I don't see you offering up any suggestions."

I stepped away from Clementine's and starting walking again. Just as I did, the third guy suddenly turned, and our eyes met. He had dark hair, cut short, incredibly tanned skin, and a broad, confident smile, which he now flashed at me. "How about," he said slowly, his gaze still locked with mine, "I just saw the hottest girl in Colby walking by?"

"Oh, Jesus," the dorky one said, shaking his head, as the other one laughed out loud. "You're pathetic."

I felt my face flush hot, even as I ignored him and kept walking. I could feel him looking at me, still smiling, as I put more and more distance between us. "Just stating the obvious," he called out, as I was about out of earshot. "You could say thank you, you know."

But I didn't. I didn't say anything, if only because I had no idea how to respond to such an overture. If my experience with friends was sparse, what I knew about boys—other than as competitors for grades or class rank—was nonexistent.

Not that I hadn't had crushes. Back at Jackson, there was a guy in my science class, hopeless at equations, who always made my palms sweat whenever we got paired for experiments. And at Perkins Day, I'd awkwardly flirted with Nate Cross, who sat next to me in calculus, but everyone was in love with Nate, so that hardly made me special. It wasn't until Kiffney-Brown, when I met Jason Talbot, that I really thought I might actually have one of those boyfriend kind of stories to tell the next time I got together with my old friends. Jason was smart, good-looking, and seriously on the rebound after his girlfriend at Jackson dumped him for, in his words, "a juvenile delinquent welder with a tattoo." Because of Kiffney-Brown's small seminar size, we spent a fair amount of time together, battling it out for valedictorian, and when he'd asked me to prom I'd been more excited than I ever would have admitted. Until he backed out, citing the "great opportunity" of the ecology conference. "I knew you'd be okay with this," he'd said to me as I nodded, dumbly, hearing this news. "You understand what's really important."

Okay, so it wasn't like he called me beautiful. But it was a compliment, in its own way.

It was crowded at Last Chance Café, with a line of people waiting to be seated and two cooks visible through a small kitchen window, racing around as orders piled up on the spindle in front of them. I gave my order to a pretty, dark-haired girl with a lip ring, then took a seat by the window to wait for it. Glancing down the boardwalk, I could see the guys still gathered around the bench: the one who'd talked to me was now sitting down, his arms stretched behind his head, laughing, as his short, stocky friend rode a bike back and forth in front of him, doing little hops here and there.

It took a while for the food to be ready, but I soon realized my dad was right. It was worth the wait. I was digging into the onion rings before I even got out the door to the boardwalk, which by then was crowded with families eating ice-cream cones, couples on dates, and tons of little kids running along the sand. In the distance, there was a gorgeous sunset, all oranges and pinks, and I kept my eyes on it as I walked, not even looking over at the bike shop until I was almost past it. The guy was still there, although now he was talking to a tall girl with red hair, who was wearing a massive pair of sunglasses.

"Hey," he called out to me, "if you're looking for something to do tonight, there's a bonfire at the Tip. I'll save you a seat."

I glanced over at him. The redhead was now giving me the stink eye, an annoyed look on her face, so I didn't say anything.

"Ah, she's a heartbreaker!" he said, then laughed. I kept walking, now feeling the redhead's gaze boring in somewhere between my shoulder blades. "Just keep it in mind. I'll wait for you."

Back at the house, I found three plates and some silverware, then set the table and put out the food. I was shaking ketchup packets out into a pile when my dad came downstairs.

"I thought I smelled onion rings," he said, rubbing his hands together. "This looks great."

"Is Heidi coming down?" I asked, sliding his burger onto a plate.

"Not sure," he replied, helping himself to an onion ring. Mouth full, he added, "The baby's having a hard night. She probably wants to get her to sleep first."

I glanced up the stairs, wondering if it was possible that Thisbe was still crying, as I'd been gone at least an hour. "Maybe I'll, um, just ask her if she wants me to bring it up to her."

"Sure, great," he said, pulling out a chair and sitting down. I stood there for a second, watching as he ate another ring, tugging a nearby newspaper over with his free hand. I'd wanted to have dinner with my dad, sure, but I felt kind of bad about it happening this way.

Thisbe *was* still crying: I could hear her as soon as I got to the top of the stairs, Heidi's dinner on a plate in one hand. When I got to the pink room, the door was ajar, and inside I could see her sitting in a rocking chair, her eyes closed, moving back and forth, back and forth. I was understandably hesitant to bother her, but she must have smelled the food, because a beat later, she opened her eyes.

"I thought you might be hungry," I called out. "Do you—should I bring this to you?"

She blinked at me, then looked down at Thisbe, who was still howling. "You can just put it down," she said, nodding at a nearby white bureau. "I'll get to it in a second."

I walked over, moving aside a stuffed giraffe and a book called *Your Baby: The Basics*, which was opened to a page with the heading "Fussiness: What Causes It, and What You Can Do." Either she hadn't had time to read it, or that book didn't know jack, I thought as I slid the plate over.

"Thanks," Heidi said. She was still rocking, the motion almost hypnotic, although clearly not to Thisbe, who continued to cry at full volume. "I just . . . I don't know what I'm doing wrong. She's fed, she's changed, I'm holding her, and it's like . . . she hates me, or something."

"She's probably just colicky," I said.

"But what does that mean, exactly?" She swallowed hard, then looked back down at her daughter's face. "It just doesn't make sense, and I'm doing all I can. . . ."

She trailed off, her voice getting tight, and I thought of my dad downstairs, eating his onion rings and reading the paper. Why wasn't *he* up here? I didn't know jack about babies either. Just as I thought this, though, Heidi looked up at me again.

"Oh, God, Auden, I'm so sorry." She shook her head. "I'm sure this is the last thing you want to hear about. You're young, you should be out having fun!" She sniffled, reaching up to rub her eyes with one hand. "You know, there's a place called the Tip, just down the road from here. All the girls at my shop hang out there at night. You should go check it out. It has to be better than this, right?"

Agreed, I thought, but it seemed rude to actually say that. "Maybe I will," I said.

She nodded, like we'd made a deal, then looked back at Thisbe. "Thanks for the food," she said. "I really . . . I appreciate it."

"No problem," I told her. But she was still looking at the baby, her face weary, so I took this as a dismissal and left, shutting the door behind me.

Downstairs, my dad was finishing his dinner, perusing the sports section. When I slid into a chair opposite him, he looked up at me and smiled. "So how's she doing? Baby asleep?"

"Not really," I told him, unwrapping my burger. "She's still screaming."

"Yikes." He pushed his chair back, standing up. "I better go check in."

Finally, I thought as he disappeared up the stairs. I picked up my burger, taking a bite: it was cold, but still good. I'd only eaten about half of it when he reappeared, walking to the fridge and grabbing a beer. I sat there, chewing, as he popped the top, took a sip, and looked out at the water.

"Everything okay up there?"

"Oh, sure," he said easily, moving the bottle to his other hand. "She's just colicky, like Hollis was. Not much you can do except wait it out."

The thing was, I loved my dad. He might have been a little moody, and definitely more than a little selfish, but he'd always been good to me, and I admired him. Right at that moment, though, I could see why someone might not *like* him that much. "Does Heidi . . . is her mom coming to help out, or anything?"

"Her mom died a couple of years ago," he said, taking another sip of his beer. "She has a brother, but he's older, lives in Cincinnati with kids of his own."

"What about a nanny or something?"

Now he looked at me. "She doesn't want help," he said. "It's like I told you, she wants to do this on her own."

I had a flash of Heidi craning her neck, looking down at my dad's office, the grateful look on her face when I brought her dinner. "Maybe," I said, "you should, you know, insist, though. She seems pretty tired."

He just looked at me for a moment, a flat expression on his face. "Auden," he said finally, "this isn't something you need to worry about, all right? Heidi and I will work it out."

In other words, back off. And he was right. This was his house, I was a guest here. It was presumptuous to show up and just assume I knew better, based on only a few hours. "Right," I said, balling up my napkin. "Of course."

"All right," he said, his voice relaxed again. "So . . . I'm going to head upstairs, get back to it. I'd like to finish this chapter tonight. You'll be okay on your own?"

It wasn't even really a question, only phrased to sound like one. Funny how intonation could do so much, change even what something was at its core. "Sure," I said. "Go ahead. I'll be fine."

three

I WASN'T FINE, though. I was bored, and Thisbe was still hollering. I unpacked my clothes, tried to crack my future Econ 101 textbook, and cleaned out all the messages on my phone. All of which took about forty minutes. At that point, with the baby still crying—still crying!—I finally grabbed a jacket, pulled my hair back, and went out for a walk.

At first, I wasn't planning to go to the Tip, whatever or wherever it was. I just wanted some air, a break from the noise, and a chance to process whatever it was that had happened between my dad and me earlier that evening. But after I walked in the opposite direction from the board-walk for about a block, the sidewalk ended in a cul-de-sac, a bunch of parked cars crowded along the edges. A path was visible off to one side, and I could see light in the distance. Probably a mistake, I thought, but then I thought of Hollis in that picture frame, and followed it anyway.

It wound through some beach grass and over a couple of dunes, then opened up to a wide swath of sand. From the look of it, it had once been all beach, until erosion or a storm or both created a peninsula of sorts, where now a bunch of people were gathered, some sitting on driftwood that was piled up in makeshift benches, others standing around a firepit where a good-size blaze was going. A large truck was parked off to one side, a keg in the bed, and I recognized the tall, skinny guy from the bike shop sitting beside it. When he saw me, he looked surprised, then glanced over at the fire. Sure enough, the guy who'd called out to me was there, in a red windbreaker, holding a plastic cup. He was talking to two girls—the redhead from earlier and a shorter girl with black hair, braided into pigtails—gesturing widely with his free hand.

"On your right!" I heard someone yell from behind me, and then there was a whizzing sound. I turned, only to see the short, stocky guy I'd seen earlier coming at me fast on a bike, pedaling wildly. I jumped out of the way just as he blasted by, rounding the dune and shooting onto the flatter sand of the beach. I was still trying to catch my breath when I heard the clatter of pedals, and two more bikes emerged from the dark of the path, the riders—a blond guy, and a girl with short, cropped hair—laughing and talking with each other as they zoomed past. Jesus, I thought, stepping back again, only to feel myself collide squarely with something. Or someone.

When I turned, I found myself facing a tall guy with long-ish dark hair pulled back at his neck, wearing a worn blue hoodie and jeans. He glanced at me quickly—his eyes were green, and deep set—barely seeming to register my face.

"Sorry," I said, although it wasn't my fault: he was the one creeping up behind. But he just nodded, as if I'd owed him this, and continued to the beach, sliding his hands in his pockets.

I hardly needed another sign that it was time to turn back. As I went to do just that, though, I heard a voice from behind me. "See? I *knew* you couldn't resist me!"

I turned, and there was the guy from the boardwalk, still holding his cup. The redhead and the girl with pigtails were now standing by the keg, watching disapprovingly as he walked toward me. I was suddenly nervous, not sure how to respond, but then I had a flash of my mom at our kitchen table, surrounded by all those graduate students. Maybe I didn't know what I would say. But I knew my mother, and her techniques, by heart.

"I can resist you," I told him.

"Well, of course you would think that. I haven't begun my offensive yet," he said.

"Your offensive?" I asked.

He grinned. His smile—bright, wide, verging on goofy— was his best trait, and he knew it. "I'm Jake. Let me get you a beer."

Huh, I thought. This wasn't so hard after all.

"I'll get it myself," I told him. "Just point the way."

*   *   *

What's your problem?

I didn't know how to answer this. Not when Jake first asked it, as I pulled away from him, gathering my shirt around me, and stumbled over the dunes back to the path. And not as I walked back up my dad's street, trying to shake the sand out of my hair. My lips felt full and rubbed raw, the closure of my bra, hurriedly snapped, digging into the skin of my back as I let myself in the side door, shutting it behind me.

I crept upstairs, down the dark hallway, glad to hear nothing but my own footsteps. Finally, Thisbe was asleep. After a long, hot shower, I put on some yoga pants and a tank top, then settled into my room, opening my Econ textbook again. But even as I tried to focus on the words, the events of the night came rushing back to me: my dad's sharp tone, Jake's easy smile, our fumbled, hurried connection behind the dunes, and how it suddenly all felt so weird and wrong, not like me at all. Maybe my mom could play the aloof, selfish bitch. But that was what I'd been doing: playing. Until the game was up. I was a smart girl. Why had I done something so stupid?

I felt tears fill my eyes, the words blurring on the page, and pressed my palm to my face, trying to stop them. No luck. Instead, they were contagious: a moment later, I heard Thisbe start up again, followed by the sound of someone—Heidi, I knew—coming down the hall and a door opening, then closing.

She kept on for an hour, long after my own tears had stopped and dried. Maybe it was the guilt I felt about what I'd done that night. Or that I just needed a distraction from my own problems. Whatever the reason, I found myself stepping out into the hallway, then walking to the door to Thisbe's room. This time, I didn't knock. I just pushed the door open, and Heidi, her face ragged, streaked with its own tears, looked up at me from the rocking chair. "Give her to me," I said, holding out my arms. "You get some rest."

*　*　*

I was pretty sure *Your Baby: The Basics* didn't say anything about sunrise walks on the boardwalk as a cure for colic. But you never knew.

At first, I wasn't sure Heidi was going to let me take her. Even after the hours of crying, and her clear and present exhaustion, she still hesitated. It wasn't until I took one more step toward her and added, "Come on," that she let out a big breath, and the next thing I knew my sister was in my arms.

She was so, so small. And writhing, which made her seem all the more fragile, although with all the screaming she had to have some strength to her somewhere. Her skin was warm against mine, and I could feel the dampness at the base of her neck, the hair wet there. Poor baby, I thought, surprising myself.

"I don't know what she needs," Heidi said, flopping back into the rocking chair, which then banged against the wall. "I just . . . I can't . . . I can't listen to her cry anymore."

"Go to sleep," I told her.

"I don't know," she mumbled. "Maybe I should—"

"*Go*," I said, and while I didn't mean for my voice to sound so sharp, it worked. She pushed herself out of the chair, sniffling past me and down the hallway to her room.

Which left me alone with Thisbe, who was still screaming. For a little while, I just tried to walk her: in her room, then downstairs, through the kitchen, around the island, back to the living room again, which quieted her a bit, but not much. Then I noticed the stroller, parked by the door.

It was about five when I strapped her in, still hollering, and began to push her down the driveway. By the time we got to the mailbox, twenty feet farther, she'd stopped.

No way, I thought, pausing myself and looking down at her. A beat passed, and then I watched her draw in a breath and start up again, louder than before. I quickly began pushing her once more, and after a few turns of the wheels . . . silence again. I picked up the pace and turned out onto the street.

By the time we got to the business district she was asleep under her blanket, eyes closed, face relaxed. Ahead of us, the boardwalk was deserted, a brisk breeze blowing across it. All I could hear was the ocean and the stroller wheels clacking beneath my feet.

We'd walked all the way to the Last Chance Café before we finally saw another person, and even then they were far off in the distance, just a speck and some movement. It wasn't until we came back up on the orange awning of Clementine's that I realized it was someone on a bike. They were in a spot where the boardwalk opened up to the beach, and I watched, squinting, as they went up on their front wheel, hopping for a few feet, then easing back down, spinning the handlebars. Then they were pedaling backward, zigzagging, before suddenly speeding forward, banking off a nearby bench, then down again. The movements were fluid, almost hypnotic: I thought of Heidi in the rocking chair, and Thisbe asleep in the stroller, the subtle, calming power of motion. I was so distracted, watching the person on the bike, that it wasn't until I got right up to him that

I recognized the blue hoodie, that dark hair pulled back at the neck. It was the same guy I'd bumped into on the path hours earlier.

This time, though, I was taking him by surprise, which was made obvious by the way he jerked, skidding to a clumsy stop when he suddenly spotted us standing not ten feet from him. Just by his glance, I knew he recognized me, too, although he wasn't exactly friendly—no hello. But then, I hadn't said anything either. In fact, we both just stood there, looking at each other. It probably would have been incredibly awkward, if Thisbe hadn't started crying again.

"Oh," I said, quickly pushing the stroller forward, then back again. She quieted immediately but kept her eyes open, looking at the sky overhead. The guy was watching her, and for some reason, I felt compelled to add, "She's . . . it's been a long night."

He looked at me again, and his face was so serious. Almost haunted, although why that word came to mind, I had no idea. He turned his gaze back to Thisbe, then said, "Aren't they all."

I opened my mouth to say something—to agree, at least—but he didn't give me the chance, was already pedaling backward. No good-bye, no nothing, just a spin of the handlebars, and then he was rising up on the pedals and riding away from us. Instead of a straight line, he moved down the boardwalk from side to side, zigzagging slowly, all the way to the end.

four

"FOR YOU."

I looked down: sitting in front of me on a little yellow plate was a plump, perfect blueberry muffin. A pat of butter sat next to it, like an accessory.

"Your dad said they were your favorite," Heidi said. "I got the berries this morning, from the farmers' market, and made them fresh."

While she was still clearly tired, now my stepmother looked a lot more like the Heidi I knew: her hair was pulled back neatly, and she had on jeans, a clean and matching shirt, and lip gloss. "You really didn't have to do this," I said.

"Yes," she replied. Her voice was flat, serious. "I did."

It was two P.M., and I'd just come down from a good seven hours of sleep to find her in the kitchen, rinsing out a mixing bowl, the baby asleep in the crook of her other arm. I was headed straight for the coffeemaker and not up for conversation, but before I even knew what was happening she'd blindsided me with a hug and baked goods.

"Because of you," she said now, sliding into a chair opposite me, shifting the baby slightly, "I got the first uninterrupted four hours of sleep since she was born. It was like a miracle."

"It really was not that big a deal," I told her, wishing she'd just leave it alone. All this fussing over a person, it just smacked of desperation to me.

"I'm serious," she said, clearly not getting the hint. "You are officially my favorite person in the world right now."

Great, I thought. Then I peeled back the muffin wrapper, taking a bite instead of responding. It was still warm, and delicious, and made me feel horribly ungrateful for everything I'd felt since laying eyes on her. "This is really good," I said.

"I'm so glad!" she said as the phone rang. "Like I said, it was the least I could do."

I took another bite as she stood, shifting the baby to her other arm, then grabbed the receiver off the counter. "Hello? Oh, Maggie, good, I've been wondering if that shipment came in. . . .Wait, are you okay?" She narrowed her eyes. "You sound like you've been crying. Are you crying?"

Good Lord, I thought, picking up the newspaper and scanning the headlines. What was it about the women in this town? Was everyone emotional?

"Okay," Heidi said slowly. "I just couldn't help but notice . . . No, no, of course. What? Well, it should be in the office, right in that left-hand drawer. It's not? Huh. Well, let me think. . . ." She looked around the room, then threw a hand over her mouth. Her voice rose as she said, "Oh, crap. It's here, I see it over by the door. God, how did that happen? No, I'll just bring it down right now. It's not a problem, I'll just pop Thisbe in her stroller. . . ."

The person on the other line was saying something, the voice equally high and shrill. I took a gulp of my coffee, then another one, just as Thisbe began to chime in as well. I wondered if emotions were like menstrual cycles, if you got enough women together. Give it time, and everyone was crying.

"Oh, dear," Heidi said, glancing at her watch. "Look, I'm going to have to feed her before we can go anywhere. Just tell the delivery guy . . . Is there enough cash in the drawer? Well, can you check?" There was a pause, during which Thisbe went from sputtering to all-out crying. Heidi sighed. "All right. No, we'll come right now. Just . . . hold tight. Okay. Bye."

She hung up, then walked across the room to the bottom of the stairs, jiggling Thisbe slightly as she went. "Robert?" she called up the stairs. "Honey?"

"Yes?" my dad replied a moment later, his voice muffled.

"Do you think you can feed Thisbe for me? I have to run the checkbook down to the store."

I heard footsteps overhead, then my dad's voice, louder and clearer, saying, "Are you talking to me?"

Thisbe chose this moment to increase her volume: Heidi had to shout over her as she said, "I was just wondering if you could give Thisbe a bottle, I need to go down to the store because I left the checkbook here, and I thought they could cover this COD charge with cash but there isn't enough. . . ."

Too much information, I thought, sucking down the rest of my coffee. Why did she always have to make everything so complicated?

"Honey, I'm not really at a good stopping point," my dad said. "Can it wait twenty minutes?"

Thisbe howled in response, pretty much answering this question. "Um," Heidi said, looking down at her, "I don't know—"

"Fine," my dad said, and instantly I recognized his tone, put upon and petulant. *Fine*, he'd said to my mom, you just support us with your job. *Fine*, I guess you do know more about what the publishing industry wants. *Fine*, I'll just give up my writing altogether, it's not like I was ever nominated for a National Book Award. "Just give me a minute, and I'll—"

"I'll take it down there," I said, pushing my chair back. Heidi glanced over at me, surprised, but not nearly as much as I was myself. I thought I'd given up this kind of co-dependent behavior years ago. "I want to go up to the beach anyway."

"Are you sure?" Heidi asked. "Because you were such a help last night, I don't want to ask you to—"

"She's offering, Heidi," my dad said. I still couldn't see him, only hear his voice, booming down from sights unseen, like God. "Don't be a martyr."

Which was good advice, I was thinking ten minutes later, as I walked down the boardwalk, the checkbook—and some muffins for the girls!—in hand. Twenty-four hours in Colby and already I didn't recognize myself. My mother would be disgusted, I thought. I knew I was.

When I walked into Clementine's, the first thing I saw was the dark-haired girl from the night before standing by

the counter talking to a UPS guy. "The thing is," she was
saying, "I know it's stupid that I'm still crying over him. But
we went out for, like, two years. It wasn't just a fling. We
were serious, as serious as things like that can be. So some
days, like today . . . it's just hard."

The UPS man, who looked decidedly uncomfortable,
brightened at the sight of me. "Looks like your checkbook's
here," he said.

"Oh!" She turned to face me, then blinked, confused.
"Is Heidi . . . are you . . . ?"

"Her stepdaughter," I explained.

"Really? That's great. Are you here to help with the
baby?"

"Not—"

"I can't wait to meet her," she said before I could finish.
"And I love her name! It's so unusual. Although I thought
Heidi was naming her Isabel or Caroline? But maybe I was
wrong. . . ."

I handed over the checkbook, then the bag. When she
glanced at it, quizzical, I added, "Muffins."

"Really?" she said excitedly, opening the bag. "Oh, these
smell delicious. Here, Ramon, you want one?" She offered
the bag to the UPS guy, who reached in and took one, then
to me. I shook my head, and she helped herself. "Thanks so
much. Here, I'll just write the check quick and send it back
with you, because I think Heidi needed it for some bill stuff,
and I wouldn't want you to have to make another trip. Although it is handy to have it here, but at the same time . . . "

I nodded—too much information, again—then walked

over to a display of jeans, leaving her to chatter on. Behind the jeans, tucked away against a back wall, were some bathing suits on sale, so I started picking through them. I was checking out a red, boy-short bikini that wasn't entirely hideous when I heard the front door chime.

"I brought caffeine," a girl's voice called out. "Double mocha, extra whip. Your favorite."

"And I," another chimed in, "have the very latest issue of *Hollyworld*. They just got dropped at the newsstand, like, ten minutes ago."

"You guys!" Maggie squealed. I glanced over, but because of the rack of suits, my view was blocked: she was all I could see now, as Ramon had clearly left the building, lucky guy. "What's the occasion?"

No one spoke for a moment, and I went back to my browsing. Then one of the girls said, "Well . . . the truth is, we have something we have to tell you."

"Tell me?" Maggie said.

"Yes," the other girl told her. There was a pause. Then, "Now, before we do, I want to stress that this is for your own good. Okay?"

"Okay," Maggie said slowly. "But I don't like the sound of—"

"Jake hooked up with another girl last night," the first girl blurted out. "At the Tip."

Oh, shit, I thought.

"What?" Maggie gasped.

"Leah!" one girl said. "Jesus. I thought we agreed we were going to break it to her gently."

"*You* wanted to break it to her gently," Leah replied. "I

said we should just do it fast and all at once, like an eyebrow wax."

"Are you guys serious?" Maggie's voice was tight, high, and I shrank farther into the bathing suits, wondering if there was a back exit. "How do you know? Who was it? I mean, how . . . "

"We were there," Leah said flatly. "We saw her show up and we saw them talking and then walk off to the dunes together."

"And you didn't stop him?" Maggie shrieked.

"Hey," the other girl said. "Calm down, okay?"

"Don't tell me to calm down, okay, Esther? Who was she?"

Another silence. Stupid Heidi and her stupid check-book, I thought, burying myself more deeply into the near-by one-pieces. "We don't know," Leah said. "Some summer girl, a tourist."

"Well, what did she look like?" Maggie demanded.

"Does it really matter?" Esther replied.

"Of course it matters! It's paramount."

"It is not," Leah said with a sigh, "paramount."

"Was she cuter than me?" Maggie asked. "Taller? I bet she was a blonde. Was she a blonde?"

Silence. I peered out from behind the rack of suits, by this point not surprised at all to see the redhead and the girl in the pigtails from the bonfire. They exchanged a look before pigtails—Esther—said, "She had black hair and fair skin. Taller than you, but kind of bony."

"And her skin wasn't that great," the redhead, who had to be Leah, added.

I felt myself flinch, hearing this. First, I was not bony. And okay, so I had a couple of zits, but they were temporary, not a condition. And anyway, who were they to say—

Suddenly, the bathing suit rack before me parted right down the middle, like the Red Sea. And just like that, with a clattering of hangers, I found myself face-to-face with Maggie.

"Did she," she said, narrowing her eyes at me, "look like this, maybe?"

"Holy crap," Leah said. Beside her, Esther slapped a hand over her mouth.

"I can't *believe* this," Maggie said as I fought the urge to try to protect myself with a nearby bandeau. "Did you hook up with Jake last night?"

I swallowed, the sound seeming louder than a gunshot. "It wasn't," I began, then realized my voice was wavering and stopped, taking a breath. "It was nothing."

Maggie sucked in a breath, her cheeks hollowing. "Nothing," she repeated. Then she dropped her hands from the suits on the rack, letting them flop to her sides. "You hook up with the love of my *life*, the boy I wanted to *marry*—"

"Oh, man," Leah said. "Here we go."

"And it's *nothing*? Really?"

"Maggie," Esther said, walking over, "come on. It's not about her."

"Then what it is about, exactly?"

Esther sighed. "You knew this was going to happen sooner or later."

"No," Maggie protested. "I didn't know that. I didn't know that at all."

"Yes, you did." Esther put her hand on her shoulder, squeezing it. "Face it. If it wasn't her, it just would have been some other girl."

"Some other stupid girl," Leah added, picking up the magazine and flipping through it. Then, as an after-thought, she glanced at me and said, "No offense. He's just an idiot."

"He is not," Maggie protested, tears filling her eyes.

"Come on, Mag. You know he is." Esther glanced at me, then slid her hand down Maggie's arm, wrapping a hand over hers. "And now, you can really start to get over him. If you think about it, this is probably the best thing that could have happened."

"That's right," Leah agreed, flipping another page.

"How do you figure?" Maggie whimpered, but she al-lowed herself to be led back to the counter, numbly taking her mocha as Leah handed it off to her.

"Because," Esther said gently, "you were still just hang-ing on, torturing yourself, thinking he was coming back. And now you have to let go. She kind of did you a favor, if you really think about it."

Maggie looked back over at me, and I made myself stand up straighter. I couldn't believe I'd actually been worried about her: she was tiny, pink as a powder puff. Thinking this, I emerged from behind the suits and started for the door.

"Wait a second," she said.

I didn't have to stop. I knew that. Still, I slowed my steps, turning back to her. But I didn't say anything.

"Do you," she began, then stopped and took a breath.

"Do you really like him? Just tell me. I know it's pathetic, but I need to know."

I just looked at her for moment, feeling all those eyes on me. "He's nothing to me," I said.

She kept her gaze on me a moment longer. Then she picked up the checkbook, walking over and holding it out to me. "Thanks," she said.

Maybe in the world of girls, this was supposed to be a turning point. When we saw beyond our initial differences, realized we had something in common after all, and became true friends. But that was a place I didn't know well, had never lived in, and had no interest in discovering, even as a tourist. So I took the checkbook, nodded, and walked out the door, leaving them—as I had so many other groups—to say whatever they would about me once I was gone.

✳ ✳ ✳

"So," my mother said, "tell me *everything*."

It was late afternoon, and I'd been dead asleep when my phone rang. Even without looking at it, I knew it had to be my mom. First, because it was her favorite time to make phone calls, right at the start of cocktail hour. It wasn't like I was expecting to hear from anyone else, except maybe my brother, Hollis, and he only called in the middle of the night, having yet to fully grasp the concept of time zones.

"Well," I said, stifling a yawn, "it's really pretty here. You should see the view."

"I'm sure it is," she replied. "But don't bore me with the scenery, I need details. How is your father?"

I swallowed, then glanced at my shut door, as if I could

somehow see through it, all the way down to his. Amazing how easily my mother could get to the one thing I didn't want to talk about. She always just knew.

I'd now been at my dad's for three days, during which I'd probably seen him a total of, oh, three hours. He was either in his office working, in his bedroom sleeping, or in the kitchen grabbing a quick bite, en route to one or the other. So much for my visions of us hanging out and bonding, sharing a plate of onion rings and discussing literature and my future. Instead, our conversations usually took place on the stairs, a quick, "How's it going? Been to the beach today?" as we went in opposite directions. Even these, though, were better than the efforts I'd made at knocking on his office door. Then, he didn't even bother to turn away from the computer screen, my attempts at dialogue bouncing off the back of his head like shots missing the rim by a mile.

It sucked. What was worse, though, was that if my father was nonexistent, Heidi was *everywhere*. If I went to get coffee, she was in the kitchen, feeding the baby. If I tried to hide on the deck, she emerged, Thisbe in the BabyBjörn, inviting me to join them for a walk on the beach. Even in my room I wasn't safe, as it was so close to the nursery that even the slightest movement or noise summoned her, as she assumed I was as desperate for companionship as she was.

Clearly, she was lonely. But I wasn't. I was accustomed to being alone: I liked it. Which was why it was surprising that I even noticed my dad's lack of attention, much less cared. But for some reason, I did. And all her muffins and chatter and over-friendliness just made it worse.

I could have told my mother all of this. After all, it was exactly what she wanted to hear. But to do so, for some reason, seemed like a failure. I mean, what had I expected, anyway? So I took a different tack.

"Well," I began, "he's writing a lot. He's in his office every day, all day."

A pause as she processed this. Then, "Really."

"Yeah," I said. "He says he's almost done with the book, just has some tightening up to do."

"Tightening up that takes all day, every day," she said. Ouch. "What about the baby? Is he helping Heidi out with her?"

"Um," I said, then immediately regretting it, knowing this one utterance spoke volumes. "He does. But she's actually really determined to do it on her own. . . ."

"Oh, please," my mom said. I could hear her satisfaction. "Nobody wants to be the sole caregiver of a newborn. And if they say they do, it's only because they don't really have a choice. Have you seen your father change a diaper?"

"I'm sure he has."

"Yes, but Auden." I winced. This was like being painted into a corner, stroke by stroke. "Have you *seen* it?"

"Well," I said. "Not really."

"Ah." She exhaled again, and I could almost hear her smiling. "Well, it's nice to know some things really never do change."

I wanted to point out that since this was what she was so sure of, she shouldn't have been surprised. Instead, I said, "So how are you doing?"

"Me?" A sigh. "Oh, the same old, same old. I've been

asked to head up the committee rewriting the English core courses for next year, with all the attendant drama that will entail. And I have several articles expected by various journals, my trip to Stratford coming up, and, of course, entirely too many dissertations that clearly cannot be completed without a large amount of hand-holding."

"Sounds like quite a summer," I said, opening my window.

"Tell me about it. These graduate students, I swear, it just never ends. They're all so *needy.*" She sighed again, and I thought of those black-rimmed glasses sitting on the countertop. "I have half a mind to decamp to the coast, like you, and spend the summer on the beach without a care in the world."

I looked out the window at the water, the white sand, the Tip just visible beyond. Yep, I wanted to say. That's me exactly. "So," I said, thinking this, "have you heard from Hollis lately?"

"Night before last," she said. Then she laughed. "He was telling me he met some Norwegians who were on their way to a convention in Amsterdam. They own some Internet start-up, and apparently they're very interested in Hollis, think he's really got his finger on the pulse of their American target audience, so he went along. He's thinking it could pan out into a position of some sort. . . ."

I rolled my eyes. Funny how my mom could see through me entirely, but Hollis takes off for Amsterdam with some people he just met, spins it into a career move, and she goes for it hook, line, and sinker. Honestly.

Just then, there was a knock on my door. When I opened it, I was surprised to see my dad standing there. "Hey," he said, smiling at me. "We're heading out for some dinner, thought you might want to come along."

"Sure," I mouthed, hoping my mother, who was still talking about Hollis, wouldn't hear.

"Auden?" No luck. Her voice was clear through the receiver, a fact made more apparent by the way my dad winced. "Are you still there?"

"I am," I told her. "But Dad just came and invited me to dinner, so I better go."

"Oh," she said, "so he's done with the tightening for the day?"

"I'll call you later," I said quickly, shutting my phone and folding my hand around it.

My dad sighed. "And how is your mother?"

"Fine," I said. "Let's go."

Downstairs, Heidi was waiting for us, her own phone clamped to her ear, Thisbe strapped into her stroller. My dad opened the door, and she pushed the baby out as she kept talking. "But that doesn't make sense! I did the payroll myself, and we had plenty of money in the account. It just . . . well, of course. The bank would know. I'm terribly sorry, Esther, this is so embarrassing. Look, we're on our way down there right now. I'll get some cash from the ATM and we'll work all this out on Monday, okay?"

My dad took a deep breath as we stepped outside. "Gotta love that sea air!" he said to me, patting his hands on his chest. "It's great for the soul."

"You're in a good mood," I said as Heidi, still talking, eased the stroller down the front steps, and we started toward the street.

"Ah, well, that's what a breakthrough can do for you," he replied, reaching over Heidi's hands and taking the stroller handles from her. She smiled at him, stepping aside as he began to push Thisbe along. "I'd been really struggling with this middle chapter, just couldn't find my groove. But then, today, suddenly . . . it came together." He snapped his fingers. "Just like that! It's going to make all the ones to follow that much easier."

I glanced at Heidi, who was now saying something about bank fees, a worried look on her face. "I thought you were mostly tightening," I said to my dad.

"What?" he said, nodding at a man who was jogging past, plugged into his iPod. "Oh, right. Well, it's all just a matter of fitting things together. A few more days like today, and I'll have this draft done by midsummer. At the latest."

"Wow," I said as Heidi shut her phone, then ran a hand through her hair. My dad reached over, grabbing her by the waist and pulling her closer, then planted a kiss on her cheek.

"Isn't this great?" he said, smiling. "All of us together, going for Thisbe's first trip to the Last Chance."

"It's wonderful," Heidi agreed. "But I actually need to stop at the shop on the way. There's apparently some problem with the payroll checks. . . ."

"It's Friday night, honey!" my dad said. "Just let it go. All that work stuff will still be there on Monday."

"Yes, but—" Heidi replied as her phone rang again. She glanced at it, then put it to her ear. "Hello? Leah, yes, what's . . . oh. No, I'm aware of it. Look, are you at the branch just down from the shop? Okay, then just walk over and I'll meet you there. I'm remedying it as we speak."

"These girls she hires," my dad said, nodding at Heidi. "Typical teenagers. It's always something."

I nodded, as if I were not, in fact, a teenager myself. Then again, to my dad, I wasn't.

"Their paychecks bounced," Heidi told him. "It's kind of a serious situation."

"Then call your accountant, let him deal with it," he replied, making a goofy face down at Thisbe, who was drifting off to sleep. "We're having family time."

"He doesn't do payroll, I do," Heidi said.

"Well, then tell them to wait until we've finished dinner."

"I can't do that, Robert. They deserve to be paid, and—"

"Look," my dad said, annoyed, "weren't you the one who said I wasn't spending enough time with you and the baby and Auden? Who *insisted* that I stop working, and have a family dinner out?"

"Yes," Heidi said as her phone rang again. "But—"

"So I knock off early. On my best day yet, I might add," he continued as we rolled up onto the boardwalk, "and now you're not willing to do the same thing."

"Robert, this is my business."

"And writing isn't mine?"

Oh, boy, I thought. Change a few details—professorship for business, committees for employees—and this was the same fight he'd had with my mom all those years ago. I glanced at Heidi: her face was stressed, as Clementine's now came into view, Esther and Leah standing outside together. "Look," she said to my dad, "why don't you and Auden take the baby and get a table and I'll meet you there. This will only take a few minutes. Okay?"

"Fine," my dad said, although clearly, it wasn't.

He wasn't the only one not happy. Twenty minutes later, just as we were about to be seated at Last Chance, Thisbe woke up and started fussing. At first, it was a low, rumbling sort of crying, but then it began to escalate. By the time the hostess arrived and began to grab menus for us, she was pretty much screaming.

"Oh," my dad said, moving the stroller forward and back. Thisbe kept wailing. "Well. Auden, can you . . . ?"

This was not followed by a verb, so I had no idea what he was asking. As Thisbe kept crying, though, now attracting the attention of pretty much everyone around us, he shot me another, more panicked look, and I realized he wanted me to jump in. Which was ridiculous. Even worse? I did it.

"I'll take her," I said, grabbing the stroller from him and backing it up to the door. "Why don't you—"

"I'll sit down and order for us," he said. "Just bring her back in when she's calmed down, all right?"

Of course. Because *that* was going to happen anytime soon.

I wheeled her out onto the boardwalk, where at least the noise wasn't enclosed, then sat down on a bench beside her. I watched her face for a while, scrunched up and reddening, before glancing back into the restaurant. Past the hostess station, down a narrow aisle, I could see my dad, at a table for four, a menu spread out in front of him. I swallowed, then ran a hand over my face, closing my eyes.

People don't change, my mother had said, and of course

she was right. My dad was still selfish and inconsiderate, and I was still not wanting to believe it, even when the proof was right in front of me. Maybe we were all destined to just keep doing the same stupid things, over and over again, never really learning a single thing. Beside me, Thisbe was now screaming, and I wanted to join in, sit back and open my mouth and let the years of frustration and sadness and everything else just spill forth into the world once and for all. But instead, I just sat there, silent, until I suddenly felt someone looking at me.

I opened my eyes, and there, standing next to the stroller in jeans, beat-up sneakers, and a faded T-shirt that said LOVE SHOVE across the front, was the guy I'd seen at the Tip and the boardwalk. It was like he'd appeared from nowhere and now was suddenly right there, studying Thisbe. As he did, I took the opportunity to do the same to him, taking in his tanned skin and green eyes, shoulder-length dark hair pulled back messily at the back of his neck, the thick, raised scar that ran up one forearm, forking at the elbow like a river on a map.

I had no idea why he was here, especially considering how he'd blown me off the last time we'd met, in this same place. But at that moment, I didn't have the energy to over-think. I said, "She just started screaming."

He considered this but said nothing. Which for some reason, God only knew why, made me feel like I needed to keep talking.

"She's *always* crying, actually," I told him. "It's colic, or just . . . I don't know what to do."

Still, he was silent. Just like he'd been that night at the

Tip, and on the boardwalk. The sick part was that I *knew* he wouldn't answer, but still insisted on talking to him anyway. Which was so not like me, as I was the one who usually—

"Well," he said suddenly, taking me by surprise yet again, "there's always the elevator."

I just looked at him. "The elevator?"

In response, he bent down and unhitched Thisbe from the stroller. Before I could stop him—and I was pretty sure I should stop him—he'd taken her out, lifting her up into his arms. My first thought was that this was the last thing I'd expected him to do. The second was how amazingly at ease he seemed with her, more than me and my dad and even Heidi, combined.

"This," he said, turning her so she was facing out (still screaming, of course), his hands wrapped around her mid-section, legs dangling down and kicking wildly, "is the ele-vator." And then he bent his legs, easing down, and straightened them, then repeated it, once, twice, three times. By the fourth, she abruptly stopped her protests, a weird look of calm spreading over her face.

I just stood there, looking at him. Who *was* this guy? Sullen stranger? Trick biker? Baby whisperer? Or—

"Eli!" Heidi said, suddenly appearing behind him. "I thought that was you."

The guy glanced at her, then flushed, but only barely, and briefly. "Hey," he said, stopping the elevator. Thisbe blinked, then burst into tears.

"Oh, dear," Heidi said, reaching out to take her from him. To me she said, "Where's your father?"

"He got a table," I told her. "We were about to sit down when she started to freak out."

"She's probably hungry," Heidi said, glancing at her watch. Thisbe wailed louder, over her shoulder, while I glanced at the guy—Eli—trying to process what I'd just seen. "What a day! You would not believe the mess I have to deal with at work. The checkbook is all out of order, somehow I missed a deposit or something, thank God the girls are so understanding. I mean, it's not like their paychecks are for huge amounts, but still, they work hard, and . . ."

Between this soliloquy and the baby melting down, not to mention Eli witnessing it all, I could literally feel my temperature rising. Why did she have to make everything such a big deal?

"I better get back to the shop," he said to Heidi. "Congratulations, by the way."

"Oh, Eli, you're so sweet, thank you," she replied, jiggling the baby. "And I'm so glad you met Auden! She's new here, hardly knows a soul, and I was hoping she'd find someone to introduce her around."

I felt my face flush even hotter; of course she had to make it sound like I was desperate for company. Which was why I barely responded as Eli nodded at me before crossing the boardwalk and pushing the door open to the bike shop, disappearing inside.

"Thisbe, sweetheart, it's okay," Heidi was saying, oblivious to all this as she strapped the baby back into the stroller. To me she added, "It's so great you and Eli are friends!"

"We're not," I said. "We don't even really know each other."

"Oh." She looked over at the bike shop, as if it would confirm this, then back at me. "Well, he is really sweet. His brother, Jake, is about your age, I think. He went out with Maggie until just recently. Awful breakup, that was. She's still reeling from it."

His brother? I thought, my face flushing. How small *was* this freaking town, anyway? And Heidi was *still talking*.

"Should we go back to the restaurant?" she asked me. "Or maybe I should take Thisbe home, she's so upset. What do you think? I mean, I'd love a dinner out, but I wonder—"

"I don't," I said, the words coming even as I knew I should bite them back, "I don't know what you should do. Okay? All I know is that I'm hungry, and I want to go eat with my father. So that's what *I'm* going to do, if it's all right with you."

I could see her draw in a breath as a hurt look spread across her face. "Oh," she said after a moment. "Well, sure. Of course."

I knew I'd been mean. I knew it, and yet I still turned and walked away, leaving her and the baby, still crying, behind me. But I could have sworn the sound followed me, hanging on, filling my ears even through the crowd on the boardwalk, into the restaurant, all the way down the narrow aisle to the table where my dad was already eating. He took a look at my face, then pushed a menu over to me as I slid into the booth across from him.

"Just relax," he said. "It's Friday night."

Right, I thought. Of course. And when the onion rings arrived a few minutes later, I tried to do just that. But for some reason, they didn't taste the same this time. Still good. But not great like before.

❋ ❋ ❋

I knew from experience when a fight was over and when it had only just begun. So I stayed gone after dinner, taking a walk on the beach and the longest way home. Not long enough, though: as I climbed the porch steps two hours later, I could hear them.

"—understand what you want from me. You asked me to stop working and come to dinner. I did that. And you're still not happy."

"I wanted us to all have dinner together!"

"And we would have, if you hadn't left to go to the store. That was your choice."

I dropped my hand from the doorknob, stepping back out of the porch light. From the sound of it, this was happening just inside, and the last thing I wanted was to walk into the middle of it.

"I just wish . . . " Heidi said, her voice cracking.

Then, nothing. The silence was almost unbearable, broken only when my dad said, "You just wish what."

"I don't know," she said. "I just . . . I thought you'd want to spend more time with us."

"I'm here all the time, Heidi," my dad said, his voice flat.

"Yes, but you're in your office. You're not with Thisbe, interacting with her. You don't rock her or get up with her. . . ."

"We discussed this as soon as you got pregnant," my dad told her, his voice rising. "I told you I cannot function on broken sleep, that I have to get my nine hours. You knew that."

"Okay, but you could take her during the day, or in the morning so I could deal with work stuff. Or even—"

"Have we not discussed," my dad said, "how important it is that I finish the book this summer? That I can't do the work I need to do during the academic year, and this is my only chance to work uninterrupted?"

"Yes, of course, but—"

"Which is why," he continued, talking over her, "I said let's hire a nanny. Or a babysitter. But you didn't want to."

"I don't need a nanny. I just need an hour here or there."

"So ask Auden! Isn't that why you wanted her to come visit?"

I literally felt like I'd been slapped: my reaction was that visceral, blood rushing to my face.

"I didn't invite Auden so she'd babysit," she said.

"Then why is she here?"

Another silence followed. This one I welcomed, though, as sometimes a question can hurt more than an answer. Finally Heidi said, "For the same reason I want you to spend time with the baby. Because she's your daughter, and you should want to be with her."

"Oh, Jesus," my dad said. "Do you really think—"

There was more coming, of course there was. My dad never said a sentence when he could go on for a paragraph. But this time, I couldn't stand to hear it. So I dug my keys out of my pocket and got into my car.

I stayed gone for three hours, driving up and down the streets of Colby, circling up to the college, down to the pier, then back again. It was too small a place to really get lost in, but I did my best. And when I pulled back into the driveway, I made sure all the lights were out in the house before I even thought about going inside.

It was quiet as I stepped into the foyer, shutting the door behind me. At least there was no sign of major disturbances: the stroller was parked by the stairs, a burp cloth folded over the banister, my dad's keys sitting on the table by the door. The only thing different was the kitchen table, which was now piled with Heidi's business checkbook, various stacks of paper, and a couple of legal pads. On one of them, she'd clearly been trying to figure out what had happened with accounts. "WITHHOLDING?" she'd written, as well as "DEPOSIT 6-11?" and "CHECK ALL DEBITS SINCE APRIL, ERRORS?" From the looks of it—messy, sort of desperate—she hadn't gotten very far.

Looking down at the mess of papers, I had a flash of her hurt face after I'd snapped at her, as well as what she'd said later to my dad about me. It was so unexpected to have her in my corner, defending me. Even more shocking was how grateful I'd felt, if only fleetingly, to find her there.

I glanced at my watch: it was twelve fifteen, early by my clock, with a full night still ahead of me. And the coffee-maker was right there on the counter, already filled for the morning and ready to go. It wasn't Ray's, but it would do. So I turned, hitting the button, and as it began to brew, I sat down with Heidi's checkbook, flipping it open, and went looking for what she'd lost.

five

"HEY, AUD. IT'S me! What's going on?"

My brother's voice, loud and cheerful, boomed through my cell phone, a loud bass beat behind it. I was sure that Hollis did spend some of his time in places other than bars, but he never seemed to call me from any of them.

"Not much," I said, glancing at my watch. It was eight thirty P.M. my time, which meant well past midnight at his. "Just getting ready to go to work."

"Work?" he said, saying the word like it was from another language. Which, to him, it sort of was. "I thought you were supposed to be having a lazy summer, just hanging out at the beach."

I was sure it was no coincidence he'd put it like this, almost verbatim the way my mother had described it during our last conversation: if Hollis was able to spin my mom's thinking any way he wanted, she had similar influence over his own. Their connection was almost eerie, really, a bond that was so strong you could almost feel it, like a tidal pull, when they were together. My mother claimed it was the result of all those nights they spent together when he was a baby, but I wondered if it was just that Hollis had a way with women, starting with the first one he'd ever known.

"Well," I said now, as the music grew louder, then dropped off again behind him, "I didn't plan on working, actually. It just sort of happened."

"That sucks!" he said. "Drop your guard, and stuff like that will sneak up on you. You gotta stay vigilant, you know?"

I knew. In truth, though, this latest situation was no surprise. If anything, I'd walked right into it, eyes wide open. I had no one to blame but myself.

"I can't believe it!" Heidi had said when I came down the day after I'd worked on her books. As always, she was in the kitchen, lying in wait, the baby strapped to her in the BabyBjörn. "When I went to bed last night, this was all such a mess, and then this morning, it's . . . it's fixed. You're a miracle worker! How did you even know how to do all that?"

"I worked for an accountant last summer for a little while," I told her, pulling the coffee out of the freezer. By the time I got up they'd long ago rinsed out the pot, so I always got a fresh one, all mine. "It was no big deal."

"I spent *two hours* last night going over this checkbook register," she said, picking it up and waving it at me. "And I could not find the problem. How did you even know to consider double withholding?"

I started the coffeemaker, wishing I could at least have a cup in me before having to converse with anyone. No chance of that, though.

"The register indicated it happened last May," I told her. "So I just figured it might have again. And then when I went to look at the tax statements—"

"Which were such a mess, too, I couldn't find a thing in them!" she said. "And now they're all organized. You must have spent hours getting all this stuff in order."

Four, I thought. Out loud I said, "No. I really didn't."

She just shook her head, watching me as the coffee-maker finally produced enough for a quarter of a cup, which I quickly poured into my mug. "You know," she said, "I've been needing to hire someone to help me with the books for months now, but I was hesitant, as it's such a sensitive job. I didn't want to give it to just anyone."

Oh, dear Lord, I thought. Please just let me drink my coffee.

"But if you were interested," she continued, "I'd make it worth your while. Seriously."

I was still waiting for the caffeine to hit as I said, "Um, I wasn't really planning to work this summer. And I'm not exactly a morning person. . . ."

"Oh, you wouldn't have to be, though!" she said. "The girls do the deposit every day, and that's the only thing that has to be done by a certain time. The rest, like the books and the payroll and keeping track of the register take, you can do later in the day. It's actually *better* if you wait, really."

Of course it was. And now I was stuck, as clearly, no good deed went unpunished. The bigger issue, though, was what had inspired this sudden burst of Good Samaritan be-havior on my part? Was it that hard to realize that it would never just stop with one thing, there would always be a next step expected, and then one beyond that?

"That's a really nice offer," I said to Heidi, "but—"

This thought was interrupted by the sound of footsteps

behind me: a moment later, my dad rounded the corner, carrying an empty plate, a Diet Coke can balanced on top of it. When he saw Heidi, and she looked back at him, I knew instantly their argument from the night before had not been resolved. It wasn't exactly a chill in the air as much as a deep freeze.

"Well," he said to me, walking to the sink and putting his plate into it, "I see you're finally awake. What time do you go to bed these days, anyway?"

"Late," I told him. "Or early, depending on how you look at it."

He nodded as he rinsed off the plate, sticking it in the dish rack. "Ah, the ease of youth. Up all night, not a care in the world. I envy you."

Don't, I thought. Heidi said, "Actually, Auden spent last night going over my books. She found the error that threw off my balance."

"Really," my dad said, glancing at me.

"I'm trying to convince her to work for me," Heidi added. "Do a few hours a day in the office at the shop."

"Heidi," he said, rinsing off his hands, "Auden's not here to work. Remember?"

It was just one comment but crafted for maximum impact. And it delivered: I watched as Heidi winced. "Of course not," she said. "I just thought that she might—"

"She should be enjoying her time with her family," he told her. Then he smiled at me. "What do you say, Auden? How about you and me have dinner tonight?"

He was good, my dad. I had to give him that. And so what if this was all about getting back at Heidi for the night before? It was exactly what I wanted, just me and him, and that was all that mattered. Wasn't it?

"That sounds great," Heidi said. When I looked at her, she smiled at me, although it seemed a little forced. "And, look, don't worry about the job thing. Your dad's right, you should just be enjoying your summer."

My dad was taking a last sip of his Diet Coke, watching her as she said this. It had been a while since I'd had to listen to my parents fight, but no matter. Same tension, same barbs. Same look on my dad's face when he knew he'd won.

"Actually," I said, speaking before I even really realized what I was doing, "I could use some extra money for school. As long as it wasn't too many hours."

Heidi looked surprised, then glanced at my dad—whose expression could best be described as annoyed—before saying, "Oh, it wouldn't be! Just, like, fifteen a week. If that."

"Auden," my dad said. "Don't feel obligated. You're here as our guest."

I knew that if I hadn't heard their argument the night before, this entire exchange would have been different. But you can't unlearn something, even if you want to. You know what you know.

Later that evening, my dad and I walked up the board-walk to a place right on the pier, where we ordered a pound of steamed shrimp and sat looking over the water. I wasn't sure if it was that I couldn't stop thinking about what he'd said, or that he was still annoyed at me taking Heidi's offer (and, in his mind at least, side), but at fi st it was a little stiff, awkward. After he had a beer and ᣾ both endured some very dull conversation, though, things loosened up, with him asking me about Defriese and my plans for my major. In turn, I got him to talk about his book ("an intricate study of a man trying to escape his family's past") and the progress he was making (he'd had to tear out the middle, it just wasn't working, but the new stuff was much, much better). It took a while, but somewhere between the second pound of shrimp and his detailed explanation about his character's inner conflict, I was reminded of everything I loved about my dad: his passion for his work, and the way, when he was talking to you about it, it was like there was no one else in the room, or even the world.

"I can't wait to read it," I told him as the waitress dropped off our check. Between us there was a huge mound of shrimp shells, translucent and pink in the sunlight slanting through the window. "It sounds great."

"See, *you* understand how important all this is," he said, wiping his mouth. "You were there when *Narwhal* came out, and saw how its success changed our lives. This could do the same for me and the baby and Heidi. I just wish she could see that." He was studying his beer bottle as he said this, turning it in his hand.

"Well, it could be she's just emotional right now. Sleep deprivation and all that."

"Maybe." He took a sip. "But in truth, she doesn't think like we do, Auden. Her strength is business, which is all about results, very calculating. It's different with academics and writers. You know that."

I did know that. But I also knew that my mother, who fit

both of these categories, had felt the exact same way about his efforts with this exact same novel. Still, it was nice to know he felt like he could confide in me.

After dinner, we parted ways and I headed toward Clementine's, where I'd told Heidi I'd look over the office and get my bearings before officially starting work the next day. I wasn't exactly looking forward to it, for any number of reasons, so I was actually grateful for once for the distraction that was my brother.

"So," I said to him now as the music began to thump again, "Tara's nice."

"Who?"

"Tara," I repeated. "Your girlfriend?"

"Oh, right." There was a pointed pause, which pretty much answered any lingering questions I might have asked. Then, "So you got your present, huh?"

I could see the picture frame, which was in my duffel bag, instantly in my mind, those words beneath his grinning face: THE BEST OF TIMES. "Yeah," I said to Hollis. "It's great. I love it."

He chuckled. "Come on, Aud. You do not."

"I do."

"No, you don't. It's totally tacky."

"Well," I said. "It's—"

"Horrible," he finished for me. "Cheap and ridiculous. Probably the stupidest graduation gift ever, which is exactly why I gave it to you." He laughed, that booming, Hollis guffaw that, despite myself, always made me want to laugh, too. "Look, I figured there was no way I could compete with all the money and savings bonds and new cars you'd be getting from everyone else. So I decided at least my offering should be memorable."

"It is that," I agreed.

"You should have seen the others!" Another laugh. "They had them with all kinds of sayings. One was HELLO FRIEND! in bright yellow. Also, PARTY QUEEN, in pink. And then there was the one that said, inexplicably, in green, CRAZY PERSON. Like anyone would want their picture in that."

"Only you," I said.

"No kidding!" He snorted. "Anyway, I figured the cool thing was that you could keep switching out the picture. Because you don't want THE BEST OF TIMES to be just one thing, forever. You have to have a lot of bests of times, each one topping the last. You know?"

"Yeah," I said. And just like that, he'd done it again: taken a thought he'd probably come to on the fly, under any number of influences, and somehow managed to make it deep enough to resonate. It was an art, what Hollis did. Never calculating, but it did have its charms. "I miss you," I said to him.

"I miss you, too," he replied. "Hey, look, I'll send a CRAZY PERSON frame. You can put that picture of me in it, set it next to you in THE BEST OF TIMES, and it'll almost be like we're together. What do you think?"

I smiled. "It's a deal."

"Cool!" There was a muffled noise, followed by loud voices. "Okay, Aud, I gotta run, Ramona and me are headed to a party. Talk soon, though, okay?"

"Sure," I said. "Let's—"

But then he was gone, just like that. Before I could ask him who exactly Ramona was, or what had happened in Amsterdam. That was my brother, the living, breathing To Be Continued. Like my dad's book, he was always in progress.

I shut my phone, then slid it back into my pocket. Hollis was a great distraction, but any regret I'd been feeling about taking the job came rushing back as soon as I opened the door to Clementine's and saw Maggie standing at the register, Leah and Esther on either side of her. There is really nothing more intimidating than approaching a group of girls who have already made up their minds about you. It's like walking a plank, no way to go but down.

"Hello," Leah, the redhead, said as I came toward them. She was one of those tall, curvy types with milky white skin and was wearing a low-cut sundress and strappy heels. Her voice was neither kind nor unkind, just sort of level as she said, "What can we do for you?"

"She's going to be doing the books," Maggie told her, although her eyes were on me. When I looked back at her, though, she flushed, turning her gaze to some papers on the counter in front of her, shuffling them busily. "Heidi's been looking for someone since the baby came, remember?"

"Oh, right," Leah said. She pushed back from the counter, hopping up on the one behind her, and folded her long legs. "Well, maybe now our checks won't bounce."

"No kidding," Esther said. Her pigtails were gone, her hair loose and topped with an army-style cap, which she was wearing with a black sundress, a denim jacket thrown over it, and flip-flops. "I mean, I love Heidi. But getting paid at the ATM is kind of sketchy."

"You did get paid, though. Heidi's a good boss; it was an honest mistake," Maggie said. Now she was making a studied point of not looking at me as she hit a button on the register, then pulled out a stack of bills, straightening them. Again, she was dressed in pink—both her shirt and flip-flops—and I wondered if this was some kind of signature thing with her. I bet it was. "Anyway, someone's supposed to show her around."

"Who?" Leah asked. "Heidi?"

"No." Maggie shut the drawer, then looked at me. A moment later, Leah and Esther both followed suit. Clearly, I'd reached the end of that plank. Nothing to do but jump.

"Auden," I said.

A pause. Then Leah pushed herself off the counter, dropping her feet to the floor with a *clunk*. "Come on," she said over her shoulder. "The office is this way."

I could feel the other girls watching me as I followed her past a couple of racks of jeans, a shoe display, and a clearance section to a narrow hallway. "That's the bathroom," she said, nodding at a door on the left. "Not for customer use, ever, it's the rule. And here's the office. Stand back, the door kind of sticks."

She reached for the knob, then pushed herself against it. A second later, I heard a *pop!* and it swung open.

The first thing I saw was pink. All four walls were painted a rosy, almost bubble-gummy shade of Maggie's favorite color. What wasn't pink (which, at first glance, didn't seem like much) was orange. Adding to the insanity, the very small space was jammed with all kinds of girly little touches: pink stacking bins, a Hello Kitty pencil cup, a bowl filled entirely with lipsticks and lip glosses. Even the filing cabinets—the filing cabinets!—had pink and orange labels, and a pink feather boa was stretched out over across the top of them.

"Wow," I said, unable to keep my silence.

"I know," Leah agreed. "It's like being in a Starburst box. So, the safe is under the desk, the checkbook lives in the second left-hand drawer, when it's here, and all the invoices go under the bear."

"The bear?"

She stepped inside the room, walked to the desk, and picked up a little stuffed pink bear. Wearing an orange hat. "Here," she said, pointing to the stack of paper beneath him. "Don't ask me, it was like that when I got hired. Any questions?"

Of course, I had several, but none she could answer. "No. Thanks."

"Sure thing. Just holler if you need us." She stepped past me, back into the hallway, where I was still standing, having not yet had the strength to actually venture inside. I heard her take a few steps before she said, "And Auden?"

I turned, facing her. "Yeah?"

She glanced over her shoulder, then took one step back toward me. "Don't worry about Maggie. She's just . . . emotional. She'll get over it."

"Oh," I said, wondering how, exactly, I was supposed

to respond to this. Even I knew better than to talk about one girl with another one, especially if they were friends. "Right."

She nodded, then walked away, back to the register, where Esther and Maggie were now bent over a box, sticking price tags onto sunglasses. As she approached, they glanced up at her, then easily adjusted themselves, making room for her to join them.

I looked back into the pink room, and for some reason thought of my mother, if only because she was the only person I knew who would have had more trouble entering it than I did. I could just imagine her face, how her eyes would narrow in disgust, the heavy, through-the-nostril sigh that would speak louder than the words that followed it. "It's like a womb in here!" she'd groan. "An environment totally ruled by gender stereotypes and expectations, as pathetic as those who chose to inhabit it."

Exactly, I thought. Then I went inside.

❋ ❋ ❋

Heidi's office might have been over-the-top, but her books were actually in pretty good shape. When I'd worked for my mom's accountant the summer before, I'd seen some crazy bookkeeping methods. There were people who came in with registers where entire months' worth of checks were missing, others who only seemed to keep their receipts on matchbooks or napkins. Heidi's stuff was organized, her files made sense, and there were only a few discrepancies, all of which had happened in the last ten months or so. Maybe this shouldn't have been a surprise to me, considering what my dad had said about her business background. But it was.

Not shocking was the fact that at first, the office was completely distracting. I actually felt a little nauseated, sitting there, a condition exacerbated when I turned on the desk lamp, which had an orange shade and made everything seem even more radioactive. But after a few minutes with the calculator and the checkbook, it all just kind of fell away. I hadn't realized how much I missed the simplicity of a project of numbers, how things just made sense in sums and division. No emotion, no complications. Just digits onscreen, lining up in perfect sequence.

I was so immersed, in fact, that at first I didn't even hear the music coming from the store behind me. It was only when it suddenly got very loud, like someone had twisted the volume from the lowest to highest setting, that it broke through the tax forms I was looking at and got my attention.

I looked at the clock—it was 9:01—then pushed my chair back and eased the door open. Out in the hallway, the music was positively deafening, some disco song with a fast beat, a girl's voice chanting some lyrics about a summer crush over it. I was wondering if maybe they were having some issue with the stereo system when I saw Esther suddenly go shimmying past the jeans display, her arms waving over her head. She was followed, moments later, by Leah, doing a slow, hip-swiveling move, and then Maggie, bouncing on her tiptoes. It was like a conga line of three, passing quickly, then gone.

I took another step forward, leaning out a bit more

into the store. I couldn't see any customers, although the boardwalk looked crowded, lots of people passing by. I'd just decided to go back to the office and wait for the silence to return when Esther popped up from behind the bathing suit rack, this time doing a step-slide, step-slide move, her hair swinging out to the side. She reached out a hand to Leah, pulling her into view, then spinning her out and back toward her as they both laughed. Then they split, and Maggie moved in between them, shaking her hips as they circled around her, still dancing.

I didn't realize I was standing there just staring at them until Esther saw me. "Hey," she called out. Her cheeks were flushed. "It's the nine o'clock dance. Come on."

Instinctively, I shook my head. "No thanks."

"You can't say no," Leah yelled as she grabbed Maggie's hand, then spun her out and back again. "Employee participation is mandatory."

Then I quit, I thought, but already they were moving on, back to the conga line, this time with Maggie in the lead, bouncing up and down, Esther snapping her fingers behind her. Leah, bringing up the rear, glanced back at me one last time. When I didn't say or do anything, she just shrugged, following the others as they wound around the displays, and headed toward the door.

I went back to the office, sitting down at the desk. I was sure they thought I was a total stick-in-the-mud, not that I cared. It was just like all the activities I'd walked past at my old schools during lunch—fake sumo wrestling, pie-eating contests, mass games of Twister on the quad—always wondering how, exactly, you did stuff like that. Maybe if you'd done it as a kid, it was all nostalgia, and that was the appeal. But I hadn't. It was all new to me, and therefore more intimidating than anything else.

I picked up my pen, going back to my 1099s. A moment later, the music stopped, as suddenly as it had begun. Another hour passed, in the silence of numbers, and then there was a tap on the door.

"Closing time," Esther said as she came in behind me, a bank bag in one hand. "Can I get in the safe?"

I pushed out my chair, making room as she dropped down to a squat, sticking the key she was holding into the lock. I watched as she put the bag in, then swung the door shut before pushing herself up again.

"We'll be out of here in about ten minutes," she told me, brushing off her knees. "You coming with us, or staying late?"

I wanted to tell her that, to me, after ten wasn't late. But I knew she wasn't really looking to make conversation, so I said, "I'm almost done."

"Cool. Just come out front and we can lock up when we're all out."

I nodded. She left the door open behind her, so as I finished up the last few things I had going, I could hear her and Maggie and Leah, out by the register chattering.

"Where did these Skittles come from?" Esther asked.

"Where do you think?" Leah told her.

"Really." I could tell by her voice, slightly teasing, that Esther was smiling. "So, Mags. More candy from Adam, huh?"

Maggie sighed. "I told you guys, it means nothing. He's a store-goer, just like all those boys."

"That may be true," Leah said, "but just because he goes to the store doesn't mean he has to buy something for you every time."

"He doesn't do it every time," Maggie grumbled.

"Sure seems like it," Esther said. "And with a store-goer boy, that is the first sign, anyway. It's how you know."

"True," Leah agreed.

"Not true," Maggie said. "It's just candy. Stop reading so much into it. You guys are ridiculous."

I could second that. It amazed me that they'd been together all night, and yet they still, seemingly, had something to talk about. Even if it was, predictably, candy and boys.

When I came out, they were all by the front door, waiting for me. "I understand if you don't want to get involved with him," Leah was saying. "I mean, he is a high school boy."

"He graduated just like we did, Leah," Esther told her.

"True. But he's not a college boy yet. There's a big difference in that one summer."

"How would you know? You refuse to date anyone *but* college guys."

"Why does that bother you so much? I mean, in college, we'll all be dating college boys anyway. So what's the harm in starting early?"

"It's not that it's harmful," Esther replied as we all filed out, Maggie swinging the door shut and pulling out her keys. "I just think that maybe you missed something, you know, by refusing to date anyone your own age."

"What would I have missed?"

"I don't know." Esther shrugged. "There is something kind of nice about having the age thing in common."

"Says the person who hasn't dated in over a year," Leah said.

"I'm choosy," Esther told her.

"Picky," Maggie said. "Nobody is good enough for you."

"I have high standards. It's better than dating just anyone."

There was a sudden, awkward pause, noticeable enough that even I felt it. Maggie, putting her keys in the door, stiffened. Esther said, "Oh, Mags. You know I didn't mean Jake."

"Okay, okay," Maggie said, shaking her off. "Let's not even talk about it."

This wouldn't be easy, though, as I realized when I looked to my right, to the bike shop, where I saw the curly-headed guy, sitting on a bike and talking to two boys I didn't recognize. Right behind him, pulling a jacket over his shoulders, was Jake. When he turned, he looked right at me.

Great, I thought, hurriedly turning my back, which left me facing Esther and Leah, who were trying to decide where to go from here. "There's always the Tip," Esther was saying. "I heard something about a keg there tonight."

"I am so tired of the sand and flat beer." Leah groaned. "Let's go to a club or something."

"You're the only one with an ID, remember?"

"I can get you guys in."

"You always say that," Esther told her. "You never can. Mags, what do you want to do?"

Maggie shrugged, dropping her keys into the bag she had slung over her shoulder. "I don't care," she said. "I might just go home."

Leah shot a glance at Jake, then at me. "Nonsense. Let's at least—"

This thought was interrupted by the curly-headed guy, who suddenly rode up right beside us, braking to a stop with a screech. "Ladies," he said. Leah rolled her eyes. "Anyone want a ride to the jump park?"

"Oh, God help us," Leah said. "Please, no more nights involving bicycles. What are we, twelve?"

"They're not just *bicycles*," the guy said, offended. "How can you even say that?"

"Easily," she replied. "And anyway, Adam—"

"I'll go," Maggie said, interrupting her. Adam smiled, then sat back on his seat as she climbed onto the handlebars, arranging her purse in her lap. "What?" she said to Leah, who sighed. "It's better than some club."

"No," Leah said flatly, "it really isn't."

"Oh, lighten up," Adam told her as he pushed off the boardwalk, starting to pedal. Maggie leaned back, closing her eyes, and then they were on their way, the other guys on bikes in front of the shop following behind them. Leah shook her head, annoyed, but allowed Esther to link her arm in hers as they brought up the rear on foot. Which left just me and Jake.

I tried to turn and start for home, but no luck. Two steps in and he was beside me. "So," he said, "what was all that about the other night, anyway? You took off awfully fast."

He was too everything: too confident, standing too close, wanting too much. I said, "It wasn't about anything."

"Oh," he said, his voice low, "I think it was. And could still be. You want to take a walk, or something?"

It was all I could do not to cringe. I'd already regretted what we'd done, and that was before he was Maggie's ex and Eli's brother. And how strange was it that I, who wanted to know as little as possible about anything here, now knew all this?

"Look," I said to him. "What happened the other night was a mistake, okay?"

"You're calling me a mistake?"

"I have to go," I told him, and started to walk away.

"You're messed up, you know that?" he said as I ducked my head down, focusing on the end of the boardwalk. "Freaking tease!"

More steps, more space. I'd just stepped off the board-walk onto the street, and finally let myself sort of relax, when I saw Eli up ahead, coming toward me. He was walk-ing slowly behind a group of older women dressed for a night out, all of them too tan and wearing bright colors. I tried to make myself too small to be seen, but just as he passed me, he looked over. Please just move along, I thought, fixing my gaze tightly on the plaid shirt of the guy walking in front of me.

But Eli was clearly different from his brother, in that he took direction well. No words shouted, nothing said. In fact, he didn't even look at me twice, just walked on.

six

"AUDEN? HAVE YOU . . ."

I stopped. Listened. Waited. But, as usual, nothing followed this but silence.

Sighing, I put down my econ textbook, stood up, and opened my bedroom door. Sure enough, there was Heidi, Thisbe in her arms, looking at me with a perplexed expression.

"Oh, for God's sake," she said. "I had a concrete reason why I came up here! And now, I have no idea what it was. Can you even believe that?"

I could. In fact, Heidi's forgetfulness had become as much a part of my routine as my morning coffee and late, late nights. I had done the best I could to keep myself segregated, my own life in Colby as separate from hers and my dad's as possible, considering we were living under the same roof. But it was no use. Two weeks in, and I was hopelessly intertwined, whether I liked it or not.

Because of this, I was now fully aware of the fact that my dad's mood depended entirely on how his writing went that day: a good morning, and he was cheerful the rest of the day, a bad one and he skulked around, sullen and muttering. I knew all the ups and downs of Heidi's ongoing postpartum issues, such as the forgetfulness, insane mood swings, and how she worried on multiple, complex levels about every freaking thing the baby did, from sleeping to eating to pooping. I was even fully versed in Thisbe's day-to-day life, from the crying (which was ongoing, it seemed) to her tendency to get the hiccups right when she was finally falling asleep. Maybe they were equally aware of me, as well, but I doubted it.

Because of all this, I'd actually come to kind of enjoy—sometimes even crave—the few hours I spent at Clementine's every day. It was a chance to do something concrete, with a beginning, middle, and end. No wild emotional swings, no wondering aloud about someone else's bathroom habits, and no hiccuping. The only thing that kept it from being perfect was its close proximity to Esther, Leah, and Maggie and all *their* various dramatics. But at least they left me alone when my door was shut.

Now, I looked at Heidi, who was still standing there, her brow furrowed as she tried to remember why she'd come upstairs. Thisbe, in her arms, was awake and staring up at the ceiling, most likely debating when she wanted to start screaming again. "Did it have something to do with work?" I asked her, as I'd learned that a few prompts could sometimes trigger her memory.

"No," she said, shifting Thisbe to her other arm. "I was downstairs, and thinking that I had to get the baby down for a nap soon, but it's been so hard because she's been switching it up so much, so no matter what I do she gets overtired. . . ."

I tuned out and began mentally reviewing the periodic table, which usually kept me occupied during these soliloquies.

" . . . so I was going to try to put her down, but then I didn't, because . . ." She snapped her fingers. "The wave machine! That's what it was. I can't find it. Have you seen it around?"

I was about to say no. Two weeks ago, when I'd first arrived, I would have, with no guilt or even a second thought. But thanks to the intertwining, I said, "I think it might be on that table by the front door."

"Oh! Wonderful." She sighed, looking down at Thisbe, who was yawning. "Well, I'll just go grab it and we'll hope for the best. I mean, yesterday I tried to put her down at this same time, she was clearly exhausted, but of course the minute I did she started up. I swear, it's like . . ."

I began easing the door shut, slowly, slowly, until at last she got the hint, stepping back and turning toward the stairs. ". . . so wish us luck!" she was saying, when I finally heard the knob click.

I sat down on my bed, looking out at the beach below. There were a lot of things about being here that I did not understand. And I was okay with that. But the wave machine? It drove me *nuts*.

Here we were, mere *feet* from the real, actual ocean, and yet Heidi was convinced that Thisbe could only sleep with the sound of manufactured waves—turned up to the highest setting, no less—supplied by her noise machine. Which meant that I had to hear them all night long as well. It probably would not have been that big a deal, if it hadn't made it impossible to hear the real sea. So I was there, in a beach-front house, listening to a fake ocean, and this just seemed to sum up everything that was wrong with this situation from start to finish.

Outside, I heard footsteps again, then a door opening and shutting. A moment later, sure enough, the waves began. Fake, loud, and endless.

I stood up, grabbing my bag, and stepped out into the hallway, moving past Thisbe's barely open door as quietly as I could. At the top of the stairs, I paused, looking into my dad's study, the door to which he always kept slightly ajar. He was at his desk, facing the wall, as usual, a Diet Coke can and a whole apple next to him. So it had been a good day.

Like I said, I'd become versed in my dad's habits. And by using my talents of observation, I'd figured out that he took an apple up to his office every day after lunch. If it was a good day, he always got too immersed in what he was doing and didn't eat it. On a bad one, though, the core was bitten down to nothing, nibbled to death, sometimes even in two pieces. On a whole-apple day, he emerged at dinnertime cheerful and talkative. On an apple-core day—especially a two-piece core—you did best to steer clear, if he even came down at all.

Most days, though, I wasn't around for dinner anyway, as I left at five or so to head to Clementine's, where I grabbed a sandwich as I worked until closing. After that, I usually walked the boardwalk for an hour or so before coming home to get my car and taking off for another three or four.

I'd found one all-night place, called the Wheelhouse

Diner, about thirty-five miles away, but it was no Ray's. The booths were narrow and stank like bleach, and the coffee was watery. Plus, the waitresses all dirty-looked you if you stayed longer than it took to eat whatever you ordered, even though the place was usually deserted. So more often than not, I'd just stop at the Gas/Gro, the closest convenience store, buy a big travel cup of coffee, and sip it as I drove around. In just two weeks, I knew about every inch of Colby backward and forward, for all the good that would do me.

By the time I got to Clementine's, it was almost six, and the shift was about to change. Which meant technically that Esther was done and Maggie was coming on, although more often than not—and for reasons I did not understand— whoever was leaving usually still hung around, unpaid, by choice. Then again, hanging around seemed to be all anyone did in Colby. The girls gathered at Clementine's, crowding the register and gossiping, flipping though fashion magazines, while the boys were on the benches in front of the bike shop, gossiping and reading bike magazines. It was ridiculous. And yet it went on, every day, all day long.

"Hey there," Esther, who was the friendliest of all of the girls, called out to me when I came in. "How's it going?"

"Good," I said, my standard reply. I'd long ago resolved to be cordial but not overly so, lest I be sucked into some conversation about what celebrity was in rehab or strap versus strapless dresses. "Any shipments in today?"

"Just these." She picked up a couple of slips of paper,

handing them off to me as I passed. "Oh, we got an extra roll of quarters at the bank today for some reason, and I put the deposit slip under the bear."

"Great. Thanks."

"No problem."

A minute later, I was in the office, door shut, all alone. Just how I liked it. If only the walls had been a cool white, everything would have been perfect.

Usually, my focus on my work allowed me to tune out anything that was going on out in the store. But occasionally, as I switched tasks, I'd hear bits here and there. When Leah was working, she was always on her cell phone. Esther seemed to spend a lot of time humming and singing to herself. And Maggie: well, Maggie was always talking to the customers.

"Oh, those look great," I heard her say around seven thirty as I started on the payroll for the week. "Petunia's are the best jeans, I swear. I live in mine."

"I don't know," a girl's voice replied. "I like the pockets on these, but I'm not sure about the wash."

"It is a little dark." A pause. "But at the same time, I think it's always good to have one pair of jeans you can always dress up, you know? And a dark wash guarantees that. Not all jeans look good with heels. But those will."

"Yeah?"

"Oh, totally. But if the wash worries you, we can pull a few other brands. The pockets on the Pink Slingbacks are great. And then there's always the Courtney Amandas. They're, like, magic for your butt."

The girl laughed. "Then I definitely need to try them."

"Done. Let me just find your size. . . ."

I rolled my eyes at no one, punching a few numbers into the calculator. Every time I overheard her going on in such detail about stuff like this, the nuances of different brands of flip-flops, or the pros and cons of boy shorts versus bikini bottoms, it seemed like such a waste. Here you had the capability to know so much about so many things, and you chose shoes and clothes. Leah at least seemed smart, while Esther, who clearly followed her own beat, was an individual. But Maggie was just . . . well, she was just like Heidi. A girl's girl, all the way, all pink and fluff and frivolity. Even worse, she was happy about it.

"Here they are!" I heard her say now. "Oh, and I grabbed a pair of these great Dapper wedges we just got in, so you could see how they do with a bit more formal look."

"Thanks," the customer said. "These look great. I love shoes."

"Of course you do!" Maggie replied. "You're human, aren't you?"

For God's sake, I thought. Where was the wave machine when you really needed it?

A little while later, I heard the front door chime. A moment later, the music cranked up, this time a loud, thumping dance beat. I didn't even have to look at my watch. By this point, I knew the nine o'clock dance when I heard it.

It happened each night, an hour before closing, regardless of whether there was only one employee or all three present, and always lasted exactly the length of one song, no longer. I didn't know how the customers reacted, although I could remember how I had, which was why I made sure to stay in the office.

From about 9:03 to ten, there were always a few more customers and a lot of idle chatter, usually concerning plans for the night or the lack thereof. Again, I tried to make it a point not to listen, but sometimes this was impossible, which was why I now knew that Leah always wanted to go out to the clubs (better chances of meeting older boys they hadn't known all their lives), while Esther preferred to go hear music (apparently she had some sort of singer-songwriter bent). Maggie, from what I could tell, didn't do much other than hang out with the boys from the bike shop, most likely pining after Jake, although she swore up and down she was over him, so over him.

This night was no different, as became clear when I heard Leah say, "So, it's Ladies in Free at Tallyho tonight."

"What was it," Esther said, "that we swore the last time we went there?"

"We didn't—"

"No, no, no to Tallyho," Maggie recited over her.

Someone snickered. Then Leah said, "I don't understand what is it you guys hate so much about that place."

"Everything?" Esther said.

"It's better than going to open mike night at Ossify and watching some guy recite his shopping list over a drumbeat."

"I don't know," Maggie said. "Is it really?"

More snickering. "Look," Esther said, "I'm not saying we have to go to Ossify. I just don't feel like getting grinded on by some drunk tourist again tonight."

"There's always the jump park," Maggie said. Loud groans. "What? It's free, there are boys there . . ."

"The boys we've known all our freaking lives," Leah said.

" . . . and it's fun," Maggie finished. "Plus, I heard Eli might be riding this weekend."

I'd been adding up a long list of numbers, and at just this moment lost track of the last one I'd punched in. I hit clear, and started over.

"That rumor," Leah said, "goes around every week."

"Maybe, but this time I heard it from Adam."

"Who heard it from Eli?" No answer from Maggie. "Exactly my point. It's like a Bigfoot sighting by now. It's urban legend."

No one spoke for what seemed like a long time. Finally Esther said, "It has been over a year. You'd think that he'd eventually . . ."

"Abe was his best friend," Leah said. "You know how tight they were."

"I know, but still. He has to get back to it sometime."

"Says who?"

"What she means," Maggie said, "is that it was his life, back then. And now he's here, managing the shop. It's like everything just stopped."

Another silence. Leah said, "Well, for him it probably did. You know?"

There was a tap on the door behind me, making me jump: at some point, Esther had slipped away from them and come back with the cash from the register. "We're about out of here," she said as she came in. I moved aside, like I did every night, as she ducked under the desk to the safe. "You almost done?"

"Yeah," I said. She swung the door shut, pulling out the safe key. "I'll, um, be out in a sec."

"All right."

When she left, I turned back to my calculator, starting to add again. Halfway down the row of numbers, though, I stopped and sat as still as I could, listening hard to see if the conversation would double back to where it had been before. When it didn't, I bent back over my numbers, punching them in slowly this time, one by one by one, so as not to make the same mistake again.

❋   ❋   ❋

By midnight, I'd already walked the boardwalk and driven a full loop of Colby proper, and still had a few hours before I even wanted to think about going home. Clearly, I needed coffee. So I headed to the Gas/Gro.

I had just parked and was digging in my ashtray for change when I heard an engine zooming up behind me. When I looked up, a beat-up green truck was pulling in a few spaces down. Even before I saw the bikes piled in the back I recognized the short, stocky guy behind the wheel, and Adam, Maggie's friend, beside him. They cut the engine and hopped out, going inside. After a moment, I followed them.

The Gas/Gro was small but clean, with neat aisles and not too bright lighting. I went straight to the full-strength GroRoast, as was my habit, pulling out the biggest cup and filling it up. Adam and his friend were at the other end of the store, by the coolers, where they grabbed drinks before proceeding to the candy aisle.

"Goobers," Adam was saying as I added a bit of cream to my cup. "Twizzlers. And . . . let me see. Maybe Junior Mints?"

"You know," his friend said, "you don't have to name each item out loud."

"It's my process, okay? I make better decisions when I vocalize as I do it."

"Well, it's annoying. At least do it quietly."

I put a lid on my cup, making sure it was secure, then started for the register, where a heavyset woman was buying some lottery tickets. A moment later, they stepped up behind me. I could see them in the mirrored reflection of the cigarette ad over our heads.

"One fourteen," the clerk said, ringing me up.

I slid my exact change over, then reached for my cup. As I turned, Adam said, "Hey, I thought you looked familiar! You, um . . . work at Clementine's, right?"

I knew that um. It was obvious my one night of bad judgment had branded me as The Girl Who Hooked up with Jake, although Adam was nice enough to not say this, at least to my face. "Yeah," I said. "I do."

"Adam," he said, pointing to himself. "And this is Wallace."

"Auden," I told him.

"Look at that," Adam said, nudging him. "She bought a single cup of coffee. Such restraint!"

"No kidding," Wallace said as they dumped their collective items onto the counter. "Who can come to the Gas/Gro and only buy one thing?"

"Well," Adam said as the clerk began ringing things up, "she's not from here."

"This is true." Wallace glanced at me. "No offense, of course. It's just that we're—"

"Store-goers," I finished for him, without even thinking.

He looked surprised, then exchanged a smile with Adam. "Exactly."

"That'll be fifteen eighty-five," the clerk said, and as they dug in their pockets, pulling out crumpled bills, I took the opportunity to slip out, back to my car. A moment later, they emerged, each carrying a bag, and climbed into the truck. I watched them back out, their lights moving across me as they pulled away.

I sat there and drank my coffee for a little while, considering my options. There was always the all-night diner. Or another loop around Colby. I glanced at my watch: only 12:15. So many hours to fill, and so little to do it with. Maybe it was for this reason that I found myself pulling out, turning in the direction they'd gone. Not looking for Bigfoot, necessarily. Just something.

✳ ✳ ✳

It wasn't hard to find the jump park. All you had to do was follow the bikes.

They were everywhere. Crowding the narrow sidewalks, on racks on the backs of cars, or sticking up from rails on the roof. I stuck close to an old Volkswagen van with a bright orange one hanging off it, following as it turned into a big lot two or three streets away from the beach. As I parked, I could see some bleachers bordered by two huge lights, which were shining down on a row of jumps, ramps made out of logs, and sand. Every once in a while, you'd see someone on a bike rise up above the sight line, suspended in midair for just a moment before disappearing again.

There was also an oval track made up of various types of berms, which some people were circling, and down from that, two large, curved ramps facing each other. I sat in my car for a moment, watching someone in a black helmet ride down one side, then up the other, back and forth, mesmerized, as if someone were swinging a watch on a chain before my eyes. Then someone slammed the door on the Volkswagen, jerking me back to attention.

I was not sure what I was doing there. It wasn't like it was exactly my scene or crowd. The bleachers were filled with girls who were probably busy comparing lip glosses and mooning over the guys as they rode below them. Further proof: as I looked closer, I spotted Maggie sitting a few rows up, in pink, naturally. I hadn't looked closely enough to see if Jake was one of the guys currently moving through the jumps, but then again, I probably didn't need to.

I sat back, picking up my cup of coffee and taking a sip. Cars were still pulling in and parking, and occasionally people would pass by my car, their voices rising overhead. Each time, I felt more self-conscious, reaching for my keys to crank the engine and get out of there. But then they'd move on, and I'd let my hand drop. After all, it wasn't like I had anything better to do. And at least this way I wasn't wasting gas.

"Yo!" I heard someone yell suddenly from somewhere

to my right. "Pretty girl! Where's the party at?"

I recognized Jake's voice instantly. Sure enough, when I turned, I spotted him one row over and two down, leaning against a silver sedan. He had on jeans and a red long-sleeved shirt, the tails of which were flapping in the breeze as he took a sip of something in the blue plastic cup in his hand. It took me a minute before I realized he hadn't even been speaking to me but to a tall blonde who was walking a few rows down, her hands stuffed in the pockets of her jacket. She glanced up at him, smiling shyly, and kept walking. A moment later, he was catching up with her just a couple of cars in front of me.

Crap, I thought, watching as he flashed her that wide smile. Leaving right then would have attracted way too much attention, but it wasn't like I wanted to sit and watch my biggest mistake in recent memory play out before me either. I considered my options a moment, then carefully opened my door, sliding my feet onto the gravel. I eased it shut, ducking down as I rounded the car beside me, then put another, and yet another between us.

Due to my zigzag escape, I ended up in an area off to the left of the jump park, where there were only a couple of bike racks and a few straggly trees. It was just out of the reach of the bright lights by the bleachers, so I could see everything without being spotted. In other words, perfect.

I leaned against a bike rack as I watched people move through the line of jumps. At first glance, each rider looked the same, but with further study I realized everyone was going at different speeds on their approach, and some stayed closer to the ground, cautious, while others rose up high, then higher still on the next. Occasionally there'd be a smatter of applause or some hooting from the bleachers, but otherwise it was strangely quiet, just the sound of tires on gravel, broken up by moments of silence as they went airborne.

After a while, I spotted Adam and Wallace, sitting on their bikes, helmets off, where people were lining up for the jumps. Wallace was eating Pringles, while Adam was looking up at the bleachers, gesturing for someone there to come join them. Following his gaze, I found Maggie again, still alone, still staring down at the ramps. You can keep looking, I wanted to tell her, but most likely, he's under those bleachers, not in front of them. Stupid girl.

Just as I thought this, she stood suddenly, like she'd heard me. I watched as she reached up, pulling her dark curls back at the base of her neck, then twisted an elastic around them. She reached into the bag beside her and pulled out a helmet, grabbing it by the strap and starting down the bleachers to the boys waiting below.

I had to admit I was surprised. What I saw next, though, left me stunned: when she got to Adam, he hopped off his bike, offering it to her, and she climbed on, pulling the helmet over her head. He said something to her, and she nodded, then pushed back slowly, flexing her fingers over the ends of the handlebars. When she was about twenty feet back, she rose up on the pedals for a moment, squaring her shoulders, and started toward the jumps.

She hit the first one at moderate speed, kicking up a bit of dust, gaining even more momentum as she approached, then cleared, the next. By the third, she was rising up re-

ally high, shoulders hunched, the bike seeming to float beneath her. Even from my limited experience, I could tell she
was good: she hit the jumps squarely, and her landings were
smooth, not clumsy like some of the other riders I'd seen. It
seemed to take her no time or effort at all to do the entire set
of them, and then she was circling back to where the boys
were waiting. Wallace offered her a Pringle, and she took it,
flipping up the visor of her helmet to pop it in her mouth.

I was so busy watching this that at first, I didn't see the
figure that had appeared off to my right, so it took a second
to realize it was Eli. His hair was loose over his shoulders,
and he had on jeans and a green long-sleeved T-shirt. Un-
fortunately, by the time I processed all this, I'd been staring
at him long enough for him to notice. He turned and looked
right at me, and I nodded at him in reply, in what I hoped
seemed like a casual way.

He nodded back, sliding his hands in his pockets, and I
thought of what Esther, Leah, and Maggie had been talking
about earlier that day, how he did or didn't ride anymore,
and the reasons, or person, behind that choice. Not that it
was any of my business. I was leaving anyway.

I started toward my car, which meant I had to walk right
by him. As I got closer, he glanced up at me again. "Already
leaving," he said in that flat voice I recognized. "Not exciting
enough for you?"

"No," I said. "Just . . . I have somewhere I have to be."

"Busy times," he said.

"That's right."

I didn't pretend to know Eli at all, but even so, I'd
noticed that his manner was slightly hard to read. It was

something in the way he talked that made it difficult to tell whether he was kidding or serious or what. This bothered me. Or intrigued me. Or both.

"So," I said after a moment, figuring I had nothing to lose in asking, "do you jump?"

"Nope," he replied. "You?"

I almost laughed, then thought of Maggie and realized this maybe was not a joke. "No," I said. "I don't even . . . I mean, I haven't ridden a bike in ages."

He considered this, then looked back at the jumps. "Really."

This too was said flatly, no intonation, so I had nothing to go on. Still, I felt defensive as I said, "I just . . . I wasn't much for outdoor stuff as a kid."

"Outdoor stuff," he repeated.

"I mean, I went outside," I added. "I wasn't a recluse or anything. I just didn't ride bikes very much. And haven't recently."

"Right."

Again, it wasn't like this was critical, necessarily. But something about it still bugged me. "What," I said, "is that a crime here or something? Like only buying one thing at the Gas/Gro?"

I meant to say this in a kidding sort of way, but I sounded shrill even to my own ears, hearing it. Or maybe just crazy. Eli said, "What?"

I felt my face flush. "Nothing. Forget it."

I turned to go, pulling my keys out of my pocket. I'd only taken two steps, though, when he said, "You know, if you don't know how to ride a bike, that's nothing to be ashamed of."

"I can ride a bike," I said. And this was true. I'd learned over Christmas when I was seven, in our driveway, on Hollis's old Schwinn, with training wheels. From what I remembered, I'd liked it, or at least not hated it. Which did not explain why I couldn't actually recall doing it very much since then. Or, at all. "I just . . . I haven't had the opportunity in a while."

"Huh," he said.

That was just it. Just Huh. Jesus. "What?"

He raised his eyebrows. Probably because again, my voice sounded high, slightly unbalanced. It was so weird, because usually I was totally nervous talking to guys. But Eli was different. He made me want to say more, not less. Which was maybe not such a good thing.

"All I'm saying," he said after a moment, "is that we *are* at a jump park."

I just looked at him. "I'm not going to ride a bike just to prove to you that I can."

"I'm not asking you to," he replied. "However, if you're looking for an opportunity . . . here's your chance. That's all."

Which, of course, made perfect sense. I'd said I hadn't had the opportunity: he was pointing out that now I did. So why did I feel so unnerved?

I took a breath, then another, so my voice was calm, level as I said, "I think I'll pass, actually."

"All righty," he said, hardly bothered.

And then I was walking back to my car. End of subject and conversation. But "all righty"? What *was* that?

Once behind the wheel, the door shut behind me, I looked back at him, already thinking of a dozen other, better ways I could have handled this conversation. I cranked my engine, then backed out of my space. The last thing I saw before turning around was Eli right where I'd left him, still looking up at the jumps. His head was cocked slightly to the side, as if he was thinking hard, the jumpers rising up in front of him. From this distance, you couldn't tell them apart, distinguish their various styles or approaches. They were all the same, moving in a steady line, up, down, in view for only a moment, then gone again.

seven

WHEN IT CAME to Thisbe, Heidi worried about everything. How much she slept. Whether she ate enough.
Whether she ate too much. What that red spot on her leg
was. (Ringworm? Eczema? The mark of the devil?) If it
hurt her to cry so much/her hair was going to fall out/her
poops were the right color. And now, she was going to give
the kid an identity crisis.

"My goodness!" I heard her saying one day when I came
down for my coffee around four P.M. She and Thisbe were
in the living room, having "tummy time"—which she did
religiously, as it was supposed to keep the baby from having
a flat head—on the floor. "Look at how strong you are!"

Initially, I was too focused on getting my caffeine levels
up to pay attention to them. Also, I'd kind of mastered tun-
ing Heidi out, if only out of necessity. But after I'd had a
half a cup I began to notice something was amiss.

"Caroline," she was saying in a singsong voice, drawing
out each syllable. "Who's my pretty Caroline girl?"

I filled my cup up again, then walked into the living
room. She was leaning over the baby, who was on her
stomach, struggling to hold up that big, possibly flat head.

"Caroline," she said, tickling the baby's back. "Miss Pretty Caroline West."

"I thought her name was Thisbe," I said.

Heidi jumped, startled, then looked up at me. "Auden," she stammered. "I . . . I didn't hear you come in."

I looked at her, then at the baby, then back at her again. "I was actually just passing through," I told her, and turned to go. I thought I was safe, but then, just as I reached the stairs, she spoke.

"I don't like the name!" When I turned back, she looked up at the ceiling, her face flushed, like someone else had said this. Then she sighed, sitting back on her heels. "I don't," she said slowly, more quietly. "I wanted to name her Isabel. It's the name of one of my best friends here in Colby, and I'd always loved it."

Hearing this, I looked longingly up the stairs in the direction of my dad's office, wishing, as I always did, that he was here to deal with this instead of me. But lately he'd been even more immersed in his book, the apples piling up uneaten.

"So," I said to Heidi, walking back over to her, "why didn't you?"

She bit her lip, smoothing her hand over the baby's back. "Your father wanted her to have a literary name," she said. "He said Isabel was too pedestrian, common, that with it, she'd never have a chance at greatness. But I worry Thisbe it's just *too* unusual, too exotic. It's got to be hard to have a name hardly anyone's ever heard of, don't you think?"

"Well," I said, "not necessarily."

Her mouth dropped open. "Oh! Auden! I wasn't saying that yours—"

"I know, I know," I said, holding up my hand to fend off this apology, which would likely have gone on for ages. "I'm just saying, from experience, it hasn't really been a hindrance. That's all."

She nodded, then looked back down at Thisbe. "Well," she said. "I guess that is good to know."

"But if you don't like it," I told her, "just call her Caroline. I mean—"

"Who's being called Caroline?"

I jumped, turning to see my dad, standing at the bottom of the stairs. Clearly, I was not the only one creeping around. "Oh," I said. "I was just saying it's the baby's middle name—"

"*Middle* name," he repeated. "And only because her mother insisted. I wanted to name her Thisbe Andromeda."

Out of the corner of my eye, I saw Heidi wince. "Really?" I said.

"It's powerful!" he replied, pounding his chest for emphasis. "Memorable. And it can't be shortened or cutified, which is how a name should be. If you were an Ashley or a Lisa, and not an Auden, do you think you'd be so special?"

I wasn't sure how I was supposed to answer this. Did he actually expect me to agree that it was his choice of name, and not all my hard work, that had gotten me where I was?

Luckily, it seemed to be a rhetorical question, as he was already en route to the fridge, where he pulled out a beer. "I think," Heidi said, glancing at me, "that while names are important, it's the person who really defines themselves. So if Thisbe is a Thisbe, that's great. But if she wants to be a Caroline, then she has that option."

"She is not," my dad said, popping his beer, "going to be a Caroline."

I just looked at him, trying to figure out when, exactly, he'd gotten so pompous and impossible. He couldn't have been like this my entire life. I would have remembered it. Wouldn't I?

"You know," Heidi said quickly, scooping the baby up and coming into the kitchen, "I don't even know your middle name, Auden. What is it?"

I kept my eyes on my dad, steadily, as I said, "Penelope."

"See?" said my dad to her, as if this proved something. "Strong. Literary. Unique."

Embarrassing, I thought. Too long. Pretentious. "That's lovely!" Heidi said too enthusiastically. "I had no idea."

I didn't say anything, instead just downed the rest of my coffee and put the cup in the sink. I could feel Heidi watching me, though, even as my dad headed out onto the front deck with his beer. I heard her take in a breath, about to say something, but luckily, then my dad was calling her, asking what she wanted to do for dinner.

"Oh, I don't know," she said, glancing at me as she put Thisbe in her bouncy seat, which was on the kitchen table. She fastened her in, then shot me an apologetic look as she stepped outside to join him. "What are you in the mood for?"

I stood there for a moment, watching them stand together, looking out at the water. My dad was drinking his beer, and as Heidi talked he looped his arm around her waist, pulling her closer to him, and she rested her head on his shoulder. You just couldn't even begin to understand how some things worked, or so I was learning.

On the counter, the baby made a gurgling noise, waving her arms around, and I walked over, looking down at her. She couldn't look you in the eye yet: instead, her gaze always found the center of your forehead.

Maybe she would be a Thisbe, after all, and never even consider Caroline. But it was the thought of my dad's face, so sure, as he stated otherwise that made me lean in close to her ear and christen her anew. Part her given name, part the one Heidi had wanted, but all mine.

"Hey, Isby," I whispered. "Aren't you a pretty Isby girl."

* * *

There's something about living at the beach in the summer. You get so used to the sun and sand that it gets hard to remember what the rest of the world, and the year, is like. When I opened the front door to an outright downpour a couple of days later, I just stood there for a moment, realizing that I'd forgotten all about rainy days.

Since I had no rain jacket, I had to borrow one from Heidi, who offered me three colors: bright pink, light pink, and, in her words, "dusky pink," whatever that meant. I picked the light one, yet still felt positively radioactive as I walked down the gray, wet sidewalk, boldly contrasting with everything around me.

At Clementine's, Maggie was behind the counter, in a miniskirt, flip-flops, and a worn T-shirt that said CLYDE'S

RIDES on it, bicycle wheels in both the *D*s. She was bent over a magazine, most likely her beloved *Hollyworld*, and gave me a sleepy wave as I approached.

"Still coming down out there, huh?" she said, reaching into the register to hand me the day's receipts.

"Yup," I replied. "Any shipments?"

"Not yet."

I nodded, and then she went back to her reading, turning a page. While Esther and Leah sometimes attempted more conversation with me, Maggie always kept it to a minimum, which I actually appreciated. It wasn't like we needed to pretend we were friends, or had anything in common other than our employer. And while I had to admit to still being somewhat surprised by what I'd seen her do at the jump park, otherwise I figured I pretty much had her pegged, and knew she probably felt that exact same way about me.

I went to the office, which for some reason was freezing, so I kept Heidi's jacket on as I got settled, pulling out the checkbook and finding my calculator. For the next hour or so, the store was pretty dead, aside from a couple of groups of girls coming in to pick through the clearance rack and moon over the shoes. Occasionally I'd hear Maggie's phone beep as a text message came in, but otherwise it was pretty quiet. Then, at around six, the door chimed.

"Hi there," I heard Maggie say. "Can I help you find anything?"

There was a pause, and I wondered if the person had heard her. Then, though, came the voice I knew better than just about any other. "Oh, dear God no," my mother said, and I could hear the shudder in her tone. "I'm just looking for my daughter."

"You're Auden's mom?" Maggie said. "That's great! She's in back. I'm sure she—"

I sat bolt upright, then pushed my chair back and scrambled to the door. Even though I got out to the floor as fast as I could, it wasn't quick enough. I found my mother, dressed in her customary all-black—dress, sweater over it, hair piled on her head—by the makeup display. She was holding a glass bottle at arm's length, her eyes narrowed as she examined the printed label.

"Booty Berry," she read slowly, enunciating each word. Then she looked over her glasses at Maggie. "And this is?"

"Perfume," Maggie told her. Then she smiled at me. "Or, actually, body spritzette. It's like perfume, but lighter and longer lasting, for everyday use."

"Of course," my mother said, her voice flat. She replaced the bottle, then took a long look around the store, her displeasure more than evident. When she finally got to me, she didn't look any happier. "Well. There you are."

"Hi," I said. She was studying me with such seriousness that I was instantly nervous, then even more so when I remembered the pink jacket I had on. "I, um . . . when did you decide to come down?"

My mother sighed, turning past Maggie—who was now smiling at her, for some reason—to the bathing suits, which she surveyed with an expression one might reserve for observing some sort of tragedy. "This morning," she said, shaking her head as she reached out to touch an orange bottom, trimmed with ruffles. "I was desperate for an escape, but I seem to have brought foul mood and weather with me."

"Oh, don't worry about that," Maggie said. "The rain's supposed to taper off tonight. Tomorrow will be gorgeous! Perfect beach weather. You'll get that suntan yet."

My mom turned back to look at her as if she were speaking in tongues. "Well," she said, in such a way I knew she was holding back everything she was actually thinking, "won't that be nice."

"Have you eaten?" I asked her, too eagerly. I took a breath, then said more calmly, "There's a really good place just a bit down the boardwalk. I can probably take off for an hour or so."

"Of course you can!" Maggie said. "You should totally hang out with your mom. The books can wait."

My mom eyed Maggie again, as if doubting she could recognize a book, much less read one. "I could use a drink, at any rate," she said, taking another look around the store before starting for the door. Even her stride was disapproving. "Lead the way."

I glanced at Maggie, who was watching her, fascinated. "I'll be back in a little bit, okay?"

"Take your time!" she said. "Really. I'm fine here alone."

My mother snorted softly, hearing this, and then, thankfully, we were out the door, back into the rain. As soon as it swung shut behind us she said, "Oh, Auden. It's even worse than I expected."

I felt my face flush, although I wasn't surprised she was so up front. "I needed a rain jacket," I said. "I wouldn't normally—"

"I mean," she continued, "I knew any business Heidi owned would probably not be to my sensibilities. But Booty Berry? And what about those Lolita-esque swimming bottoms? Are we packaging women to look like little girls now? Or little girls to look even more so, in order to exploit their innocence? How can she be a woman, not to mention a mother, and condone this sort of thing?"

Hearing this, I relaxed, as my mother's rants were as familiar to me as nursery rhymes. "Well," I said, "the fact is, she knows her market. That stuff really sells."

"Of course it does! But that doesn't make it right." My mother sighed, opening her umbrella and raising it over her head, then offering me her arm, which I took, stepping beneath it with her. "And all that *pink*. It's like a giant vagina in there."

I stifled a laugh, covering my mouth with my hand.

"But I guess that's the point," she said, sighing. "It's just so bothersome because it's the most shallow, base depiction of the female experience. Sugar and spice and everything nice, peddling packaging, not substance."

We were at the Last Chance now, where for once there was no line. "This is the place," I said, nodding at it. "The onion rings are to die for."

My mother peered in the door. "Oh, no, no. I'll require at least tablecloths and a wine list. Let's keep looking."

We ended up back at the hotel where she was staying, a small boutique place called the Condor just off the boardwalk. Its restaurant was tiny, crowded with only a few tables, and dim, heavy red curtains hanging from the windows, the carpet a matching shade. My mother settled into a booth, nodded her approval at the flickering candle on the table, and ordered a glass of cabernet from the hostess as she shed her sweater. After a pointed look, I took off Heidi's jacket, stuffing it under my bag, out of sight.

"So," she said, once her wine had arrived and she'd taken a big gulp. "Tell me about your father's book. He must be done by now, ready to send it off to his agent. Has he let you read it?"

I looked down at my water glass, moving it in a circle on the table. "Not yet," I said carefully, as I knew she was looking for more than just the answer to this question. "He's working day and night, though."

"Sounds more like writing than revising," she observed, picking up the menu and scanning it before setting it aside. I didn't say anything. "But then, your father did always have odd work habits. Writing never came easily for him, as it does for some others."

Right, I thought. Time for a subject change. "The baby's pretty cute," I said. "She still cries a lot, though. Heidi thinks she has colic."

"If you *think* a baby has colic, it probably doesn't," my mother said, taking another sip of her wine. "You know. With Hollis, there was no question. From the first night home, he screamed his lungs out. It lasted for three months."

I nodded. "Well, Thisbe's pretty fussy. . . ."

"Thisbe." My mother shook her head. "I still cannot believe that name. Your father and his delusions of grandeur. What's the middle name? Persephone? Beatrice?"

"Caroline."

"Really?" I nodded. "How quaint. And unlike him."

"Heidi fought for it, apparently."

"She should have fought harder," my mom said. "It's only a middle name, after all."

The waiter came by then, asking if we wanted appetizers. As my mother picked up the menu again, ordering us some scallop ceviche and a cheese plate, I looked down at Heidi's jacket, the pink now barely visible against the dark red of the booth all around it. I had a flash of her face the day we'd been discussing names, how she'd rushed to compliment my own cumbersome middle name, just because she assumed it would make me feel better.

"Then again," my mom said as the waiter left, "I doubt your father picked Heidi for her fortitude. Quite the opposite, in fact. I think all he really wanted was someone fluffy and insubstantial, so that he could be absolutely sure she'd always follow his lead."

I knew that she was probably right. After all, it wasn't like Heidi had showed any great backbone in the last few weeks. And yet, somehow, I heard myself say, "Heidi's not completely ditzy, though."

"No?"

I shook my head. "She's actually a pretty sharp businesswoman."

She turned to face me, her dark eyes meeting mine. "Really."

"Yeah. I mean, I know because I'm doing her books." I'd forgotten how penetrating my mother's looks could be, and I broke quickly, turning my attention back to my water glass. "Clementine's could be just a seasonal business, but somehow she's managing to turn a monthly profit all year long.

And she's really savvy when it comes to catching trends. A lot of the stuff she ordered last year at this time went on to be huge."

"I see," she said slowly. "Like, Booty Berry, for instance?"

I flushed. Why was I even defending Heidi, anyway? "I'm just saying," I said. "She's not just what she appears."

"No one is," she said, once again managing to both have the last word and make it seem like she'd been right all along. How she always did that, I had no idea. "But enough about Heidi. Let's talk about you. How's the reading going for next year? You must be getting a lot done."

"I am," I said. "It's slow going, though. The textbooks are pretty dry, especially the econ stuff. But I think—"

"Auden, you can't expect any subject to simplify itself for you," she said. "Nor should you want it to. A challenge only means you'll retain the information that much better."

"I know," I replied. "It's just kind of hard, doing the reading without any direction from a professor. I think once I'm in the class, it'll be easier to know what's important."

She shook her head. "But you shouldn't *need* that. Too often I have students who are happy to just wait for me to explain to them what a line of dialogue or stage direction means within the context of the play. They don't even think to try to figure it out themselves. But in Shakespeare's time, you had only the text. It's up to you to decipher the meaning. It's the only pure way to learn."

She was getting fired up, clearly. Which was probably why it was a mistake to say, "But this is economics, not literature. It's different."

Now she really zeroed in on me, narrowing her gaze.

"No, Auden, it's not. That's exactly my point. When have I ever taught you to take another person's view on anything?"

I just sat there, this time knowing better than to answer. Thankfully, then our food arrived, and she got this last word, as well.

Things did not really improve from there. She gave up on me as a source of conversation, instead ordering another glass of wine before launching into a long, protracted story about some curriculum dispute that was apparently draining all her time and energy. I half listened, making affirming noises when necessary, and picked at my salad and pasta. By the time we were done, it was past eight, and when we stepped back outside, the rain had stopped, and the sky was now streaked with pink.

"Well, look at that," my mother said, taking it in. "It's your favorite color."

I felt this like a sudden slap, which was exactly how it was intended. "I don't like pink," I said, my voice as stiff as I felt.

She smiled at me, then reached over, ruffling my hair. "Methinks you doth protest too much," she said. "And your choice of outerwear says otherwise."

I looked down at Heidi's jacket. "This isn't mine. I told you that."

"Oh, Auden, relax. I'm just kidding." She took a deep breath, then let it out, closing her eyes. "And besides, maybe it's to be expected that you'd change a bit, down here with Heidi and these people. I suppose I couldn't expect to keep you as my very own doppelgänger forever. Eventually, you'd want to try the Booty Berry, so to speak."

"I don't," I said, and now I could hear the edge in my voice. She did, too, her eyes widening, but just slightly. "I mean, I'm not. I just work there. That's all."

"Honey, it's fine," she said, ruffling my hair again, but this time I stepped out of her reach, hating her condescension, the way she smiled, shrugging. "We all have our dirty little secrets, don't we?"

It was only pure chance, and nothing else, that led me at this exact moment to look over the fence behind us to the hotel pool, which was deserted, save for one person. One person in black, square-framed glasses, his skin pale enough to be translucent, wearing red trunks and reading a small, hardback book that you knew at one glance was Literature. I glanced at my mother, catching her eye, then turned back to him, making sure her gaze followed mine. When it did, I said, "I guess we do."

She tried to keep her face relaxed, but there was one, quick twitch as this remark hit home. But I didn't feel good about it. I didn't feel anything.

"Well," she said after a moment. "I'm sure you need to get back to your job." She said these last two words the same way she referred to my dad's book, making it clear that she doubted it mattered or even existed.

She leaned closer, offering me her cheek to kiss, but I stayed where I was. She smiled at me again, then said, "Oh, darling, don't be bitter. It's the first instinct of the weak."

I bit my lip, turning away from her, and didn't respond to this. Instead, I dug my hands deep into Heidi's jacket, as if to tear the pink right off it, as I walked away. Someone else might have called after me, but I knew my mother wouldn't. She'd gotten her last word, and it was a good one, and to her, that was all that mattered.

On the way back to Clementine's, I kept my head down, trying to swallow over the thick lump that had appeared in my throat. Clearly, it was my defending Heidi that had set her off, even though I'd only said that she wasn't "that much of a ditz," and then paid her two small compliments. But that was enough, in my mother's eyes, to put me squarely in the big pink camp. If I wasn't in total agreement with her, I might as well have been Heidi. There was no middle ground.

Thinking this, I felt tears fill my eyes, just as I pulled open the door to Clementine's. Luckily, Esther and Leah were clustered at the counter with Maggie, all of them discussing their evening plans, as always. They barely paid me any attention as I walked past to the office, where I sat down at the desk, fully intending to get back to work. But after about twenty minutes of my numbers blurring as I wiped my eyes with the back of my hands, I decided to call it a night.

Before I left the office, I pulled my hair back in a rubber band, then arranged my face to as stoic and unbothered an expression as I could manage. Two deep breaths, and then I was walking to the door.

"The thing is," Leah was saying as I came onto the floor, "I'm never going to meet a hot guy at a coffee shop."

"Says who?" Esther asked.

"General logic. They just don't hang out there."

"What about the hot, sensitive, artistic type? They *live* at coffee shops."

"See, but," Leah said, "artistic isn't hot to me."

"Oh, right. You only like greased-up frat boys," Esther replied.

"Grease is your specialty, actually. It's the artistic types who don't bathe."

I was hoping that this conversation was engrossing enough that they'd hardly notice me. But no luck. When they saw me coming, I had their full attention.

"So, I've got to go," I said, keeping my voice casual. "The receipts are done, and I'll come in early to finish payroll tomorrow."

"Okay," Maggie said. "Hey, did you have fun with your—"

"You know," Esther said suddenly to Leah, "I kind of resent that remark. I have *never* dated anyone as greasy as that air force guy you met last summer."

"That wasn't grease," Leah said, picking up her phone and scanning the screen. "That was hair gel."

"I think it counts."

"It doesn't."

"You sure about that? Because . . . "

Thankfully, due to this, I was able to pretend I hadn't heard Maggie's half question, and slip out the door without further explanation. Not that she seemed to notice: when I glanced back, she was laughing at something Leah was saying, while Esther rolled her eyes, the three of them securely in their little pink world, as always.

I hit Beach Beans, which was a few stores down, for a

large coffee, then found a place on the sand and drank it while the sun set. After downing the last drop, I pulled out my phone and hit number one on my speed dial.

"Dr. Victoria West."

"Hi, Mom. It's me."

There was a slight pause. Then, "Auden. I thought I might hear from you."

Not a good start, but I pressed on anyway. "I just," I said, "I wanted to see if you might want to have breakfast tomorrow morning."

She sighed. "Oh, darling, I'd love to, but I'm heading back very early. I fear this trip was ill advised, to be honest. I forgot how much I dislike the beach. Everything is just so . . . "

I waited for the adjective that would fill this gap, knowing it probably was meant to describe me, as well. But she let it trail off, sparing both the coast and myself.

"Anyway," she said after a moment of too-noticeable silence, "it was lovely to see you. Do let me know how your summer progresses. I want to know *everything.*"

It was not lost on me that this was exactly what she'd said to me the day I left. Then, though, we'd both known she meant the gory, mockable details of my dad and Heidi and their silly lives. The life that I, with one pink raincoat, was now living as well.

"I'll do that," I said. "Have a safe drive back."

"I will. Good-bye, sweetheart."

I shut my phone, then just sat there, feeling that lump rise in my throat again. I'd always had to work so hard to keep my mother's interest, wresting it away from her work, her colleagues, her students, my brother. I'd often wondered if it was ridiculous to feel this way. Clearly, though, my instincts had been right: her attention was not only hard come by, but entirely too easy to lose.

I sat there for a long time, watching as people walked up and down the beach in front of me. There were families, kids running ahead and dodging the waves. Couples holding hands. Groups of girls, groups of guys, surfers dotting the distant breakers, even as darkness began to fall. Eventually, though, the sand grew empty, as lights came on in the houses behind me and on the pier in the distance. The night was only just starting, and there was still so long to go until morning. The very thought made me tired, so tired.

"Auden?"

I jumped, then turned my head to see Maggie standing beside me. Her hair was blowing in the breeze, her bag over her shoulder. Behind her, the boardwalk was a row of lights, one right after the other.

"You okay?" she said. When I didn't respond, she added, "You seemed kind of sad when you left."

I had a flash of my mother, the dismissive way she'd looked at Maggie, the bikini bottoms, the Booty Berry, and then me, all of us grouped in the category of Not to Her Liking. But it was vast, that place I'd struggled to avoid for so long, as wide and long as the beach where we were right then. And now that I finally found myself squarely in it, I realized I was kind of glad to have company.

"No," I said to her. "I don't think I am, actually."

I wasn't sure what I expected her to do or say to this.

It was all new to me, from that second on. But clearly, she'd been there before. It was obvious in the easy way she shrugged off her bag, letting it fall with a thump onto the sand, before sitting down beside me. She didn't pull me close for a big bonding hug, or offer up some saccharine words of comfort, both of which would have sent me running for sure. Instead, she gave me nothing but her company, realizing even before I did that this, in fact, was just what I needed.

eight

"WHAT I FIND," Maggie said, "is that when you get gum, you always need something else. Because gum isn't really a snack."

"So true," Esther agreed.

"If I *do* get gum, I always grab some chips, or maybe a cookie two-pack, as well. That way you know you've got your food and something refreshing for afterward."

Leah shook her head. "I don't know," she said. "What about Tic Tacs? They're like gum, but I've been known to eat them for a meal before."

"Tic Tacs you actually swallow, though," Esther pointed out. "You own a Tic Tac. Gum is just borrowed."

Maggie turned to her, smiling. "Impressive."

"Thank you," Esther replied. "I always feel inspired here at the Gas/Gro."

I, however, was not feeling inspired. Or impressed. If anything, I felt completely out of my element, a stranger in a strange world. One minute I was alone on the beach, and the next, I was here, a girl among girls, maybe even a store-goer.

When Maggie had first sat down beside me, I'd had no

idea what to expect. I had friends from the various schools I'd attended, but the one common denominator was that I'd never really done the girly thing with any of them. Our interactions, instead, were mostly limited to academic discussions, our solid common ground. So all I had to go on were the snippets of chick flicks I'd caught here and there on basic cable, where women only seemed to bond while drinking too much, playing disco music, dancing together, or all of the above. But since none of these things was going to happen on my watch, even in my depressed state, I had to wonder what, exactly would. When Maggie finally spoke, though, she managed to surprise me. Again.

"So your mom's kind of a badass, huh."

I turned to look at her. She was staring out at the water, her hair blowing around her face, knees pulled to her chest. I said, "That's one word for her."

She smiled, then reached over for her bag, plopping it between us and then reaching a hand in to dig around for something. After a moment, she pulled a magazine out, and I braced myself for some celebrity analogy, God help me. Instead, I was shocked to see it was a college catalog from the U as she pulled it into her lap, flipping through a few pages until she found one with the corner folded down. Then she handed it to me.

U ENGLISH AND YOU it said. The words were somewhat hard to read, as I had only the distant glow of the house behind us to go on. But the picture of my mom—sitting at the head of a seminar table, her glasses in one hand, clearly mid-lecture—I would have known in any light, any distance.

"Where did you get this?" I asked her.

"It came with my application package. The English department was the main reason I applied there."

"You're going to the U?"

She shook her head, and I felt bad for asking, as a rejection had to be a sore subject. "I did tons of research, though. I knew your mom looked familiar in the store today. But I couldn't figure out why until I went home and found that."

I looked down at my mom's picture again, then slowly shut the catalog. "She's . . . complex," I said. "It's not always easy being her daughter."

"I think," she said, "sometimes it's hard no matter whose daughter you are."

I considered this as I handed the catalog back to her and she returned it to her bag. For a moment we just sat there, both of us quiet, looking at the water. All I could think was that of everyone I'd met so far in Colby, she was the last person I ever would have thought I would end up with like this. Which reminded me of something else.

"You know," I said finally, "Jake really was nothing to me. I'm embarrassed I ever had anything to do with him."

She nodded slowly. "He tends to have that effect on people."

"Really, though. If I had it to do over . . . " I took in a breath. "I wouldn't."

"And you," she said, stretching her legs out in front of her, "were only with him for one night. Imagine wasting two years of your life, like I did."

I couldn't, of course. I'd never even had a real boyfriend, even a crappy one. I said, "You must have really loved him."

"I did." This was said simply, easily. The truth. "I guess everyone has that, though, right?"

"Has what?"

"That first love. And the first one who breaks your heart. For me, they just happen to be the same person. At least I'm efficient, right?" She reached into her bag, rummaging around again, before finally pulling out a pack of gum. She went to pull out a stick, then furrowed her brow. "Empty. Time to hit the Gas/Gro."

I looked up at her as she got to her feet, brushing sand off herself before grabbing her bag. "Well," I said. "Thanks. For checking in on me."

"You're not coming?" she asked.

"To the Gas/Gro?"

"Or wherever." She hiked her bag over her shoulder. "I mean, you can just sit here, I guess. But it seems kind of lonely. Especially if you're already feeling rotten."

I just sat there, looking at her for a moment. I felt like I should be honest, let her know that lonely actually appealed to me, even at my most rotten, and at times was actually preferable. But then I remembered how I'd been feeling, sitting there watching the sun go down, and wondered if this was still true. Maybe. Maybe not. It seemed a lot to decide, right in that moment. So instead, I went with another truth, one that was never in doubt.

"Well," I said, "I guess I could use some more coffee."

Then, somehow, I was standing up. Chucking my empty cup in a nearby trash can. And falling into step beside her, down the sand to the boardwalk, past the gathered tourists,

132 @ Sarah Dessen

to the Gas/Gro, where Esther and Leah were sitting outside on the bumper of a beat-up Jetta, waiting for us.

Now, I watched as Maggie grabbed a pack of cookies and her gum, and paused, her hand over the Twizzlers, before deciding against them. Esther, beside her, was studying a package of sunflower seeds.

"All night I've been thinking about these," she said. "But now, here in the moment, I'm just not sure they have enough snack bang."

"Snack bang?" I asked.

"It's the amount of taste and sustenance you get from any given snack," Maggie explained as Leah grabbed a box of Tic Tacs, shaking them. "So, like, sunflower seeds have very little. But beef jerky has tons."

I said, "You know, I have to be honest. I just don't *get* this."

"Get what?" Leah asked.

"This whole obsession with stores, and snacks, and analyzing the minutiae of every single choice and pairing," I said. "What is that all about?"

They all looked at one another. Then Esther said, "I don't know. It's like, we're headed out somewhere. You never know what's going to happen. So you stop for supplies."

"The store-going comes first," Maggie added, "and then the adventure follows."

They headed for the register, and I grabbed a fresh cup, filling it up with GroRoast. It was simple: I required nothing else. But on my way to the register, I found myself suddenly reaching out to grab a pack of two chocolate cup-

cakes. I knew they were extraneous, highly caloric, a waste
of money. And yet I had to wonder if they were right. When
you don't know where you're going, maybe it wasn't such a
bad thing to have more than you need.

* * *

"Oh, God," Esther groaned. "Like we haven't been *here*
before."

We were standing in the driveway of a big house right
on the beach. There were people packed on the front steps,
moving in shadows across lit-up windows, filling both decks
and scattered across the sand below. Plus, there still were
cars arriving, parking behind those already lining the narrow road and cluttering the cul-de-sac. In the two minutes
we'd been standing there, at least fifteen people had walked
past us, heading in.

"And because we have been here before," Esther continued as a car drove by behind us, radio blaring, "I vote that
we leave now, while we still have our dignity."

"I'm not planning to be undignified," Leah said, opening
her Tic Tacs and popping one in her mouth. "I just want to
have a good time."

"Same thing."

"Oh, for God's sake, it is not," Leah said. "Would you
just relax, for once? This might be fun."

"This kind of party is never fun," Esther said. "Unless you
like having beer spilled on you, or some meaty guy grab your
ass in some crowded hallway. Which, apparently, you do."

Leah sighed, blowing her hair out of her face. "Look.

Last night, I went to Club Caramel and sat there while that
girl played the xylophone and sang ten songs about commu-
nism. And did I complain?"

"Yes," Maggie and Esther said in unison. Esther added,
"Loudly."

"But I went," Leah continued, ignoring this. "And in return, I got to choose what we did tonight. And I pick this.
So let's go in."

She didn't wait for agreement, instead just pocketing
her Tic Tacs and starting toward the house with long, confident strides. Esther followed along behind her, decidedly
less enthusiastic, while Maggie glanced at me. "It won't be
that bad," she said. "I mean, it's just your typical weekend
house party. You know."

I didn't, though. I had no idea, not that I was going to say
so. I just followed Maggie up the driveway, taking care to
step over the many beer cans that were littering the driveway and stairs.

Inside the house, the hallway was crowded, people
packed in on either side. The only way through was navi-
gating a narrow passage, single file, and even then it was a
tight squeeze. It smelled like cologne and sweat and beer, an
odor that just grew more potent the farther we proceeded.
I tried to look straight ahead, but occasionally, out of the
corner of my eye, I'd see a guy watching me, his brow damp
with sweat, or hear a voice say something—"Hey baby, how
you doing?"—maybe meant for me, or anyone.

We finally reached the living room, where there was a
bit more breathing room, and a lot more people. Music was
blaring from a stereo I couldn't see, and there was a group of

people dancing off to one side, mostly girls, while a bunch of guys looked on. In the kitchen directly to my right, I could see a keg, as well as a bunch of various liquor bottles cluttering the counter by the sink. There was also, inexplicably, two trays of pastries: one of beautiful cupcakes, clearly hand-iced, each dotted with roses, and another of various bars—lemon, chocolate chip, raspberry—carefully arranged on tiny paper doilies.

Maggie, seeing me notice this, motioned for me to lean closer to her. Then she said, right in my ear, "Belissa's parents own Sweet Petite bakery. This is her house."

She nodded toward a girl with long, dark hair streaked with blonde, wearing a white tank top and jeans, who was dancing with the group in the living room. She had her head thrown back, laughing, and her lipstick was bright, bright red, the same color as the tiny roses on each of the cupcakes.

"We need beer," Leah announced from Maggie's other side. She grabbed a couple of red cups from somewhere, then handed them to me. "Here. You're closest."

I looked down at the cups, then at the keg beside me. Leah and Maggie were now talking about something— Esther had vanished—so neither of them noticed me hesitate before turning to face the keg, where I assumed I was supposed to get the beer. It seemed simple enough, so I picked up the spigot attached to it and turned the top. Nothing happened.

I glanced around me. Leah and Maggie were still talking, and the only other people nearby—a couple, making out against the fridge—weren't paying me, or anything else, any attention. I twisted the top again—nothing—and felt my face flush, embarrassed. I had never been good at asking for help with anything, especially something that people assumed you already knew. And I knew plenty, but this simple, stupid thing was all new to me.

I took a breath, about to try again, when suddenly a hand appeared over mine, the fingers pressing down on the spigot, and beer began to fill the cup I was holding.

"Let me guess," Eli said, his voice that low, even timbre, as always. "Drinking from kegs also falls under outdoor activity."

I just looked at him, standing there in jeans and the same blue hoodie he'd had on the first time I met him. Maybe it was the embarrassment, which had been bad enough before I had an audience, but I was instantly annoyed. I said, "Are we outside?"

He glanced around, as if needing to confirm this. "Nope."

"Then no." I turned my attention back to the keg.

He removed his hand from the spigot, then stood there watching me as I filled another cup. "You know," he said, "I've noticed you're kind of defensive."

"And I," I replied, "have noticed that you are very judgmental."

"Oh," he said. "So you're still upset about the bike thing."

"I know how to ride a bike!" I said.

"But not how to work a keg."

I sighed. "And you care about this because?"

He shrugged. "It's kind of required here. Like buying more than one thing at the Gas/Gro."

I was kind of impressed he remembered me saying this from the jump park—it was nice to be memorable, even in a somewhat embarrassing way—but I ignored him, instead moving to get Maggie's and Leah's attention so I could give them their beers. When I turned to them, though, they both were staring at me, their eyes wide. "What?" I said, but they just took the cups, then stepped a bit farther away from me, exchanging a look as they each took a sip.

I moved back to the keg with the last cup, reaching to fill it. Once I had, they were still watching me with these weird expressions, so I just took a sip from my cup instead. The beer was warm and flat. Clearly, I had not been missing much.

Beside me, Eli was now studying the pastries, and I realized that maybe I had been a little short with him. In an attempt to be conciliatory, I said, "Apparently the people who own this house have a bakery. Or something."

He glanced at me. "Really."

I took another sip, why I had no idea, as it tasted terrible. "She's the girl in the white shirt, over there. With the red lipstick."

He glanced in the direction I indicated, watching the people dancing for a moment. "Oh, right. I see her."

The girl was really moving now, her hair swishing down her back from side to side as she moved her hips in a circle, a pumped-up guy with, yes, hair gel pressing up behind her. "Wow," I said. "That's really something."

"Meaning what?"

I shrugged. The girl glanced over at us, her eyes meeting

mine, and I took another sip of my beer. "Just . . . sometimes less is more. You know?"

He sort of smiled, as if this was cute, which was kind of annoying. I glanced over at Maggie and Leah, who, for some reason, were now looking at me totally goggle-eyed.

"Which is not to say," I said to Eli, "you shouldn't have one of her cupcakes. They look great."

"Nah," he said. "I'll pass."

"You know," I told him, "if you don't know how to eat a cupcake, that's nothing to be ashamed of."

Now he did smile. "I know how to eat a cupcake."

"Sure you do."

"I do," he said. "I just don't want one of those."

"Yeah?" I put my cup down, then reached into my bag for the packaged ones I'd bought at the Gas/Gro, pulling them out and placing them on the counter between us. "Prove it."

"You really want me to?" he asked.

"It's kind of required here," I said. "Like riding a bike."

He studied my face for a second, then picked up the pack of cupcakes, opening it and pulling one out. I was watching him, about to take another sip of beer, when I felt a hand suddenly clench my arm. "Abort," Maggie hissed in my ear. "Abort, abort, right now."

"What?" I said, but I barely got the word out before she was yanking me sideways, past Eli—who was chewing, watching us—and out onto the back deck, where Leah was clearing a path through the people there.

"Hurry," she yelled over her shoulder, and Maggie nodded, still dragging me behind her. "I think if we go down the stairs this way, we can get out faster and maybe avoid this."

"Right," Maggie replied, "let's *definitely* avoid this."

"What are you guys talking about?" I asked as Maggie dragged me down a short flight of stairs to a lower deck, which was a bit less crowded. "Avoid what?"

She turned, as if to answer me, but didn't get the chance. Because right then, a glass door to our right slid open, and the girl from the dance floor—Miss Red Lipstick, cupcake, less is not more—appeared, planting herself squarely in our path. Two of the girls she'd been dancing with, a redhead in a black dress and a shorter, pudgy blonde girl, spilled out behind her.

"Okay," she said, holding up both hands, palms facing us. Her voice was kind of nasal, thin. "What just happened in there? And who the *hell* is this?"

She was looking right at me, as were both her friends, and I felt myself break into a cold sweat, instantly, something that I'd read about but never actually experienced before in my entire life. Maggie, releasing her hold on my arm, said, "Belissa, it's really nothing."

"Nothing?" Belissa took a step toward me. Up close, I could see the bumpy texture of her skin, how her nose was a little pointier than she probably liked. "What's your name, skank?"

At first, I thought this was both a question—what's your name?—and an answer. Then I realized she was actually waiting for a response. "Auden," I said.

Her eyes narrowed. "Auden," she repeat d, the way you'd

say *scrotum* or *excrement*. "What kind of a name is that?"

"Well—" I said.

"It doesn't matter," Leah said, cutting me off. "Like Maggie said, nothing happened."

"Was she, or was she not, in there hitting on Eli?" Belissa demanded.

"She wasn't," Leah said, her voice flat. Certain. The blonde and the redhead exchanged looks. "She's not from here, she doesn't know anybody."

"Or anything," Maggie added, sounding less confident. Belissa glanced at her. "You know what I mean."

"I saw how he was talking to her," Belissa said. It was weird how she was staring at me, and yet at the same time ignoring me completely. "He was *smiling*, for God's sakes."

"He's not allowed to smile?" Leah asked. Maggie shot her a look, and she added, "Look, Belissa, it was an honest mistake, and we're leaving. Okay?"

Belissa considered this, then stepped even closer to me. "I don't know who you are," she said, punctuating this with a jab of her finger, the tip touching my chest. "And I don't really care. But you better stay away from my boyfriend, especially when you're under my roof. Understood?"

I looked past her, to Maggie, who nodded, her head bobbing wildly. I said, "All right."

"All right," Belissa repeated. Behind her, Leah sighed, looking up at the sky. "Now get off my property."

And with that, Maggie was yanking my arm again, dragging me down the nearby stairs. She continued her death grip on me as we followed Leah down to the beach, around a dune, and then over a public walkway, back to the street, not letting go until we were back at the car, where Esther was waiting.

"Where the hell have you been?" Leah demanded. "We could have used you back there."

"Let me guess," Esther said as Maggie and I got in the backseat. "Something undignified happened."

"If you call Auden just about getting all our asses kicked undignified, then yes," Leah told her. She slammed her door shut, then turned around in her seat to look at me. "Are you crazy? Flirting with Eli Stock in front of Belissa Norwood, in Belissa Norwood's house, while eating Belissa Norwood's cupcakes?"

They were all looking at me now. I said, "We weren't eating those cupcakes."

Leah threw her hands up, turning back around as Esther cranked the engine. Maggie, beside me, said, "You guys, she didn't know about any of that."

"She didn't know about you and Jake, either," Leah said. "But that didn't stop you from wanting to flatten her when she hooked up with him."

"True," Maggie said. "But, like Belissa, I was in the wrong. She and Eli are broken up. He can talk to whoever he wants."

"But that's just the point," Leah told her, turning to face me. "Eli doesn't talk. To anyone. Ever. So why is he talking to her?"

No one said anything. Finally, I cleared my throat and said, "Well, I don't know. He just does, ever since this one night when I saw him riding his bike."

Silence. They were all staring at me, even Esther, who used the rearview. Maggie said softly, "You saw Eli on a bike? What was he doing?"

I shrugged. "I don't know. Tricks? He was jumping around, at the end of the boardwalk."

Maggie and Leah looked at each other. "You know," Leah said, "I think maybe . . ."

"Agreed," Esther said, hitting her turn signal as the Gas/Gro came up in the distance. "We definitely need some snack bang for this one."

* * *

"The thing is," Maggie began, "if we're going to tell you about Eli, first we have to tell you about Abe."

We were at the very tip of the pier, lined up on a bench and looking out over the water. On the way out to the end, we'd passed several fishermen, standing with their rods leaning over the side, focused on the water. Here, we were all alone, except for the wind and the splashing below.

"Abe and Eli," Maggie said, "were inseparable. Best friends since, like, kindergarten. You hardly ever saw them apart."

"But they were totally different," Esther added. "You know, Eli's got that dark, quiet thing going on. And Abe was . . ."

They were all quiet for a moment. Then Leah said, "A total goofball."

"Total," Maggie agreed. "Like, the silliest person you have ever met. He could make anybody laugh."

"Even Eli."

"*Especially* Eli." Leah smiled. "God, do you even remember what Eli was like before Abe died? He was actually . . . funny."

"Abe died?" I said.

Maggie nodded solemnly, opening up a pack of gum. "It was May of last year. He and Eli were down in Brockton, at this event at Concrete Jungle? They were both sponsored, had been for a couple of years now. They both started out straight BMX, you know, but then Eli took up the half-pipe, and Abe stuck more to flatland, at least in competition. But they were both really good at urban, although that's not surprising, considering where we're from."

I just looked at her. Leah said, "Maggie, nobody here but you understands all that bike shit. Speak English."

"Oh, sorry." Maggie pulled out a piece of gum, popping it in her mouth. "Eli and Abe were both really, really good at riding bikes. So good they got paid to go around and compete at various events, and that's why they were in Brockton."

"And it was after the event," Esther said, "when they were driving back from a party, that the accident happened."

"The accident," I said.

Leah nodded. "Eli was driving. And Abe was killed."

I heard myself gasp. "Oh, my God."

"I know." Maggie folded the gum wrapper she was holding, first once, then twice, down to a tiny square. "I was with Jake when Eli called. We were at his house, and I could hear Eli on the phone. He was at the hospital, and he was trying to talk, but all I could hear was this awful sound he was making. . . . "

She didn't finish, instead just looked out over the water, dark on either side of us. Esther said, "It wasn't his fault. They were going through a four-way stop, and someone just ran it and hit them."

"A drunk," Leah added.

Esther nodded. "It tore Eli up, big-time. It was like Abe took some part of him when he went, you know? He's never been the same."

"He gave up all his sponsorships, the riding, everything," Maggie said. "He'd gotten into college at the U and deferred to keep competing, but he didn't go there either. He just got a job managing the bike shop and stopped riding altogether."

Leah glanced at me. "Or so we thought."

"I just saw him doing it that one night on the boardwalk," I told her. "It was really late. Or early, actually."

"Well," Maggie said, "I guess that means something. What, I don't know. But something."

There was a sudden burst of noise from behind us: when I turned, I saw one of the fisherman pulling something over the rail of the pier. It was flopping, catching the light here and there, before he eased it down behind a tackle box, out of sight. The other people fishing took note, then returned to their own lines.

"And Belissa," I said, warming my hands around my cup. "What's the story there?"

"They'd dated since sophomore year," Leah told me.

"She stuck with him through the funeral, and a couple of months after, but eventually things just fell apart. She dumped him, is what I heard. Although apparently she sees it differently."

"Apparently," I said.

Leah smiled, shaking her head. "I swear, when she asked you what kind of a name that was, and you were about to answer her . . . I almost just took off running and left you there to fend for yourself."

"She asked me a question," I said.

"She didn't want an answer, though."

"Well, then why did she ask?"

"Because," Leah said, "she was gearing up to smacking your face. God! Don't you know anything about dealing with jealous ex-girlfriends?"

"No," I said. "Not really."

Maggie smiled. "Well, you just got a crash course, then."

"*Crash* being the operative word," Leah added. "I mean, did you see how pissed off she was? And then she tells you to get lost, or else, and you say . . ."

"'All right,'" Maggie said.

Esther's eyes widened. "No."

"She *totally* did. And said it just like that, too. Like she was doing her a favor by agreeing."

"I did not," I said. Leah and Maggie just looked at me. "Did I?"

"Yup." Leah shook her cup, then took another sip off her straw. "Which was either incredibly ballsy, or incredibly stupid. I'm still not sure which."

Esther laughed, and I just sat there, looking down at my

coffee and remembering how completely out of my element I'd been at that party, and that moment. Never before had it been so obvious that although I'd spent my entire life learning, there was a lot of stuff I still didn't know. Enough to get me into big trouble, apparently, if someone hadn't been there to help me out.

"It was stupid," I said out loud, thinking this. They all looked at me. "I mean, what I said. The truth is, I didn't have much of a social life in high school. Or ever, for that matter."

This was greeted with an extended silence. Or maybe it just felt that way to me.

"You know," Leah said, "that actually explains a *lot*."

"It does," Maggie agreed.

"What's that supposed to mean?" I asked.

"Nothing," she said quickly. Then, glancing at Leah, she added, "I mean, just how you came to town, and hooked up with Jake right away, and then were surprised when people, um, drew conclusions about you."

"And by people," Leah said, "she means us."

"Got that," I replied. "Thanks."

"Plus," Esther added, "there's the way you've always kept to yourself."

"Except for tonight," Leah pointed out.

"Except for tonight," Maggie agreed. "I mean, we just figured you thought you were better than us. But maybe you just didn't know how to hang out."

I wanted to believe it was the latter. But I knew in my heart of hearts, my truest place, that I had assumed my superiority. In Maggie's case, with a single glance.

"Like I said," Leah said, "only a girl who didn't have any real girlfriends would actually begin to answer the question, 'What kind of a name is that?'"

"I thought she wanted to know!" I said.

"I doubt Belissa Norwood has much interest in learning about the life of a modern poet famous for his works on politics, nature, and unrequited love," Maggie said.

I turned, facing her. "You know about Auden?"

"I wrote my senior thesis on the use of loss in his poems," she replied. "It's what got me into Defriese. Hey, Leah, you have any Tic Tacs left?"

I just sat there, stunned into silence as Leah pulled out the pack, passing it to her. I'd had a lot of surprises that day: my mom showing up, almost getting my butt kicked, and learning about Eli's past. But this was the thing that left me speechless. Maggie was going to Defriese. Just like me.

"Shoot," Esther said, glancing at her watch. "It's past midnight. I better get home. Who needs a ride?"

"I guess I do," Leah said, standing up and wiping off her jeans with her hands, "considering I didn't get to meet some hot guy to drive me home from that party."

"Sorry," I said.

"Oh, she'll survive," Esther said, sliding her arm around Leah's shoulders as we started back down the pier. "Tomorrow night, we'll go to Bentley's for open mike, and maybe you can find yourself a nice, greasy artist type there."

"Maybe I will," Leah replied, "just to spite you."

"What about you, Auden?" Maggie asked, falling into step beside me. "You want a ride back to Heidi's?"

I looked down the pier to the boardwalk and the road beyond it, the streetlights breaking up the dark. "Nah," I said. "I think I'll grab some more coffee before I head home."

"More coffee?" Esther said, eyeing my cup. "Doesn't that keep you up, though?"

I shook my head. "Nope. It doesn't."

At the end of the pier, we said our good-byes, and they headed back to the car. I could hear them still talking, their voices carried by the wind, as I turned and started in the other direction, back to the Gas/Gro, where I was the only customer as I filled up a fresh cup, adding milk, a stirrer, and, after a moment of consideration, a candy bar. The cashier, an older woman with blonde hair and a name tag that said WANDA, was working on a crossword. She put it down, then rang me up while stifling a yawn.

"Late night," she said as I slid my money across to her.

"Aren't they all," I replied.

Out in the parking lot, the wind was warm and blowing hard, and for a moment I just closed my eyes and stood there, feeling it on my face. Earlier that night, I'd taken off to be alone, only to find—to my surprise—that company was just what I needed. Still, I knew it must have been hard for Maggie to come looking for me, not knowing how I'd react when I saw her. The easiest thing would have been to just leave me alone. But she didn't go for the easiest thing.

I was a girl who liked a challenge, too. Or at least I liked to think of myself that way. So I went looking for Eli.

On the way to the boardwalk, I passed a cop, driving slowly, his radio crackling. Two girls, arm in arm, one stumbling, the other pulling her forward. The bars still had an hour or so left until closing, with people and music spilling out their open doors. Farther down into the business district, though, all the stores were dark. But in the bike shop, way in back, a light was on.

I raised my hand to knock, then dropped it, reconsidering. So I'd spent a night in the world of girls, big deal. Did it really mean anything had changed, especially me? As I stood there, debating this, I saw someone move across the lit, open back door of the shop: dark hair, blue shirt. Before I knew what I was doing, my hand was rapping the glass, hard.

Eli looked up, his face wary. When he came closer and saw it was me, he didn't really look relieved. Or surprised, actually. He unlocked the door, pushing it open. "Let me guess," he said. "You want to learn to ride a bike, and it can't wait until morning."

"No," I said. He dropped his hand from the door, and just stood there, looking at me. I realized he was waiting for me to explain myself. "I was in the neighborhood, saw the light." I held up my coffee, as if this proved something. "Long night, and all that."

He studied my face for a moment. "Right," he said finally. "Well, come on in."

I stepped through the door, and he shut it, locking it behind me. I followed him through the dark shop to the back, which was some kind of repair area. There were parts of bikes up on stands, wheels leaning against workbenches, a pile of gears on a table, tools everywhere. In one corner, where a bike was partially assembled, a handwritten sign said ADAM'S WORKSPACE—TOUCH AND DIE! with a skull and crossbones underneath it.

"Have a seat," Eli said, waving a hand at a stool right beside this.

"Seems dangerous."

He glanced at the sign, then rolled his eyes. "It's not."

I sat down, my cup in hand, as he slid behind a nearby cluttered desk, which was piled with papers, various bike parts, and, not surprisingly, a collection of empty soda bottles and various convenience store items. "So," he said, picking up an envelope and glancing at it, "you say you're not here for a bike."

"No," I said.

"Then what? You're just out walking the boardwalk in the middle of the night?"

Eli doesn't talk, Leah had said. *To anyone. Ever.* But he had to me, and maybe that did mean something, even if it wasn't clear just what.

"I don't know," I said. "I just . . . I thought you might want to talk, or something."

Eli shut the drawer, slowly, and looked at me. The click noise it made seemed very loud. "Talk," he said, his voice flat.

"Yeah." He was just sitting there, staring at me, expressionless, and I felt not unlike when my mom got me in her sights, a serious squirm coming on. "You're up, I'm up. I just figured . . ."

"Oh, I get it," he said, nodding. "Right. You know now."

"Know . . . " I said.

He shook his head. "I should have known when I saw you at the door. Not to mention at that party. Maggie isn't exactly known for holding back information."

I just sat there, not sure what to do. I said, "Look, I'm sorry. I just thought . . ."

"I know what you thought." He picked up a stack of papers, rifling through it. "And I appreciate you wanting to help me, or whatever. But I don't need it. Okay?"

I nodded numbly. Suddenly the room seemed too bright, illuminating every single one of my failings. I slid off the stool. "I should go," I said. "It's late."

Eli looked over at me. I remembered how that first night, I'd thought of him as haunted, before I even knew this was true. He said, "Do you want to know why I talk to you?"

"Yeah," I said. "I do."

"Because," he said, "from that first day on the board-walk, you were different. You never tiptoed around me, or acted all weird and sorry for me, or gave me that look."

"What look?"

"That one," he said, pointing at my face. I felt myself blush. "You were just . . . normal. Until tonight."

Until tonight, I thought, hearing Maggie and Esther saying these same words, only an hour earlier. Eli was still rummaging around in the drawer, his head ducked, and I thought of him that day on the pier with Thisbe, how easily he'd reached down to pick her up. There are a lot of ways to comfort someone. The elevator was only one of the un-expected ones.

"You know," I said, leaning against the doorjamb, "I'm actually really relieved to hear you say that. Because I don't want to feel sorry for you."

"You don't," he said, not looking up.

"Nope. The truth is, I'm actually kind of angry with you."

"Angry?" I nodded. He lifted his head: now, I had his attention. "And why is that?"

"Because you almost got my ass kicked tonight."

"I did?"

I rolled my eyes. "Like you didn't know that was your girlfriend I was talking about," I told him. "Not to mention looking at *while* I was talking about."

"Hold on," he said. "She's—"

"You just let me stand there and shoot off my mouth," I continued, ignoring this, "and then, when she came after me . . ."

"She came after you?"

"She poked me in the chest and called me a skank," I said. He raised his eyebrows. "And meanwhile, you're off eating cupcakes somewhere."

"Excuse me," he said, pushing the drawer shut, "but *you* were the one who told me to eat the cupcakes."

"When I didn't know my life was in danger!" I sighed. "All I'm saying is that you kind of left me out there to fend for myself. Which was not very cool."

"Look," he said, "Belissa is not my girlfriend."

"You might want to tell her that," I replied. "If you can, you know, make time during all that cupcake eating."

Eli was just looking at me, his expression hard to read, and again I felt like squirming. But not for the same reasons. At all.

"What are you really doing out so late?" he asked.

"I don't sleep at night."

"Why not?"

"It used to be because my parents were up fighting," I said. "But now . . . I don't know."

This answer was like a reflex, coming without thinking. Eli nodded, then said, "So what do you do to pass the time? Other than not riding bikes."

I shrugged. "Read. Drive. At home, I have a twenty-four-hour diner I really like, but here there's only the Wheelhouse, which is less than ideal."

"You've been going to the Wheelhouse?" He shook his head. "The coffee there is terrible."

"I know. Plus the waitresses are mean."

"And it's not like you're taking up a table someone else wants." He sighed. "You should be going where I go. Open twenty-four/seven, great coffee, *and* pie."

"Really," I said. "That's the trifecta."

"I know."

"Wait, though," I said. "I have Googled every single restaurant for fifty miles, and nothing came up but the Wheelhouse."

"That," he said, "is because my place is a local secret."

"Oh, right." I leaned back against the doorjamb. "Of course. The local thing again."

"Yep," he said, reaching down to grab a canvas bag from

beside the desk, and hoisting it over his shoulder. "But don't worry. I think I can get you in."

*   *   *

"This," I said, "is not a restaurant."

That much was obvious by the row of coin-operated washing machines on one side of the room, the dryers on the other. Not to mention the tables lined up for folding in between, a few plastic chairs, and a machine dispensing small boxes of detergent and fabric softener with an OUT OF ORDER sign taped over it.

"I didn't say it was a restaurant," Eli said as he walked over to a machine, plopping his canvas bag down on top of it.

"You didn't say it was a Laundromat," I pointed out.

"True." He pulled a bottle of Tide out of the bag, then dumped the bag's contents inside. After he fed in some quarters, and water began to slosh across the glass front, sudsing immediately, he said, "Follow me."

I did, albeit hesitantly, down the row of washers and dryers to a narrow hallway, which ended with a plain, white door. He knocked twice, then pulled it open, gesturing for me to go through first. Initially, I hesitated. But then, sure enough, I smelled coffee. And that was enough to push me over the threshold.

Which, honestly, was like stepping into a different world. Gone was the linoleum and shiny appliances. This place was dim, the walls painted a deep purple. There was one window, a string of multicolored lights tacked up over it, and a few small tables. Right by the back door, which was open, a warm breeze blowing through, was a small counter.

An older guy with black hair streaked with white was sitting behind it, reading a magazine. When he looked up and saw Eli, he smiled.

"Yo," he called out. "I thought you might turn up tonight."

"I was running out of shirts," Eli replied.

"Well, then." The guy put his magazine aside, then stood up, rubbing his hands together. "What can I get for you?"

"That depends, " Eli said, walking over to the counter and pulling out a stool. I was about to do the same when he gestured at it, and I realized it was for me. "What's on the menu?"

"Well," the guy said, stepping back from the counter and looking beneath it, "let's see . . . there's some rhubarb. Apple. And some razzleberry."

"Razzleberry?"

The guy nodded. "Raspberry and blueberry. Sort of tart, sort of mellow. It's a little intense. But worth trying."

"Sounds good." Eli glanced at me. "What do you want?"

"Coffee?" I said.

"Just coffee?" the guy asked.

"She's not from here," Eli explained. To me he said, "Trust me. You want pie."

"Oh." They were both looking at me. I said, "Um, apple, then."

"Good choice," Eli said as the guy turned around, grabbing two mugs from a rack behind him and filling them from a nearby coffeepot. Then, as we watched, he pulled two plates out from under the counter, followed by two pies. He cut hefty slices of each, arranged them neatly with a fork beside, and them pushed them over to us.

I picked up my mug first, taking a tiny sip. Eli hadn't been joking after all: the coffee was incredible. But not as good as the pie. Sweet Jesus.

"I told you," Eli said. "Beats the Wheelhouse by a mile."

"The Wheelhouse? Who's eating there?" the guy said. Eli nodded at me. "Oh, man. I hate to hear that."

"Clyde," Eli said to me, "is a man who takes pie very seriously."

"Well," Clyde said, flattered, "I mean, I endeavor to. But I'm only a beginner at this whole baking thing. I got a late start."

"Clyde owns the bike shop," Eli told me. "And this Laundromat. And about four other businesses here in Colby. He's a mogul."

"I prefer the term renaissance man," Clyde said as he picked up his magazine again, which, I saw now, was a copy of *Gourmet*. "And just because I'm good at business does not mean I can do a perfect piecrust. Or so I'm learning."

I took another bite of the pie—which tasted pretty close to perfect to me, actually—and looked around the room again.

"You have to admit," Eli said as Clyde flipped a page, studying a recipe for potatoes au gratin, "this is better than driving or reading."

"Much," I agreed.

"She doesn't sleep either," Eli told Clyde, who nodded. To me he said, "Clyde bought this place just so he'd have something to do at night."

"Yep," Clyde said. "The coffee shop part, though, that was Eli's idea."

"Nah," Eli said, shaking his head.

"It was." Clyde turned another page. "Used to be, we'd just hang out during the spin cycle, share a thermos and whatever pastry I was working on. Then he convinced me maybe we weren't the only ones looking for a place to go other than a bar late at night."

Eli poked his fork into his piecrust. "Spin cycle," he said. "That's not a bad one, actually."

"Huh." Clyde considered this. "You're right. Write it down."

Eli pulled out his wallet, then took out a piece of yellow folded paper. From the looks of it, it was a list, and a long one. Clyde handed him a pen, and I watched as he added SPIN CYCLE to the bottom.

"We need a new name for the bike shop," Clyde explained to me. "We've been trying to come up with one for ages."

I had a flash of my first day in Colby, the conversation I'd heard among Jake, Wallace, and Adam as I passed them on the boardwalk. "What's it called now?"

"The Bike Shop," Eli said, his voice flat. I raised my eyebrows. "Nice, right?"

"Actually, it's called Clyde's Rides," Clyde said, picking up my coffee mug to refill it. "But the sign got blown off during Hurricane Beatrice last year, and when I went to replace it, I thought maybe it was time to give it a new name . . ."

" . . . which we've been trying to do ever since," Eli said. "Clyde can't make up his mind."

"I'll know it when I hear it," Clyde said, hardly bothered. "Until then, it's fine if everyone calls it the Bike Shop. Because that's what it is. Right?"

A phone rang behind him then, and he turned to grab it. As he stepped outside, the receiver pressed to his ear, Eli turned to look at me. "What did I tell you?" he said. "Pretty good, huh?"

"It is," I agreed. "And you're right. I never would have found this place in a million years."

"Nope," he said.

We sat there for a minute, eating. On the other side of the wall, I could hear a load bumping through a drying cycle, *thump thump thump*. My watch said two fifteen. "So," I said. "What else you got?"

✻ ✻ ✻

I'd thought I was pretty good at both staying up and staying productive. But Eli was the master.

After the Laundromat, we got back into his car—an old Toyota truck with a cab on it, the back of which was filled with bike parts that clanked and rattled with every turn—then headed fifteen miles west, to the twenty-four-hour Park Mart. There you could, at three A.M., not only buy groceries, linens, and small appliances, but also get your tires rotated, if you so desired. As we walked the aisles, a cart between us, we talked. Not about Abe. But about almost everything else.

"So, Defriese," he said as he compared brands of microwave popcorn. "Isn't that where Maggie's going?"

"I think so," I said as he pulled down a box, examining it.

"Must be a really good school, then. That girl's brilliant." I didn't say anything, and a moment later he added, "So I guess that makes you brilliant, too, huh?"

"Yep," I said. "Pretty much."

He raised an eyebrow at me, sticking the popcorn in our cart. "If you're such a brain, though," he said, "how come you didn't know not to flirt with another girl's boyfriend in her own kitchen?"

"I'm book smart," I said. "Not street-smart."

Eli made a face. "I wouldn't exactly call Belissa street. She gets her jeans dry-cleaned."

"Really?"

He nodded.

"Wow."

"I know."

We walked down the aisle a bit. He didn't seem to have a list and yet still knew exactly what he wanted. "Seriously, though," I said. "You're right. I was kind of . . . "

I trailed off, and he didn't jump in, pushing me to finish. I was finding that I liked that.

"I guess," I said, "that I just missed a lot in high school. Like, socially."

"I doubt it," he replied, stopping to throw a roll of paper towels in the cart. "A lot of that stuff is overrated."

"You can say that because you were popular, though."

He glanced at me as we turned the corner, to the soup aisle. Halfway down, a guy in a long coat was muttering to himself. That was the one thing about being out so late, or early. The crazies were, too. Watching Eli, I saw he had the same attitude about it that I did, which was three pronged: don't stare, keep a wide berth, and act normal. "What makes you think I was popular?"

"Oh, come on," I said. "You were a bike pro. You had to be."

"For all you know," he replied, "I was a nerdy bike pro."

I just looked at him.

"Okay, fine. I wasn't exactly a wallflower." He grabbed a can of tomato rice soup off the shelf, then another. "But big deal. It's not like it makes a difference in the long run."

"I think maybe it does." I leaned over the cart, looking down into it. "I mean, I did all the academic stuff. But I never had that many friends. So there's a lot I don't know."

"Like . . ."

"Like not to talk to a girl's boyfriend in her own kitchen."

We moved out of the aisle away from the guy in the coat, who was still muttering, and headed to the dairy section, passing a sleepy-looking employee restocking cold cuts along the way. "Well," he said, "nothing like almost getting your ass kicked to hammer a lesson home. You're not likely to forget it now."

"Yeah," I said. "But what about everything else?"

"Such as?"

I shrugged, leaning over the cart as he pulled out some milk, checking the expiration date. Watching him, I thought, not for the first time that night, that maybe it should have felt strange to be with him, here, now. And yet it didn't, at all. That was one of the things about the night. Stuff that would be weird in the bright light of day just wasn't so much once you passed a certain hour. It was like the dark just evened it all out somehow. I said, "I just think that it's too late, maybe. All the things I should have been doing over the last eighteen years, like going to slumber parties, or breaking curfew on Friday night, or—"

"Riding a bike," he said.

I stopped pushing the cart. "What is it," I said, "with you and the whole bike thing?"

"Well, I am in the business. Plus, it's a big part of growing up," he replied, moving down to the cheese display. "And it's not too late."

I didn't say anything as we headed toward the registers, where one girl was standing by the only one that was open, examining her split ends.

"Of course," Eli said as he began unloading the cart onto the belt, "it's not too late for slumber parties or any of that other stuff either. But breaking curfew I think you can go ahead and knock off your list."

"Why?"

"Because it's past four A.M. and you're at the Park Mart," he said as the girl began to scan the groceries. "It counts, I think."

I considered this as I watched some apples roll down the belt. "I don't know," I said. "Maybe you're right, and all that stuff I think I missed is overrated. Why should I even bother? What's the point, really?"

He thought for a moment. "Who says there has to be a point?" he asked. "Or a reason. Maybe it's just something you have to do."

He moved down to start bagging while I just stood there,

letting this sink in. *Just something you have to do.* No excuse
or rationale necessary. I kind of liked that.

From Park Mart, we headed over to Lumber and Stone,
the home improvement superstore, which Eli informed me
opened early for contractors. Which we were not, but they
didn't seem to care, letting us walk right in. I tagged along
as Eli stocked up on a new wrench set, a box of nails, and
a value pack of lightbulbs: while he checked out, I sat on a
bench by the front door, watching the sun begin to rise over
the parking lot. By the time we left, it was almost six, and
the rest of the world was finally waking up to join us.

"I saw that," he said as I stifled a yawn while sliding into
the front seat of his car.

"This," I said, "is about the time I usually crash."

"One last stop," he replied.

It was, of course, the Gas/Gro, where the same older
woman, now reading the newspaper, was behind the counter, a cell phone pressed to her ear.

"You need anything?" Eli asked, and I shook my head,
sliding down in the seat a bit as he got out and went in.
Just as he walked up to the door, a little blue Honda pulled
in a few spaces down. I was in the midst of another yawn
when I saw someone get out, shutting the driver's-side door
and also leaving a passenger to wait. He was tall, wearing
rumpled khakis, a plaid shirt, and black-framed glasses.

I leaned closer, taking in his profile as he went in. Then
I turned slowly to look down at the Honda, where, sure
enough, I saw my mother sitting in the passenger seat. She
had her hair piled up on her head, her favorite black sweater
tied over her shoulders, and she looked tired. Inside, her

grad student was pouring himself a coffee. I watched him grab a pack of gum, and then an apple pie, as he headed up to the register, where Eli was chatting with the woman working as she rang him up. What do you know, I thought. My mother was dating a store-goer.

When Eli came out, a bottled water and bag of Doritos in hand, I watched her study him as he passed, eyes narrowed as she took in his too-long dark hair, the worn T-shirt, the way he jangled his keys in his hand. I knew she was cataloging him instantly: high school education, not college bound or even interested, working class. The same things, if I was honest, that I would have thought, once. But I was one night, and many hours, further away from my mother now. Even with this short distance between us.

She might have still been watching when Eli got in the truck, shutting the door behind him. I didn't know, because by then I'd already turned to face him, my back to her, unrecognizable. Just any girl, nodding in reply as he asked if I was ready, finally, to go home.

nine

"IT'S DONE!"

I opened my eyes, blinked, then shut them again. Maybe I was dreaming. A moment later, though, I heard it again.

"Done! Finished!" A door opened and shut, followed by footsteps, coming closer. "Hello? Where *is* everybody?"

I sat up, then glanced at my watch. It was four fifteen, and I'd been up until six A.M. the morning before. Or that morning, actually. These days, it was kind of hard to draw a distinction.

I slid off my bed, then walked to my bedroom door, easing it open just in time to see my dad approaching Thisbe's room, one hand already outstretched to the knob. "Hey," he said to me, "Guess what! I—"

Lightning quick, I reached out, intercepting his fingers just as they made contact and pulling them back. "Wait," I whispered. "Don't."

"What?" he said.

I wrapped my hand around his, pulling him into my room and shutting the door gently behind us. Then I motioned for him to follow me across the short distance to the window, the farthest spot from the wall between the baby's room and mine.

"Auden," he said, his voice still loud. "What are you doing?"

"The baby was really colicky last night," I whispered. "And this morning. But she's finally sleeping, so I bet Heidi is, too."

He glanced at his watch, then at my closed door. "How do you know she's sleeping?"

"Who?"

"The baby. Or Heidi, for that matter," he said.

"Do you hear crying?" I asked him.

We both listened. All that was audible was the noise machine. "Well, this is anticlimactic," he said after a moment. "I finally finish my book and nobody cares."

"You finished your book?" I asked. "That's great."

Now, he smiled. "Just wrote the last paragraph. Want to hear it?"

"Are you kidding?" I replied. "Of course I do."

"Come on, then."

He opened the door, and I followed him—quietly—down the hallway, back to his office, where he'd pretty much been living for the last couple of weeks. This was obvious by the collection of mugs, empty water bottles, and broken apple cores in various states of decomposition that I spied as soon as I stepped inside.

"Okay," my dad said, sitting down in front of his laptop and punching a few keys. A document appeared, and he rubbed his hands together, then moved the page down so only a couple of lines were showing. "Ready?"

I nodded. "Ready."

He cleared his throat. "'The path was more narrow now, the lacy boughs of the trees bending to meet each other as I walked beneath them. Somewhere, ahead, was the sea.'"

When he finished, we just stood there, letting the words settle around us. It was a big moment, although I was somewhat distracted as distantly, I was pretty sure I heard a yelp. "Wow," I said, hoping I was wrong. "That's great."

"It's been a long haul, that's for sure," he said, leaning back in his chair, which creaked beneath him. "Ten years, all leading up to those twenty-seven words. I can't really believe it's finally done."

"Congratulations," I said.

Thisbe was definitely crying now, the sound growing louder from down the hall. My dad sat up straighter, hearing it, then said, "Sounds like they're up! Let's go share the good news, shall we?"

And with that, he was out of his chair, a bounce in his step as he walked back down to Thisbe's room, pushing the door open. Instantly, the crying went from low level to full on. "Honey, guess what?" he was saying as I caught up with him. "I finished my book!"

All it took was one look at Heidi to know that, frankly, she probably couldn't have cared less. She was still in her pajamas from the night before, a pair of yoga pants and a rumpled T-shirt with some kind of damp stain on the front. Her hair was flat and stringy, her eyes red as she looked at both of us, as if we looked familiar, but she wasn't quite sure why.

"Oh, Robert," she managed as Thisbe squirmed in her arms, her own face red and twisted, "that's just wonderful."

"I think a celebration is in order, don't you?" he asked, then turned to look at me for confirmation. I was still trying to decide whether I should nod or not when he added, "I was thinking we'd do a nice dinner. Just the two of us. What do you think?"

It was hard to ignore Thisbe when she was screaming. I knew, because I had been trying since, oh, the day I'd arrived. And yet my dad could somehow do it. Apparently.

"I don't know," Heidi said slowly, looking down at the baby, who was clearly in a state. "I don't think I can take her out like this. . . ."

"Of course not," my dad said. "We'll find a sitter. Didn't Isabel say she'd love to come help you out one night?"

Heidi blinked at him. She honestly looked like pictures of prisoners of war I'd seen in history books, that out of it and shell-shocked. "She did," she said. "But . . . "

"Let's call her, then," my dad said. "Get her earning those godmother stripes. I'll do it, if you like. What's her number?"

"She's out of town," Heidi said.

"Oh." My dad considered this. And then, slowly, he turned to me. "Well . . . Auden? Think you can help us out here?"

Heidi looked at me, then shook her head. "Oh, no, that's not fair. We can't put you on the spot like that."

"I'm sure Auden doesn't mind," my dad said. To me he added, "Do you? It would only be for a couple of hours."

I probably should have been annoyed by this easy

assumption, but honestly, looking at Heidi, agreeing felt more like an intervention than a favor. I said, "Sure. No problem."

"But you've got to go to work," Heidi said, shifting Thisbe to her other arm, which did not stop or even slow down the crying. "The books . . . payroll is tomorrow."

"Well," my dad said, glancing at me again. "Maybe . . . "

I was noticing that he did this a lot, the half-sentence-trailing-off thing, leaving you (or me, in this case) to finish his thought for him. It was like Mad Libs, but passive-aggressive. "I'll just take her with me," I said to Heidi. "Then you can pick her up when you're done."

"I don't know," she said, jiggling Thisbe. "She's not exactly in good shape for an outing."

"The sea air will do her good!" my dad said, reaching over to take the baby from her. He smiled down at her screaming face, then sat down in the nearby rocking chair, cradling her in one arm. Heidi followed the baby's movement with her eyes, her expression unchanging. "And you, too, honey. Go jump in the shower, and take your time. We've got it from here."

Heidi glanced at me, and I nodded. A moment later, she started moving toward the door. Out in the hall, she looked back at my dad, who was still rocking Thisbe, seemingly unaffected by her continued fussing, as if she wasn't quite sure who he was. Truth be told, at that moment, I wasn't either.

With Heidi gone, I half expected my dad to hand the baby right over to me. But he didn't. He sat there, rocking her and patting her back with one hand. I wasn't even sure he was aware I was in the doorway, watching him, even as I lingered there, wondering if he'd done this same thing with Hollis and me. If my mother was to be believed, probably not. I certainly wouldn't have thought so even ten minutes earlier. But maybe people can change, or at least try to. I was beginning to see evidence of it everywhere, even though I knew enough to not be convinced, just yet.

❋   ❋   ❋

It had been about a week since my long night out, and since then, my knowledge of Colby nightlife only continued to expand. All those nights by myself, driving to the Wheelhouse, and then through the neighborhoods and streets, stopping now and then at the Gas/Gro: they'd been as boring as treading water. It was only now, with Eli, that I was finding the real night.

It was at the Laundromat, sharing pie and coffee with Clyde as he detailed his latest culinary adventures. Dodging the crazies at Park Mart while on the hunt for dental floss, wind chimes, and whatever else was on the list Eli carried in his head. Going to the boardwalk after last call, when a guy named Mohammed set up a pizza cart outside the most popular clubs to sell the best slice of cheese—at a dollar fifty a pop—I'd ever had in my life. Fishing on the pier and watching the phosphorescence lighting up the water below. I'd leave Clementine's after closing, spend some time shooting the breeze with the girls, and then make my excuses and head off by myself. Fifteen minutes, half an hour, an hour later, at the Gas/Gro, or Beach Beans, I'd cross paths with Eli, and the adventures would begin.

"How does anyone get to the age of eighteen," he'd said to me the night before, "without *bowling?*"

We were at the Ten Pin, a bowling alley open late a couple of towns over from Colby. The lanes were narrow, the benches sticky, and I didn't even want to know what the story was with the shoes I'd had to rent. But Eli had insisted we come, once he'd heard that this was one of the many things my childhood had excluded.

"I told you," I said as he sat down at the head of the lane, sliding our score sheet beneath a rusty clip, "my parents were not sports oriented."

"You bowl indoors, though," he said. "So you should be, like, a pro at this."

I made a face at him. "You know, when I told you I'd missed out on a lot of things, I didn't mean that I was necessarily sorry about *all* of them."

"You would be very sorry if you never bowled," he told me, holding out the ball he'd picked out for me. "Here." I took the ball, putting my fingers in the holes the way he showed me. Then he gestured for me to follow him to the top of the lane. "Now, when I was a kid," he said, "we learned by squatting down and just pushing the ball forward with both hands."

I looked down the lanes on either side of us, which were empty, as it was two A.M. The only people around were sitting up at the bar behind us, which was barely visible due to a fog of cigarette smoke. "I'm not squatting down," I said firmly.

"Fine. Then you have to learn the proper release." He lifted his hands, holding an imaginary ball, then stepped forward, lowering it to his side, and then ahead of him, opening his fingers. "Like that. Okay?"

"Okay."

I lifted up the ball. He didn't move, still standing right beside me. I shot him a look and he shrugged, retreating back to the sticky bench.

Since our first night out together a week earlier, this was pretty much how it had been. A constant back-and-forth, sometimes serious, more often not, stretched out across the hours between when everyone else went home and the sun came up. I knew if I'd spent the same amount of time with Eli during the day, or even early evening, I probably would have gotten to know him, too. But not like this. The night changed things, widening out the scope. What we said to each other, the things we did, they all took on a bigger meaning in the dark. Like time was sped up and slowed down, all at once.

So maybe that was why we always seemed to be talking about time as we wandered the aisles of stores under fluorescent lights, or drank coffee in a dark room while his clothes fluffed, or just drove through the mostly empty streets, en route to somewhere. Time ahead, like college, and behind, like childhood. But mostly, we discussed making up for lost time, if such a thing was possible. Eli seemed to think it was, at least in my case.

"You know what they say," he'd said to me a few nights earlier, as we helped ourselves to Slurpees at the Gas/Gro around three A.M. "It's never too late to have a happy childhood."

I picked up a straw, poking down the   nk slush in my

cup. "I wouldn't say my childhood was unhappy, though. It just wasn't . . . "

Eli waited, fitting a lid onto his cup with a click.

" . . . very childlike," I finished. I took a sip of my Slurpee, then added a bit of blue flavor for variety, a trick he'd taught me a few nights before. "My brother had kind of worn my parents out on the whole kid thing. They didn't have the patience to do it again."

"But you *were* a kid," he pointed out.

"I was," I agreed. "But in their minds, that was something I could overcome, if I just tried hard enough."

He gave me one of the looks I'd come to recognize, his expression a mix of befuddlement and respect. You kind of had to see it to understand. Then he said, "In our house, it was the total opposite. Kid central, all the time."

"Really."

"Yup. You know how there's one house in the neighborhood where everyone goes to ride bikes, or watch cartoons, or sleep over, or build a tree house?"

"Yeah," I said. Then I added, "I mean, I've heard of such things."

"That was our place. Because there were four of us, we were always halfway to any game of kickball or dodgeball. Plus my mom was always around, so we had the best snacks. Her pizza wraps were *legendary*."

"Wow," I said, following him up to the register. The cashier, the older woman I'd come to recognize, looked up from her magazine, smiling at him as she rung us up. "Your mom sounds great."

"She is." He said this so simply, matter-of-factly, as he pushed a couple of bills across to the cashier. "She's so good it's hard for her to convince anyone to move out. It took her forever to get rid of my sister and older brother. And Jake's the baby, and totally spoiled, so she's probably stuck with him until some girl is stupid enough to marry him."

Hearing this, I felt my face flush, remembering our fast, fumbled moment in the dunes. I swallowed, focusing on Wanda as I paid for my Slurpee.

It wasn't until we were headed outside that he said suddenly, "Look, no offense. I mean, about what I said. About Jake. I know you two—"

"I'm not offended," I said, cutting him off before he could begin to try and define this. "Just humiliated."

"We don't have to talk about it."

"Good." I took a long draw off my straw. We walked in silence to the car, but then I said, "In my defense, though, I don't have a lot of experience with, um, guys. So that was . . ."

"You don't have to explain," he said, opening his door. "Really. My brother is a piece of work. Let's just leave it at that."

I smiled gratefully, as I slid into the front seat. "I have one of those, too. A piece-of-work brother. Except he's in Europe, where he's been mooching off my parents for a couple of years now."

"You can mooch from overseas?"

"Hollis can," I told him. "He's got it down to an art form, practically."

Eli considered this as we stepped out into the hot, windy night. "Seems kind of selfish," he observed. "Considering he got the only childhood."

I hadn't ever thought of it that way. "Well, like you said. Maybe it's not too late. For my happy childhood, and all."

"It's not," Eli said.

"You sound awfully sure of that," I told him. "So sure I have to wonder if you've done this kind of making-up thing before."

He shook his head, taking a sip off his straw. "Nope. I have the opposite problem, actually."

"Which is?"

"Too much of a childhood." We walked over to the truck, and he pulled his door open. "All I've ever done was goof around. I even managed to make playing a living."

"With the bike thing."

He nodded. "And then you wake up one day, and you've got nothing of value to show for all those years. Just a bunch of stupid stories, which seem even stupider the more time passes."

I looked at him over the top of the car. "If you really feel that way," I said, "then why do you keep encouraging me to do all this stuff?"

"Because," he said, "you can always break curfew or have a slumber party. It's never too late. So you should, because . . . "

He trailed off. By now, I knew not to fill in the gap.

" . . . that's not the case with everything," he said. "Or so I'm learning."

Now, ahead of me, the lights were blinking over the pins, on and off. The lane stretched out ahead, the wood polished and worn, and I tried to imagine how, as a kid, it would look even longer, almost endless.

"You're overthinking," Eli called from behind me. "Just throw it down there."

I stepped back, trying to remember his form, and swung the ball out in front of me. It took flight—which I was pretty sure was not supposed to happen—then landed with a loud *thud*. In the next lane. Before rolling, oh-so-slowly, into the gutter.

"Hey!" a voice bellowed from the smoking section. "Careful there!"

I felt my face flush, totally embarrassed, as the ball rolled to the end of the lane, disappearing behind the pins. A moment later, there was a *thunk*, and Eli appeared back beside me, holding it out to me.

"I think I'd better not," I said. "Clearly, this is not my strong suit."

"It was your first shot," he replied. "What, you thought you'd get a strike or something?"

I swallowed. In fact, this was exactly what I'd thought. Or at least hoped for. "I just . . ." I said. "I'm not good at this kind of thing."

"Because you've never done it." He reached over, taking my hands, and put the ball in it. "Try again. And this time, let go earlier."

He went back to the bench, and I forced myself to take a deep breath. It's just a game, I told myself. Not so important. Then, with this still in mind, I stepped forward and released the ball. It wasn't pretty—wobbling crookedly, and very slowly—but I took out two pins on the right. Which was . . .

"Not bad," Eli called out as the machine reset itself. "Not bad at all."

We'd played two full games, during which he bowled constant strikes and spares, and I focused on staying out of the gutter. Still, I managed a couple of good frames, which I surprised myself by actually being kind of happy about. So much so that as we left, I plucked the score sheet from the trash can where he'd tossed it, folding it down to little square. When I looked up, I realized Eli was watching me.

"Documentation," I explained. "It's important."

"Right," he said, keeping his eyes on me as I slipped it into my pocket. "Of course."

Outside, we walked across the rain-slicked parking lot to my car, leaving the blinking BOWL neon sign behind us. "So now you've done bowling, breaking curfew, almost getting your ass kicked at a party," he said. "What else is on the list?"

"I don't know," I said. "What else did you do for your first eighteen years?"

"Like I said," he said as I unlocked the car, "I'm not so sure that you should go by my example."

"Why not?"

"Because I have regrets," he said. "Also, I'm a guy. And guys do different stuff."

"Like ride bikes?" I said.

"No," he replied. "Like have food fights. And break stuff.

And set off firecrackers on people's front porches. And . . . "

"Girls can't set off firecrackers on people's front porches?"

"They can," he said as I cranked the engine. "But they're smart enough not to. That's the difference."

"I don't know," I said. "I think food fights and breaking stuff are equal-opportunity activities."

"Fine. But if you're going to do the firecracker thing, you're on your own. That's all I'm saying."

"What," I said, "you afraid or something?"

"Nope." He sat back. "Just been there, done that. Done the getting hauled down to the police station thing because of it, too. I appreciate your quest and everything, but I have to draw the line somewhere."

"Wait," I said, holding up my hand. "My *quest*?"

He turned to look at me. We were at a red light, no other cars anywhere in sight. "Yeah," he said. "You know, like in *Lord of the Rings*, or *Star Wars*. You're searching for something you lost or need. It's a quest."

I just looked at him.

"Maybe it's a guy thing," he said. "Fine, don't call it a quest. Call it chicken salad, I don't care. My point is, I'm in, but within reason. That's all I'm saying."

Here I'd thought we were just hanging out. Killing time. But gender specific or not, I kind of liked the idea of searching for something you'd lost or needed. Or both.

The light finally changed, dropping down to green, but I didn't hit the gas. Instead I said, "Chicken salad?"

"What? You never said that as a kid?"

"'Call it chicken salad'?" I asked. He nodded. "Um, no?"

"Wow." He shook his head. "What *have* you been doing all your life?"

As soon as he said this, a million answers popped into my head, each of them true and legitimate. There were endless ways to spend your days, I knew that, none of them right or wrong. But given the chance for a real do-over, another way around, who would say no? Not me. Not then. Call it crazy, or just chicken salad. But within reason, or even without it, I was in, too.

* * *

"Well," Maggie said, *"that's* an interesting outfit."

We all looked down at Thisbe, who was strapped in her stroller, still in the trance she'd fallen into as soon as I wheeled her down the driveway, eyes wide open, fully silent. "Interesting," I repeated. "What's your point?"

"Did Heidi put this on her?" Leah said, crouching down so she was at Thisbe's eye level.

"No. I did." Leah looked at Maggie, who raised her eyebrows. "What? I think she looks cute."

"She's wearing black," Maggie said.

"So?"

"So how often do you see infants in black?"

I looked down at the baby again. When my dad went to go get ready for dinner, I'd realized she, too, probably needed a change, so I went to her bureau to find a fresh Onesie. Since everything was pink, or had pink incorporated somewhere, I'd decided to be contrary, digging in the very bottom drawer until I found a plain black Onesie and some bright green pants. I thought she looked kind of rock and roll, personally, but judging by the looks I was getting now—not to mention the odd expression Heidi had given me as we said good-bye—maybe I was wrong.

"You know," I said, "just because you're a girl doesn't mean you have to wear pink."

"No," Leah agreed, "but you don't have to dress like a truck driver, either."

"She doesn't look like a truck driver," I said. "God."

Leah cocked her head to the side. "You're right. She looks like a farmer. Or maybe a construction worker."

"Because she's not in pink?"

"She's a baby," Maggie told me. "Babies wear pastels."

"Says who?" I asked. Esther opened her mouth to answer, but before she could I said, "Society. The same society, I might add, that dictates that little girls should always be sugar and spice and everything nice, which encourages them to not be assertive. And that, in turn, then leads to low self-esteem, which can lead to eating disorders and increased tolerance and acceptance of domestic, sexual, and substance abuse."

They all looked at me. "You get all that," Leah said after a moment, "from a pink Onesie?"

Just then, Thisbe began to whimper, turning her head from side to side. "Uh-oh," I said, pushing the stroller forward, then back. "This does not bode well."

"Is she hungry or something?" Esther asked.

"Maybe it's her low self-esteem," Leah said.

I ignored this as I bent down to unbuckle the baby, scooping her up into my arms. Her skin was warm, her cries just starting to get loud as I turned her around, locking my hands around her waist, and bent my knees. Up, down. Up, down. By the third round, she was quiet.

"Wow," Maggie said. "You've got the touch, huh?"

"It's called the elevator," I told her. "Works every time."

They all watched me for a moment. Then Esther said, "You know, I think Auden's right. The black isn't so weird. It's kind of radical, actually."

"Of course *you'd* say that," Leah said. "Look what you're wearing."

Esther glanced down at her dark T-shirt. "This isn't black. It's navy."

The other two girls snorted. Then Leah turned to me, saying, "That's what she said all during her goth period, when she wouldn't wear anything but black. Black clothes, black shoes . . . "

"Black eyeliner, black lipstick," Maggie added.

"Are you guys ever going to let that go?" Esther asked. She sighed. "It was a phase, all right? Like you two never did anything you regretted in high school."

"Two words," Maggie replied. "Jake Stock."

"No kidding," Leah agreed.

"And you," Esther said, pointing at her, "dyed your hair blonde for Joe Parker. Which—"

"No real redhead should ever do," Leah finished. "I'm still ashamed."

Through all of this, I was still doing the elevator with Thisbe in my arms. She'd gone back into her trance, quiet, and for a moment we all just watched her moving up and down. Finally Maggie said, "Isn't it weird to think we were all that little, once?"

"Totally." Leah reached out, taking Thisbe's hand and squeezing it. "She's like a clean slate. No mistakes yet."

"Lucky girl," Esther said. Then, leaning closer, she added, "A word of advice: don't do the goth thing. Nobody *ever* lets you forget it."

"And don't change for a guy, ever," Leah added. "If they're worthy, they'll like you just the way you are."

"Always wear your helmet on the dirt jumps," Maggie said.

"Don't eat beef jerky before you get on a roller coaster," Leah said.

"A nose piercing," Esther chimed in, "does not look good on everyone. Trust me."

Thisbe took all this in with her same, solemn expression. I shifted her in my arms, leaning down to breathe in her smell, a mix of milk and baby shampoo. "Come on, Auden," Leah said. "You must have some wisdom to share."

I thought for a moment. "Don't flirt with a girl's boyfriend in her own kitchen," I said. "Or answer the question 'What kind of a name is that?'"

"And you know someone will ask her that," Leah said. "With a name like Thisbe, it's guaranteed."

"What about this," Maggie said. "Stay clear of cute boys on bikes. They'll only break your heart." I glanced over at her, and she smiled. "Of course, that's easier said than done. Right?"

I just looked at her, wondering what she meant. I hadn't told anyone about me and Eli, mostly because I knew they would just assume we were hooking up. What else would you be doing all night, every night, with someone else? The very fact that there were so many answers to that question made me want to leave this one, that Maggie was asking and yet not asking, unanswered.

"God, Maggie," Leah said, "I thought you'd let that Jake thing go, already."

"I have," Maggie told her.

"Then why are you bugging Auden about it now?" Leah shook her head.

"That's not what I was—"

This thought was interrupted, suddenly, by a crash from the front entrance. We all looked over just in time to see Adam bending back from the glass, rubbing his arm.

"Pull open," Maggie called out. As Leah rolled her eyes, she said, "He never remembers. It's so weird."

"Can't say I don't make an entrance," Adam said, hardly bothered by what some would consider a public humiliation of sorts as he walked toward us, carrying a plastic grocery bag in one hand. "So, ladies. An announcement."

Leah shot a wary look at the bag. "Are you selling candy bars to raise money for math club again?"

Adam just looked at her. "That was eighth grade," he said. "And school's over, remember?"

"Ignore her," Maggie told him as Leah shrugged, going back behind the counter. "What's the announcement?"

He grinned, reaching into the bag. "Hot-dog party," he said, pulling out a value pack of wieners. "The first of the summer. After work, at me and Wallace's. Bring your own condiments."

"Count me out," Esther said, hopping up on the counter. "I'm a vegetarian."

Adam reached back into the bag, pulling out another pack of dogs. "Bam!" he said, shaking it at her. "Tofu Pups! Just for you!"

"Is the bathroom going to be clean?" Leah asked.

"Isn't it always?"

"No," Leah, Maggie, and Esther said in unison.

"Well, it will be tonight. I'll bust out my Clorox Clean-Up and everything."

Maggie smiled as he dropped the dogs back into the bag, twisting it shut. "It's been a long time since the last hot-dog party," she said. "What's the occasion?"

"The housewarming party we forgot to have two months ago when we moved in," he said. "Plus, it's been a while, you know? It just seemed like maybe it was time."

"Is Eli coming?" Esther asked.

"He's invited," Adam said. "So we'll see."

Maggie turned to me, saying, "The hot-dog party was one of Abe's big traditions. He used to have them every Saturday at Eli's and his place. Hot dogs, baked beans . . . "

" . . . potato chips for the vegetable," Leah said.

"And Popsicles for dessert. He called it the perfect summer meal." Maggie reached up, twisting one of her curls around her finger. "He and Eli always bought all the stuff in bulk at Park Mart, so they could have one at a moment's notice."

"IHDP," Esther said. When I raised my eyebrows, she added, "Impromptu Hot-Dog Party."

"Right," I said. My knees were starting to hurt, so I stopped the elevator, shifting Thisbe across my right arm. Adam came closer, making a googly face at her.

"You might be too young for an HDP," he said, poking her tummy before turning toward the door. "As for the rest of you, I expect to see you with condiments, at Wallace's, after closing. No excuses."

"You know," Leah said, "I liked you better when you were selling candy bars."

"See you later!" he replied. This time, he got the door right, disappearing out onto the boardwalk as the chime sounded overhead.

Leah looked at Maggie. "Great," she muttered. "He's got the hots for you, and now we all have to eat wieners because of it."

"He does not have the hots for me," Maggie said, walking over to the earring display and adjusting a couple of pairs.

"Well, I'm not going," Leah said, pushing a button on the register. The drawer slid open, and she picked up some bills, straightening them. "The summer is almost half over, and the only guys I've hung out with are the ones I've known since grade school. This is getting ridiculous."

"There might be new boys at the hot-dog party," Esther suggested.

"Oh, please," Leah said.

"Hey, they have tofu dogs. Anything is possible."

But it wasn't new boys I was interested in as I sat in the office for the next hour, my foot locked around the back wheels of Thisbe's stroller, pushing her back and forth as I paged through the day's receipts. It was just one boy, that same boy I always started to think about more and more as the hours passed.

Despite my best efforts, it was hard, as the hour got later, not to look ahead, wondering what the night might hold for me and Eli. This was something I'd missed out on thus far, the sense of expectation when it came to someone else. So while a hot-dog party sounded fun and all—and might even have qualified for part of my quest, actually—if Eli wasn't going to be there, I was pretty sure I didn't want to be, either. Even if there were tofu dogs.

At around eight thirty, my dad and Heidi showed up to pick up the baby. Their arrival was heralded by a burst of squealing from the sales floor.

"Oh, my God, you look so good!" Maggie said. "You're super skinny already!"

"Please," Heidi said. "I could not wear a single thing in this store right now. Not even the ponchos."

"Stop it," Esther told her. "You're gorgeous."

"And so is Thisbe," Leah added. "We love her name, by the way."

"See?" I heard my dad say. "I told you. It's a powerful name! It has *presence*."

"Although," Maggie said, "the story of Thisbe is kind of tragic, really. Dying for her lover, and her soul blooming in the mulberry tree."

Even with the door shut between us, and no visual on this interaction, I could literally *feel* how impressed my dad was as he said, "You know the story of Thisbe?"

"We read it in my classics class, when we were studying myth and women," Maggie replied.

"I thought it was from Shakespeare," Heidi said.

"It was reprised in Shakespeare, in a farcical way," my

dad told her. "But this young lady is right. The true story is actually quite sad."

"That's our Maggie," Leah said. "Expert on all things tragic."

"Is Auden in back?" I heard Heidi say. A moment later, she tapped on the door, sticking her head in. When she saw Thisbe, dozing in the stroller, she smiled. "Look at that. And here I was worried she was screaming her head off the entire time."

"Not the entire time," I said. "How was dinner?"

"Lovely," she said. Then she yawned, putting her hand over her mouth. "It was good that we went and celebrated. This is a great accomplishment for your father. He's worked so hard these last few weeks."

I looked down at Thisbe. "So have you," I said.

"Oh, well." She waved this off, then stepped forward, easing the stroller out the door. "I can't thank you enough, Auden, really. I can't remember the last time we got out alone, together."

"It was no problem," I said.

"Still. I appreciate it." She glanced out at the sales floor. "I'd better get your father out of here while he's still cheerful. He claims this place gives him a headache. Too much pink. Can you even imagine?"

I could. But I didn't say anything, instead just nodding as she wheeled Thisbe down the hallway, waving to me over her shoulder.

For the next two hours, I focused on my work, taking only passing notice of the customers that came and went

(there was a run on flip-flops), the nine o'clock dance (El-
vis this time, from his rockabilly days), and the ongoing
debate about attending the hot-dog party (Maggie was in,
Leah out, Esther on the fence). At ten on the dot, I locked
the safe, shut the door, and went out to join them as they
headed out onto the boardwalk, still in discussion. All of
this was part of my routine now, as was what came next:
making my excuses, and going to find Eli.

"We could just go for a little while," Maggie was saying.
"To make an appearance."

Leah turned to me. "What about you, Auden? Are you
in or out?"

"Oh," I said. "Actually, I think I'm going to just . . ."

I was going to use one of my standards, like "go home,"
or "go run some errands," but just then, I looked over Maggie's shoulder to the bike shop, and there was Eli, sitting on
the bench, the shop locked up and dark behind him. No
searching for once, so simple. Or it would have been, except
that he wasn't alone.

Belissa Norwood was standing in front of him, her hair
blowing around her face, hands in her pockets. She wasn't
dressed up like she'd been at the party, now wearing just
jeans and a simple blue sleeveless shirt, a sweater tied
around her waist, and I was struck, immediately, by how
much prettier she looked. Less is more, indeed.

She was saying something to Eli, who wasn't looking
at her, instead just leaning forward on the bench, his head
propped in his hands. Then she said something else, and
he looked up at her and nodded. I just stood there, staring,

as she slid down to sit beside him, her knee resting against his. After a moment, she leaned her head on his shoulder, closing her eyes.

"Auden?" Leah said. Seeing my face, she turned, looking behind her, just as a group of big-shouldered guys in tracksuits came out of the adjacent Jumbo Smoothie shop, blocking everything behind them. "What is it?"

"Nothing," I said quickly. "I'm in."

*　*　*

Wallace's apartment was the lower level of a green house two streets back from the beach. The yard was mostly dirt with a few clumps of grass, there was a washing machine on the side porch, and a sign hanging over the garage read, inexplicably, SENTIMENTAL JOURNEY.

"Interesting name choice," I said as I followed Maggie and Esther up the driveway, the bag of condiments we'd bought at the Gas/Gro—ketchup, mustard, mayo, and chocolate sauce—in my hand. Leah was lagging behind, her phone to her ear, still networking in hopes of finding a better destination.

"It wasn't up to the guys," Maggie explained over her shoulder. "The landlords picked it. It's a beach thing, you know, naming houses. The last place Wallace lived was called GULL'S CRY."

"Which was a terrible name," Esther said. "Hey, Mags, remember when Eli and Abe were living over in that dump on Fourth Street? What was that—"

"SUMMER LOVIN'," Maggie finished for her as we climbed

the front steps. "And there was nothing to love about it, let me tell you. *Such* a dump."

Just as she said this, Adam appeared in the open door, an oven mitt on one hand. "Hey," he said, holding it over his heart, offended. "You haven't even come inside yet!"

"I wasn't talking about this place," Maggie told him as he stepped aside, letting us in. "This is . . . very nice."

Which was kind of an overstatement. The living room was small, crowded with worn, mismatched furniture: plaid couch, striped recliner, very beat-up coffee table, stained with rings upon rings upon rings. Clearly, though, someone had taken steps to spruce it up, as was evident by the bowl of nuts on the table and what looked like a brand-new scented candle burning on the bar that led to the kitchen.

"Decor," Adam said, having caught me noticing this. "It really makes a difference, don't you think?"

"Still stinks like beer," Leah informed him as she came in, dropping her phone in her purse.

"Does that mean you don't want one?" Wallace yelled from the kitchen.

"No," Leah said.

"Didn't think so," he replied, emerging with a twelve-pack of cans. He moved down the line, handing them off. I was going to pass but ended up taking one anyway, if only to be polite.

"There are coasters to your left," Adam said to Leah as she popped her can.

"Coasters?" she said. "On this coffee table? It's already covered with rings."

He glanced at it, then at her. "Just because something's damaged doesn't mean it shouldn't be treated with respect."

"Ad," Wallace said, "it's a coffee table, not an orphan."

Esther snickered. But Maggie, true to form, reached over and set a coaster on the table before putting her beer down. As she did, Adam reached behind him to the island, grabbing a camera sitting there. "Our first hot-dog party," he said, raising it to his eye. "I *have* to get a shot of this."

The reaction in the room was swift, and unanimous: every single person except me raised their hands at once to cover their faces. The accompanying utterances, though, were varied. I heard everything from "Please no" (Maggie), to "Jesus Christ" (Wallace), to "Stop it or die" (I'm assuming it's obvious).

Adam sighed, lowering the camera. "Why," he said, "can you guys not allow one shot, once in a while?"

"Because that was the deal," Wallace replied, his face muffled by his fingers, which were still over his mouth.

"The deal?" I asked.

Maggie separated her thumb and forefinger, then said through them, "Adam was yearbook editor for the last two years. He was *relentless* with the camera."

"I only had one person on staff!" Adam protested. "I had no choice. Somebody had to take pictures."

"So we told him," Wallace continued, around his palm, "that we would tolerate it until the yearbook was done. But after that . . . "

"No more pictures," Maggie said.

"Ever," Leah added.

Adam put the camera back on the island, a glum expression on his face. "Fine," he said, and everyone dropped their hands. "But years from now, when you're feeling nostalgic about this summer and yet can't really reminisce because of a lack of documentation, don't blame me."

"We've been fully documented," Maggie told him. "The yearbook candids were of nothing *but* us."

"Which is great, because you'll never forget anything," he told her. "But that's already history. This is now."

"The now in which we are spared being photographed." Leah picked up her beer—no coaster—and took a sip, then said, "So who else is coming to this shindig?"

"You know, the usual suspects," Wallace replied, sitting down in the armchair, which sagged noticeably beneath him. "The guys from the shop, some of the locals from the bike park, that cute girl from Jumbo Smoothie, and—"

This thought was interrupted by the sound of someone banging up the steps. "Yo!" a voice bellowed. "You guys better have some beer, because I am ready to get—"

Jake Stock—in a form-fitting black tee and a deeper tan than ever—stopped talking and walking the minute he came through the door and saw me and Maggie, side by side on the couch. Talk about a buzz kill.

"Get what?" Leah asked him, sipping her beer.

Jake looked at her, then at Wallace, who shrugged. "Lovely to see you as always," he said to Leah, then walked past her and us, heading to the kitchen. I glanced sideways at Maggie, but she was staring straight ahead at her beer on its coaster, her expression unreadable.

"It's not too late to hit the clubs," Leah said to her. "New boys, new chances."

"Grill's on!" Adam hollered from the back door. "Who wants the first dog?"

Maggie stood, picking up her beer. "Me," she called back, walking past Jake, who was leaning against the bar, sniffing the candle. "I do."

An hour later, I'd had one beer, two tofu dogs, and, despite my efforts to keep up with the party and conversation around me, entirely too much time to run over what I'd seen on the boardwalk with Eli and Belissa. I looked at my watch: it was almost midnight. This time the night before, Eli and I had just been leaving Clyde's, where he'd done a load of whites and we'd shared a piece of butterscotch almond tart. I looked down at the bowl of nuts, untouched on the table in front of me, and took another sip of my beer.

Really, it had been stupid to expect anything anyway. A few late nights does not a habit, or a relationship, make.

Just then, my phone rang, and I felt stupid by how quickly I jumped to answer it, thinking it might be Eli. Who, I realized a beat later, did not have my phone number. I flipped it open, only to see the number of another man who always seemed to keep me wondering: my brother.

"Aud!" he said as soon as I answered. "It's me! Guess where I am?"

As we'd played this game before, and I'd always lost, I just said, "Tell me."

"Home!"

At first, I thought he'd said Rome. It wasn't until I asked

him to repeat himself, and he did, that I realized he was two hundred miles away instead of however many thousand.

"Home?" I said. "Since when?"

"About two hours ago." He laughed. "I am jet-lagging like crazy, let me tell you. I have no freaking idea what time it is. Where are you?"

"At a party," I said, standing up and walking to the front door, pushing it open.

"A party? Really?"

He sounded so shocked I probably should have been offended. Then again, a few weeks earlier, I would have been surprised, too. "Yeah," I said, walking down to sit on the bottom step. "So . . . what brings you back?"

There was a pause. For dramatic purposes, as it turned out. "Not what," he said. "Who."

"Who?"

"Aud." Another pause. Then, "I'm in love."

As he said this, I was looking up at a streetlight, bright and buzzing overhead. A few bugs were circling it, tiny specks up high. "You are?" I said.

"Yeah." He laughed. "It's crazy, I know. But I'm sick with it. So sick I cut the trip short and jumped a plane to follow her back here."

The trip had been going on for a couple of years, which I wouldn't exactly have called short. But with Hollis, it was always about the bigger picture. "So," I said, "who is she?"

"Her name," he said, "is Laura. She's amazing! I met her at a youth hostel in Seville. I was there for this big three-day festival-slash-rave . . . "

I rolled my eyes at no one, there in the dark.

" . . . and she was there for some genetic conference. She's a scientist, Aud! Doing grad work at the U, of all places. She was studying in the library where I was sleeping. Said my snoring was disturbing her research and I needed to get up and get out. Crazy, right? It's the story we'll tell our grandchildren!"

"Hollis," I said, "you're messing with me right now, aren't you? You're in Paris, or somewhere, and just—"

"What?" he replied. "No! God, no. This is the real deal. Here, I'll prove it."

There was a muffled noise, followed by some static. Then, I heard my mother recite, at a distance, in her most droll, flat tone, "Yes. It is true. Your brother is in love and in my kitchen."

"Hear that?" Hollis asked, even as I sat there, startled at her voice. "It's no joke!"

"So . . . " I said, still grappling, "how long are you home for, then?"

"As long as Laura will have me. We're looking for an apartment, and I'm going to sign up for fall classes. Might even hit up the English department, you never know." He laughed. "But seriously, before then I want to come down, visit you and Dad and Heidi and the munchkin, introduce my girl around. So let them know, okay?"

"All right," I said slowly. "I'm glad you're back, Hollis."

"Me, too. See you soon!"

I hung up, then looked out at the quiet street, the ocean somewhere in the dark beyond. It was so early and yet, between what I'd seen with Eli and my brother's strange homecoming, I felt, for the first time in a long while, like all I wanted to do was go crawl into bed. Pull the covers over my head, finding my own dark, and wake up when this night was over.

Thinking this, I went inside to say my good-byes, but the living room was empty, stereo still playing, beer cans scattered—mostly uncoastered—across the coffee table. I picked up my purse, then walked through the kitchen to the back door. Through it, I could see everyone gathered on the back deck: Adam at the grill with Maggie beside him, Leah and Esther sitting side by side on the rail. Wallace was opening a can of baked beans while Jake looked on from a nearby rusted lawn chair.

"You knew he probably wouldn't show," he was saying to Adam, who was busy turning dogs over the flame. "He's been antisocial ever since it happened."

"It's been over a year now, though," Adam said. "He's got to start hanging out again sometime."

"Maybe he is hanging out," Maggie said. "Just not with you."

"Meaning what?" Wallace asked. I stepped back behind the open door, waiting for Maggie to respond, but she didn't. "Belissa? I can assure you, that is *not* happening."

"No kidding. They've been broken up for months, idiot," Jake said.

"Yeah, but she's still been hung up on him," Wallace replied. "But then tonight, she came by the shop to tell him she's got a new boyfriend. Some guy from the U, down for the summer working at the Cadillac tending bar. Said she wanted to tell him in person, so he didn't find out from someone else."

There was a short silence. Then Leah said, "And how do you know this, exactly?"

"I might have been just inside the door, checking the air on the display bikes."

Someone snorted. Adam said, "You are the worst gossip, Wallace. Worse than a girl."

"Hey!" Esther said.

"Sorry. Just an expression," Adam told her. "Seriously, though, Maggie might be right. Maybe he does have something going on, somewhere else. When I invited him tonight, he said he'd try to make it, but he already had plans with someone to run some errands."

"Errands?" Leah said. "Who runs errands at night?"

"It didn't make sense to me either," Adam told her. "But that's what he said."

I looked around the kitchen, then walked over to a nearby drawer, pulling it open, then the one beneath it. In the third, I found what I was looking for: the Colby phone book. It was such a small town, only one Laundromat was listed.

"The Washroom, Clyde speaking."

I glanced outside again, then stepped closer to the fridge. "Hey, Clyde. It's Auden. Is Eli there?"

"You bet. Hang on."

There was a bit of interference, and a short exchange, as the receiver was handed over. Then Eli said, "You are missing out on some *serious* apple crumble right now."

"I got dragged to a hot-dog party," I said.

A pause. "Really."

"Yeah." I turned around, shutting the phone book. "Apparently, they are a very important rite of passage. So I figured I should check it out, for my quest and all."

"Right," he said.

For a moment, neither of us said anything, and I realized that it was the first time in a long while that I'd felt nervous or uncomfortable around Eli. All those crazy nights, doing so many crazy things. And yet this, a simple phone conversation, was hard.

"So let me guess," he said. "Right about now, Adam's probably still cooking hot dogs, even though no one wants any more."

I glanced outside. Sure enough, Adam was at the grill, opening up another pack. "Um," I said. "Yeah, actually."

"Leah and Esther are probably starting to argue about leaving."

Another look proved that yes, they did look like they were having a somewhat spirited conversation. Leah, at least, was gesturing pretty widely. "They are. But how did you—"

"And my brother," he continued, "having arrived talking big about throwing down and scoring with women, is most likely drunk and dozing off somewhere. Alone."

I peeked back at Jake. His eyes were definitely closed. "You know," I said, "with all the time we spent together, you could have mentioned you were a psychic."

"I'm not," he said. "You need a ride?"

"I do," I replied, without even hesitating.

"Be there in ten."

*　　*　　*

Seventeen minutes later, and I was out on the deck with everyone else, watching Leah and Maggie argue.

"The deal was," Leah was saying, her voice slightly slurred, "that I would come as long as we could leave at some point and do something else."

"It's past midnight!" Maggie replied. "It's too late to go anywhere."

"Which was exactly your plan. Get me here, get me drunk—"

"You got yourself drunk," Adam pointed out.

"—and get me stuck. Same as always," Leah finished. "What happened to our big, fun summer before college? The one that was supposed to be full of new experiences and great memories we'd take with us for when we were apart? It was supposed to be . . . to be . . . "

She trailed off, clearly grasping for words. I said, "The best of times."

"That's right!" She snapped her fingers. "The best of times! What happened to the best of times?"

Everyone fell completely silent, I assumed because they were all contemplating this question. Then I realized it was because Eli had appeared behind me in the open kitchen door.

"Don't ask me," he said. We were all staring at him. "I just came for the hot dogs."

"Hot dogs!" Adam burst out excitedly. "We've got hot dogs! Tons of hot dogs! Here! Have one!"

He grabbed a bun, stuffing a dog into it, and thrust it out toward him. Eli raised his eyebrows, then took it. "Thanks."

"No problem!" Adam said. "Lots more where that came from, too. Plus there's chips, and baked beans, and—"

"Adam," Wallace said, his voice low. "Chill out."

"Right," Adam replied just as loudly. Then, in a somewhat more subdued tone, he added, "We have Popsicles, too."

Everyone looked at Eli again. It was so awkward and tense, you would have thought we were at a wake, not a cookout. Then again, maybe we kind of were.

"So, Eli," Maggie said after a moment, "how's it going with the shop? Come up with a name yet?"

Eli glanced at her, then down at his hot dog. "It's still in the discussion phase."

"Personally," Adam said, "I like The Chain Gang."

"That makes us sound like a singing group," Wallace told him.

"A *bad* singing group," Leah added.

"It's better than Pump Cycles."

"What's wrong with Pump Cycles?" Wallace asked. "That's a great name."

"It sounds menstrual," Adam told him. Esther swatted at his arm. "What? It does."

"I think," Jake said, surprising everyone, as we'd assumed he was fast asleep, "that we need a name with edge. Something dark, kind of dangerous."

"Like?" Eli said.

"Like," Jake went on, eyes still closed, "Barbed Wire Bikes. Or Flatline Bikes."

Adam rolled his eyes. "You can't call a tourist bike shop Flatline Bikes."

"Why not?"

"Because people on vacation want to think about happy, relaxing things. When they rent a bike, they don't want to think about dying in some accident."

I could tell, by Adam's face as he said this—relaxed, opinionated—followed by just after—shocked, then ashamed—that he'd had absolutely no idea what was going to come out of his mouth until it was too late. And now it was.

Another silence fell. Adam's face was flushed, and I watched Maggie and Esther exchange a desperate kind of look. Beside me, Eli just stood there, the awkwardness tangible, something solid you could feel. All I could think was that it was my fault he was there, that any and all of this was happening. But I had no idea what to do about it until I saw the pot of baked beans on the table next to me.

It was a split-second decision, the kind you hear about people making in the most dangerous or serious of situations. This was really neither, but I still was not thinking, just doing, as I reached my hand into the beans, scooping out a big gob with my fingers. Then, before I could reconsider, I turned and launched it right at Eli.

The beans hit him square in the forehead, then splattered back into his hair, a few falling to hit the deck at his feet. I could hear the inhaled breath of everyone else on the deck, indicating their absolute shock, watching this. But I kept my eyes on Eli, who blinked, then reached up, wiping some beans from the tip of his nose.

"Oh, man," he said to me. "It's *so* on."

And just like that, he was reaching across me, lightning quick, and grabbing the pot of beans. One smooth movement—too fast to even think, much less stop him—and he'd overturned it on my head. I felt heat on my hair, something slimy trickling down into my eyes, even as I grabbed for a discarded plate nearby, launching the half-eaten hot dog back at him.

"What the hell . . . " I heard Leah say, but the rest of the sentence was lost as Eli pelted me with buns from the bag he'd grabbed off the kitchen counter. I ducked my head— still covered with beans—and ran across the deck, picking up along the way a bag of Cheetos for ammo.

"Wait!" Adam yelled. "That's my breakfast for the week!"

"Oh, lighten up," Maggie said, picking up a handful of coleslaw from her plate and tossing it at him. When Leah gasped, she threw another fistful at her.

Leah's jaw dropped. She looked down at her shirt, then up at Maggie. "Oh, boy," she said, picking up a beer can and shaking it, hard, before popping the top, "you better *run*."

Maggie squealed, taking off down the stairs with Leah behind her, the beer already fizzing over. Meanwhile Adam and Wallace were now exchanging rapid fire with the leftover nuts while Esther, arms over her head, ducked behind Jake, who was asleep with a sprinkling of coleslaw over his face. All of this I noticed before running back into the house while trying to simultaneously dodge the Popsicle pieces Eli was tossing at me and chucking potato chips back at him behind me. I was so busy defending myself and keeping up my offensive that I didn't realize he had me trapped in the kitchen until it was too late.

"Wait," I said, gasping for breath as I leaned against the fridge. I held up my hands. "Time-out."

"There's no time-outs in food fights," Eli informed me, throwing another slushy piece at me. It hit my shoulder, knocking off some beans.

"Then how do they end?"

"Whoever runs out of food first has to formally surrender," he said.

I looked at my hands, covered with bean residue and pieces of chips, but basically empty. "I'm not good at surrendering."

"No one is," he said. "But sometimes, you lose. Nothing you can do but admit it."

We were both so filthy, standing there, beans in our hair, food all over our clothes. It was the last moment you'd think would mean anything, and yet somehow, it did. Like only in all this chaos could it finally feel right to say the one thing I'd wanted to, all along.

"I'm really sorry about your friend," I told him.

Eli nodded slowly. He kept his eyes right on me, not wavering a bit, as he said, "Thanks."

Outside, I could hear someone still shrieking, other battles going on. But in the bright light of the kitchen, it was just us. The way it had been those other nights, yet suddenly something felt different. Not like we'd changed so much as that we could. And might.

I was looking right at Eli, thinking this, and he was staring right back at me, and it was suddenly so easy to imagine myself reaching my hand forward to brush his hair from his face. It was all there: how his skin would feel against my fingertips, the strands against my palm, his hands rising up to my waist. Like it was already happening, and then, suddenly, I heard the door bang behind me.

"Hey," Adam called out, and I turned to see him holding up the camera again, the lens pointing right at us. "Smile!"

As the shutter snapped, I knew it was likely I'd never see this picture. But even if I did, it wouldn't come close to capturing everything I was feeling right then. If I ever did get a copy, I already had the perfect place for it: a blue frame, a few words etched beneath. The best of times.

ten

"BOOT CUT OR boyfriend fit?"

There was a pause. Then, "Which do you think looks better?"

"You know, it's not an either/or kind of thing. It's more about how you want your butt to look."

I sighed, then put the deposit book into the safe and pushed the door shut with my foot. Another day, another opportunity to hear Maggie go on about the gospel of denim. I liked her and all—surprising as that was—but I still had trouble stomaching the seriously girly stuff. Like this.

"See?" I heard her say a moment later as the customer emerged again from the fitting room. "The boot gives you that nice flow from thigh to ankle. The upturn at the cuff draws your eye right to it, rather than other areas."

"Other areas," the woman grumbled, "are my problem."

"Mine, too." Maggie sighed. "But the boyfriend fit has its strengths also. So you should try them and we'll compare."

The woman said something, although I couldn't hear her over the front door chiming. A moment later, Esther came into the office. She had on army pants and a black tank top, and her expression was grave as she flopped into the chair behind me without comment.

"Hey," I said to her. "Are you—"

Maggie suddenly appeared in the open door, eyes wide, her phone in one hand. She glanced at it, then at Esther. "I just got your text! Is this for real? Hildy is . . . dead?"

Esther nodded, still silent.

"I can't believe it." Maggie shook her head. "But she was, like, one of us. I mean, after all this time . . . "

I opened my mouth to say something, offer some kind of condolence. But before I could, Esther finally spoke. "I know," she said, her voice tight. "She was a great car."

Outside, the fitting room door swung open again. "Car?" I asked.

They both looked at me. "The best Jetta ever," Maggie said. "Hildy was our sole source of transportation in high school. She was one of the girls."

"Such a trooper," Esther agreed. "I bought her for three thousand bucks with eighty thousand miles on her, and she never let us down."

"Well," Maggie said, "I wouldn't say that. What about that time on the interstate, on the way to the World of Waffles?"

Esther shot her a look. "Are you really going to bring that up? Now? At this moment?"

"Sorry," Maggie said. Outside, the fitting room door swung open again. "Oh, crap. Hold on."

She disappeared back down the hallway. A moment later, I heard the customer say, "I just don't know about these. Now I feel like my ankles are huge."

"That's just because you're used to the flare," Maggie assured her. "But look at how good your thighs look!"

By the door, Esther tipped her head back, looking at the ceiling. I said, "So what now? You're walking?"

"Not an option," she said. "I leave for school soon, and I have to take a car with me. I've got some money saved, but not nearly enough."

"You could take out a loan."

"And be in more debt?" She sighed. "I'm already going to be paying college off until I'm dead."

"I don't know," I heard the customer say outside. "Neither have really looked right so far."

"That's because finding the perfect jeans is a process," Maggie replied. "I told you, you have to find the ones that speak to you."

I rolled my eyes again, picking up my pen and going back to my balance sheet. A moment later, I heard the customer go back into the fitting room, and Maggie reappeared in the office.

"Okay, so let's talk options," she said to Esther, who was still staring at the ceiling. "What about a loan?"

"I'm already going to be paying off college until I'm dead," she repeated, her voice flat. "I guess I'll just have to cash the savings bonds my grandparents gave me."

"Oh, Esther! I don't know if that's a good idea."

I knew this really didn't concern me, but I felt bad for Esther. So I figured someone should jump in to clarify. "She doesn't want to be in more debt," I explained to Maggie, wishing there was a way to draw a parallel between this and jeans, somehow. "If she takes out a loan, she'll owe more."

Outside, the fitting room door banged open again. "I don't know about these. . . ." I heard the customer say. "Are my legs supposed to look like sausages?"

"No," Maggie called down to her, shaking her head. "Try the other boot cuts, the ones with the embellished pockets, okay?"

The door shut. Esther sighed. I said to Maggie, "More money borrowed is more money owed. It's basic."

"True," Maggie agreed. "But a car is a consumable item, not an asset. Esther's not investing the money she puts into it, because it will automatically begin to depreciate. So while it's tempting to liquidate her savings, and cash in the bonds, the better bet is probably to take advantage of the rate you can get from the local credit union on a loan."

"You think?" Esther asked.

"Absolutely. I mean," she continued, "what is the rate right now, like, 5.99 percent or something? So you do that, and keep your bonds in savings where they retain their full market value. It's a more cost-effective use of the money."

I just looked at her. Who was this girl?

"What about these?" the customer called out.

Maggie glanced down the hallway, her face breaking into a big smile. "Oh, man," she said, clapping her hands. "What do you think?"

"I think," the woman said, "that they're speaking to me."

Maggie laughed, and as I watched her head back down to the fitting rooms, I sat there, trying to process what I'd just seen. It wasn't easy. In fact, later that night, when she came in before locking up, I was still thinking about it.

"That financial stuff," I said to her as she slid the cash drawer onto the desk. "How did you know all that?"

She glanced up at me. "Oh, mostly from my riding days. My mom wasn't exactly supportive of it as a hobby, so I had to finance my bikes and equipment and stuff."

"It's pretty impressive."

"Maybe," she said. "Too bad it's not what impresses my mom."

"No?" She shook her head. "What does, then?"

"Oh, I don't know," she said. "Maybe if I'd agreed to do the debutante thing like she wanted. Or taken up pageants instead of riding jump bikes with a bunch of grungy boys. I'd always tell her, why can't I do both? Who says you have to be either smart or pretty, or into girly stuff or sports? Life shouldn't be about the either/or. We're capable of more than that, you know?"

Clearly, she was. Not that I'd seen it, really, until now. "Yeah," I said. "That does make sense."

She smiled, then grabbed her keys off the desk, sliding them into her pocket. "I'm going to go clean up the denim section while you finish up. Finding those slim boot cuts for that woman was work. But it was so worth it. Her butt looked *great* when she left here."

"I bet," I said, and then she was gone back down the hallway to fold. I sat there for a minute, in that pink-and-orange room, thinking about what impressed my mom, and the either/or I'd been stuck in for so long. Maybe it was true, and being a girl could be about interest rates and

skinny jeans, riding bikes and wearing pink. Not about any
one thing, but everything.

*   *   *

Over the next couple of weeks, I fell into the perfect routine. Mornings were for sleep, evenings for work. My nights
were for Eli.

These days, I didn't have to make it look like I was bumping into him accidentally. Instead, it was understood that we
met each evening after I got off work at the Gas/Gro, where
we fueled up on both gas (coffee) and gro (you never knew
what you might need) and planned our evening's activities.
Which meant errands, eating pie with Clyde, and working
on my quest, one item at a time.

"Really?" I said, one night around one as we stood outside Tallyho, Leah's favorite club. There was a neon sign
in the window that said HOLA MARGARITAS! and a beefy,
bored-looking guy sitting on a stool by the door, checking
messages on his phone. "You think I need to do this?"

"Yup," Eli said. "Hitting a club is a rite of passage. And
you get extra points if it's a bad club."

"But I don't have an ID," I told him as we walked closer,
passing a girl in a red dress, puffy eyed and stumbling.

"You don't need one."

"Are you sure?"

Instead of answering, he reached down and grabbed my
hand, and I felt a jolt run through me. Since that night at
the hot-dog party, we'd been closer, but this was the first
real physical contact between us. I was so busy worrying

about what it might mean that it took me a minute to realize how natural and easy his palm felt against mine. Like it wasn't new at all, but something I'd done recently and often, that familiar.

"Hey," Eli said to the bouncer as we approached. "What's the cover?"

"You got ID?"

Eli pulled out his wallet, then handed over his license. The guy glanced at it, then at him, before giving it back. "What about her?"

"She forgot hers," Eli said. "But don't worry, I'll vouch for her."

The guy gave him a flat look. "Honor system doesn't fly here, sorry."

"I hear you," Eli replied. "But maybe you can make an exception."

I expected the guy to react in some way, but if anything he looked even more bored than before. "No ID, no exceptions."

"It's fine," I said to Eli. "Really."

He held up his hand, quieting me. Then he said, "Look. We don't want to drink. We don't even want to stay long. Five minutes, max."

The bouncer, now starting to look annoyed, said, "What part of no ID, no entry, do you not understand?"

"What if I told you"—Eli pressed on as I squirmed, worrying my palm was now entirely sticky against his— "that this was a quest?"

The guy just looked at him. Through the door, I could

hear bass thumping, thumping. Finally he said, "What kind of quest?"

No way, I thought. There's just no way.

"She's never done anything," Eli told him, gesturing at me. "No parties in high school, no prom, no homecoming. No social life, ever." The bouncer looked at me, and I tried to look adequately culturally stunted. "So we're just, you know, trying to make up for lost stuff, one thing at a time. This is on the list."

"Tallyho is on the list?"

"Going to a club is," Eli told him. "Not drinking at a club. Not even staying at a club. Just going."

The bouncer looked at me again. He said, "For five minutes."

"Maybe even four," Eli replied.

I just stood there, feeling my heart beat, and then the guy was reaching for my hand, pulling a rubber stamp out from his chest pocket. He pressed it against mine, then gestured for Eli's so he could do the same. "Stay away from the bar," he said. "And you've got five minutes."

"Awesome," Eli said, and with that, he was tugging me inside.

"Wait," I said as we headed down a dark, narrow hallway that led to a room full of flashing lights, "how did you *do* that?"

"I told you," he said over his shoulder. He had to yell over the music, which was just getting louder. "Everyone understands a quest."

I wasn't sure how to reply to this. Not that I could have

anyway, as we emerged into the club, which was so loud I couldn't hear anything, even my own voice. It was a single room, square, lined with booths on three sides, a bar on the other. The dance floor was in the middle, and it was packed with people: girls in tight shirts, holding beer bottles, guys with deep tans and faux-surfer gear shuffling their feet alongside them.

"This is crazy," I yelled to Eli, who was still holding my hand. He either didn't hear or just didn't reply, though, pulling me alongside the dance floor.

I was trying to step over feet and purses, and barely succeeding, the floor thumping beneath me with every beat. The air felt thick and sticky, and smelled like perfume and smoke, and already I'd broken a sweat, even though we'd been in there for mere seconds. It was like being in a carnival fun house, but with a copious amount of hair gel.

"Last dance!" I heard a voice yell from somewhere overhead, filtering through the pounding music. "Grab someone and hit the floor, it's already tomorrow!"

Suddenly, the song changed, in midbeat, to something slow with a more quiet, sensual beat. There was a bunch of hooting from somewhere on the floor, and the crowd there changed, with some people leaving, the remainders pairing up as new couples joined them. I was so immersed in watching this that when Eli suddenly hung a sharp left, pulling me into the crowd, I almost lost my footing and went down entirely.

"Wait," I said as we brushed past one couple in midgrope, followed by a guy and a girl totally grinding on each other. She was still holding her beer, the bottle dangling from two fingers. "I don't know if I—"

He stopped walking. I pulled up short beside him, my hand still in his, and realized we were in the center of the floor, a bunch of spinning lights over our heads. I looked up at them, then at everyone around us, before turning back to him.

"Come on," he said. Then he stepped forward, letting loose of my hand and sliding his arms down to my waist. "We've still got a good two minutes."

I smiled at him, in spite of myself, and felt my feet step forward, closer. It came so naturally to put my arms around his neck, my fingers finding each other there. And just like that, we were dancing.

"This is insane," I said, looking around me. "It's . . ."

"Worth doing once," he finished for me. "But only once."

I smiled, and then, in the middle of Tallyho, in the middle of the night, in the middle of everything, Eli kissed me. It was not at all how I'd imagined it happening, and yet totally perfect anyway.

When he pulled back moments later, the song was winding down. And yet everyone kept dancing, kept holding on, until the very end. I rested my head against Eli's chest, letting it last, knowing that what the DJ had said was true. It was already tomorrow. But I had a feeling it was going to be a really good day.

❊　❊　❊

When I woke up at noon, the house was quiet. No waves, no crying. Nothing, except . . .

"Are you kidding? Of course I'll come. I wouldn't miss it!"

I blinked, rolling over, then got out of bed and made

my way to the bathroom, where I woke up slowly while brushing my teeth. My dad's voice, louder now, kept drifting down the hallway.

"No, no, there's a couple of daily flights. . . ." There was the sound of keys clacking. "Sure. The timing couldn't be better. I'll bring the draft with me. Yes. Great! See you then."

By the time I came down for coffee ten minutes later, he was in the kitchen, pacing back and forth. Heidi was at the table, looking bleary, with Isby in her arms.

" . . . a great opportunity to get my name back out there," my dad was saying. "Lots of industry types, just the people I need to make contact with. It's perfect."

"It's tonight?" Heidi asked. "Isn't that kind of short notice?"

"Does it matter? I'll just book a flight, head up there for a night, and then come back."

I pulled a mug out of the cupboard, watching Heidi as she processed this information. It took a while, but then everything did on the mornings after Isby was up crying, as she had been most of the night before. Sleep deprivation dulled all Heidi's edges, but especially the cognitive ones.

"When?" she said finally.

"When what?"

In her arms, Isby squawked, and she winced, putting her over her shoulder. "When will you be back?"

"Sometime tomorrow. Maybe in the evening," my dad replied. He was all jacked up, still moving around. "As long as I'm there, I might as well try to take some meetings. At least set up a lunch."

Heidi swallowed, then looked down at Isby, who was

snuffling into her shoulder. "I just," she began, then stopped. "I'm not sure this is a good time for you to go away."

"What?" my dad said. "Why?"

I took a sip from my mug, making a point of keeping my back to all of this.

"Well," Heidi said after a moment, "it's just that the baby's been really fussy lately. I haven't slept in so long. . . . I just don't know if I can . . ."

My dad stopped walking. "You want me to stay."

It was not a question. Heidi said, "Robert, I'm just wondering if you could wait a couple more weeks. Until we're on more of a schedule."

"This party is tonight," he said slowly. "That's the whole point."

"I know. But I just think—"

"Fine."

I grabbed the carafe, filling my cup again, even though I'd barely taken two sips of what I had.

"Robert—"

"No. I'll just call Peter and tell him no, sorry, I can't make it. I'm sure there will be another Writers' Guild benefit in a few weeks."

I didn't want to be part of this. Not ever, but especially not today, which I'd started so happily on the floor of Tallyho, with Eli. So I made it a point not to look at Heidi or my dad as I slipped out of the kitchen and back upstairs to my room, where I pushed open my window and sat on the sill, letting the ocean drown out anything else I might have heard.

Still, I was not surprised when I came down a couple

of hours later to see a small carry-on suitcase by the door.
My dad might have made an effort to sound like he would
compromise. But again, he had gotten his way.

By the time I left for work, he was already gone, and
Heidi was in the pink room, rocking Isby in her chair. I
paused outside the door, thinking I should probably check
in with her, but then I stopped myself. It wasn't like she'd
asked me for help. And I was tired of always offering it anyway.

At Clementine's, I busied myself in the office, trying to
focus on Eli and the night ahead. Out on the floor, Maggie
had a steady stream of customers, thanks to an outdoor con-
cert that was going on at the boardwalk pavilion. Around
nine thirty, she stuck her head in the office door.

"Have you seen anything about a Barefoot special order?"

I glanced up at her, my head still swimming with numbers. "A what?"

"Barefoot flip-flops?" she said. "There's someone here
who said they set up a special order for, like, twenty pairs
with Heidi ages ago. I can't find a record of it anywhere."

I shook my head. "Did you call her?"

"I hate to bother her. The baby might be sleeping."

"Unlikely," I said. Then I handed her the phone, dialing
it first.

She glanced back out at the floor, the receiver cocked
between her ear and shoulder, as I turned back to the payroll. "Heidi? Hi, it's Maggie. Look I just . . . are you okay?"

I pulled the calculator closer, clearing the screen. Outside, I could hear some girls squealing over the clearance
rack.

"No, it's just, you sounded . . ." Maggie paused. "What? Yeah, I can tell. She's really crying, huh? Look, I'm so sorry I bothered you, but there's this special order thing. . . ."

Eli, I thought, punching in a number. Tonight. Hit the plus sign. Not my problem, subtotal, total. It took three different transactions, but finally, Maggie hung up.

"She says they're in the storeroom, in one of the jeans boxes," she reported, handing the phone back to me. "At least, I think that's what she was saying. It was hard to tell with all the crying."

"Yeah," I said, clearing the screen again. "Isby can really let it rip."

"Not her," she replied. "It was Heidi. She sounds miserable. Is she all right?"

I turned, looking at her. "Heidi was crying?"

"She acted like she wasn't. But you can tell, you know?" The door chimed again. "Crap. I gotta get back out there. Can you go look for that box for me?"

I nodded. Then I sat there for a second before pushing out my chair and heading into the storeroom, where I found the flip-flops right where Heidi said they'd be. I picked up the box, carrying it out to the floor, where Maggie shot me a grateful look as I slid it onto the counter. Then I pushed out the front door and turned toward home.

* * *

I actually would have felt better if I'd heard Isby's familiar wailing as I stepped into the foyer, but instead it was quiet. I went down the dark hallway to the kitchen, where a single light was on over the sink. The living room was dark, so dark that at first I didn't even see Heidi.

She was sitting on the couch, Isby in her arms, and she was crying. Not with gasps and shrieks, the kind I was used to, but a silent, constant weeping that gave me a chill up the back of my neck. It was such a raw, personal moment that I wanted to turn around and let her have it in peace. But I knew I couldn't.

"Heidi?" I said. She didn't respond. I moved closer, squatting down beside her. When I reached out, touching her leg, she sobbed harder, tears dripping down onto my hand. I looked at Isby, who was awake and staring up at her. "Give me the baby."

She shook her head. Still crying, her shoulders shaking.

"Heidi. Please." No response. She was scaring me, so I reached out, taking Isby from her arms. As soon as I did, she curled into herself, pulling her knees to her chest, and turned her face away from me.

I looked at her, then at Isby. I had no idea what to do. And while I knew I should probably call my dad, or even my mom, I instead walked to the kitchen and dialed the one number I thought might put me in contact with someone who could help.

"Gas/Gro, Wanda speaking."

In my mind, I could see the cashier that was always there at this time of night, with her dangling earrings and blonde hair. I cleared my throat.

"Hi, Wanda." I jiggled Isby, who was sputtering a bit. "I, um . . . this is Auden, I come in there a lot around this time of night for coffee? I'm trying to find Eli Stock? It's kind of an emergency, I mean, not really, but he's about twenty or so, dark hair, drives a black—"

"Hello?"

At the sound of Eli's voice, I felt some small part of me relax. "Hi. It's me." I paused, then clarified, "Auden."

"I had a feeling," he replied. "I am not sure who else would actually call me at the Gas/Gro."

"Yeah," I said, glancing at Heidi, who was harder than ever to see now in the dark of the living room, curled into the couch. "Sorry about that. I just kind of have a situation here, and I'm not sure what to do."

"A situation," he repeated. "What's going on?"

I stepped into the foyer, putting Isby over my shoulder, and told him. As I did, faintly, distantly, I could hear Heidi, still sobbing.

"Sit tight," he said when I was done. "I know just what to do."

❊　❊　❊

Twenty minutes later, there was a knock at the door. When I walked over and opened it, there was Eli, carrying four cups of GroRoast and a pack of cupcakes. "Coffee?" I said. "This is your solution?"

"No," he replied. "This is."

And he stepped aside, revealing a small, middle-aged woman with short dark hair. She had familiar olive skin and green eyes, and was wearing a sensible cardigan and slacks, a purse strapped across her, and spotless white tennis shoes.

"Mom, this is Auden. Auden, my mom. Karen Stock."

"Hi," I said. "Thank you for coming. I just . . . I don't know what to do."

She smiled at me, then leaned closer, looking down at Isby, who was now starting to fuss. "How old's the baby?"

"Six weeks."

"And where's Mom?"

"In the living room," I said, stepping back from the door. "She's just crying, she won't even talk to me."

Mrs. Stock came inside. Then she looked at Eli and said, "Take the baby upstairs and swaddle her. I'll be up shortly."

He nodded, and then looked at me. "Should I . . . " I asked. "I mean—"

"She'll be just fine," she said. "Just trust me."

And the weird thing was, I did. Even as I stood there, watching this stranger walk past me into the living room. She put her purse down on the kitchen table, then moved over to Heidi, sitting down beside her. When she began to speak, I couldn't make out a word she was saying. But Heidi was listening. It was clear in the way that, after a moment, she let Mrs. Stock pull her into her arms, patting her on the back as she allowed herself to be the one soothed, finally.

❊ ❊ ❊

By the time we got to the pink room, Isby was all-out fussing, working up to one of her fits. Eli stepped inside, flicking on the light, then said, "Got a blanket?"

"A blanket?" He nodded. "In the dresser. Third drawer, maybe?"

I watched, jiggling Isby a bit as he walked over, rummaging around for a minute before pulling out a pink one with brown dots. He glanced at it, then shut the drawer. "We need a bed," he said. "Something flat. Where's your room?"

"Next door," I said. "But I don't—"

He was already walking next door, leaving me no choice but to follow. Once there, he spread the blanket out on the bed sideways, then folded down the top corner. "Okay," he said, holding out his hands. "Give her here."

I shot him a doubtful look. "What are you doing?"

"Didn't you hear my mom?" he asked. "You're supposed to trust me."

"She said to trust *her*," I pointed out.

"You don't trust me?"

I looked at him, then at the blanket, then at Isby, who was all-out squawking, and had a flash of him leading me to the center of the floor at Tallyho, not even a full day ago. I handed her over.

Isby was wailing, her face getting redder and redder as he carefully laid her down, her head just on the edge of the folded blanket. Then, as she writhed around, he put her left arm to her side and pulled the bottom tip of the blanket up and across her, then tucked the bottom corner over her shoulder. With each step, Isby wailed louder.

"Eli," I said, raising my voice to be heard. "You're making it worse."

He didn't hear me, moving to the last corner, which he pulled tight across her waist and around her. Isby was all-out screaming now.

"Eli," I said again, practically yelling, as he pulled the

last corner tight and started to tuck it into one of the other folds, "stop it. She's not—"

And then, suddenly, it was silent. It happened so abruptly and completely that for a moment I was sure Isby had died. But when I looked at her, and she was just lying there, all wrapped up like a tiny burrito, blinking at us.

"—crying," I finished. Eli reached down, picking her up, and handed her back to me. "How did you do that?"

"It's not me," he said as I eased myself carefully onto the bed. Isby opened her mouth, but only yawned, then settled against me. "It's the swaddle. It's like magic. My mom swears by it."

"It's amazing," I said. "How does she know all this?"

"She was a maternity ward nurse," he replied. "Just retired last year. Plus my brother and sister have four kids between them. Add in all of us, and she's had a lot of practice."

There was a light tap on the door, and then Mrs. Stock stuck her head in. "Heidi's going to take a little rest," she said. "Let's go downstairs."

Eli and I followed her down the hall, past Heidi's room, where I could see a small sliver of light under the closed door. Just as I started down the steps, it went out.

In the kitchen, Mrs. Stock went to the sink, where she washed her hands, then dried them on a paper towel. "All right," she said, turning to me with a smile. "Give me that baby."

I did, and she took her, easing down into a chair, and I watched as she brushed her fingers over Isby's forehead. "This is a good swaddle," she said.

"Eli's a pro," I told her.

"Just well trained," he said, and we both watched as she rocked Isby slowly, patting her back with her hand.

"Thank you for coming," I said finally. "Heidi's been having kind of a hard time. But when I got home and found her like that . . . I didn't know what to do."

"She's a new mom," Mrs. Stock said, still looking down at Isby. "She's exhausted."

"My dad tried to convince her to get help. But she wouldn't do it."

Mrs. Stock adjusted the blanket a bit. "When I had Steven, my oldest, my mother came and lived with me for a month. I couldn't have done it without her."

"Heidi's mom died a couple of years ago."

"She mentioned that," she said, and I thought of Heidi's face, crumpled, as she curled into Mrs. Stock, there in the dark. I wondered what else she'd said. "The truth is, being a mom is the hardest job in the world. But she'll be fine. She just needs some rest."

We all considered this as Isby, way ahead of us all, closed her eyes. Mrs. Stock looked at Eli. "You," she said, "would be well advised to go to bed as well. Don't you work in the morning?"

"Yeah," he said. "But—"

"Then get on home," she replied. "Leave me your keys. You can pick up the truck tomorrow."

"So I'm walking?" he asked.

She gave him a flat look. "Eli Joseph. It's four blocks. You'll survive."

Eli grumbled, but he was smiling as he dropped his keys

onto the table. "Thanks, Mom," he said. She offered him her cheek, and he kissed it, then turned toward the door. I followed him out onto the porch.

"So," I said, glancing back into the kitchen, where Mrs. Stock was still rocking Isby, "guess it's an early night."

"Guess so," he said. "Mom doesn't exactly know about my nocturnal habits."

"She wouldn't approve?"

He shook his head. "Nope. In her mind, no good can come after midnight."

I looked up at him, then smiled. "Well, I have to say, your mom's amazing. But I don't agree with that."

"She is amazing," he said. "And I don't either." Then he leaned down, kissing me, and I slid my arms around his neck, pulling him a little closer. I could have stood there all night, good or no good, but then he was pulling back, glancing over my head at the kitchen. "I better go."

I nodded. "See you tomorrow."

He smiled, then stepped off the porch and started down the front walk. I waved one last time, then watched him until he disappeared into the dark just past the streetlight's glow. Up in my room, I leaned out my window and looked down the road in the direction he'd gone. It was a long, flat road, and as it got later there were only a few lights visible, here and there. I picked one that I figured was about four blocks down. Then I watched it like a star, burning bright, all the way until morning.

eleven

IT WAS A week later, and my brother was scheduled to ar-
rive around five P.M. At four thirty, my phone rang.

"I'm only calling," my mother said, "to warn you."

She and I had not spoken since her own visit to Colby
had ended so disastrously, a fact that seemed to now be
behind us, if this contact was any indication. Still, I was
cautious as I said, "Warn me about what?"

There was a pause as she took a sip of what I assumed
was her early glass of wine. Then she said, "The Laura."

The qualifier pretty much said it all, but I bit anyway.
"What? You don't like her?"

"Auden," she said. I could almost hear her shudder.
"She's horrible. *Horrible.* I don't know what your brother
got into over there, but clearly, it's given him brain damage.
This girl, she's . . . she's . . . "

Rarely had my mother ever been at a loss for words. I
was actually starting to get a little worried.

" . . . a *scientist*," she finished. "One of those cold, metho-
dical types, all about hypotheses and control groups. And
her ego in assuming that everyone else is interested in it as

well? Unparalleled. Last night she bored us for an entire dinner talking about myelinated cells."

"About what?"

"Exactly," she said. "There's no heart to this girl, no soul. She's only a few years older than your brother but acts like a Puritan schoolmarm. I have no doubt she'll take everything unique about Hollis and suck it out of him. It's horrifying."

I looked out my open door, down the hall, where I could see Heidi sweeping out my father's office, which had been converted into a second guest room. Thisbe was parked in her bouncy seat, watching her.

Since that bad night, things had been a little better. In the end, Mrs. Stock had stayed over, tending to Isby, and when I came down late the following morning, she had just left. I found Heidi in the kitchen, with the swaddled baby in her arms, looking more rested than she had in weeks.

"That woman," she said in lieu of a hello, "is a miracle worker."

"Yeah?"

She nodded. "She was here for three hours this morning, and I already know about a hundred percent more than I did yesterday. Did you realize that swaddling helps a baby feel secure and fuss less?"

"I did not," I said. "But it appears to be true."

"And she helped me raise the baby's mattress, which will reduce her gas, and said I should buy a swing to help her sleep. Plus, she knew exactly what to do about my nipples being so sore!"

I winced. "Heidi. Please."

"Sorry, sorry." She waved her free hand at me. "But really.

I'm so grateful to you for bringing her here. I mean, she's even offered to come by again, if I need help, but I don't know. Last night was just so strange. I don't know what happened. I was just so tired. . . ."

"It's fine," I said, as always wanting to avoid a big emotional moment. "I'm just glad you feel better."

"I do," she said, looking down at Isby again. "I really do."

Since then, she had seemed to be in better spirits, and Isby was sleeping a bit more, which was good for everyone. Still, Mrs. Stock had dropped by a couple more times, although I always seemed to miss her. When she'd visited, though, I could always tell. Heidi just seemed happier.

Unlike my mother, who was still going on about Laura and how she was sucking out my brother's joie de vivre, one myelinated cell at a time. "I don't know," I said to her now. "He seems to really like her."

"Your brother likes everyone! That's always been his fatal flaw." Another dark sigh. "You'll see when you meet her, Auden. She's just . . ."

I glanced back out my window, just in time to see a silver Honda pulling into the driveway. "Here," I finished for her. "I better go."

"God help you," she muttered. "Call me later."

I told her I would, then closed my phone and walked out into the hallway just as my dad was yelling up to Heidi that Hollis had arrived.

"Ready to go meet your brother?" she said to Thisbe, bending down to unbuckle her from her seat. Together, we walked to the top of the stairs just as my dad opened the front door.

I could see Hollis getting out of the car, and even though it had been more than two years that he'd been gone, he looked pretty much the same. A little skinnier, his hair somewhat shaggier. When Laura stepped out of the passenger side, she, too, looked awfully familiar, although at first I couldn't figure out why. Then Heidi gasped.

"Oh, my God," she said. "Laura looks just like your mother!"

She was right. Same long dark hair, same dark clothes, same pale, pale skin. Laura was a little shorter and curvier, but still, the resemblance was striking. The closer they got, the more it freaked me out.

"There he is!" my dad said, pulling Hollis in for a hug as he stepped over the threshold. "The world traveler returns!"

"Look at you, proud papa! Where's that baby girl?" Hollis said, grinning.

"Right here," Heidi said, starting down the stairs. I made myself follow her, even as Laura came in the door, taking off her sunglasses and folding them. Her eyes were dark, too. "This is Thisbe."

Hollis immediately reached for the baby, lifting her up high over his head. She looked down at him, as if trying to make up her mind whether to start crying or not. "Oh, boy," he said. "You're gonna be trouble. I can just tell!"

My dad and Heidi laughed, but I kept my eyes on Laura, who was standing just off to the side, still holding her sunglasses, watching this scene with a somewhat clinical expression. After a moment of Hollis making googly faces at the baby, she very quietly—but pointedly—cleared her throat.

"Oh, babe, sorry!" Hollis handed Thisbe off to my dad, then reached an arm over Laura's shoulders, pulling her in closer to everyone else. "Everyone, this is my fiancée, Laura."

"Fiancée?" my dad said. "You didn't mention that in your phone call. When did you . . ."

Laura smiled, showing no teeth. "We didn't," she said. "Hollis is just . . . "

"Confident," my brother finished for her. "And ready. Even if she isn't."

"I keep telling Hollis that marriage is serious," Laura said. Her voice was very even and clear, like she was used to having the room's attention. "You can't just jump into it like an airplane."

Dad and Heidi and I just stood there, not sure what to make of this, but Hollis just laughed. "That's my girl! She'll break my impulsive streak yet."

"Oh, don't do that," my dad said to Laura, clapping Hollis on the shoulder again. "We *love* that about this guy."

"Impulsiveness can be charming," she agreed. "But deliberation can have an appeal, as well."

My dad raised his eyebrows. "Actually," he said, his tone a bit sharper than before, "I—"

"You must be exhausted from your trip!" Heidi said, reaching to take Thisbe from my father. "Let's go and have a cold drink. We've got lemonade, beer, wine. . . ."

She turned, starting for the kitchen, and Hollis and my dad immediately fell in behind her, leaving me with Laura. I watched as she examined her sunglasses, then took a corner of her black shirt, slowly rubbing a spot on one lens clean before again folding them shut. Then she looked up at me, as if surprised to find me still standing there.

"It's really nice to meet you," I said, for lack of anything better. "Hollis seems . . . he's very happy."

She nodded. "He's a very happy person," she said, although from her tone, I couldn't tell if she thought this was an asset or not.

"Babe!" my brother yelled. "Get in here! You gotta see this view!"

Laura gave me another tight smile, then walked into the living room. I waited a beat or two, then followed her, stopping in the kitchen, where my dad and Heidi were huddled together by the sink, pouring lemonade into glasses.

" . . . her first time meeting us," Heidi was saying. "She's probably just nervous."

"Nervous? You call that nervous?" my dad replied.

Heidi said something else, but I didn't hear her, having turned my attention to my brother and Laura. They were standing in front of the open glass doors, the ocean a wide, clear blue in front of them. Hollis had his arm around her shoulders, gesturing with one hand as he said something about the horizon, but even from the back I could tell Laura was not particularly impressed. It was something about the posture, the way her head was slightly tilted to the side. Sure, she was a stranger. But I'd seen it before.

❋   ❋   ❋

"So you don't like her."

I looked over at Eli. "I didn't say that."

"You didn't have to."

He pulled a container of milk off the shelf, sticking it in the cart. It was one thirty A.M., and we were at Park Mart, doing a little shopping. As it was a Monday night, we had the place pretty much to ourselves, and the quiet was just what I'd needed, having earlier endured a two-hour family dinner that had basically devolved into an argument between my dad and Laura about capital punishment. This followed their spirited discussion about university funding (liberal arts versus sciences) over cocktails, which had come after a protracted debate about environmental policy during lunch. For me, it was like watching an adaptation of the last couple of years of my parents' marriage, just with someone else playing the role of My Mom.

"It's just," I said to Eli, pushing the cart forward to follow him out of the grocery section and into sporting goods, "she's really different from all the other girls Hollis has dated."

"And what were they like?"

A blur of gorgeous, friendly faces appeared in my mind. "Nice," I finally said. "Sweet. More like Hollis."

Eli stopped to check out a camping stove, then moved on. "He didn't want to marry any of the others, though. Right?"

I considered this as we passed a collection of catcher's mitts. "Not for more than a few minutes."

"But this girl, he says is the one." We were coming up on

the bike section now, several lined up in a row, from kids' sizes to adult. He pulled a midsize bike off the rack, bouncing it on its front tire. "So it seems to me, it doesn't matter what you or your mom or dad think. Relationships don't always make sense. Especially from the outside."

"But this is Hollis," I pointed out. "He's never been serious about anything."

He climbed onto the bike, then rose up on the pedals, moving slowly forward. "Well," he said, "maybe he just found the right person. People change."

He was riding around me and the cart, and as I watched him I thought of my mother, saying these same two words with a *don't* between them, with equal conviction. "You know," I said finally, "everyone thinks you never ride anymore."

"I don't."

I rolled my eyes, since he was passing me again as he said this. "Then how come I'm watching you do it right now?"

"I don't know," he said. "What do you think?"

The truth was, I wasn't sure. But I wanted to keep believing people could change, and it was certainly easier to do so when you were in the midst of it. The way I imagined I was as I stood there, aware of a slight breeze each time he passed, like a wave, the feeling of motion.

❋　❋　❋

I'd been at Clementine's for over an hour, catching up on paperwork, when I got the distinct feeling someone was watching me. And that someone was Maggie.

"Hi," she said when I looked up to find her standing in the half-open doorway. She had on a white eyelet sundress and orange flip-flops, her hair pulled back at her neck, and was holding a pricing gun. "Got a minute?"

I nodded, and she glanced back out at the store before taking a step inside, then clearing a stack of catalogs off a nearby chair and sitting down.

She didn't say anything, and neither did I. All I could hear was a pop song, playing from the sales floor. Something about roller coasters and sweet tangy kisses.

"So, look," she began. "About you and Eli."

This wasn't a question. Or even a statement. It was a fragment, and this was my justification for not responding. How can there even be a whole answer to a part of something?

"I know you guys have been hanging out all night, like, every night," she continued. "And it's not exactly my business, but . . ."

"How?" I said.

She blinked at me. "How is it not my business?"

"How do you know?"

"I just do."

"What, you're all-knowing and all-seeing now?" I asked. "Who are you, Big Brother?"

"This is a small town, Auden. In many ways, minuscule. Word gets around." She sighed, looking down at the gun. "Look, the thing is, I've known Eli a long time. I don't want to see him get hurt."

I'd honestly had no idea what she was getting at. None.

But when I heard this, I felt like a fool for not having seen it coming. "You think I'm going to hurt Eli?"

She shrugged. "I don't know. After what happened with Jake . . ."

"That was totally different," I said.

"See, but I don't know that." She sat back, folding her legs. "All I have to go on is what I've seen. And while the thing with Jake pissed me off because I was jealous, it was also somewhat karmic. He had it coming. Eli doesn't."

"We're just . . ." I trailed off, not sure how much I wanted to explain this. "We're friends."

"Maybe so." She looked down at the gun again, turning it in her lap. "But we both know you're the reason he showed up at the party the other night. I heard you call him."

I raised my eyebrows. "You *are* like Big Brother."

"I was in the bathroom. The walls are so thin there! I sometimes can't even pee if anyone's in the kitchen." She waved her hand. "Anyway, then there's the bike thing, and the fact that you threw beans at him and he didn't *completely* go ballistic—"

"It was just a food fight."

"You don't understand, though," she said. "Eli hasn't done anything since Abe died. No parties, no hanging out, hardly even any conversation. Definitely no food fights. He's been under this cloud. And then suddenly you show up, and all that changes. Which is great."

"But," I said, because there is always a *but*.

"But," she continued, "if you *are* just jerking his chain and playing around, he might not just bounce back like

Jake did. There's more at stake here, and I just wasn't sure you knew that. So I wanted to tell you. Because that's what friends do."

I considered this as the music outside changed to something slower, more dreamy-sounding. "Well," I said, "I guess he's lucky he has you. As a friend, I mean."

"I wasn't talking about Eli."

I looked up at her. "What?"

"*We're* friends," she said, moving her hand back and forth between us. "And friends are honest with each other. Even if the truth hurts. Right?"

I would have agreed with this, but my own truth was that I really didn't know. All of this was new to me. So instead, I said, "You don't have to worry. Nobody's getting hurt. We're just . . . we're hanging out. Nothing more."

She nodded slowly. "Okay, then. That's all I need to know."

There was a beep from the sales floor, signaling a customer entering. Maggie got to her feet, then stuck her head out the door. "Hi," she called out. "I'll be right with you!"

"No worries," a voice I recognized replied. "Just tell Auden to get her butt out here!"

Maggie turned to look at me. "My brother," I explained, pushing my chair back.

"You have a brother?"

"Come and see for yourself."

When we got out to the floor, Hollis was standing by a box of half-off swimsuits, examining a purple thong bikini.

"Not your size," I said as I approached. "Or color, either."

"Too bad," he replied. "I think it would look boss on me, don't you?"

"I think you should stick to trunks," I told him.

"Actually," Maggie piped up, "in Europe, men often wear a more bikini style. Every summer we have at least one group of German tourists who show up in them."

"No way," Hollis told her. "Over there, you just go to the nude beach. No suit needed, period!"

"This is Maggie," I said to him. "Maggie, my brother, Hollis."

"You went to a nude beach?" she asked him. "Seriously?"

"Sure, why not? You know what they say. When in Rome. Or Spain . . ." He tossed the thong back into the box. "So, Aud, you up for a little very late lunch or super early dinner? Dad says there's a place with great onion rings I should try."

"The Last Chance," Maggie told him. "End of the boardwalk, on the left. I recommend the tuna melt."

Hollis sighed. "I love a tuna melt. That, you can't get in Spain. Even if you are naked."

I glanced back at the office. "I actually have a lot of work to do. . . ."

"Oh, come on! You haven't seen me in two years." Hollis shook his head at Maggie. "My sister. She got all the drive in this family, obviously."

"Go," Maggie said to me. "You can just stay later tonight, or something."

"Listen to Maggie," Hollis said. He said her name casually, like they'd known each other for years. "Come on. Let's go bond."

along *for the* ride

Out on the boardwalk, it was that golden time of the afternoon, past the heat of the day but before it began to cool off for evening. Hollis and I fell in behind a group of women with strollers, their wheels clacking across the boards beneath us.

"So, where's Laura?" I asked him. "She doesn't like onion rings?"

"Loves them," he replied, sliding on his sunglasses. "But she has work to do. She's applying for some grant for the spring and has some essays to write for it."

"Wow," I said. "She sounds like the driven one."

"No kidding. She's unstoppable."

He tipped his head back, looking up as a row of pelicans flew overhead, toward the water, and I watched with him for a moment. Then I said, "She seems really nice, Hollis."

"She is." He smiled at me. "She's not like any of the other girls I've dated, huh?"

I wasn't sure how to answer this. But he was asking, so I said, "Not really, no."

"You should have heard Mom," he said, laughing. "For years she's on me for only dating vapid, mindless drones—her words, of course—"

"Of course."

"—and now I show up with someone smart and amazing, and she totally freaks out. You should have seen her at dinner when Laura was talking about her work. So jealous she was almost sputtering."

Wow, I thought. Out loud I said, "Jealous? You think?"

"Oh, come on, Aud. You know Mom's used to being the smartest woman in the room. It's her thing." He reached up, adjusting his sunglasses. "She kept pulling me aside, telling me I was making a mistake, that I was too serious about Laura too quickly. Like I'm going to take relationship advice from her, with that grad student lurking outside, sleeping in his car like some kind of stalker."

"What?" I said.

He glanced at me. "Oh, you know. She was sleeping with some grad student, he got serious about her and actually wanted something from her, so she cut him loose, and now he's hanging around, licking his wounds."

I had a flash of the guy in the dark-framed glasses, sitting out by the pool with his book. I didn't even know his name.

"I felt so bad for the guy," Hollis was saying now. "Although God knows he should have seen it coming. It's not like she hasn't done it before."

It took me a minute to absorb all this, so I focused on the bike shop, which was coming up ahead. I could see Wallace and Adam on the bench outside, sharing a bag of potato chips. "You think she does that a lot?"

"Oh, God, yes. Since the divorce, anyway." He slid his hands in his pockets, then glanced at me. "I mean, you knew that, right? You had to."

"Sure," I said quickly. "Absolutely."

He watched my face for a moment. Then he said, "Not that I can say anything, though. Considering I used to be just like her."

Again, I was speechless. What do you do when you finally hear everything you've always thought said aloud? This time, though, I was saved from having to reply, as Adam spotted us. "Hey, Auden! Come settle an argument!"

Hollis glanced over at him and Wallace. "Friends of yours?"

"Yeah," I said as Adam waved us over. Hollis looked surprised, which I tried not to take personally. "Come on."

When we got over to them, I introduced my brother as Adam hopped off the bench, landing in front of us. "Okay," he said, holding up his hands. "We're finally on the brink of a new name for the shop."

"Which is to say," Wallace piped in from behind him, his mouth full of chips, "that we've narrowed the list of possibilities to ten."

"Ten?" I said.

"But only five are any good," Adam added. "So we're taking an informal poll to see who likes which ones."

Hollis, always game, looked up at the bare awning. "What's it called now?"

"The Bike Shop," Wallace told him. Hollis raised his eyebrows. "It's temporary."

"For the last three years," Adam said. "So, okay. The list in no particular order, is as follows: Overdrive Bikes, the Chain Gang, Colby Cycles . . . "

I was distracted temporarily as Eli came out of the shop, pushing a small pink bike with training wheels. He had a helmet in his free hand, and a couple with a little girl in tow were right behind him.

" . . . the Crankshaft and Pedal to the Metal Bikes," Adam finished. "What do you think?"

Hollis thought for a second. "The Chain Gang or the Crankshaft," he said. "Overdrive is boring, Colby Cycles too corporate. . . ."

"That's what I said!" Wallace said, pointing at him.

"And Pedal to the Metal . . . I don't even know what to say about that."

Adam sighed. "Everyone hates it. The only reason it's still on the list is that it's my favorite. Auden, what do you think?"

I was still watching Eli, though, as he bent over the pink bike, adjusting one of the pedals. The little girl for whom it was clearly intended, a redhead wearing blue shorts and a T-shirt with a giraffe on it, stood holding her mom's hand, looking apprehensive.

"Like I said," he was saying, "this is a really good starter bike."

"She wants to learn," her mom was saying, running a hand over her daughter's head. "But she's kind of nervous."

"Nothing to be nervous about." Eli stood up, then looked at the girl. "The training wheels will keep you up until you get the hang of it. And then one day, you just won't need them anymore."

"How long does it usually take, though?" the father, who had on a baseball cap and leather sandals, asked. "What's the norm?"

"Different for everyone," Eli told him. "When she's ready, she'll know."

"What do you say, honey?" the woman asked. "Want to try it out?"

The girl nodded slowly, then stepped forward. I watched as Eli held out his hand, helping her onto the bike, then strapped the helmet on her head. She reached for the handlebars, carefully stretching her fingers over them.

"All right, sweetie," her dad said. "Just pedal, like you do on your trike."

The girl put her feet down, tentatively pushing on the pedals, and moved about a half an inch forward. She glanced back at her parents, who smiled at her, then tried again. After another incremental budge, I watched as Eli put his hand on the back of the bike, nudging it forward just slightly. She was still pedaling and didn't even notice. But when she really began to move, she looked back at him, grinning.

"Auden?"

I turned my head to see Adam looking at me, his face expectant. "Um," I said, "I don't really like any of them that much. To be honest."

His face fell. "Not even the Crankshaft?"

I shook my head. "Not really."

"I told you they all sucked," Wallace said.

"He liked two of them!" Adam shot back.

"Not that much," Hollis said.

Adam sighed, flopping back down on the bench, and I waved good-bye as Hollis and I started walking again toward the Last Chance. After a few steps, though, I looked back at that little girl again. After that initial push, she'd gotten going for real, and now had passed two storefronts and was almost at Clementine's. Her mom was trailing behind her, close but not too close, as she slowly made her way, all on her own.

The Last Chance was empty for once, and we got a booth right by the window without having to wait. As Hollis perused the menu, I looked out on to the boardwalk, watching the people walk by.

"So, Aud," he said after a moment. "I gotta say, I'm really happy you did this."

I looked over at him. "Did what?"

"This," he said, gesturing around the restaurant. "Coming here for the summer, hanging out, making friends. I was worried you'd spend this summer like all the others."

"Like all the others," I repeated.

"You know." He picked up his water, taking a sip. "Hanging out at the house with Mom, refilling wineglasses at her little superior get-togethers, studying for classes that haven't even started yet."

I felt myself stiffen. "I never refilled wineglasses."

"You get the idea." He smiled at me, clearly unaware that he might have offended me. Or at least hurt my feelings. "My point is, you're different here."

"Hollis, I've only been here for a month."

"A lot can happen in a month," he replied. "Shoot, in two weeks I met my future wife, changed my entire life's trajectory, and bought my first tie."

"You bought a tie?" I asked. Because honestly, this was almost the most shocking part.

"Yup." He laughed. "Seriously, though. Seeing you here, with your friends . . . it just really makes me happy."

"Hollis," I said. Now I was uncomfortable again, but for different reasons. My family was a lot of things—and changing daily, or so it seemed—but sentimental was not one of them. "Come on."

"I'm serious!" He looked down at his menu again, then up at me. "Look, Aud. I know the divorce was hard for you.

And living with Mom afterward had to be even harder. She's not exactly kid-friendly."

"I wasn't a kid," I told him. "I was sixteen."

"You're always a kid around your parents," he replied. "Unless they're acting like children. Then you don't get the chance. You know what I'm saying?"

I realized, suddenly, that I did. Just about the same time that it hit me why my brother had stayed gone for so long, careful to keep an ocean and a telephone line between us and him. It was the reverse of most families: to be a kid, you had to leave home. It was returning that made you grow up, once and for all.

Just as I thought this, Adam and Wallace whizzed by on a pair of bikes, zigzagging through the pedestrians. Hollis said, "Speaking of which, it's not too late."

"Too late for what?"

"To learn to ride a bike." He nodded back at the shop. "I bet your friends could teach you."

"I can ride a bike," I said.

"Yeah? When did you learn?"

I just looked at him. "When I was six," I said. "In the driveway."

He thought for a moment. "You sure about that?"

"Of course I am."

"Because all I remember," he said, "is you getting a bike, falling off it right away, and then it sitting in the garage and slowly rusting until Dad gave it away."

"That," I said, "is not what happened. I rode all over the driveway."

"Did you?" He squinted, thinking hard. "Well, you're probably right. God knows I've killed a few brain cells in the last few years."

This was the truth: between the two of us, there was no question whose memory was more reliable. And wouldn't I know my own history better than anyone else? Still, even as we ordered, I couldn't stop thinking about what he'd said. He was going on about Laura, and Europe, but I was only half listening as I thought back, back, to that day in the driveway. It was all so clear: climbing on, pushing down on the pedals, rolling forward, it had to be true. Didn't it?

twelve

"SO THE WORD on the street," my mother said in her formal, cool way, "is that you've changed."

I took my toothbrush out of my mouth, already wary. "Changed?"

These days, she always called around five, when I was waking up and she was ending her workday. I wanted to believe it was because she missed me, or had realized how important our connection really was to her. But I knew that really, she just needed someone to vent to about Hollis, who was back under her roof, still madly in love with Laura, and completely on her nerves.

"For the better, if that's what you're asking," she said now, although her tone suggested she was not entirely convinced. "I believe the exact word your brother used was *blossomed*."

I looked at myself in the mirror: my hair was uncombed, I had toothpaste on my lips and was still wearing the scoop-necked tee I'd had on last night at the bowling alley, which reeked of smoke. Not exactly flowery. "Well," I said, "that's nice, I guess."

"He was particularly impressed," she said, "with your

newfound social life. Apparently you've got scads of friends and a serious boyfriend as well?"

The fact that this last part was phrased as a question pretty much said everything about how she felt about it personally. "I don't have a boyfriend," I told her.

"Just a boy you spend your nights with." A statement, this time.

I looked at myself in the mirror again. "Yep," I told her. "That's about right."

Among all the other sudden changes in my brother, he was now an early riser—Hollis, who'd always slept past noon—as well as a jogger. He and Laura ran every day at sunrise, then came home to do yoga stretches and meditate. Although apparently, he wasn't that immersed in his *oms* and *namastes*. When he heard me come in the morning after their arrival, he immediately came to investigate.

"Auden Penelope West," he said, wagging a finger at me as I carefully shut the door behind me. "Look at you, doing the walk of shame!"

"I'm not ashamed," I replied, although I did kind of wish he'd keep it down.

"And who is this young man dropping you off?" he asked, pulling aside a blind to peer out at Eli, who was backing his truck out of the driveway. "Shouldn't he have to show himself, get my approval before taking you out courting?"

I just looked at him. From the living room, I could hear Laura chanting.

"My little sister," he said, shaking his head. "Staying out all night with a boy. Seems like just yesterday you were playing Barbies and skipping rope."

"Hollis, please," I said. "Mom considered Barbies weapons of chauvinism, and nobody's skipped rope since 1950."

"I just can't believe," he said, ignoring this, "you're growing up so fast. Next you'll be married and bouncing a baby on your knee."

I ignored this, walking past him to the stairs, but it didn't stop him, not then, and not the mornings that followed, when he always managed to be waiting for me, opening the door as I came up the front walk. One day he was actually sitting on the porch when we pulled up, necessitating both an introduction and a conversation with Eli.

"Nice guy," he'd said, when I'd finally wrangled him away. "What's with the scars on his arm, though?"

"Car accident," I told him.

"Really? What happened?"

"I don't really know, actually."

He shot me a doubtful look as he pulled the front door open for me. "Seems kind of weird, considering how much time you two spend together."

I shrugged. "Not really. It just hasn't come up."

I could tell he didn't believe me, not that I cared. I'd long ago stopped trying to explain my relationship with Eli to anyone, including myself. It wasn't any one thing, but many strung together: long nights, trips to Park Mart and Builder's Supply, pie with Clyde, bowling in the early morning, and my quest. We didn't talk about our scars, the ones you could see, and the ones you couldn't. Instead, I was having all the fun and frivolousness I was due in one summer, night by night.

Now, my mother took another sip of her wine as I left

the bathroom, heading back down the hall. Thisbe's door was slightly ajar, and I could hear her waves, steady and crashing, over and over again.

"Well," she said, "frankly, I'm glad to hear you're not getting involved with someone. The last thing you need before you head off to Defriese is some boy begging you to stay with him. A smart woman knows a fling is always best."

There had been a time when I liked my mother to think we were similar. Even craved it. But hearing this, I felt a weird twinge, something not settling right. What I was doing with Eli wasn't like her and her graduate student(s).

"So," I said, shaking this off, "how's Hollis doing?"

She sighed, loud and long. "He's insane. Completely insane. I came home yesterday and do you know what he was doing?"

"I don't."

"Wearing a tie." She gave this a minute to sink in, then added, "She had him interviewing for a *job* at a *bank*. Your brother! Who this time last year was living in a tent on the side of a mountain in Germany!"

It was just too easy to get my mom off my back these days. One mention of Hollis, and she was off and running. "A bank," I said. "What's he going to be, a teller or something?"

"Oh, I don't know," she said irritably. "I didn't even ask, I was so horrified. He did volunteer, however, that Laura thinks employment might help him to be 'more responsible' and 'prepared for their future together.' Like that's a *good* thing. I don't even think this is a relationship, it's so dysfunctional. I don't know what to call it."

"Call it chicken salad."

"What?"

Too late, I realized this had slipped out, without me even realizing it. "Nothing," I told her.

I heard footsteps, and looked down the hall just in time to see Heidi and my dad coming upstairs. From the looks of it they, too, were having a pretty intense conversation: my dad was throwing his arms around, his annoyed face on, while she just shook her head. I eased my door shut, switching my phone to my other ear.

" . . . ridiculous," my mom was saying now. "Two years of culture and travel, and for what? To sit and process deposits all day long? It's heartbreaking."

She really sounded sad. Still, I couldn't help but say, "Mom, most people Hollis's age have jobs, you know. Especially if they aren't in school."

"I didn't raise either of you to be like most people," she replied. "Don't you know that by now?"

I had a flash of myself the night before, standing at the Park Mart with Eli, in the toy section. He'd stopped by a big display of rubber sport balls, pulling one out and bouncing it on the floor. "Oh, yeah," he said. "Hear that?"

"The bouncing noise?"

"It's more," he told me, "than a bouncing noise. That is the noise of imminent pain."

I looked at the ball, still moving up and down under his open palm. "Pain?"

"In dodgeball," he explained. "Or kickball, if you were playing the way we did."

"Wait!" I said, holding up my hand. "I have played dodgeball. And kickball."

"Really."

I nodded.

"I'm impressed. And they aren't even indoor sports."

"Oh, it was, actually. At school, in the gym." He raised his eyebrows. "What? It's the same game."

"Actually it's not," he said.

"Come on."

"Seriously. There's school rules, and neighborhood rules. The two are *very* different."

"Says who?"

"Anybody who has played both," he said, tossing the ball back. "Trust me."

Now, my mother took another sip of her wine. "Oh, I almost forgot," she said. "A packet has arrived for you. From Defriese. Orientation information, I'm assuming. Would you like for me to open it?"

"Sure," I said. "Thanks."

There was the sound of paper tearing, then crinkling. She sighed. "As I suspected. Meal plan info, updated transcript requests, a roommate questionnaire . . . which is due at the end of the week, apparently."

"Really."

"For God's sake." She groaned. "It's like a compatibility test! 'What activities do you enjoy?' 'Would you say you are a workaholic, or more carefree with your studies?' What is this, higher education or Internet dating?"

"Just stick it in the mail to me," I said. "I'll get it back as fast as I can."

"And if you're late, you'll end up with some carefree, activity-loving roommate. We're better off filling it out now," she muttered. "Oh, wait a moment. There's a second page here, where you can request 'alternate living arrangements.'"

"Meaning what?"

She didn't say anything for a moment, busy reading. Then, "There are certain floors and dorms you can request where everyone has a specific focus, such as foreign languages or sports. Let me just . . . ah. Perfect."

I heard a pen scritching. "What's perfect?"

"The Pembleton Program," she replied. "I just signed you up for it."

"What?"

She cleared her throat, then read aloud. "'Housed in a dorm removed from the main campus, the Pembleton Program offers academically strong students an environment dedicated solely to their studies. With single rooms, on-site research materials, and close access to both libraries, members of Pembleton are free to focus on their work without the distractions of regular dorm life.'"

"Which means . . . "

"No roommate, no parties, no nonsense. It's just what you want."

"Um," I said. "I don't know. It sounds kind of restrictive, don't you think?"

"Not at all," she replied. "You won't have to deal with drunk frat boys and hormonal, gossiping girls. It's ideal.

Now, I'll just sign your name here, and we can—"

"Don't," I said quickly. I could feel her surprise, could see her on the other end of the phone, pen in hand, eyebrows raised. "I mean, I'm not really sure I want to live there."

Silence. Then, "Auden. I don't think you understand how distracting it can be to live in a dorm environment. There are people who come to college purely for the social life. Do you really want to be stuck in a room with someone like that?"

"No," I said. "But I don't want to spend every single second studying either."

"Oh." Her voice was flat. "I suppose this is part of your blossoming, then? Suddenly school isn't important anymore, just boys and girlfriends and clothes?"

"Of course not. But—"

A sigh, loud, filling my ear. "I should have *known* spending the summer with Heidi would do this to you," she said. "I spend eighteen years teaching you about the importance of taking yourself seriously, and in a matter of weeks you're wearing pink bikinis and totally boy crazy."

"Mom," I said, my voice rising. "This isn't about Heidi."

"No," she shot back. "It's about your sudden lack of drive and focus. How could you let yourself get this way?"

Hearing this, I had a flash of my dad, attributing all I'd done to the name he'd chosen for me. All the good was their doing; the bad, mine. I bit my lip. "I haven't changed," I told her. "This is just me."

Silence. And I knew, within it, that the fact this might be true was worse than any frat boy or pink bikini ever could be.

"Well, I'll just stick this in the mail." She drew in a

breath, stiff, formal. "You make your own decision."

I swallowed. "Okay."

For a moment, neither of us said anything, and I wondered what could possibly follow this. How we could come back from such an impasse, this huge expanse stretching between us. There were a million different ways, I was sure, but my mom surprised me by not choosing any of them. Instead, she hung up, leaving me with a simple click, the last word, and no idea where to go from here.

* * *

Apparently, conflict was contagious, or at least in the air. When I left my room about twenty minutes later to head to work, Thisbe's waves had stopped, and another steady noise was coming from her room: the sound of bickering.

"Of course you deserve a night out," my father was saying. "I'm just not sure tonight is the right one, is all I'm saying."

"Why not?" Heidi asked. I could hear Thisbe making noises in the background. "I'll be back for the nine o'clock feeding, the baby's just had a nap. . . ."

"Nine o'clock! It's only five thirty right now!"

"Robert, we're having cocktails and dinner."

"Where? Istanbul?" my dad said. "There's no way that will take three and a half hours."

There was a prolonged silence. I didn't have to peek inside to imagine the look on Heidi's face. Finally my dad said, "Honey, I want you to go have fun. But it's been a long time since I've been alone with a newborn for that long, and I just . . ."

"She's not a newborn. She's your daughter." Thisbe sputtered, as if agreeing with this. "You've raised two lovely children. You can do this. Now go ahead and take her so I can go finish getting ready."

I heard my dad start to say something, but then the door was opening, and I darted out of sight. Not fast enough, though.

"Auden?" he called out. "Could you—"

"No, she can't," Heidi said over her shoulder. Then she nudged me forward. "Keep walking. He's fine."

When we got to the stairs, I turned to look at her. Instead of the Heidi I'd gotten used to seeing, clad in sweats and a ponytail, dark circles perennially under her eyes, this was a different woman entirely. Her hair was sleek, her makeup done, and she was wearing dark jeans, heels, and a fitted black top, a silver necklace with a key studded with red stones around her neck. This I recognized: we'd just gotten them in at the store the previous week, and they were already selling like hotcakes.

"Wow," I said. "You look great."

"You think?" She glanced down at herself. "It's been so long since I could wear this stuff I didn't even know if it would fit. I guess stress does burn a lot of calories, after all."

Down the hall, I could hear Thisbe beginning to fuss. Heidi looked over, then turned on her heel, walking to her bedroom. I followed her to the doorway, leaning against it as she picked up her purse from the bed.

"So I have to say," I said as she rummaged around, finally pulling out a lip gloss, "you sure seem different all of a sudden. And it's not just the clothes."

Thisbe was really crying now. Heidi bit her lip, then un-capped the gloss, putting some on. "You're right," she said. "I just . . . I've realized over the last couple of weeks that I needed to take some time for myself. We've talked about it a lot, actually."

"You and Dad?"

"Me and Karen."

"Really," I said.

She nodded, dropping the gloss back in the bag. "Ever since the baby was born I've been so hesitant to ask your dad for any help. I'm so used to doing everything myself, and it wasn't like he was really offering much."

"Or any," I said.

"But Karen kept pointing out that you and your brother were just fine, and he was your dad as well. She said it takes two to make a baby, and at least that many to raise one well. Usually more." She smiled. "She made me promise her that I'd set up that girls' night my friends have been wanting forever. I was dragging my feet, though, until Laura came. When she said pretty much the same thing, I figured they had to be onto something."

I watched as she checked her hair in the mirror, adjust-ing a piece in front. "I didn't realize you and Laura talked when she was here."

"Oh, we didn't at first," she replied, picking up her purse. "To be honest, she kind of scared the crap out of me. Not exactly the warmest person, you know?"

I nodded. "No kidding."

"But then the night before they left, I was up late with Thisbe, and she came down for a glass of water. At first she

Sarah Dessen

was just sitting there, watching us, and eventually I asked her if she wanted to hold her. She said yes, so I handed her over, and then we just started talking. There's a lot more to her than it seems at first glance."

"You should tell my mother that," I said. "She hates her."

"Of course she does," she said. "It's because they're so similar. They both have that whole cold, bitchy, wary-of-all-other-women thing going on. It's like two magnets repelling each other."

I thought of my mother just moments earlier on the phone, her voice so sharp and dismissive. If I wasn't like her, she didn't care to know who I was. "So you think my mom has more to her than that, as well?"

"Of course she does. She has to."

"Because . . ."

She looked at me. "Because she raised you. And Hollis. And she was in love with your father for a very long time. Truly cold bitches don't do that."

"What do they do?"

"They end up alone."

I raised my eyebrows. "You sound awfully sure about that."

"I am," she said. "Because I was one."

"You?" I said. "No way."

She smiled. "Someday I'll tell you all about it. But now, I've got to run and kiss my daughter and then try to leave without having a breakdown. Okay?"

I nodded and was still standing there, trying to process this, as she started into the hallway. When she passed me, she paused, bending down to quickly kiss my forehead

before moving on, the smell of her perfume lingering behind her. Maybe it was to prove her point. Or just instinct.
Either way, it was surprising. But not as much as the fact
that I didn't really mind it, not at all.

❋   ❋   ❋

Later that night, I was walking to the Gas/Gro after work
when I heard a car coming up behind me. A moment later,
a newspaper landed with a slap at my feet.

I looked at it, then at Eli, who was now pulling up beside me. "So you have a paper route now?"

"Technically," he replied as I picked up the paper, noticing the stacks of others piled up in the back of the truck,
"my friend Roger has a paper route. But he also has the flu,
so I'm helping him out. Plus, I thought it might apply to
your quest."

"Delivering papers?"

"Sure." He stopped the car, gesturing for me to open the
passenger door. When I did, he said, "It's a rite of passage.
My first job was delivering the *Colby Coupon Clipper* on my
bike."

"I've had jobs," I told him.

"Yeah? What were they?"

"I worked for a professor in the English department one
summer, helping with a bibliography for his book," I said,
as I slid inside. "Then I worked for my mom's accountant
as an office assistant. And all last year I did test prep at
Huntsinger."

Personally, I'd always thought this was a pretty impressive résumé. Eli, however, just gave me a flat look. "You," he

said, hitting the gas, "definitely need a paper route. At least for one night."

And so it was that, after hitting the Washroom, and Park Mart for a few incidentals, we pulled into a neighborhood just past the pier, driving slowly with a stack of papers between us, and a list of subscriber addresses in his hand. It was just after two A.M.

"Eleven hundred," Eli said, nodding at a split-level off to the right. "That's all you."

I picked up a paper, getting a good grip, then tossed it toward the driveway. It hit the curb, then bounced into a pile of lawn clippings, disappearing entirely. "Whoops," I said. He pulled to a stop and I jumped out, retrieving it and throwing it again, this time doing a bit better, hitting the far right of the driveway. "It's harder than it looks," I told him when I finally got back in the car.

"Most things are," Eli said. Then, of course, he grabbed a paper, launching it at a house across the street in a perfect arc. It landed right on the front stoop, the delivery version of a perfect ten. When I just looked at him, speechless, he shrugged. "*Colby Coupon Clipper*, I told you. Two years."

"Still," I said. My next shot was a bit better, but too wide. It hit the lawn, and again I had to get out to move it to a safer, less wet spot. "God, I suck at this."

"It's your second one," he said before launching another perfect shot at a bungalow with a plastic flamingo in the front yard.

"Still," I said again.

I could feel him watching me as I threw another one,

concentrating hard. It hit the steps (good) but then banked into the nearby bushes (not so good). When I came back from retrieving it, some brambles in my hair, my frustration must have been obvious.

"You know," Eli said, tossing another paper and hitting another front stoop—*thwack!*—"it's okay not to be good at everything."

"This is delivering papers."

"So?"

"So," I said as he did another perfect throw, Jesus, "I'm all right if I suck at, say, quantum physics. Or Mandarin Chinese. Because those things are hard, and take work."

He watched, silent, as I missed yet another driveway. By about a mile. When I returned he said, "And clearly, this doesn't."

"It's different," I told him. "Look, achievement is my thing, okay? It's what I do. It's all I've ever been good at."

"You're good at doing well," he said, clarifying.

"I'm good," I said, throwing another paper and doing marginally better, "at learning. Because I never had to involve anyone else in that. It was just me, and the subject matter."

"Indoors, working away," he added.

I shot him a look, but, as usual, he did not seem deterred. Or bothered in the least. He just handed me another paper, which I launched at the next house. It hit the driveway, a bit too much to the left, but he drove on anyway.

"Life is full of screwups," he said, chucking another paper at a split-level before taking the corner. "You're supposed to fail sometimes. It's a required part of the human existence."

"I've failed," I told him.

"Yeah? At what?"

I blanked for a moment, not exactly good for my argument. "I told you," I said, "I was a social failure."

He took another turn, tossing a couple more papers as we cruised down a dark street. "You didn't try to be homecoming queen and lose, though."

"Well," I said, "I never wanted to be homecoming queen. Or any of that stuff."

"Then you didn't fail. You just opted out. There's a difference."

I considered this as we cruised down another street. He wasn't even handing me papers anymore, just throwing them all himself. "What about you, then?" I asked. "What did you fail at?"

"The better question," he said, slowing for a stop sign, "is what didn't I fail at."

"Really."

He nodded, then held up a hand and began to count off, finger by finger. "Algebra. Football. Lacey McIntyre. Skateboarding on a half-pipe . . ."

"Lacey McIntyre?"

"Eighth grade. Spent months working up to asking her to a dance, and she shot me down cold. In full view of the entire lunchroom."

"Ouch."

"Tell me about it." He turned again, going down a narrow street with only a few houses on it. *Thwack. Thwack.*

"Winning over Belissa's dad, who still hates me. Convincing my little brother not to be such a chump. Learning to fix my own car."

"Wow. This *is* a long list."

"I told you. I'm very good at being bad at things."

I glanced over at him again as we came to another stop sign. "So you never get discouraged."

"Of course I do," he said. "Failing sucks. But it's better than the alternative."

"Which is?"

"Not even trying." Now he did look at me, straight on. "Life's short, you know?"

I'd never met Abe. Or even heard much about him, aside from the few things Maggie and Leah had said. But suddenly, in that moment, it was like I could feel him. Sitting in the very seat where I was, riding along with us. Maybe he'd been there the whole time.

Eli took another turn, and I realized we were in my dad's neighborhood, the surroundings suddenly familiar. His house was quickly approaching, and on my side to boot. It had to be a sign. I reached over, picking up a paper from the stack between us. "Okay," I said. "This one's mine."

I drew back my hand, trying to use my elbow for leverage the way I'd seen him do, and this time aimed not for the driveway but the porch. It came closer, closer, and at the exact right minute, I let it fly, watching as it arced high over the lawn . . . before landing with a slap on the windshield of Heidi's Prius.

Eli slowed to a stop. "I know it's family," he said, "but that demands a do-over."

I slid out of the car—again—and walked over to grab the paper, tucking it under my arm. Then I crept up as slowly as possible to the porch, trying to be quiet as I bent to slide it onto the perfect center of the mat. Just as I did, though, I heard my dad's voice.

" . . . just my point! I wanted you to have what you wanted. But what about what *I* want?"

I shrank from the door, backing down one step as I glanced at my watch. It was almost three A.M. Entirely too late for most people to be up, unless something bad was happening.

"Are you saying you don't want the baby?" Heidi said. Her voice was higher, shaky. "Because if that's true . . . "

"This isn't about the baby."

"Then what is it about?"

"Our lives," he replied, sounding tired. "And how they've changed."

"You've done this before, Robert. *Twice.* You knew what it was like to have an infant in the house."

"I was a child myself then! I'm older now. It's different. It's . . ."

Silence. All I could hear was Eli's car, the engine murmuring behind me.

" . . . not what I expected," my dad finished. "You want the truth, there it is. I wasn't ready for all this."

All this. Such a round, all-encompassing term, as wide as the ocean, which I could also hear, distantly—the real waves this time. But even with all that vastness, it was impossible to tell what, or who, it really included. It seemed safest to just assume everything.

"This," Heidi said, "is your *family*. Ready or not, Robert."

I had a flash of all those cul-de-sac games I never really played, but knew the rules to nonetheless. You hide: whoever is It counts down, and then—ready or not!—they came looking for you. If they got close, you had no choice but to stay put, hoping not to be found. But if you were, there was no wiggle room. Game over.

I could hear my father starting to say something, but I wasn't a child this time, and didn't have to stay and listen. I could leave, disappear into the night, which was vast, too, wide and all-encompassing, with so many places to hide. So I did.

*   *   *

"Forgive the mess," Eli said, reaching inside the dark room for a light switch. "Housework is another one of my failings."

In truth, his apartment was simply plain. One large room, with a bed on one side, a single wooden chair and TV on the other. The kitchen was tiny, the counters bare except for a coffeemaker, a box of filters beside it. Still, I appreciated his efforts to pretend otherwise, if only because it meant we weren't talking about the fact that I'd pretty much lost it only moments earlier.

I thought I'd been fine as I backed away from my dad's house, walking across the already dew-damp grass to the truck. Fine as I slid in, picking up another paper to throw. But then, Eli had said, "Hey. You okay?" and the next thing I knew, I wasn't.

It's always embarrassing to cry in front of anyone. But bursting into tears in front of Eli was downright humiliating.

Maybe it was the way he just sat there, not saying anything, the only sound my hiccuping sobs and loud sniffles. Or how, after a moment, he just drove on, throwing papers at houses while I looked out the window and tried to stop. By the time he'd pulled into the dark driveway of a green split-level house a block from the boardwalk, I'd gotten calmed down enough to be racking my brain for some way to play the whole thing off. I was thinking I'd blame sudden-onset PMS, or maybe my devastation at sucking so entirely at paper delivering. Before I could say anything, though, he cut the engine, pushing his door open.

"Come on," he said. As he got out, I sat there for a moment, watching as he began to climb a narrow flight of stairs beside the garage. He never looked back to see if I was following him. Which was probably why I did.

Now, he shut the door behind me, then walked over to the kitchen, dropping his keys on the counter en route to turning on the coffeemaker. Only when it began to brew, the smell wafting toward me, did I go to join him.

"Have a seat," he said, his back to me as he bent into the fridge, rummaging around for something. "There's a chair."

"And only *a* chair," I said. "What do you do when you have company?"

"I don't." He stood up, shutting the fridge. He had a stick of butter in one hand. "I mean, usually."

I didn't say anything, instead just watching as he pulled a saucepan out of a cabinet, sticking the butter in it before placing it on the stove. "Look," I said as he turned on the burner, "what happened back there—"

"It's okay," he said. "We don't have to talk about it."

I was quiet for a minute, watching as he melted the butter in the pan, tipping it from side to side. It was just another courtesy that he'd given me this easy out, the chance to move on, and I thought it was a gift I'd take, and gratefully. Until I heard myself say, "Remember how you were asking me what I'd failed at, earlier?"

He nodded, jiggling the pan over the stove. "Yeah. The social thing, right?"

"That," I said, "and keeping my parents together."

It wasn't until I said this that I realized it was true. That I hadn't blanked out at this question earlier so much as thought of an answer I couldn't say aloud. At least until I'd overheard my dad and Heidi fighting, and it all came rushing back to me: those awkward dinners, with the picky little arguments, the unsettled feel of the house as the hours went on and on, closer to my bedtime. The way I learned to stretch the night all around me, staying awake and alert to keep all the things that scared me most at bay. But it hadn't worked. Not then. And not now either.

I blinked, feeling a tear roll down my cheek. Three years of total stoicism, blown in one night. Talk about humiliating.

"Hey. Auden."

I looked up to see Eli watching me. He'd taken out a box of Rice Krispies at some point, and instead of looking back at him I focused on the faces of Snap, Crackle, and Pop, all gathered happily around a big cereal bowl. "I'm sorry," I said, because for some reason, even with these cartoon distractions I *still* seemed to be crying. "I just . . . I don't even think about this anymore, but then when I went to throw that paper, they were fighting, and it was so . . ."

He put the box down, then came over to the opposite side of the island. He didn't try to reach out for me, or touch me. He just stood there, near, as he said, "Who was fighting?"

I swallowed. "My dad and Heidi. Things have been pretty bumpy since Isby came, and tonight I guess things just blew up, or something."

God, I was still blubbering. My voice was all choked, coming in little gaspy sobs. Eli said, "Just because people fight doesn't mean they're splitting up."

"I know that."

"I mean, my parents used to go at it sometimes. It just kind of cleared the air, you know? It was always better afterward."

"I know my dad, though," I said. "I've seen him do this before."

"People change."

"Or they don't," I replied. Finally I made myself look at him. Those green eyes, long lashes. His haunted face, not as haunted anymore. "Sometimes, they don't."

He just stood there, looking at me, and I had this flash of us, here in this little garage apartment, in the middle of the night. From up above, in a plane passing over, you'd just see one little light in all this dark, with no idea of the lives that were being lived within it, and in the house beside, and beside that one. So much happening in the world, night and day, hour by hour. It was no wonder we were meant to sleep, if only to check out of it for a little while.

There was a sudden crackling *pop* from the stove, and Eli looked over his shoulder. "Whoops," he said, turning back to the saucepan and pulling it off the heat. "One sec, let me just finish these."

I wiped my hand beneath my eyes, trying to collect myself. "What are you doing over there, anyway?"

"Making Rice Krispie treats."

This seemed so odd, and incongruous, it almost made sense. Along with everything else that night. Still, I felt compelled to ask "Why?"

"Because it's what my mom always did when my sisters were crying." He glanced back at me. "I don't know. I told you, I never have company. You were upset, and it just seemed . . . "

He trailed off, and I looked around the room, taking in the plain bed, the one chair. The single light outside the door, glowing yellow and bright, all night long.

" . . . perfect," I finished for him. "It's perfect."

❊   ❊   ❊

Of course, nothing is really perfect. But Eli's Rice Krispie treats were pretty close. We ate half a pan while we split the pot of coffee, using the one chair as a table, each of us sitting on the floor on either side of it.

"So let me guess," I said, putting my mug on the floor by my feet. "You're a minimalist."

He glanced around the room, then back at me. "You think?"

"Eli," I said. "You have one chair."

"Yeah. But just because all the furniture at my old place was Abe's."

Hearing this, it was all I could do not to start, or jump,

so jarring was it to hear him say his name, after all this time. Instead, I took another sip of my coffee. "Really."

"Yeah." He sat back, picking a bit of sticky crumb off the side of the Rice Krispie pan. "The minute he made some prize money riding, he was all about decorating our place. And he bought the stupidest stuff. Huge TV, singing fish . . . "

"A singing fish?"

"You know, those plastic ones that you hang on the wall, and when you walk by they start singing, like, some Motown song?" I just looked at him. "Okay, so you don't know. Consider yourself lucky. Ours was, like, the center of our apartment. He put it right by the door, so it went off constantly, and everyone had to listen to it."

I smiled. "Sounds interesting."

"That's not the word I'd choose." He shook his head. "Plus he insisted on buying these big papasan chairs, you know the ones that are circular, filled with squishy cushions? I wanted a plain, normal couch. But no. We had to have these stupid things that everyone was always getting sucked down into. No one could ever get up and out of them on their own. We were always having to pull people out, like a freaking rescue mission."

"Come on."

"I'm totally serious. It was ridiculous." He sighed. "And then there was the whole water bed thing. He said he'd always wanted one. Even when it leaked, and gave him a crazy backache, he would not admit it was a mistake. 'I must have spilled something,' he'd say, or 'I really pulled a muscle on that last ride.' He was hobbling around like an old man, complaining constantly. All night long, all I could hear was him thrashing around, trying to get comfortable. It was, like, an *endless* squishing."

I laughed, picking up my mug again. "So what happened? Did he finally give it up?"

"No," he said. "He died."

I knew this, of course. But even so, hearing it this way was like a shock to the system, all over again. "I'm sorry," I said. "I—"

"See, but that's the thing, though." He sat back, shaking his head. "Everyone always wants to tell these stories, all the stories. It's all anyone wanted to do at the funeral, and after. Oh, remember this thing, and this, and what about this? But the ending to every story is the same. He dies. That's never going to change. So why even bother?"

We were both quiet for a moment. "I guess," I said finally, "that for some people, it's how they remember. You know, by telling the stories. It keeps the person close."

"But I don't have that problem," he said quietly. "Not remembering."

"I know."

"You want to talk about failure?" He looked up at me, meeting my eyes. "Try being the one who was driving. Who got to live."

"Eli," I said. I tried to keep my voice low, even, the way his had been when he'd been reassuring me. "It wasn't your fault. It was an accident."

He shook his head. "Maybe. But the bottom line is, I'm here and he's not. And everyone who sees me—his parents, his girlfriend, his friends—they know that. In all the uncertainty, it's the one thing they know for sure. And it *sucks*."

"I'm sure they don't hold it against you," I said.

"They don't have to." He looked down at his mug, then up at me. "The whole do-over thing, that's all I think about since it happened. What if we'd left that party earlier, or later. If I'd seen the car coming at us and not stopping, a moment sooner. If he'd been driving instead of me. There are a million variables, and if even one was different . . . maybe everything would be."

We were both quiet for a moment. Finally I said, "You can't think like that, though. You'll make yourself crazy."

He gave me a wry smile. "Tell me about it."

I started to say something, but then he was getting to his feet, picking up the tray and taking it to the kitchen. Just as he did, I heard a thump from the wall by his bed, followed by another. I stood up, walking closer, and listened again.

"That's the McConners," Eli said from the kitchen.

"The who?"

He came over, standing behind me. "The McConners. They own this house. Their son's room is right through that wall."

"Oh," I said.

"He usually wakes up once or twice a night. Asks for water, you know, the whole thing." Eli sat down on his bed, the springs creaking beneath him. "If it's really quiet, I can hear every word."

I sat down beside him, listening hard. But all I could

make out was two voices murmuring: one high, one lower. It was kind of like Heidi's waves, distant white noise.

"I used to do that," Eli said. We were both whispering. "The whole waking up, wanting water thing, when I was a kid. I remember it."

"Not me," I told him. "My parents needed their sleep."

He shook his head, lying back on the bed, folding his arms over his chest. Through the wall, the negotiations continued, the higher voice rising, urgent, the lower one staying level. "You were always thinking of them, huh?"

"Pretty much." I stifled a yawn, then looked at my watch. It was four thirty, about when I usually headed home. Through the wall, the voices kept going, and, still listening, I slid down next to Eli, resting my head on his chest. His T-shirt was soft beneath my head, and smelled like the detergent I knew he used at the Washroom.

"It's late," I said quietly. "He should go to sleep."

"Not always so easy." His voice was low, slow, too, and I felt his lips brush the top of my head, gently.

The light was still on in Eli's kitchen, but it became muted as I closed my eyes, still hearing those murmurings behind me. *Shh, shh, everything's all right,* I was sure I heard a voice say. Or maybe it was the one in my head, my mantra. *Shh, Shh.* "It's not your fault," I said to Eli, my voice sounding thick to my own ears. "You're not to blame."

"Neither are you," he answered. *Shh. Shh. It's all right.*

It was so late. Late for children, late for anyone. I knew I should get to my feet, go down those stairs, and find my way home, but already I could feel something happening.

A feeling, thick and heavy, creeping over me. It had been so long since I'd done this that for a moment a part of me was scared, wanting to fight it off, stay vigilant. But instead, just before it took me, I rolled over, pressing myself closer against him. I felt his hand rise to my head and then, I was gone.

❄   ❄   ❄

When I woke up the next morning, it was seven thirty and Eli was still sleeping. His arm was around my waist, his chest moving slowly up, down, up, down, beneath my cheek. I closed my eyes again, trying to drift back, but the sunlight was slanting in overhead, the day already begun.

I eased myself away from him, getting to my feet, but then stood watching his face, relaxed and dreaming, for a few moments. I knew I should tell him good-bye, but I didn't want to wake him. Plus, I had no idea what I could say in a note that would possibly convey how grateful I was to him for everything he'd done for me the night before. In the end, I did the closest thing I could: I refilled the coffee-maker, put fresh grounds in a new filter, and flipped the switch. It was already brewing as I slipped outside and made my way down his steps to the street.

It was one of those gorgeous beach mornings, bright and sunny already, everything enhanced with the benefit of actual nighttime sleep. Walking the four blocks or so back home, I was more aware than ever of the salt in the air, the beauty of the rambling roses climbing along some-one's fence, even the friendliness I felt toward the bicyclist I passed, an older woman with a long braid, wearing a crazy orange jogging suit and whistling to herself. She returned my wide smile, lifting a hand to wave as I made my way up the front walk.

I was so immersed in all this—the night, the sleep, the morning—that I didn't even see my dad until I was about to walk right into him. But there he was, in the foyer at this early hour, already showered and dressed.

"Hey," I said. "You're up early. Did inspiration strike or something? Ready to start another book already?"

He glanced up the stairs. "Um," he said. "Not exactly. Actually I was just . . . I'm headed out."

"Oh." I stopped. "Where are you going? Campus?"

A pause. Right then, in that too-long beat of silence, I got the first inkling that something was wrong. "No. I'm going to a hotel for a couple of nights." He swallowed, then looked down at his hands. His face was tired. "Heidi and I . . . we have some things to work out, and we decided this was the best thing. For now."

"You're leaving?" Even the word sounded wrong, said aloud.

"It's only temporary." He took in a breath, then let it out. "Trust me, this is better. For the baby, for everyone. I'll just be at the Condor, we can still see each other every day."

"You're leaving?" I said again. Still weird.

He bent down, picking up the bag I'd not spotted until now, which was by the stairs. "It's complicated," he said. "Just give us some time. Okay?"

I just stood there, speechless, as he walked past me to the door, pulling it open. Here I was, with finally a chance to say everything I hadn't two years earlier, the do-over of all do-overs. I could have asked him to reconsider, to think of other options. To stay. And yet nothing came. Nothing. I just watched him go, again.

I stood there for a long time, thinking this had to be a joke. It wasn't until I had watched him pull out of the garage, flip down his sun visor, and drive off that I walked over and locked the door.

When I went upstairs, Heidi's door was closed, but as I passed Isby's room, I heard something. Not surprisingly, at first, I assumed it was a cry. But listening another minute, I realized it wasn't. Tentatively, I pushed open the door, peering in. She was in her bassinette, looking up at her mobile, waving her arms around. Not wailing. Not shrieking. Even though these would have been perfectly acceptable and expected any day, but especially this one. Instead, she was just murmuring, making little baby noises.

I went closer, to the edge of her bassinette, and peered down at her. For a moment, she kept kicking, intent on the ceiling, but then she suddenly looked at me. Her face relaxed, changing entirely into something new, something amazing. A smile.

thirteen

"I DIDN'T EVEN want to call you," I heard Heidi say. "I was sure you'd just tell me you told me so."

For three hours I'd been up in my room, trying to fall back asleep, but with no luck. Instead, I'd just lain there, remembering it all again: waking up so happy with Eli, my walk home, and then being blindsided by my dad's departure, take two. But of all these images, it was Isby's smile, so sweet and unexpected, that had stuck with me the most. Whenever I closed my eyes to try and sleep, it was all I could see.

"No, not really," Heidi continued. "But I wouldn't blame you. It's just such a mess. I still can't believe any of this is happening."

I walked past the table, where she was sitting, the baby in her arms, and headed to the cupboard to get myself a mug. Outside, it was another bright and sunny day, gorgeous like all the others.

"Hey," Heidi said suddenly, glancing at me, "let me call you back. No, I will. Okay, then you call me. Ten minutes. All right. Bye."

She hung up, and I could feel her watching me as I

poured myself a cup of coffee. Finally she said, "So, Auden. Can you sit down a sec? I . . . I have to talk to you about something."

She sounded so sad and worried I could barely stand it. "It's okay, I already know," I said, turning around. "I talked to Dad."

"Oh." She swallowed, looking down at the baby again. "Well, that's good. What did he . . . "

Isby suddenly let out a little squawk. Instead of crying, though, she just buried her face in Heidi's chest, closing her eyes.

"He said you guys had some stuff to work out," I said. "And that he was staying at the Condor for a while."

She nodded, her face looking pained. "So," she said, "are you doing okay?"

"Me?" I said. "I'm fine. Why wouldn't I be?"

"Well, this is kind of unsettling, I'm sure," she said. "I just . . . you can talk to me anytime, all right? If you have questions, or concerns . . . "

"I'm fine," I said again. "Really."

Just then, I heard a buzzing noise: Heidi's phone. She glanced at it, then sighed, putting it to her ear. "Hello?" she said. "Hi, Elaine. No, no, I got your messages, I just . . . How are you? Right. Of course. Well, to be honest, I haven't had much of a chance to think about the Bash yet. . . ."

She stood, shifting Isby in her arms, and walked over to the glass doors, still talking. I sat there, thinking of how I watched my dad driving away earlier, the way it felt like another do-over, but with the same outcome. Maybe some things could never change, or be fixed, even with time.

A moment later, Heidi returned to the kitchen, putting her phone down on the counter. "That was Elaine, the chair of the Colby Visitors' Council," she said in a flat voice. "She wants a theme for the Beach Bash, and she wants it now."

"The Beach Bash?" I said.

"It's this annual event we have at the end of every summer," she explained, sitting down again. "It's in the hall on the boardwalk. We sell tickets, all the merchants participate, it's the last big thing of the summer. And for some reason, I always volunteer to organize it."

"Really."

"It's total masochism." She shook her head. "Anyway, last year, I did a pirate theme, which was kind of cute. The year before, we did a whole Renaissance thing. But this year . . . I mean, what am I going to do? I'm not exactly in a festive place right now."

I watched her as she ran a hand over Isby's cheek, then tucked the blanket more tightly around her. "You'll think of something."

Just then, her phone rang again. She picked it up, settling it between her ear and shoulder. "Hi, Morgan. No, it's fine. I was just talking to Elaine." She sighed, shaking her head. "I know. And I appreciate that. But it's just . . . I can't believe this, you know? Last year at this time, all I wanted was for Robert and me to get pregnant, and now . . ."

She gulped, then moved a hand to cover her face, even as I heard whoever was on the other end start talking, their voice low and soothing. I pushed out my chair, then put my cup in the sink as once again, I found myself on the outside, watching something I'd never really known and didn't

understand. Most perplexing of all, though, was the tight-
ness of my own throat and the sudden lump I felt there. I
pushed back my chair, slipping out of the room, into the
foyer, thinking again of my dad walking out that same door,
bag in hand. It *was* terrible and awful when someone left
you. You could move on, do the best you could, but like Eli
had said, an ending was an ending. No matter how many
pages of sentences and paragraphs of great stories led up to
it, it would always have the last word.

※　※　※

By the time I left the house two hours later, Heidi and the
baby were both sleeping. The house seemed almost peace-
ful, if you didn't know better.

I, however, felt entirely unsettled, which made no sense,
because first, Heidi was not my mother, and second, when
this *had* happened with my parents, years earlier, I'd been
just fine. Sure, I was disappointed and a little sad, but from
what I remembered, I'd adapted pretty quickly to the new
arrangements. Aside from the whole not-sleeping thing, of
course, but that had been going on already. What I didn't
remember was the weird, panicky feeling, now still lingering, that had come over me watching my dad drive away
from the house earlier. It was the way I usually felt around
midnight, knowing that so much of the night was still to
come and I had to find a way to fill it, the certainty of time
passing so slowly until daylight.

Thank God I had work to do. I'd actually never been
so happy to walk into Clementine's, which was bustling
with customers in a late afternoon rush. Maggie, consulting

with a mother and daughter on some jean shorts, waved as I passed, grabbing the receipts and invoices on my way to the office. Once inside, I shut the door, flicked on the light, and prepared myself to buckle down into the numbers until closing. I'd just managed to lose myself in the check register when my phone rang.

MOM, the caller ID said. I watched the screen, the little phone jumping up and down as it logged one ring, then another. For a moment, I considered answering and telling her everything. Then, just as quickly, I realized that this was the worst possible idea ever. It would be like Christmas and her birthday rolled into one, the satisfaction she'd get, and I just couldn't take her smugness. And besides, she'd hung up on me the day before, making it more than clear that she didn't want to know me. Now it was my right to distance myself, as long as I wanted.

For the next two hours, I immersed myself in Heidi's books, more grateful than ever for the dependability and static nature of numbers and calculations. When I finished the register and the payroll, I turned my attention to the desk, which had been cluttered since the day I started. I could almost feel my blood pressure dropping, bit by bit, as I organized Heidi's pens, throwing out the ones that didn't work and making sure the rest had caps snugly on and were all facing upright in the pink mug where they lived. Then I moved on to the top drawer, sorting little scraps of paper, stacking random business cards into neat piles, and collecting all the paper clips into an empty Band-Aid box I found lying nearby. I was just about to tackle the next one, when there was a tap on the door and Maggie stuck her head in.

"Hey," she said. "Esther's going to Beach Beans, you want anything?"

I reached into my pocket, pulling out my wallet. "Large triple-shot mocha."

Her eyes widened. "Wow. You pulling an all-nighter, or something?"

"No," I said. "I'm just . . . kind of tired."

She nodded, running a hand through her hair. "I hear you. My mom started in on me first thing this morning about my roommate forms. Apparently she wants me to fast track my pick because she's worried otherwise we won't have enough time to properly coordinate our linens. As if anyone else cares about that."

I had a flash of my own mother, her clipped tone when I dared to question her choice of the Pembleton Program. "That's what she's worried about?"

"She's worried about everything," Maggie said, flipping her hand. "In her mind, if I don't have the perfect college experience, it will be an unparalleled tragedy."

"That's not such a bad thing, though," I said, "is it?"

She sighed. "You don't know my mother. I'm never, you know, enough for her."

"Enough?"

"Girly enough," she explained, "because I was so into dirt bikes. Social enough, because I only had one boyfriend all through high school and didn't 'play the field.' Now I'm not embracing college enough. And it hasn't even started yet!"

"Tell me about it," I said. "My mom's riding me about

the roommate thing, too. Except she wants me to enroll in some program where you do nothing but study twenty-four/ seven and fun is not allowed under any circumstances."

"Really?"

I nodded.

"I should sign up for that. My mom would lose her *mind*."

I smiled. Then the front door chime sounded, and she looked down at the money in her hand. "Large triple-shot mocha," she said. I nodded. "I'll let Esther know."

"Thanks."

The door shut back with a click, and I pulled open the second desk drawer. Inside was a stack of old checkbook registers, topped with a couple of yellow legal pads, covered with scribbles. As I pulled them out, I glanced at the writing, which was clearly Heidi's. There were lists for inventory, various phone numbers, and a few pages in, this:

Caroline Isabel West
Isabel Caroline West
Emily Caroline West
Ainsley Isabel West

Each was written carefully: you could almost feel her deliberation as she added them, one by one. I thought back to the day she'd admitted her dislike of the name Thisbe, and how I—and my mother—had judged her for giving in to it anyway. My father was selfish. He got what he wanted, and even then, it wasn't enough.

I closed the pad, pushing it aside and digging down

deeper into the drawer. There were various invoices, which I set aside to file properly, a flyer for the previous year's Annual Colby Beach Bash—*Ahoy, Mateys!*—and, at the very bottom, a stack of pictures. Here was Heidi, with a paintbrush dabbed with pink paint, standing with a wide smile in front of a white wall. Heidi again, posing before the front door, the CLEMENTINE'S sign arcing over her head. And finally, at the very bottom, a shot of her with my dad. They were on the boardwalk, her in a white dress, her belly round and full, him with his arm around her. The date stamp was early May, just a few weeks before Isby was born.

"Auden?"

I jumped. Somehow Esther had managed to slip in the door right behind me. "Oh," I said, looking down at the drawer, the contents spread across the desk, "I was just—"

"Your caffeine," she said. She was holding out the cup to me when suddenly, something blurred past behind her. Something red, which then crashed against the end of the hallway with a loud, bouncy bang.

"Hey!" Esther yelled out the door. "What the hell was that?"

"What do you think?" I heard a male voice—Adam, I thought—yell back.

She opened the door wide, just as a red rubber ball rolled slowly past in the opposite direction, heading back toward the sales floor. "Oh, man. Seriously?"

"That's right," Adam hollered. "Kickball. Tonight. Get ready to get wet."

"And who," I heard Maggie say, "decided this?"

"Who do you think?"

Esther stepped out into the hallway, picking up the ball. "Not Eli."

"Yup." I heard footsteps, and then Adam came into view, holding out his hands. Esther handed over the ball, and he nodded at me. "Came in late today, with this under his arm. He actually seemed cheerful."

"Really."

"Yup. We were all *totally* freaked out." He gave the ball a bounce. "But he was serious. First game of the season, tonight after closing. Drawing for second base commences sharply at ten oh five."

"Oh, God." Maggie groaned, joining them in the hall-way. "If I have to be second base, I'm not playing."

"That," Adam said, pointing at her, "is a quitter attitude."

"Last time I got totally soaked!" she protested.

"Last time was over a year ago. Come on! Eli's finally pulling out of this thing. The least you can do is get a little wet."

"It is pretty major that he's up for it," Esther said to her. "I wonder what changed."

I started to turn back to the desk, taking another sip of my drink. But not before I saw Maggie look right at me.

"Who knows?" Adam said. "Let's just be glad and get on with it. See you at ten!"

And with that, he was gone, bouncing the ball as he went. Esther sighed, then followed him, but I could feel Maggie's eyes still on me as I carefully stacked everything back in the drawer, stuffing the pictures in on top. "Hey," she said. "You all right?"

"Yeah," I said. "I'm fine."

This should have been true. After all, I'd had the same night as Eli, and he'd woken up with a whole new attitude. I should have been just coasting and happy, more ready than anyone to jump into kickball, especially with Eli there. And yet, as the nine o'clock dance passed and the minutes of the next hour ticked down, I could feel my stomach getting tighter and tighter.

At ten on the nose, Maggie appeared in the doorway to the office, keys in her hand. "Come on," she announced. "The second base drawing is in five minutes, and believe me, you don't want to get stuck with it. You're basically in the water."

"Oh," I said, "actually, I think I'm going to stay late tonight. I have this payroll to do, and some filing. . . ."

She looked at me, then at the pens arranged neatly in the jar next to my elbow. "Really."

"Yeah. I'll be along eventually."

"Eventually," she repeated. I nodded, then turned back to the desk. Her voice was flatter as she said, "All right. We'll be waiting for you."

Finally she left, and I busied myself labeling some file folders as she and Esther shut down the registers and headed outside. Once the door was locked behind them, I pushed back from my desk. After fifteen minutes of just sitting there, I went out to the now dark store, walking up to the front windows.

Everyone was gathered just down the boardwalk, at the main entrance to the beach. I could see Maggie sitting on a bench next to Adam, with Esther beside him. Wallace and some other guys from the bike shop I knew by sight if not by name were milling around, joking with one another: I watched as they said something to Leah when she showed up, and she rolled her eyes, swatting at them before Maggie slid over to make room for her. More and more people came along, some I recognized, others I didn't. But then suddenly everyone began to move in closer, converging, and I knew Eli had arrived.

He had on the same blue hoodie he was wearing the first time I saw him, the red ball tucked under one arm. His hair was loose, blowing over his eyes, and as he approached he bounced the ball once, catching it as he turned his head, scanning the assembled group. When he turned, looking behind him right at Clementine's, I stepped back from the window, out of sight.

After a moment of discussion, teams were organized, and some sort of decision was made. From the looks of it, Adam came out on the losing side, if the jeers and pointed fingers in his direction were any indication. Then, en masse, everyone headed onto the beach, with one group assembling by the dunes while another spread out across the sand. Adam, I saw, took his place right by the surf itself, reaching down to roll up his pant legs, while Eli moved to the center, the ball still in his hands. He was just rolling out the first pitch when I turned and went back to the office.

An hour later, I went out the back door, then made my

way across a parking lot and down two alleys before finally
popping out by the Gas/Gro. I'd been planning to just go
home, thinking Heidi might need the company, but instead
I found myself walking back to the boardwalk. I sat down
on a bench in front of the Last Chance, which was still bustling, to watch the game from a distance. Just as I arrived,
Leah was up: she kicked the ball far and long, out into the
water, and a guy I didn't recognize, now at second base,
dove in after it.

"Auden?"

I jumped, then turned slowly, bracing myself. Of course
Eli would sneak up on me, especially when I was doing my
best to stay lost. But as I turned, I saw instead the last person I ever would have expected: my former almost-prom
date, Jason Talbot. He was in khakis and a collared shirt,
hands in his pockets, smiling at me.

"Hey," I said. "What are you doing here?"

He nodded back at the restaurant behind him. "Just
finishing up some dinner. I've been sitting in there for the
last fifteen minutes, wondering if that was you, but I wasn't
sure. I didn't think I'd seen your name on the list for the
conference, but . . . "

"Conference?"

"The FCLC? It just started today. Isn't that why you're
here?"

"Um," I said. "No. My dad lives nearby."

"Oh. Right. Well . . . that's great."

There was a sudden burst of voices from down the
boardwalk. We both looked over, just in time to see Maggie

running the bases, laughing, while Adam started to wade out into the water. "Wow," Jason said. "Kickball. Haven't seen that since third grade."

"So what's the FCLC, again?" I asked.

"Future College Leadership Course," he replied. "It's a monthlong series of lectures, workshops, and symposiums, with incoming freshmen from schools all around the country. It's basically designed to give attendees skills they'll need to make an impact on their campuses from day one."

"Wow," I said. There was another round of cheering from behind him, but this time I didn't look. "That sounds great."

"Oh, I think it will be. I've already met, like, twenty people from Harvard who are already involved in campus leadership," he said. "You know, you should check it out. I know you weren't that into student government, but it's a great networking opportunity. It's not too late to sign up, and there are tons of people from Defriese there."

"I don't know," I said. "I'm kind of busy."

"Oh, tell me about it," Jason replied, shaking his head. "I got the syllabi from my fall classes and have been reading already, and it's really intense. But everyone I've met is doing the same thing."

I nodded, even as I noted that my heart was already beating a bit faster. "I bet," I said.

"That's really what I'm hearing again and again. That you can't just come in on the first day of the semester and hit the ground running anymore."

"Really."

"Oh, yeah. You need to prep early, and seriously."

"I've been doing my reading, too," I said. "I mean, between working and everything else. . . ."

"Working?" I nodded. "What are you doing? Like, internship stuff? Service projects?"

I thought of the office at Clementine's, all that pink. "More business-related. I'm working for a small business that's in the process of expanding, helping with accounting and marketing during the transition. I figured it would be a good way to experience some real-time economics while at the same time studying the larger trends."

"Wow," he said, nodding. "That sounds really interesting. Still, though, you should think about the FCLC. I mean, if you're here anyway. I think you'd be a real asset to the conversation."

There was a loud *whoop!* noise from the beach, followed by a round of applause and laughter. I said, "Maybe I will."

"Good." Jason smiled. "Look, I should get back to dinner, I guess. We were in the middle of this big discussion about class rank, the pros and cons, and I don't want to miss it."

"Sure," I said. "Of course."

He took a step back, then paused. "Are you at the same number, though? Because while I'm here, maybe we could get together, you know. Just to catch up, compare notes."

Everyone was coming off the beach now. I could see Maggie and Adam, who was soaked, in front, with Leah and Esther following. "Yeah," I said. "Sure."

"Great!" He smiled again. "So I'll just see you soon."

I nodded. And then, before I could even begin to react,

he was stepping forward, pulling me into a hug. An awkward, too-much-elbow, faceful-of-fabric-softener hug, but at least it was over quickly.

But not quickly enough. Because as he walked away, there was Eli. Standing with the ball under his arm, watching me, his expression unreadable. For a moment, we just looked at each other, and I had a flash of that first long night, near this same place. *Aren't they all.*

"Hey," I said. "How was the game?"

"Good." He bounced the ball once. "We won."

Two couples, dressed for a night out, walked between us, chattering happily among themselves. For a fleeting instant, I just wanted to fall in with them, go wherever they were going.

"So," he said, coming closer, "what happened?"

"I had to work," I said. "We're behind on payroll, and there was all this filing. . . ."

"No." He bounced the ball again. "I mean to you."

"Me?"

He nodded. "You're acting different. What's going on?"

"Nothing," I said. He kept his eyes on me, steady, unconvinced. "What, you mean that?" I said, nodding at the Last Chance, where Jason had now disappeared inside. "He's just this friend of mine from home. My prom date, actually, although he ditched me at the last minute. Not that I was that upset, we were never, like, serious. Anyway, he's down here for some conference, and he saw me out here, so—"

"Auden." The way he said my name was like a brake,

applied hard. I stopped in mid-breath. "Seriously. What's wrong?"

"Nothing," I said again. "Why do you keep asking me that?"

"Because you were fine last night," he said. "And then tonight you duck out and hide from me and now you won't even look me in the eye."

"I'm fine," I said. "God, I just had to work. Why is that so hard to believe?"

This time, he didn't answer. But he didn't really have to. It was a total lie, paper thin. And yet I stood there, holding on to it for dear life anyway.

"You know," he said finally, "if this is about what happened with your dad and Heidi . . . "

"It's not." My voice was sharp. Defensive. Even I could hear it. "I told you, I had to work. I have a lot on my plate right now, okay? I can't just spend my whole summer playing kickball. I have classes to prepare for, and books to read, if I want to hit the ground running at Defriese this fall. I've been slacking off so much, and now . . ."

"Slacking off," he repeated.

"Yes." I looked down at my hands. "It's been fun and all. But I'm totally behind. I have to get serious."

As I said this, down the boardwalk I could hear all those familiar voices, laughing, jeering, happy together. I knew it instantly, as the sound was much more familiar at a distance than from within it.

"Right," Eli said. "Well. Good luck. Getting serious, and all that."

There was something in his tone—final, distant, exactly what I'd thought I wanted—that made me suddenly realize maybe I didn't. "Eli," I said quickly. "Look. I just . . . "

But no words followed. I just let this hang there, open-ended, waiting for him to jump in, finish it, do the hard part for me. It was my dad's signature trick, and now I understood why. It was just so much easier than having to say what you didn't want to aloud. But Eli didn't fall in, doing the hard part for me. He just walked away. Not that this should have surprised me. What did he care if this sentence was finished or not? He was.

fourteen

1:05 P.M.: Just on a break from a panel, thought you might want to grab lunch?
3:30 P.M.: Are you free for dinner tonight? Last Chance, around 6?
10:30 P.M.: Heading back to the dorms. Talk to you tomorrow.

I put my phone down on the desk. Leah, who was paging through some receipts, glanced at the screen. "Well," she said, *"someone's* popular tonight."

"It's just this guy I know," I told her. "From home."

"Just a guy," she repeated. "Is there even such a thing?"

We were in the office after closing, where everyone was waiting for me to do a few last-minute things before locking up. "In this case," I told her, "yes."

My phone beeped again. I sighed, turning it over.

10:45 P.M.: If you have time to chat tonight, give me a call. Got some ideas to run by you.

"He seems awfully persistent," Esther observed.

"I think he's just trying to make up for standing me up at prom," I said. "Or something. I don't know."

Really, this hadn't occurred to me until right at that moment. But now that I thought about it, it kind of made sense.

"You got stood up on prom night?" Maggie asked. She looked truly upset. "That's horrible."

"It wasn't quite that bad," I said. "He called the day before, said he'd gotten invited to this big environmental meeting up in D.C. It was a once-in-a-lifetime opportunity."

"So is your senior prom," Leah said. "It's a good thing you're blowing him off. He deserves it."

"That's not why I'm . . ." I sighed. "I'm just not interested in revisiting that particular part of my past. That's all."

My phone beeped again. This time, I didn't even look at it. Later, though, back at home, I studied my phone, reading over Jason's messages again. Maybe it would be my own kind of do-over to answer back, go meet him, try again for something I didn't get before. But unlike bowling and food fights and breaking curfew, I didn't feel like I'd missed out on Jason. Instead, what had happened—or not—with us was just a twist of fate, meant to be. Like we hadn't even needed a first chance, much less a second one.

❋ ❋ ❋

A week earlier, at eleven thirty P.M., I would have been out already an hour, just starting the night's adventures. These days, though, I was usually back at home, in my room, hitting the books.

That night Eli had walked away from me, I'd come home

around midnight to find the entire house quiet. Isby was asleep in her room, and Heidi was down for the count, although she'd left her bedside light on. I'd gone to my own room, planning to just grab a few things before heading out, but then I'd remembered what Jason had said about reading ahead and hitting the ground running. The next thing I knew, I was pulling my suitcase out from under my bed.

When I opened it up, the first thing I saw was the picture frame Hollis had given me, which I promptly pushed aside. Beneath it was my econ textbook. Within ten minutes, I was reading chapter one, a yellow pad half covered with notes beside me.

It was so easy. Academics, like an old friend, had just waited patiently for me, and returning to it felt safe and right. Unlike all the things I'd been doing with Eli, which were new and challenging and way out of my comfort zone, studying was my strength, the one thing I did well, no matter what else was going badly.

So instead of driving around that night, I stayed in my room, the window open beside me, reading chapter after chapter as the waves crashed below. Still, whenever I took a break to go get more coffee, or hit the bathroom, I'd find myself glancing at my watch, wondering what Eli was up to. At midnight, probably the Washroom. By one thirty, Park Mart. And then, who knew? Without me and my stupid quest to deal with, he could have been anywhere.

Where I ended up, though, surprised me most of all. At seven A.M., I jerked awake, lifting my head off my legal pad, where it had apparently dropped when I actually fell asleep at some point the night before. My neck was aching, and I had ink stains on my cheek, but none of these felt as odd as the sensation that I had actually slept at night for the second time in a row. I wasn't really sure I wanted to know why.

Whatever the reason, this sudden change in sleeping habits—which continued over the next three nights—completely threw me off my schedule. For the first time in recent memory, I was awake and lucid in the morning. At first, I tried to just keep studying, but by day three, I decided to go to Clementine's.

"Oh, my God," I heard Maggie say as soon as I walked in. "This is *unbelievable*."

I rolled my eyes, then slid off my sunglasses, bracing myself for the inevitable questions, and required explanation, of what I was doing there so early. Then I realized that she hadn't seen me at all. Instead, she, Leah, and Adam were crowded around a laptop open on the counter, watching something on-screen.

"Tell me about it," Adam said. "None of us had any idea. Not even Jake. He just got a text from someone saying they'd seen it online, and so he looked it up."

"What's the date on it, again?" Leah asked as Maggie hit a button, leaning in closer.

"Yesterday. It was the Hopper Bikes exhibition thing, in Randallton."

They all focused on the screen again, not seeming to notice me as I came closer, picking up the previous day's receipts. I glanced at the screen: there was a bike going up a ramp, then down the other side.

"He looks good," Maggie said.

"He looks *great*," Adam told her. "I mean, it was his first competition in over a year and he placed second."

"Look at that," Maggie murmured.

"No kidding. It's serious vertical." Adam shook his head. "I can't believe Eli just got on the bike after all that time and did that well. It's crazy."

I looked at the screen again. The figure on the bike was small, but now I noticed the longer hair sticking out beneath the helmet.

"Well," Maggie said, "maybe he didn't."

"Meaning what?"

She didn't answer at first. Then she said, "Just because we didn't see him riding didn't mean he wasn't."

"Yeah, but," Adam said, "to be that good, still, he'd have to have been practicing a lot. Someone would have seen something. Unless he was, like . . ."

" . . . doing it in the middle of the night or something," Leah finished for him.

I glanced up. Both she and Maggie were looking at me, straight on. Adam, seeing this, looked at me, then back at them. "Wait," he said. "What am I missing?"

"Did you know about this?" Leah asked. "About Eli competing again?"

I shook my head. "No."

"You sure about that?" Maggie said. "You two seem to have a lot of secrets."

"Yeah," I told her. "I'm positive."

They were all still watching me as I picked up my receipts,

then went back into the office, shutting the door behind me. I listened as they watched the video again and again, commenting on how impressive Eli looked, how much he had surprised everyone. Especially me. It made me realize how lucky I'd been to get the tiniest glimpse into what was in his head, like pushing a door open just enough for a sliver of light to fall through. At the same time, though, it made it clear how much still remained unexplored, unseen.

Aside from glimpsing the video, I didn't want to see Eli. In fact, I was so embarrassed about how I'd acted and what I'd said that I took great pains to avoid the bike shop whenever possible. I came and went from Clementine's by the back door most of the time, claiming that way got me home faster. I wasn't sure whether Maggie and everyone else believed me, and didn't really care either. In a couple of weeks, I'd pack up for home, and then from there, Defriese. This part of my life, strange and transitory, was almost over. Thank God.

Later that night, when I took a study break, Heidi had pulled the rocking chair to the sliding glass doors, and had Isby swaddled and asleep in her arms, her phone at her ear.

"I don't know," she was saying. "Whenever we talk, he just sounds so defeated. Like he's convinced this won't work no matter what we do. I know, but . . ."

She was quiet for a moment, and all I could hear was the rocking chair creaking, back and forth, back and forth.

"I'm scared it's too late," she said finally. "Like he's right, and this is unfixable. I know, I know, you say it's never too late. But I'm not so sure."

My phone, which was in my back pocket, suddenly beeped. I pulled it out, checking the screen.

You free for coffee? I'm buying.

I read these words once, twice, three times. Never too late, I thought. Then there was another beep.

Name the place, I'm new here! J.

"Who's texting you so late?" Heidi called out as she came back inside, carrying Isby, her phone in her free hand.

"Just my ex prom date," I told her. "It's a long story."

"Really," she said. "What . . . oh, my God!"

I jumped, startled, then looked behind me, expecting to see something crashing down or on fire. "What?" I said. "What is it?"

"Prom!" Heidi shook her head. "I can't believe we didn't think of it earlier! For the Beach Bash theme. Prom Night. It's perfect!" She flipped open her phone, punching in a few numbers. A second later, I heard someone pick up. "Prom," she announced to them. There was a pause, then, "For the theme! Isn't it perfect? Well, think about it. People can dress up, and we can do a king and queen, and play cheesy music, and . . ."

She kept talking, but I headed back upstairs to my room, where my books and notes were waiting. Once I settled onto the bed, though, I found I couldn't concentrate, so I sat back, breathing in some sea air. Then I saw my laptop on my bedside table. Before I could stop myself, I was booting it up and hitting LiveVid, the video site.

HOPPER BIKES EXHIBITION, I typed in. RANDALLTON. Ten videos popped up. After scrolling through them, I found one tagged STOCK and RAMP, and clicked on it.

It was the same one they'd been watching at Clementine's: I recognized the helmet and the background. I remembered what I'd seen at the jump park, and even to my untrained eye what Eli was doing was different. There was a grace to it, an effortlessness, that made it clear how hard it really had to be. As he moved across the screen, each time going higher, higher in the air, I felt my heart jump. It was so risky and so scary, and yet at the same time, so beautiful. Maybe the truth was, it shouldn't be easy to be amazing. Then everything would be. It's the things you fight for and struggle with before earning that have the greatest worth. When something's difficult to come by, you'll do that much more to make sure it's even harder—if not impossible— to lose.

* * *

The next morning, after about a week of awkward phone calls, I finally went to visit my dad at the Condor. I found him in his room with the shades drawn, sporting a desert island–style beard. After opening the door for me, he flopped onto the unmade bed, stretching his arms over his head and closing his eyes.

"So," he said, after emitting a long, loud sigh, "tell me. How is my life without me?"

Simultaneously, I resisted the urge to answer this question and to roll my eyes. Instead, I said, "Haven't you and Heidi talked?"

"Talk." He scoffed, flipping a wrist. "Oh, we talk. But nothing ever really gets said. The bottom line is, we don't see eye to eye. I worry we never will."

The truth was, I didn't really want to know all the sticky details of their problems. It was enough to know they had them, and that they were Big and Unresolved. But since I was the only one there, I felt I had no choice but to wade in deeper. "Is this . . . is it about the baby?"

He sat up slightly and looked at me. "Oh, Auden. Is that what she's saying?"

"She isn't saying anything," I told him, pulling open the heavy shades. "I'm just asking because I want you guys to work it out, that's all."

He watched me, studious, as I walked around his room, picking up coffee cups and fast-food bags. "Your concern is intriguing," he said finally. "Considering I thought you didn't like Heidi."

"What?" I threw a couple of sticky, ketchup-covered napkins in the overflowing trash can. "Of course I do."

"So you don't think she's some vapid, soulless Barbie doll?"

"No," I said, pushing aside the thought that, okay, this might have once been true. "Why would you think that?"

"Because that's what your mother said," he replied, his voice heavy. "And you two tend to think alike."

I was in the bathroom as he said this, washing my hands, and hearing it I looked up, then away from my own eyes in the mirror. Maybe this had once been true, as well. "Not about everything," I said.

"Oh, but that is what is great about your mother," he mused as I looked around for a clean towel to wipe my hands on. "You always know what she's thinking. There's none of this guessing around, speculating, having to read all the hidden signs and codes. When she was unhappy, I knew it. But Heidi . . . "

I stepped back into the room, sitting down on the other bed. "Heidi what?"

He sighed again. "She hides everything. Keeps it deep down, and you think everything's fine, but then one day, out of nowhere, it suddenly explodes in your face. She's not fine, she's unhappy. You haven't been doing enough after all. Oh, and you're the worst father ever, also."

I waited a beat or two before asking, "Did she actually say that, though?"

"Of course not!" he snapped. "But in marriage, all is *subtext*, Auden. The fact of the matter is that in her mind, I have failed her and Thisbe. From day one, apparently."

"So you try again," I said. "And do better."

He gave me a sad look. "It's not that easy, honey."

"What's the alternative, though? Just staying here, alone?"

"Well, I don't know." He got off the bed, walking over to the window and sliding his hands in his pockets. "I certainly don't want to make things any worse than I already have. It's possible they'd be better off without me. Even probable."

I felt my stomach twist, unexpectedly. "I doubt that," I said. "Heidi loves you."

"And I her," he said. "But sometimes, love isn't enough."

The weird thing was that what bothered me most about him saying this was that it was such a lame, throwaway line. He was a great writer: I knew he could do better.

"I've got to go to work," I said, picking up my bag from the bed beside me. "I just . . . I wanted to see how you were."

He walked over to me, pulling me close for a hug. I could feel that beard, itchy and out of place, rubbing my forehead as he murmured, "I'm okay. I'll be okay."

Outside, I walked to the elevator and hit the button, which did not light up. I hit it again. Nothing. Then I stepped closer, and bashed it with my fist.

I realized—as it finally lit up, and fast—that I was furious. No: heart-pounding, can't-even-think-straight pissed off. When I got inside the elevator, the doors closed, mirroring my reflection back at me. This time, I looked at myself full-on.

It was the strangest thing, to be suddenly infuriated, like something he'd said, or done, had uncapped a valve within me, long sealed, and suddenly something was shooting out, gushing like a geyser. As I crossed the lobby to the boardwalk, all I could think was that regardless of the performance I'd just witnessed, it didn't make you noble to step away from something that wasn't working, even if you thought you were the reason for the malfunction. *Especially* then. It just made you a quitter. Because if you were the problem, chances were you could also be the solution. The only way to find out was to take another shot.

I was almost to Clementine's before I realized how fast

I was walking, passing people on both sides. When I finally pushed the door open, I was breathing so heavily and so flushed that Maggie jumped, startled, when she saw me.

"Auden?" she said. "What's—"

"I need a favor," I told her.

She blinked at me. "Okay," she said. "What is it?"

When I told her, I expected her to be confused. Or maybe laugh at me. But she did neither. She just considered it for a moment, and then nodded. "Yeah," she said. "I can do that."

fifteen

IT WAS, TO say the least, embarrassing.

"Now, see," Maggie said as I got up off the ground, "that's what we *don't* want to happen."

"Got it." I looked down, noting my newly scraped knee, which now matched my other one. "I just . . . it feels so weird."

"I bet." She sighed. "I mean, there's a reason you're supposed to learn this when you're little."

"Less self-conscious?"

"Less distance to fall."

She reached down, picking up the bike and putting it back into a standing position. Once more, I climbed on, resting my feet flat on the ground. "Okay," she said. "Try again."

We were at the clearing by the jump park, bright and early the following morning, and one thing was now clear: I did not know how to ride a bike.

If I had, it would have come back to me, along with the confidence that I *did* know what to do once I was up on the pedals and rolling forward. Instead, each time I got moving—even at a snail's pace—I panicked, wobbled, and

fell. I'd managed to go about forty yards once, but only because Maggie was holding on to the back of the seat. As
soon as she let go, I veered off into some bushes and wiped
out once more.

Of course I wanted to quit. I had since the first wreck,
which had been over an hour earlier. It was completely humiliating to have to keep picking myself up off the ground
and wiping sand and gravel off my knees, not to mention
facing Maggie's cheerful, go-team expression, which was
usually paired with a thumbs-up, even after I'd gone down
hard. This was just such a simple thing. Little kids did it
every day. And yet, I kept failing. And falling.

"You know," she said, after the next crash, which involved full-body contact with a garbage can, yuck, "I'm
thinking I'm approaching this the wrong way."

"It's not you," I told her, picking up the bike again. "It's
me. I'm terrible at this."

"No, you're not." She smiled at me, which made me feel
even more pathetic. "Look, riding a bike involves a great
deal of faith. I mean, you're not supposed to be able to be
aloft on two skinny rubber tires. It goes against all logic."

"Okay," I said, picking some gravel off my elbow, "now
you're really being condescending."

"I'm not." She held the bike as I climbed back on and
flexed my hands over the bars. "But I do think that maybe
we could use some reinforcements."

I looked at her. "Oh, no. No way."

"Auden. It's all right." She pulled her phone out of her
back pocket, flipping it open.

"Please don't," I said. "Leah will laugh me out of town.

And Esther . . . she'll just feel sorry for me, which would be even worse."

"Agreed," she replied, punching some keys. "But I'm calling the one person you literally cannot make an ass of yourself in front of. It's guaranteed."

"Maggie."

"Seriously." She hit another button. "Trust me."

At the time, I had no idea who she was talking about. But ten minutes later, when I heard a car door slam in the parking lot behind us and turned my head, it made total sense.

"This is a 911?" Adam said as he walked up. "You know you only text that when someone is dead or dying. You scared the crap out of me!"

"Sorry," Maggie told him. "But I needed you here fast."

He sighed, then pulled a hand through his curly hair, which, I now noticed, was sticking up on one side. Also, there were sheet crease marks on his face. "Fine. So what's the emergency?"

"Well," she said, "Auden can't ride a bike."

Adam looked at me, and I felt myself flush. "Wow," he said solemnly. "That *is* serious."

"See?" Maggie said to me. "I told you he was the right person to call!"

Adam came closer, checking out both the bike and me on it. "All right," he said after a moment. "So what method of instruction have you been using here?"

Maggie blinked. "Method of . . . "

"Did you start with the buddy system, and then move on to assisted riding? Or do assisted riding first, with the intention of a slow, incremental build toward independent movement?"

Maggie and I exchanged a look. Then she said, "I just kind of put her on and let her go."

"Oh, man. That's the fastest way to make a person hate the bike." He gestured for me to get off and roll it toward him, which I did. Then he climbed on. "Okay, Auden. Get on the handlebars."

"What?"

"The handlebars. Climb on." When I just stood there, clearly doubtful, he said, "Look. If you want to learn to ride a bike, you have to *want* to learn to ride a bike. And the only way to do that is to see how fun it is, once you know what you're doing. Hop on."

I shot a look at Maggie. When she nodded encouragingly, I eased myself up on the handlebars, trying to be graceful about it. "Okay," Adam said. "Now hold on tight. When we get going really fast, you can let go, but only for a second, and only when you really feel ready."

"I'm not letting go," I told him. "Ever."

"That's fine, too."

Then he started pedaling. Slowly at first, and then a bit faster, so that the wind was blowing back my hair and ruffling my shirt. Once we reached the end of the parking lot, he hung a right and kept going.

"Wait," I said, looking back at Maggie, who was watching us, her hand shielding her eyes. "What about . . ."

"She's fine," Adam said. "We won't be gone long."

We were on the main road now, moving swiftly along the shoulder, the occasional car passing us on the left. The sun was fully up now, and the air smelled sweet and salty, all at once. "Okay," Adam yelled as another car passed us, "tell me what you're feeling."

"I'm hoping I don't fall off the handlebars," I told him.

"What else?"

"I . . . " I said as we bumped off the road, onto the board-walk, "I don't know."

"You have to be feeling something."

I considered this as we started down the boardwalk, which was mostly empty, save for a few early morning walkers and a bunch of seagulls, which scattered as we approached. "It's like flying," I said, watching them rise up. "Kind of."

"Exactly!" he said, picking up the pace a bit. "The speed, the wind . . . and the best part is, it's all you doing it. I mean, it's me, now. But it will be you. And it will feel just like this. Or even better, actually, because it will be you doing it, all on your own."

We were really going now, the boards clacking beneath us, and I leaned back farther, letting the wind hit my face straight on. To my right, the ocean was so big and sparkling, and, as we whooshed along, it was a steady blue, blurring past. Despite my worry about falling, and my various embarrassments, I felt a strange sense of exhilaration, and I closed my eyes.

"See?" Adam said, his voice somehow finding my ears. "This is a *good* thing."

I opened my eyes, intending to respond to this. To tell him he was right, that I understood now, and how grateful I was that he'd given me this chance, and this ride. But just as my vision cleared, I realized we were passing the bike shop, and turned my head, looking at it. The front door was open, and in the second we blew by it I could see the back lights were on and someone was standing at the counter. Someone holding a plastic coffee cup. Maybe we were going so fast that Eli didn't even see, or if he did, had no way of knowing it was me. But regardless, for one instant, I decided to let go for real, and held up my hands anyway.

✳ ✳ ✳

For the next week, Maggie and I practiced almost every morning. It was a ritual: I picked up two coffees at Beach Beans, then met her at the jump park clearing. At first, on Adam's advice, we incorporated what he called "assisted riding," i.e., me pedaling with her holding on to the back of the seat. Then we worked up to her letting go for small increments, while still running behind, so I didn't topple over. Now, we were increasing those periods, bit by bit, while I continued to work on my balance and pedaling. It wasn't perfect—I'd had a couple of wipeouts, and still sported scabs on both knees—but it was much better than that first day.

More and more lately, I'd been realizing that my life had again shifted, almost reversing itself. I now stayed home at night, studying and sleeping, and was out in the early morning and afternoon, almost like a normal person. Unlike a normal person, though, I was still spending most of my time alone. If I wasn't at work or practicing with Maggie, I was at home, avoiding texts from Jason—which were still coming, although not with such regularity, thank God—and phone calls from my parents.

I knew they both had to be wondering what was going on, as I hadn't talked to either of them in ages, ignoring their calls and subsequent messages. I knew this was childish, and for some reason this actually made it okay to me. Like it was another part of my unfinished quest, making up for lost time. Really, though, some part of me was worried that if I did speak to either of them—even for a moment, one word—whatever I'd barely tapped into that day leaving the Condor would spill out like a big wave, engulfing us all.

The only family member I was talking to was Hollis, but even our contact was sporadic at best, if only because he was so caught up in his new life with Laura. If my dad's relationship was falling apart, and my mom's, as usual, never really even starting, Hollis was still bucking convention and his own history. Weird enough that he was still madly in love, long after he usually had lost interest and moved on. Now, he'd done something else shocking.

"Hollis West."

Even though I had dialed his number and so *knew* this was my brother, I was still taken aback by his professional tone. "Hollis?"

"Aud! Hey! Hold on, let me just step outside."

There were some muffled noises, followed by the sound of a door shutting. Then he was back. "Sorry about that," he said. "We're just on a break from this meeting."

"You and Laura?"

"No. Me and the rest of the personal finance specialists."

"Who?"

He cleared his throat. "My coworkers. I'm at Main Mutual now, didn't Mom tell you?"

Vaguely, I remembered my mother saying something about a bank. "I guess," I said. "How long have you been there?"

"Three weeks or so," he said. "It's gone fast, though. I'm really clicking here."

"So," I said slowly, "you like it?"

"Totally!" I heard a horn beep. "Turns out I'm really good at customer relations. I guess all that bullshitting around Europe did train me for something after all."

"You relate to customers?"

"Apparently." He laughed. "I got hired on as a teller, but after a week they moved me to the customer service desk. So I handle all the account changes, and safety-deposit applications, stuff like that."

I was trying to picture Hollis behind a desk at a bank, or anywhere. But all I could see was that shot of him grinning in his backpack in front of the Taj Mahal. This was the best of times?

"So, Aud," he said. "I've only got a few minutes before I go back in. What's up down there? How's Dad and Heidi and my other sister?"

I hesitated, knowing I should tell him about my father moving out. He had a right to know. But for some reason, I didn't want to be the one to tell him. It was like my dad trailing off another sentence, leaving me to do his dirty work. So instead I said, "Everything's all right. How's Mom?"

He sighed. "Oh, you know. Crabby as always. Apparently I have disappointed her beyond belief by turning my back on my independent spirit and joining the bourgeoisie."

"I bet."

"And she misses you."

Honestly, hearing this shocked me almost as much as hearing his new job title. "Mom doesn't miss anyone," I said. "She's completely self-sustaining."

"Not true." He paused for a second. "Look, Aud. I know you guys have had your issues this summer, but you should really try to talk to her. She's still having all this drama with Finn, and . . . "

"Finn?"

"The graduate student. Car sleeper? I told you about him, right?"

I thought of those black-framed glasses. "Yeah. I think so."

"You know the drill. He's in love with her, she won't commit, blah blah blah. Usually they scare off easy, but this one, he's tenacious. He is not giving up. It's kicking up all her issues."

"Wow," I said. "Sounds intense."

"Everything is, where she's concerned," he replied. "Look, Aud, I gotta get back inside for this brainstorming session. But seriously. Give her another shot."

"Hollis. I don't . . ."

"At least consider it, then. For me?"

I didn't feel like I owed Hollis all that much, to be honest. So I suppose it said something about his people skills that I still heard myself say, "All right. I'll think about it."

"Thank you. And hey, call me later, all right? I want to hear what else is going on."

I assured him that I would, and then he was gone, back into his meeting. And I kept my word, and did think about talking to my mom. I decided against it. But I did consider it.

Then it was back to the same old, same old. I tried to steer clear of Heidi, who had thrown herself full throttle into planning the Beach Bash. Ignored my parents' messages. Read another chapter, did another set of study questions. Turned off the light when I felt my eyes get heavy and then lay there in the dark, never believing that sleep would come until the exact moment when it did. The only time I let my mind go to anything other than school and work, actually, was when I was on the bike. And then, I thought only of Eli.

Since that day we'd blown past him on the boardwalk, I'd seen him a handful of times. He was passing by the front windows of Clementine's as I took stuff out of the register, or standing in front of the shop, showing a bike to a prospective customer. It was easy to tell myself that we were only not talking because we were so busy with other things, and I could almost believe that. But then I'd remember what I'd said to him about slacking off, and the look on his face just before he'd walked away from me, and I knew otherwise. This was my choice, my decision. He was the closest thing I'd ever had to something, or someone, that mattered. But in the end, close didn't count. You were either in, or you weren't.

What I thought about most, though, when I was on

the bike, was my quest. At the time, it had seemed like a silly little game, something to pass the time, but now, I was understanding it was so much more than that. Night after night, task after task, he'd helped me to return to my past and make some things—if not everything—right. Eli had given me all these second chances, presented like a gift. In the end, though, I was one short. Still, as I pedaled around the jump park lot, Maggie either holding on or right behind me, I wished I could just show him this one thing. I knew it wouldn't make up for everything else. But for some reason, I wanted him to know anyway.

So in the mornings, I practiced my riding, slowly gaining speed and confidence. At night, I sat in front of my laptop, searching for clips on LiveVid of him in one competition after another. Watching him move across the screen, so quick and sure, it hardly seemed like they could be related, my fledgling efforts and his complete skill and mastery. But at their core, they were the same thing. Each was about propelling yourself forward, into whatever lies ahead, one turn of the wheel at a time.

*   *   *

First, there was squealing. Then, giggling. But it wasn't until I heard the music start up that I put down my pen and went to investigate.

It was ten fifteen, and I was doing what I always did in the evenings, these days: getting ready to do some schoolwork. After finishing up the books at Clementine's, I'd grabbed a sandwich from Beach Beans, which I ate alone in the kitchen, savoring the fact that I had the house to myself. Once I was settled and ten minutes into *World Economic Theory and Practices*, though, I suddenly had company. The loud kind.

I went halfway down the stairs, then peered into the kitchen to see a crowd. Heidi, in shorts and a black tank top, was piling plastic bags on the kitchen table as Isby, strapped in her stroller, watched. A blonde Heidi's age was popping a beer as another girl, a brunette, dumped some tortilla chips into a bowl. Maggie, Leah, and Esther were all seated around the table, more plastic bags piled up in front of them.

There's a certain sound that can only be made by a group of women. It's not just chatter, or even conversation, but almost a melody of words and exhalations. I'd spent a lot of my life listening to it from just this kind of distance, but still, it never failed to make me acutely aware of every bit of the space between me and its source. At the same time, though, this was where I preferred to be, which was why it was so unsettling when Heidi looked up and spotted me.

"Auden," she called out as someone turned up the music, which sounded like salsa, fast with a lot of horns. "Hey. Come join us!"

Before I could react, everyone had turned and looked at me, making a fast retreat not just awkward but impossible. "Um," I said. "I—"

"This is Isabel," she continued, pointing at the blonde, who nodded at me. Then she gestured to the brunette.

"And this is Morgan. My oldest friends in Colby. Guys, this is Auden, Robert's daughter."

"So nice to finally meet you!" Morgan said. "Heidi just raves about you. Raves!"

"Did you get my messages?" Heidi asked as she lifted Isby out of her stroller. "I tried to let you know we were coming, but your mailbox was full."

"Wow," Leah said, raising her eyebrows. "Someone's popular."

"Actually," I said as Esther upended a bag onto the table, spilling out a pile of little picture frames, "I'm making a bunch of calls right now."

"Oh. Well, when you're done, then." Heidi reached over, taking the beer that Isabel was offering her as Morgan put the chips on the table. "We'll be here, I'm sure. We've got at least three hundred favors to make."

"Three hundred?" Leah said. She narrowed her eyes at Maggie. "You said . . ."

"I said it would be fun, and it will be," Maggie replied. "What else were you going to do tonight, anyway?"

"A lot of things! It's Ladies' Night at Tallyho."

"No, no, no to Tallyho," Esther said, picking up a picture frame.

"Amen to that," Isabel agreed. "That place gives me the skeevies."

Back in my room, I picked up my pen again and tried to immerse myself in the politics of global currency. After a few bursts of laughter from downstairs, I got up and shut the door. I could still hear the music through the floor, though, the beat insistent and distracting. Finally, I picked up my phone, flipping it open and dialing into my mailbox.

Heidi was right: it was full, mostly with old messages from my parents I'd never gotten around to really listening to. I worked my way through them, one by one, my eyes on the dark ocean outside.

"Auden, hello, it's your mother. I'll try you again later, I suppose."

Delete.

"Hi, honey, it's your dad. Just taking a break from doing some revisions, thought I'd give you a call. I'll be here in the room all day if you want to call or drop by. I'll keep an eye out for you."

Delete.

"Auden, this is your mother. Your brother is now working at a bank. I hope you are adequately horrified. Good-bye."

Delete.

"Hi, Auden, Dad here again. Wondering if you might want to meet at the Last Chance, I'm getting a little sick of room service. Give me a call, okay?"

Delete.

"Auden. I am getting tired of your voice mail. I will not be calling again until I hear from you."

Delete.

"Honey, Dad again. I guess I'll call the house number, maybe you're not answering this one anymore?"

Delete.

They just went on and on, endlessly, and yet I felt nothing as I kept hitting the same button, erasing them. Until I got to this one.

"Oh, Auden. You are clearly avoiding me." There was a sigh, as familiar to me as my own face. Then, though, she said, "I suppose this is what I deserve? As always, I seem to be especially adept at alienating the few people I actually want to talk to. I don't know why that is. Maybe you've figured it out, in your summer of transformation? I wonder. . . ."

I pulled the phone away, looking down at it. This message was from two days ago, at around five P.M. Where had I been, when she'd left it? Probably alone as well, in the office at Clementine's, here in my room, or somewhere in between.

I thought of my mother, sitting at her kitchen table, with Hollis off working at a bank, and me, for all she knew, riding in a car with boys while wearing a pink bikini. How different we had to be from what she had expected, or planned, all those days when, like Heidi, she rocked us and carried us and cared for us. It was so easy to disown what you couldn't recognize, to keep yourself apart from things that were foreign and unsettling. The only person you can be sure to control, always, is yourself. Which is a lot to be sure of, but at the same time, not enough.

Now, as there was another round of laughter from downstairs, I hit number one on my speed dial, and waited.

"Hello?"

"Mom, it's me."

A pause. Then, "Auden. How are you?"

"I'm okay," I said. It felt strange, talking to her after all this time. "How are you?"

"Well," she said. "I suppose I am okay, also."

My mother was not the touchy-feely type. Never had been. But there was something in her voice, in that message, that gave me the courage to say what I did next.

"Mom? Can I ask you something?"

I could hear her hesitate before she said, "Yes. Of course."

"When you and Dad decided to split up, was that . . . did you do it right away? Or did you, like, try and work it out for a long time first?"

I don't know what she'd been expecting me to ask. But based on the long silence that followed, it wasn't this. Finally she said, "We tried very hard to stay together. The divorce was not a decision we made lightly, if that's what you're asking. Is that what you're asking?"

"I don't know." I looked down at my book, my pad lined up beside it. "I guess . . . forget it. I'm sorry."

"No, no, it's all right." Her voice was closer to the phone now, filling my ear. "Auden, what's going on? Why are you thinking about this now?"

I was embarrassed, suddenly, to realize that I had a lump in my throat. God, what was wrong with me? I swallowed, then said, "It's just . . . Dad and Heidi are having problems."

"Problems," she repeated. "What kind of problems?"

From downstairs, I heard another round of laughter. I said, "He moved out a couple of weeks ago."

She exhaled slowly, the kind of sound someone makes as they watch a baseball fly over a fence, way, way gone. "Oh, my. I'm sorry to hear that."

"Are you?"

I said this without really realizing it, and instantly regretted how surprised I sounded. Her tone was a bit sharper as she said, "Well, of course. One never likes to see a marriage in trouble, especially when a child is involved."

And just like that, I was crying. The tears just came, filling my eyes and spilling over, and I sucked in a breath in an attempt to maintain my composure.

"Auden? Are you all right?"

I looked out my window at the ocean again, so steady and vast, seemingly never changing and yet always in flux. "I guess I just wish," I said, my voice wavering, "that I'd done some things differently."

"Ah," she said. Like she understood totally, even with so little given. Subtext, indeed. "Don't we all."

Maybe with normal mothers and daughters, it was more straightforward. They had the kind of back-and-forth that left no ambiguity or question, saying exactly what they meant, when they meant it. But my mom and I weren't normal, so this—stilted and vague as it might be—was the closest we'd come to each other in ages. It was like reaching out for someone's hand, then missing their fingers, or even their arm, and hitting their shoulder instead. But no matter. You hang on tight anyway.

For a moment, we just sat there on the line, neither of us saying anything. Finally I said, "I should go. My friends are downstairs."

"Of course." She coughed. "Call me tomorrow, though?"

"Yes. Absolutely."

"All right. Good night, Auden."

"Good night."

I closed my phone, then put it on the bed, on top of my textbook, and walked over to the door. As I went down the hallway and then the stairs, I could hear that same familiar melody, playing louder than ever.

" . . . just don't understand why suddenly we're all acting like prom night was so great," Isabel was saying.

"Because it was," Morgan replied.

"For some of you."

"Exactly," Esther said. "Some of us got stuck with drunk dates who never made it out of the parking lot."

Morgan snorted. Isabel said, "Shut up."

"Personally," Heidi was saying, "I think prom is one of those high school things that you either really loved or really hated. Like high school itself."

"I loved high school," Maggie said.

"Of course you did," Leah told her. "You dated the hottest guy, you had the best grades, and everyone loved you."

"You never wanted everyone to love you," Esther said to Leah.

"I wouldn't have minded if *somebody* did, though," she replied.

"My high school boyfriend broke my heart, remember," Maggie told her.

"Mine, too!" Morgan sighed. "God, that sucked."

"He was a tool," Isabel told her. "Way too much hair gel."

Now Esther snorted. Leah said, "Shut up."

"See, though," Heidi said, "this is why this is such a good

theme! People who loved prom can relive the experience. People who hated it get another shot. Everyone wins."

"Except the losers stuck doing three hundred favors," Leah grumbled. Then she looked up and saw me. "Hey. You decide to come be a loser, too?"

I swallowed, aware of Heidi looking at me, noticing my red eyes, her expression suddenly concerned. "You bet," I said.

Maggie scooted over in her chair, making a space for me, and I sat down beside her. "So," Isabel said. "Auden. Prom love or prom hate?"

"Prom hate," I replied. "I got stood up."

There was a round of gasps. "You what?" Morgan said. "That's terrible!"

"And," Leah added, "the guy is down here now and won't stop texting her."

"You know what you should do," Morgan said. "You should ask him to the Beach Bash, and then stand *him* up."

"Morgan." Isabel raised her eyebrows. "Listen to you, going all vigilante!"

"I think," Heidi said, "that you should find someone you really want to go with, and do it right. That's my opinion."

"I don't know," I said. "I think it's a little late for that."

"Not necessarily," Leah told me. "It's Ladies' Night at Tallyho."

I smiled. "No, no, no to Tallyho."

"That's my girl!" Maggie beamed, then bumped me with her shoulder.

Everyone laughed, and just like that, the conversation

shifted, jumping to another topic. It was fast and furious, the talking, the emotion, the back-and-forth and forth-and-back. I realized that if I tried to focus on it too much, I got overwhelmed. So I just decided to relax into it, bumpy and crazy as it might be, and try for once to just go along for the ride.

sixteen

"WOW. NICE ROAD burn."

I looked up to see Adam standing in the doorway to Heidi's office, a box under one arm. "Well," I said, putting down my tube of Neosporin, which I'd been applying to the latest scrape on my shin, the result of a wobbly crash that morning. "I guess that's one way of looking at it."

"It's the only way." He put the box down on the file cabinet, then yanked up his shirt, showing me a scar on his stomach. "See this? Seventh grade, wiped out on a ramp. And then here"—he slid up his shirtsleeve, showing another shiny white spot—"I crashed on a mountain bike trail when I hit a log."

"Ouch."

"But the pièce de résistance," he continued, tapping his chest, "is right here. All titanium, baby."

I just looked at him. "What is?"

"The plate they used to put my sternum back together," he replied cheerfully. "Two years ago. Broke it with my full-face helmet going over a jump."

"You know," I said, considering my scrape again, "you're kind of making me look like a wimp."

"Not at all!" He smiled. "It all counts. If you're not getting hurt, you're not riding hard enough."

"Then I," I said, "am riding really hard."

"That's what I hear," he said, picking up the box again.
"Maggie says you're like an animal out there."

I was horrified. "She what?"

"I'm paraphrasing," he said easily, flipping his hand. "She
says you're really working hard, that you're doing great."

I shrugged, capping the Neosporin. "I don't know. If I
was good, I wouldn't be all banged up like this."

"Not true."

I looked up at him. "No?"

He shook his head. "Of course not. Look at me. I'm
a great rider, and I've bit dirt more times than I can even
count. And the pros? They're, like, bionic, they've crashed
so much. Look at Eli. He's broken his elbow, and his collarbone multiple times, and then there's that arm thing. . . ."

"Wait," I said. "The arm thing? You mean the scar?"

"Yeah."

"I thought that was from the accident."

Adam shook his head. "No. He was doing some tricks
out on the pier and landed wrong. Sliced it wide open on
the edge of a bench. There was blood *everywhere*."

I looked back down at my knee scab, small and almost a
perfect circle, shiny with ointment.

"It all counts," Adam said again. "And the bottom line
is, what defines you isn't how many times you crash, but the
number of times you get back on the bike. As long as it's one
more, you're all good."

I smiled, looking up at him. "You know," I said, "you

should be a motivational speaker, or something."

"Nah. Entirely too dorky," he replied easily. "Hey, is Heidi around?"

"No. She's at lunch." I didn't add that she was with my dad, their first formal meeting since he moved out. Heidi had been so nervous all morning, walking around the store, straightening displays and hovering over me in the office, that I'd been relieved when she finally strapped Isby into the BabyBjörn and headed off. As soon as the door shut behind her, though, I'd gotten uneasy myself, wondering what she'd have to say when she returned. "She'll be back in an hour or so, probably."

"Oh. Well, I can just leave these, then." He put the box down on the desk to my left. When I glanced at them, he added, "Prom shots from my yearbook days. She said she wants them for decor for the Beach Bash, or something."

"Really," I said. "Can I take a look?"

"Sure."

I lifted the lid. Inside was a big stack of pictures, mostly five-by-sevens, all black and white. The one on the top was of Maggie, standing with Jake by the tailgate of a car. She had on a short, dark A-line dress and strappy heels, her hair spilling over her shoulders. There was a corsage on her wrist and she was laughing, holding out a bag of Doritos to Jake, who was in a tux shirt and pants, barefoot on the sand. I flipped to the next picture: also Maggie, this time alone, the same night, standing on tiptoe to check her reflection in a mirror that said COCA-COLA across its center. In the next shot, there was Leah, in a more formal pose with a guy in a military uniform, both of them looking at the camera, followed by one of Wallace on a dance floor, cummerbund loose, in the midst of busting some sort of move. Then Maggie again, another year, in another dress, this one white and longer. In the first shot, she was walking down the boardwalk, holding the hand of someone whose shoulder alone made it into the picture. In the one beneath it, she was reaching out for the camera, fingers blurred, her mouth half-open as she laughed.

"Wow," I said as I kept flipping through them. There was Leah again. Esther. Maggie. Wallace and Leah. Jake and Esther. Maggie. Wallace and Esther. Maggie. Maggie. Maggie. I looked up at him. "You're not in any of these."

"Nah. I was always behind the camera."

I moved past yet another shot of Maggie, this time on a bike, her white dress gathered up in one hand, her helmet in the other. "Lots of her here."

He kept his eyes on the picture, his tone noncommittal, as he said, "I guess so."

"What are you guys looking at?"

Adam and I both jumped as Maggie herself—in the flesh and flip-flops and jeans—appeared behind us in the doorway. "Prom pictures," I told her, casually flipping back to the one of Leah and Wallace. "Heidi wanted them for the Beach Bash."

"Oh, no." She sighed, then stepped forward to lean over my shoulder. "I can't bear to . . . look! Junior year. Leah's date was that marine, remember?"

Adam nodded. "I do."

"And I had my white dress. I *loved* that dress." She sighed again, this time happily, and reached over me to flip to the next picture. "There it is! Man. I agonized over that outfit like you would not believe. Kept it clean all night, even when I was on a bike on a dare. And then Jake threw up all over it on the way home. The stain . . . "

"Never came out," Adam finished for her. "I have a shot of it somewhere."

"Hopefully not in this box." She plucked out the one of her on the bike. "That was a great night, though. I mean, until the end. What other ones are in there? Any more of me?"

I felt Adam glance at me as I eased the box shut, saying, "Not really."

"Oh," she said. "Well, I guess that's a good thing. I don't think I necessarily want my prom memories up on display for the whole town to see anyway."

"No?" I said. "It seems like you had a pretty good time."

She shrugged. "I guess. But I was with Jake then. The last thing I need right now is another reminder of how much of my life I wasted on him."

"You were happy at the time, though," I said. "That has to count for something."

"I don't know," Maggie said. "Lately I've been thinking it would have been better to have just been by myself. That way, at least all of high school wouldn't be, you know, tinged with his memory."

"*Tinged?*" Adam said. "Is that even a real word?"

"You know what I mean," she said, poking his arm. "Anyway, my point is that if I'd wised up to what he was sooner, my entire experience might have been different."

"Yeah," I said. "You could have spent all of high school alone, and never gone to prom at all."

"Exactly," she replied. "And that might have been good, too. Or even better."

I looked down at the box again, remembering all those shots inside, trying to picture myself in even one of them. What if I'd had a boyfriend? What if I'd gone to the prom? What kind of tinge could I have had, given another chance? "Maybe," I said to Maggie. "Or maybe not."

She gave me a weird look, then opened her mouth to say something, but then the front door chime sounded. "Duty calls," she said, turning on her heel, and then she was thwacking back down the hallway, her voice cheery as she greeted a group of customers.

Adam watched her go, then leaned back in the doorjamb. "You know," he said, "if you want to remedy that, you can."

I looked up at him. "Remedy what?"

"The whole not-going-to-the-prom thing," he said. "Eli's at the shop right now, doing inventory."

"What," I said, "are you *talking* about?"

"You just walk over there and into the office and say, 'Hey, be my prom date,'" he said. "It's that simple."

I wanted to tell him that nothing concerning me and Eli was simple, especially lately. Instead, I said, "What makes you think I want to go with him?"

"Because," he said, "you're sitting here going on about spending high school alone, never going to prom at all. . . . It was kind of obvious who you were talking about."

"Maggie. I was talking about Maggie."

He crossed his arms over his chest. "Sure you were."

I just looked at him for a second. Then I said, "Well, what about you?"

"Me?"

I nodded. "When are you planning to ask her?"

"Ask her what?"

I rolled my eyes.

"Oh, no. We're just friends."

"Right." I opened up the box again and started flipping through the pictures, taking out the one of her on the bike, and walking, and laughing, and in front of the mirror, laying them on the desk side by side. "Because, of course, you took this many pictures of all your *friends*."

He glanced at the shots, then swallowed. "Actually," he said stiffly, "I do have a lot of shots of Wallace."

"Adam. Come on."

I watched as, defeated, he slumped into the chair, folding his arms behind his head. For a moment we just sat there, neither of us saying anything. Outside, I could hear Maggie chattering on the pros and cons of one-piece bathing suits. "The thing is," he said finally, "I've made it this far, you know? We start college in a matter of weeks."

"So?"

"So," he continued, "I just don't know if I want that tinge on the summer. Not to mention our friendship. An *awkward* tinge, that will then color everything else."

"You're assuming she'll say no."

"No," he said, "I'm assuming she'll say yes, because she'll figure it'll be fun. And then I'll work it up to be this big deal, like it's a real date, which is not how she'll see it, which will become crushingly obvious at the prom itself when she abandons me to dance, and then leave, and eventually marry some other guy."

Outside, Maggie laughed, the sound light and cheery, like music.

"Well," I said. "At least you haven't put much thought into it."

He gave me a wry smile. "Just like you haven't thought about asking Eli, right?"

"I haven't."

He rolled his eyes.

"No, really. We had a falling-out. . . . We're not even talking right now."

"Well, then. You know what you need to do."

I said, "I do?"

"Yep." He pushed himself to his feet. "Get back on that bike."

I just looked at him. "It's not that simple."

"Sure it is," he said. "Just takes one more time. Remember?"

I considered this as he started for the door, sliding his hands in his pockets. "On the same note," I said, "there's a worse thing than an awkward tinge."

"Yeah?"

I nodded.

"What's that?"

"Always wondering if it might have gone the other way." I nodded at the prom shots, still laid out in front of me. "That *is* a lot of pictures. You know?"

He glanced at them, then back at me. "Yeah," he said. "I guess it is."

My phone beeped then, and I glanced down at it. Jason.

Are you free for lunch? I'm en route to the Last Chance, have an hour.

"Gotta go," Adam said. Then he pointed at the scab on my knee. "Remember. Back on the bike!"

"Right," I replied. "Got it."

He flashed me a thumbs-up, then was gone, whistling—always so damn cheery, how was that?—as he headed back toward the front of the store. I looked down at Maggie's pictures, end to end, and then at my phone, where Jason's text was still on the screen. I knew I'd really screwed up with Eli, turning away from him the way I had, but perhaps it wasn't too late to have a tinge of my own. Maybe good, maybe bad, but at least it would add some color, somewhere. So I picked up my phone and gave Jason his answer.

Okay. On my way.

*   *   *

When I got home that evening, Heidi was on the back deck, looking out at the water. Even from a distance and through the sliding glass door, I recognized the tenseness in her shoulders, the way her head leaned a little sadly to the side, and so was not surprised when she turned, hearing me, to see her eyes were red and puffy.

"Auden," she said, reaching to brush back her hair, taking a breath. "I didn't think you'd be home until later."

"I finished up early." I slid my keys into my bag. "Are you okay?"

"I'm fine." She came inside, shutting the door behind her. "Just doing some thinking."

We stood there for a moment, neither of us saying anything. Upstairs, I could hear Thisbe's waves, crashing. "So . . . how did it go?"

"Good." She swallowed, biting her lip. "We did a lot of talking."

"And?"

"And," she said, "we agreed that for the time being, it's better if we keep things as they are."

"With him at the Condor," I said, clarifying. She nodded. "So he didn't want to come back."

She walked over to me, putting her hands on my shoulders. "Your father . . . he thinks he'd be a hindrance more than a help right now. That maybe, until the Beach Bash and summer is over, it's better if I just focus on me and Thisbe."

"How could that be better?" I asked. "You're his family."

She bit her lip again, then looked down at her hands. "I know it doesn't sound like it makes sense."

"It doesn't."

"But I understand what he's saying," she continued. "Your father and I . . . we had a whirlwind courtship and marriage, and I got pregnant so fast. We just need to slow down a bit."

I put my purse down on the table. "So this is a slowing. Not a full stop."

Heidi nodded. "Absolutely."

To be honest, I wasn't fully convinced. I knew my dad and how he operated: if things got complicated, he extricated himself, somehow managing to make it seem like it was the most selfless of gestures, instead of just the opposite. He wasn't abandoning Heidi and Thisbe: he was simplifying their lives. He hadn't left my mom over professional envy: he'd stepped aside to give her the spotlight she needed. And he certainly hadn't basically ignored the fact that I was his child all those years: he was just teaching me to be independent and a grown-up in a world in which most people were too infantile. My dad never got back on the bike. He never even let himself crash. One wobble, or even the hint of one, and he pulled over to the side, abandoning the ride altogether.

"So," Heidi said, pulling out a chair and sitting down at the table, "enough about me. What's going on with *you*?"

I slid in opposite her, folding my hands on top of my bag. "Well," I said, "it looks like I have a date to the prom."

"Really?" She clapped her hands. "That's great!"

"Yeah. Jason just asked me."

She blinked. "Jason . . . "

"My friend from home," I said. She still looked quizzical, so I picked up my phone, flashing it at her. "The texter."

"Oh! The one who stood you up!"

I nodded.

"Well. That's very . . . "

"Lame?" I said.

"I was going to say full circle, actually, or something to that effect," she said slowly. "What, you don't want to go?"

"No, I do." I looked down at my hands again. "I mean,

it's a second chance. I think I'd be stupid not to take it."

"True." She sat back, running a hand through her hair. "They don't come around that often."

I nodded, thinking of Jason at the Last Chance, how he'd been waiting for me in a booth and smiled broadly when I came in the door. Over burgers and onion rings, he'd gone on and on about the leadership conference, and how great it was going, and listening to him felt so familiar, but not in a bad way. It was like reversing, going back to the spring when we'd shared lunches and talked about school and classes. And when he cleared his throat and said he had something to ask me, that was familiar, too, and I'd agreed easily. It was just that simple.

Now, I looked at Heidi, who was staring out the window over the sink, and remembered how I'd once seen her based on her effervescent e-mails and girly clothes, all flash, no substance. I'd thought I knew so much when I'd arrived here, the smartest girl in the room. But I'd been wrong.

"Hey," I said, "can I ask you something?"

She looked over at me. "Of course."

"A few weeks back," I began, "you said something about how my mom wasn't a truly cold bitch. How she couldn't be, because they always end up alone. Do you remember that?"

Heidi furrowed her brow, thinking. "Vaguely."

"And then you said you knew all about cold bitches, because you used to be one yourself."

"Right," she said. "So what's your question?"

"I guess . . . " I stopped, taking a breath. "Were you really, though?"

"A cold bitch?" she asked.

I nodded.

"Oh, yeah. Totally."

"I just can't picture that," I said. "I mean, you that way."

Heidi smiled. "Well, you didn't know me before I came here and met your father. I was just out of business school, totally uptight. Ruthless, actually. I was killing myself gaining capital so I could open a boutique in New York. I had a business plan, and all these investor contacts, a loan, the whole deal. Nothing else mattered."

"I never knew you lived in New York."

"It was my plan, after I graduated," she said. "But then my mom got sick, and I had to come home here to Colby for the summer to take care of her. I'd known Isabel and Morgan since high school, so I got a job with them waiting tables, just to make some extra cash for my move."

"You worked at the Last Chance?"

"That's how I met your dad," she said. "He'd just had his faculty interview at Weymar and came in for lunch. It was slow, so we started talking. And it just went from there. At the end of the summer, my mom got better for a little while, so I said good-bye to your dad and left. But once I was in New York, it just didn't feel right. I didn't have the hunger for it anymore."

"Really."

She drew in a breath. "I'd come here planning to leave as soon as I could. It was a pit stop, not a destination. I had my whole life mapped out."

"So what happened?"

"I guess that map didn't turn out to be mine after all,"

she said. "So I left New York, married your dad, and used my money to open Clementine's. And weird as it sounds, it felt perfectly right. Totally different, but perfectly right."

I thought of her face when I'd come home that night, the sad way she'd told me about her talk with my dad. "Does it still? Feel right, I mean."

She looked at me for a moment. Then she said, "Actually, yes. Of course, I wish things were different with your dad and me right now. But I have Thisbe, and my work. . . . I have what I wanted, even if it isn't perfect. If I'd stayed in New York, I would have always wondered if that was possible."

"No tinge," I said.

"What?"

I shook my head. "Nothing."

Heidi pushed her chair out, getting to her feet. "In the end, I went away for the summer, fell in love, and everything changed. It's the oldest story in the world."

The way she was looking at me as she said this made me suddenly uncomfortable, and I turned my attention back to my purse in my lap. "Yeah," I replied, pulling my phone out. "I guess I have heard that before."

In response, she said nothing, instead just running a hand over the top of my head as she passed by me. "Good night, Auden," she said, stifling a yawn. "Sleep well."

"You, too."

And the thing was, I knew I would. Sleep, that is, and maybe even well. That was one thing that had definitely changed for me in my time here. The love part, and everything else . . . that didn't apply. But you never knew. I had a prom date, with it another chance to draw my own map. The summer wasn't over yet, so maybe the story wasn't either.

✳   ✳   ✳

"Okay," Leah said, hiking up her dress to examine the hem. "I am having major flashbacks right now. Didn't we just do this?"

"We did," Esther told her. "In May."

"And *why* are we doing it again?"

"Because it's the Beach Bash!" Maggie said.

"That's a statement, not an explanation," Leah replied. "And it's definitely not reason enough to go through all this again."

We were in Heidi's bedroom, where she'd sent us after hearing us complain, en masse, about not being able to find anything decent to wear to the Beach Bash Prom. My stepmother continued to surprise me. Not only was she a former cold bitch, but a shopaholic, as well. She had *tons* of dresses, in a variety of sizes, that she'd bought over the years. Vintage, classic, entirely eighties, you name it and it was there.

"We need dates, too, remember," Leah said. "Unless Heidi's got some hot guys tucked away behind those shoe boxes."

"You never know," I said, peering into the deep recesses of the closet. "At this point, I wouldn't be surprised."

"Dates aren't mandatory, this time," Maggie said. "Let's just all go together. It'll be easier not having to deal with boys anyway."

Leah shot her a look. "No way. If I'm having to get all

dolled up and wear a nice dress, I want a cute boy to go with it. It's a deal breaker."

"Well," I said, opening up the other side closet door, "tonight *is* Ladies' Night at Tallyho."

"Finally!" Leah pointed at me. "Someone understands."

"Easy for her to say," Esther said. "She's the only one with a date."

"But not a dress," I replied, pulling out a black, low-cut sheath, then immediately putting it back. It was a small detail, I knew. And it wasn't like this was a real prom. But it would probably be the only one I'd ever attend, so I was determined to make the most of it. So far, though, everything I'd found had been too something: too bright, too short, too long, too much.

"Oh, man!" Esther spun around, holding against herself a pink fifties-style dress with a full, stiff crinoline. "How much will you bet me to wear this without any sense of irony?"

"You have to," Maggie said, reaching out to touch the skirt. "God. It's perfect for you."

"Only if you wear that black one you had on earlier, the Audrey Hepburn–looking one," Esther told her.

"You think? It's so dressy."

"So wear flip-flops with it. They are your trademark."

Maggie walked over, picking up the black dress from the bed. "That could work. What do you think, Leah?"

"I think," Leah, who was pulling a bright red number over her tank top, said, "that if I'm going to go to this thing dateless, I could wear a garbage bag and it wouldn't matter."

"Why do you need a guy to dress up?" Maggie asked. "Aren't we, your oldest and dearest friends, good enough company?"

"Maggie." Leah yanked the dress down farther. "It's a prom. Not a sisterhood retreat."

"And this may be the last big thing we all do together before college. It's almost August, the summer is practically over."

"Don't," Esther threatened, pointing at her. "Remember the rules. No waxing nostalgic until the twentieth. We agreed."

"I know, I know," Maggie said, fluttering her hands in front of her face. She walked over to the bed, sitting down with the black dress across her lap. "I just . . . I can't believe that it's all really going to be over soon. This time next year, everything will be different."

"God, I hope so."

"Leah!"

Leah looked over from the mirror, where she was eyeing her reflection. "What? So I'm hoping a year from now I'll have a great boyfriend and total life satisfaction. A girl can dream, can't she?"

"This is not so bad, though," Maggie said. "What we have, and had. It's not."

"No," I said, pushing aside another couple of dresses. "It isn't."

I just sort of said this, not really thinking. It wasn't until the room got quiet that I realized they were all looking at me. "See," Maggie said, nodding at me. "Auden understands."

"She understood about Tallyho, too," Leah grumbled. "Not that anyone else cared about *that*."

"Seriously, though." Maggie looked at me. "She didn't get to do all this, back then. If you need a reason to go to the prom, and dress up, and do it all over again, do it for Auden. She missed it the first time around."

Leah glanced at me, then back at her reflection. "I don't know," she said. "It's a lot to ask."

"So what," Esther said, bouncing up and down, her crinoline rustling. "It gives you an excuse to go to Tallyho."

"True," Leah agreed.

"You don't have to, you know," I said to Maggie, who was watching me as I pulled on another dress. "I've got Jason to go with. I'll be fine."

"No way," she replied. "For the true prom experience, you need your friends there."

"Because who else *but* your friends," Esther said, "would agree to help you re-create your past, just to fix some wrong that's been niggling you ever since?"

"Nobody," Leah said.

"Nobody," Maggie repeated.

They were all looking at me. "Nobody," I said, although I could think of one other answer besides this one, even if I couldn't say it out loud.

Even with my affirmation, though, they continued to stare at me, to the point that I started to wonder if I had ink on my face, or my underwear was showing. I was just about to do a panicked mirror check when Maggie said, "Wow. Auden. That's the one."

"The what?" I said.

"Your dress," Esther said, nodding at me. "It looks amazing."

I looked down at the purple dress I'd pulled on moments earlier, which I hadn't even really looked at that closely, yanking it from the closet only because it was not red or black or white, like everything else I'd tried on. Now, though, as I stepped in front of the mirror, I saw that it did fit me pretty well. The neckline was flattering, the skirt full, and I liked how it brought out my eyes. It wasn't a dress to stop traffic, but maybe I didn't need that anyway.

"Really?" I said.

"Definitely." Maggie came over to stand beside me, reaching out a hand to touch the skirt. "Don't you like it?"

I studied my reflection. I'd never been one for dresses or bold colors, and had never owned anything that shade of purple before in my life. I looked like a different girl. But maybe that was the point. And like having the right snacks, for a true adventure, the proper attire is everything.

"Yeah," I said, reaching down with my fingers to pull the skirt to one side. When I dropped it, it swished back, rearranging itself, as if it already knew where it belonged. "It's perfect."

seventeen

THE MORNING OF the Beach Bash, I woke at eight A.M. to the sound of Isby crying through our shared wall. I rolled over, burying my head in the pillow, and waited for Heidi to come and quiet her down. A few minutes later, the crying turned to sobbing, and I began to wonder what was going on. When she started to all-out scream, I went to investigate.

I found her on her back in her crib, red faced, hair matted down with sweat. When she saw me lean over her, she yelled louder, waving her arms madly in front of her face. When I picked her up, cradling her against me, she quieted down, emitting only a bunch of little gasps, like hiccups.

"You're okay," I told her, jiggling her slightly as I stuck my head out in the hallway. No sign yet of Heidi, which was sort of worrisome, so I went back in and changed the baby's diaper, which cheered her up considerably. Then I swaddled her up and headed downstairs, where I came upon Heidi sitting at the kitchen table, boxes of prom favors stacked all around her, the phone to her ear.

"Yes, Robert, I understand your predicament," she was saying as she fiddled with a coffee mug in front of her. "But the truth is I was counting on you, and I don't know if I can find someone else on such short notice."

I could hear my dad's voice, distant, replying to this through the receiver. It made me realize how long it had been since I'd spoken to him: a week, maybe even two. He'd finally got the message of my not replying to his messages, though. My voice mail had been empty for a while now.

"You know what," she said suddenly, "it's fine. I'll just find someone. No, don't worry about it. Really. But I need to go now. I have a ton of stuff to do today, and . . ."

She stopped talking, and I heard my dad's voice again. Whatever he was saying, it elicited nothing from Heidi but a sigh and a shake of her head.

I hesitated, wondering if I should just go back upstairs. But then Isby let out a squawk, and Heidi turned, spotting us.

" . . . I have to go," she said, then hung up without a good-bye. She pushed out her chair. "Oh, Auden, I'm so sorry she woke you up! I thought I heard her, but I was on the phone and . . ."

"It's fine," I said as she reached for the baby, smiling at her as she lifted her from my arms. "I was kind of up anyway."

"You and me both." She tucked Isby over her shoulder, patting her back as she walked to the coffeemaker, pouring herself a fresh cup, then one for me. As she handed it over, she said, "I jolted awake at four, thinking about everything I had to do in the next fifteen hours. And of course, then when I was feeling just a *little* bit on top of things, your father called to say he can't watch the baby tonight after all, because he's got to jet off to New York to meet with his agent first thing Monday morning about his book."

I considered this as she sat down at the table again, arranging Thisbe in her lap. "Well," I said. "I can stay with her, if you want."

"You?" She shook her head. "Of course not! You're going to the Beach Bash."

"I don't have to."

"Yes you do! You have a date and everything."

I shrugged, looking down at my coffee.

"What's wrong? I thought you were excited."

I wasn't sure exactly how to explain the hesitation that had come over me ever since I'd found my dress. It was just this weird sad feeling, like the prom had already fallen short before it even happened. "I don't know," I said. "I guess it's just that it's not the real prom, you know? I mean, it'll be fun and everything. But it won't be the same as if I'd gone the first time around, to the real one."

Heidi considered this, still patting Isby's back. "Well, I guess you could look at it that way," she said. "Or, you *could* realize you're lucky to have another try, and that it's up to you to make it memorable."

"Yeah," I said. "I guess."

"Look," she said, putting down her cup. "The basic fact of the matter is that no, this isn't ideal. Very few things are. Sometimes, you have to manufacture your own history. Give fate a push, so to speak. You know?"

Right away, I thought of me and Eli, working our way down my quest. Each of those things—bowling, food fights, tossing newspapers—had happened late and out of order, not exactly as they probably should have. But the memories and experiences were no less real because of it. If anything, they were more special, because they hadn't happened to me, but because of me. And him.

"You know what?" I said to Heidi. "You're absolutely right."

"Am I?" She smiled. "Well, that's a nice thing to hear. Especially considering the day I still have ahead of me."

"It'll be fine," I told her, drinking down the rest of my coffee and going for a refill. On the way, I picked up her cup, taking it with me. "I'm up and ready to help. What can I do?"

She groaned, pulling a yellow legal pad out of one of the favor boxes and flipping up a page. "Well, there are favors to bring to the hall. And the punch bowl to pick up. And the DJ to meet at ten A.M. for a sound check. Oh, and the balloon people are demanding payment before they'll do anything, and now I have to find a babysitter. . . ."

I slid her now-full mug in front of her, then took my seat again. In her arms, Isby looked at me, and I reached out, running a hand over her head. Her skin was warm and soft, and she kept her eyes on me for a moment before tucking in tighter to her mother's chest and closing them, drifting off even in the midst of everything.

❊   ❊   ❊

By noon, I'd dealt with the balloon people, made two trips to the hall where the prom was happening, and pulled a muscle in my shoulder helping Heidi move the photo backdrop—a large, wooden fake wave dotted with fish made by the local senior arts group—into place. I was sticky and sore and on my way back to the house to pick up a box of punch glasses when I saw Jason.

He was getting out of his car, which was parked right by the top of the boardwalk. When he turned and saw me, he stiffened, then lifted a hand to wave.

"Auden," he called out, hurrying closer. "I've been trying to call you."

I had a flash of my phone, which I was pretty sure I'd left on the kitchen table. "Oh," I said. "I've been running around all morning."

"Your stepmother said," he replied. "I finally looked up your dad's home number. Luckily there are only a couple of Wests here."

Behind him, I could see Adam coming out of the bike shop, wheeling a red bike with a sign that said READY TO GO! hanging from its handlebars. He parked it by the bench, then went back inside, the door banging behind him.

"So look," Jason said. "I need to talk to you about tonight."

"Okay."

"I'm not . . . " He stopped, then took a breath. "I'm not going to be able to make it."

I was surprised by the way I reacted, hearing this. My face flushed, my heartbeat jumped. It was like every time I got on the bike, a mix of fear and inevitability, all at once. "You're canceling on me?" I said. "Seriously? Again?"

"I know." He winced. "It's totally rude of me. I wouldn't blame you if you never spoke to me again."

This was when I was supposed to proclaim otherwise. I didn't. I just waited for the excuse, because there always was one.

"It's just, there's this speaker coming today to the conference," he said quickly. "She's a leader in student activism, has really made some big changes at Harvard, where she went undergrad, and now Yale, where she's in law school. I mean, incredible policy-changing stuff. So she's a great contact for me."

I said nothing as Adam came out once again, this time pushing a smaller green bike. It had fatter tires, a glossy black seat, and was polished so clean it was glinting in the sun. ENJOY YOUR RIDE! said its sign, which was swinging in the breeze.

"Anyway," Jason continued, "her talk is this afternoon, but then she's going to dinner with a select few attendees to talk about some of her experiences one on one. No first years were supposed to be invited, but apparently she'd heard about that recycling initiative I did junior year, so . . ."

I was listening, even as I watched Adam push out another bike, this one a two-seater. YOU'LL LOOK SWEET! said its sign, with a heart around it.

"It's just," Jason finished finally. "It's something I have to do. I'm sorry."

Right then, I realized something. I wasn't upset that Jason was ditching me. That racing of my heart, the flushing of my face I was feeling: it was what happened when you got hurt, true, but also when you got back up and went on. Maybe Jason had never been meant to be part of my second chance anyway, and this was just the push that I, and fate, needed.

"You know what?" I said to him. "It's fine."

He blinked at me. "Really?"

"Really." I took a breath, making sure this true. Weirdly, it was. "I'm okay with this."

"You are?" I nodded. "Oh, God, Auden, thanks for understanding. I figured you'd be so angry with me! But you of all people understand the academic thing, right? I mean, this is a once-in-a-lifetime opportunity, and . . ."

He was still talking as I stepped around him and started toward the bike shop. Vaguely, I heard him saying something about understanding and obligation, commitment and future endeavors, all the buzzwords and concepts I did understand, and knew so well. Unlike what I was now approaching. Still, more than ever this summer, I'd learned that it's not just where you go, but how you choose to get there. So I pulled that sign off the green bike—ENJOY YOUR RIDE!—and went inside to take the first step toward doing just that.

✻   ✻   ✻

"Guess what?" Maggie said as soon as I walked into Clementine's.

"What?"

She clapped her hands. "I have a date for the prom!"

"Guess what?" I replied.

"What?"

"I don't." Her mouth dropped open. "Oh, and," I added, "I bought a bike."

"What?" she said, but I was already walking past her. I heard her fall in behind me, yelling to some customers by the jeans that she'd be with them in a second, and when I pushed open the door to the office, she was right on my heels.

"Okay, let's just slow down." She held up her hands, palms facing me. "First things first. What do you mean, you don't have a date?"

"Just that," I said, sitting down at the desk. "Jason bailed on me."

"Again?"

I nodded.

"When?"

"About twenty minutes ago."

"Oh, my God." She put a hand over her mouth: her expression was so horrified, like someone had died. "That's the worst thing ever."

"No," I said, swallowing. "It's actually not."

"No?"

I shook my head. "The worst thing is that right afterward, I marched right into the bike shop to ask Eli to go with me, and he said no."

She threw up her other hand, clapping it over the one already covering her mouth. "Holy crap," she said, her voice muffled. "Where does the bike come in?"

"I don't know," I said, waving my hand. "That part's kind of a blur."

Her eyes widened, and she dropped her hands, sticking her head back out in the hallway. After checking on the customers, she whipped out her phone. "Don't move," she said, fingers flying over the keyboard. "I'm calling for backup."

"Maggie." I groaned. "Please don't."

"Too late." She pushed one last button. "It's done."

Which was how, twenty minutes later, I found myself sitting in the same spot, now surrounded by not only Maggie but also Leah and Esther, with a large cup of coffee and two packs of chocolate cupcakes on the desk in front of me.

"Cupcakes?" Maggie said to Esther. "Really?"

"I panicked," Esther replied. "What kind of snack does a situation like this call for?"

Leah thought for a moment. "The pharmaceutical kind."

"Well, they don't have that at the Gas/Gro. So cupcakes it is." Esther looked at me. "Okay. We're all here now. What happened?"

I picked up the coffee, taking a sip, and immediately wanted to drain the whole thing. Instead, I told them.

❊   ❊   ❊

It wasn't like I had a solid plan when I pulled open the bike shop door. All I could think was that here I had another chance, and this time, I was going to do it right.

It seemed like the best sign possible, maybe even ideal, that I spotted Eli the minute I stepped inside the door. He was behind the counter, his back to me, stuffing something into a duffel bag, and seeing him, I had the same reaction I'd had for weeks now, a sudden embarrassment about how I'd acted, followed by an urge to run in the other direction as fast as I could. Instead, I gripped the sign in my hand even tighter, and pressed on.

"Hey," I said as I came up on the counter. My voice

sounded loud and ragged, rushed, and I told myself to take a breath. Which got considerably more difficult as he turned around to face me.

"Hey." He was looking at me with a wary expression. "What's up?"

In a perfect world, I would have eased into what I had to say gradually. Worked up to it, phrasing it neatly and succinctly with all the right adjectives. As it was, I just blurted out, "Do you remember that first time we went bowling?"

Eli raised his eyebrows. Then he looked in the repair room behind him, where, distantly, I could see Adam and Wallace, standing in the door that led out to the back alley, their backs to us. "Yeah," he said after a moment. "Why?"

I swallowed, the sound seeming incredibly loud in my own ears. "I was all annoyed, because I wasn't good at it. And you said I shouldn't have expected to be, because I'd never done it before, and what mattered was that I keep trying."

"Right," he said slowly. "I remember."

I knew I was on the verge of losing my nerve. I could literally feel it slipping away, second by second, like a wave slowly pulling itself back out to sea. But I kept going anyway.

"That's what happened with us," I said. "With me. What we were doing . . . what we had . . . it was my first time. You know, where it mattered. And I wasn't good at it. I sucked, actually."

He narrowed his eyes. Oh, Jesus, I thought. *That* didn't come out right.

"At being with you," I added quickly. "I was bad at, you know, us. It was all new to me. I screwed it up because I didn't know what I was doing, and that scared me so I didn't even want to try. It's like the bike. Which you were also right about, by the way."

It was very, very quiet in the shop all around us, which made all of this sound that much more loud. In fact, I probably would have been completely humiliated, if I'd let my words catch up with me. All the more reason to keep going.

"What I'm saying," I said, because God knew I needed some clarification, "is that I'm sorry. You can call it crazy, or call it chicken salad, or whatever. But I want to do what you said, keep trying. So I'm doing that by coming here and asking you to go to the prom with me tonight."

"Yo, Eli!" I heard Wallace yell, suddenly, from behind him. "Train's leaving. Time to go!"

Eli didn't respond, though. He was still looking at me, his face serious. As I stared back at him I tried to remember all those hours we'd spent together, and how they'd begun and ended in pretty much this very same space. Because of this, it seemed more right than ever to be there now, when I'd know for sure whether we'd continue, or end for good. I knew, too, that these were the two possibilities. But for some reason, I figured he'd pick the other one.

"I'm sorry," he said. And the thing was, it seemed true as he picked up his bag, slinging it over one shoulder. "But I can't."

I felt myself nod stupidly. And then, with one last look—

intense, and almost sad—he was gone, turning his back and walking through the office, past Adam and Wallace, and out of sight. A second later, the door banged shut behind him. Done.

"Auden!" I turned my head, still stunned, to see Adam coming toward me. "Are you looking for Eli? Because he just—"

"No," I said too quickly. "I'm not."

"Oh. Okay." He glanced at Wallace, who shrugged. "Well, is there something else you needed?"

I was really just looking for a way to save face, to get out of there gracefully. But then, I looked down again at the sign still in my hand—ENJOY YOUR RIDE!—and it seemed, suddenly, to be just that. A sign.

"Actually," I said. "There is one thing."

*　　*　　*

"Call it chicken salad?" Esther laughed, clapping her hands. "That is so retro! I haven't heard that since grade school."

"I," Leah said, "never understood what that meant."

"So *that's* how you ended up with the bike," Maggie said.

"Bike?" Leah said. "What does a bike have to do with any of this?"

"I just bought one," I told her. "Apparently."

"Because she also just learned how to ride one," Maggie explained. "I've been teaching her every morning, on the sly. She never knew before."

"Really?" Esther looked at me. "Wow. That's impressive."

"That I didn't know, or I learned?" I asked.

Esther considered this. "Both," she said finally.

"People! Let's stay focused." Leah turned to me. "Okay, so Eli shot you down. It's not the end of the world."

"No," I said, "it's just incredibly humiliating, and now I can never face him again."

"I wonder why he said no?" Maggie mused.

"Because he's Eli," I told her.

Leah rolled her eyes. "That's a statement, not an explanation."

"What I mean is," I said, "I know what he's like. I had my chance with him, and I blew it. So he's done."

"Wait." Esther held up her hand. "Back up. When were you and Eli an item?"

Once again, I had everyone's attention as I said, "Um, we were hanging out a lot, a few weeks back."

"Doing what?" Leah asked.

I thought of Eli and me, in the car, driving through the dark streets of Colby, alone and together, all those nights. Shopping, eating, talking, questing. We'd done so much it seemed impossible to narrow it down to any one word. So instead, I decided to go with the one thing we hadn't done, at least until the very end. "We couldn't sleep," I said. "So we were just up, together."

"Until you blew it," Esther said, clarifying.

I nodded.

"What'd you do?"

I looked down at my cold coffee. "I don't know," I said. "Something happened, and I got scared and pulled away."

"Okay, well, *that's* not vague," Leah said.

"Leah!" Esther said.

"What? 'Something happened'? What does that mean?"

They all looked at me again, and under their gazes I realized that this, too, was a point where I usually pulled back. Folded into myself, hiding away. But considering what I'd already been through that day, it seemed only fitting to go for broke. "My dad and Heidi separating," I said. "It . . . it kicked up a lot of stuff for me. And I dealt with it the way I did when my parents split."

"Which was?" Esther asked.

I shrugged. "Throwing myself into books and school, basically blocking everyone out. Especially anyone who might call me on it."

"Like Eli," Maggie said.

"Especially Eli," I replied. "We'd had this one night where we really connected . . . and the next day, I just shut down on him. It was so stupid of me."

"Did you tell him that, though?" Maggie asked. "Today?"

"Yep," I said. "But like I said, it was too late. He's done."

There was a moment of quiet as this was processed and considered. I picked up the pack of cupcakes, then put them back down.

"Well," Leah said finally, "I say, screw it."

"Leah." Esther sighed. "Honestly."

"No, really. So you're humiliated. It happens. And who needs boys anyway? We'll all just go to the prom together tonight and have a good time."

"I thought," Esther said to her, "that you were determined to have a date, or you weren't going."

"That was before I'd exhausted all my options," Leah explained. "Now, I'm embracing my single status and just hanging with the girls. Like we all are. Right?"

"Right," Esther said.

They both looked at me. I said, "You know, having been rejected twice, I'm thinking I might just stay home."

"What?" Leah shook her head. "That's a total quitter attitude."

"*Twice,*" I said again, holding up two fingers. "In fifteen minutes, within a hundred feet of each other. What's next? An anvil on my head?"

"This," Esther said to me, "is exactly when you *need* to go out with the girls. It's a textbook situation. You go with us, we dance together, you'll feel better. Right, Mags?"

I hadn't noticed until right then that Maggie had kind of shrunk back toward the door, one foot actually already out in the hall. When we all turned our attention to her, she flushed. "Well," she said. "Actually . . . "

Silence. Then Leah said, "Actually what?"

"I kind of have a date."

"What?" Esther said. "What happened to sisterhood?"

"You guys were totally blowing that off up until this very second!" Maggie protested. "How was I supposed to know you'd actually come around?"

"If you tell me you're going with Jake Stock," Leah warned, "my head is going to explode."

"No." Maggie flushed again, then looked down at her hands. "Adam asked me."

Leah and Esther looked at each other. Then at Maggie. Then at each other again. "Holy crap," Esther said, exhaling. "Finally!"

"No shit," Leah said. "He finally got up the nerve!"

Maggie brightened, stepping back into the office. "So you're not mad?"

"Of course we are," Leah said.

"But," Esther added, "we're also happy that this sexual tension that's been going on for years—"

"*Years*," Leah agreed.

"—will finally be resolved, one way or another," Esther finished.

"Oh, it's not like that," Maggie said, flipping her hand. "We're just going as friends."

"No," I said. "You're not."

She looked at me. "What?"

"He likes you," I told her. "He told me. And I'm telling you because if you blow your chance, you'll be really sorry. Trust me."

"Excuse me?" I heard someone yell from the sales floor. "Is anyone working here?"

"Whoops," Maggie said, turning around.

"I'm on it," Esther told her, brushing past her to the hallway. Leah followed her, tossing her cup in the trash as she went. A moment later I heard them burst out, already chattering at the customer, as if to compensate for the silence.

Maggie leaned against the doorjamb, looking in at me as I sat back in the office chair. "I wish you'd reconsider about tonight," she said after a moment. "It's still a memory worth having, even if it's not exactly what you imagined."

"I know," I told her. "But honestly, I just don't think I have it in me."

"Well, if you change your mind, we'll be there. Okay?"

"Okay." She nodded, then pushed off the door, heading back to work.

"Oh, I meant to tell you," she said. "Your bike? It's awesome."

"You think?"

"A Gossie with Whiplash cranks, a Tweedle fork, and those fat Russel tires? You can't go wrong."

I sighed. "Well. At least I'll be leaving at the end of the summer with something."

"I think," she said, "that was already the case."

And then she patted the doorjamb twice and was gone again. I looked back at my cupcakes, noting that somehow Esther had remembered that they were the one thing I'd bought, on impulse, all those weeks ago. I unwrapped them, pulled one out, and took a bite. It was too rich, the icing sticky. But weirdly enough, it did match the coffee perfectly.

eighteen

"ARE YOU *SURE* about this?" Heidi asked, for about the millionth time as she stood in the open door. "Because I can probably still—"

"Heidi." I shifted Isby to my other hip. "Go."

"But it just seems so wrong! If anyone should miss this, it's me. It's not like I haven't been to—"

"Go," I repeated.

"Look, if I find someone there who can relieve you, I'll just send them—"

I narrowed my eyes, shooting her the best cold bitch look I could muster. She recoiled slightly, and stepped out onto the porch.

"Okay, fine," she said. "I'm going."

I stood there, watching, as she started down the steps. After much debate, she'd selected a long, coral-colored dress with spaghetti straps. It had looked strange on the hanger—too plain, the color odd—but once on, she was a total knockout. All the more reason not to wear the Baby-Björn over it, which had been her original plan, as she'd never found a babysitter.

"I'm fine," I'd assured her, hours ago, when I volunteered.

"I don't want to go to the prom, I told you that."

"But it's your one chance!" She sighed, looking at Isby, who was on the bedroom floor between us on her little play gym, kicking her feet at the ladybug hanging overhead. "I just hate how all this turned out for you."

"I'm really okay," I said. She studied me, doubtful. I said, "I am."

Weirdly enough, this was kind of true. Even with my morning of double rejections. Even though I'd walked my new bike home, instead of riding it, as I just was not up for another bruise to my shins, elbows, or ego. Even after I'd taken that violet dress out of my room and laid it across Heidi's bed, and slipped on my sweats and a tank top, dressing down just as everyone else began dressing up. In some ways, maybe this was what I'd done back in May, my first time around. But it was also totally different.

I realized now why Maggie was so sure I'd be leaving with more than a bike at the end of the summer. Because it was obvious, this true difference in me now: I had these experiences, these tales, more of this life. So maybe it wasn't the fairy tale. But those stories weren't real anyway. Mine were.

Once Heidi was gone, I carried Isby out to the deck, holding her up so she could see the water. There were still people out on the beach, soaking up the last of the daylight, while others were already out for their evening walks, proceeding past in couples, or groups, dogs and children running out ahead or lagging behind. We watched for a while, then headed back inside, where I heard someone knocking at the door.

As I passed the kitchen table, I saw Heidi's phone, sitting right next to the saltshaker. She'd missed two calls—whoops—before realizing and doubling back for it. When I pulled the door open, holding the phone out with my other hand, I saw it wasn't Heidi after all. It was my mother.

"Hi, Auden," she said. "Can I come in?"

In response, Isby let out a squawk. My mom looked at the baby, then at me. "Sure," I said, then realized I needed to step back to make room for this to actually happen. "Of course."

I retreated, she advanced, and then, somehow, I was shutting the door behind me and shoving Heidi's phone into my back pocket before following her as she walked, slowly, through the foyer and toward the kitchen. I wasn't sure what it was about her that was so jarring, especially since she looked just the same: dark hair piled on her head, black skirt and tank top, the onyx necklace that hung right at her collarbone, emphasizing its sharpness. But still, something was different.

"So," I said slowly, shifting Isby back to my other hip. "What are you doing here?"

My mom turned and looked at me. Under the brighter lights of the kitchen, I saw she looked tired, even kind of sad. "I've been worried about you. Ever since our last conversation. I kept telling myself I was just being silly, but then . . ."

She trailed off, and I realized how rare this was, her using my dad's old trick. My mom never liked to leave any of her meaning in another person's hands. "But then," I repeated.

"I came anyway," she finished. "Call it a mother's pre-
rogative. I wonder if your dad and Heidi can spare a cup of
coffee?"

"Of course," I said, walking over to the cupboard to pull
out a mug. I was trying to reach up to get one and manage
Isby, who had suddenly decided to go all squirmy on me,
when I looked over at my mom, who was watching me with
a curious expression. "Do you think you could—"

"Oh," she said. Then she sat up straighter, as if about
to be graded on something, and held out her hands. "Certainly."

I handed Isby over, feeling my mom's fingers brush mine
as she left my hands for hers. Before I turned back to get the
coffee, it struck me how strange it was to see my mother
with a baby. She looked awkward sitting there, her arms
bent at the elbow, studying Isby's face with a clinical expression, as if she was a puzzle or riddle. In turn, Isby stared
back at her, googly eyed, moving her little hands in circles,
around and around again. Still, when I slid the coffee in
front of her a few moments later, I stood at her side, prepared to take over. But she kept her eyes on the baby, so I
sat down instead.

"She's very cute," she said finally. "Looks a little like you
did at this age."

"Really?"

My mom nodded. "It's the eyes. They're just like your
father's."

I looked at Isby, who seemed to be not at all worried
about being held by a stranger, much less one who was

clearly somewhat uncomfortable. As far as she knew, every-one she met had her best interest at heart.

"I didn't mean to worry you," I said to my mom now. "I've just . . . there's just been a lot going on."

"I could tell." She eased Isby into a seated position, pick-ing up her coffee with her other hand. "But I still got wor-ried, when in that last call, you started asking about the divorce. You sounded so different."

"Different how?" I asked.

She considered this for a minute. Then she said, "The word that comes to mind is *younger*, actually. Although for the life of me, I can't explain why that is."

It made sense to me, but I didn't say so. Instead, I reached out, taking one of Isby's fat fingers and squeezing it. She looked at me, then back at my mom.

"The truth is, I thought I was losing you," she said, more to Isby than to me. "When you came down here, to your father and Heidi, and made all these friends. And then with the argument we had about the dorms . . . I suppose I'd just gotten comfortable thinking we were on the same page. And then, suddenly, we weren't. It was very strange. Al-most lonely."

Almost, I thought. Out loud I said, "Just because we don't see eye to eye on everything doesn't mean we can't be close."

"True," she agreed. "But I suppose it was just very jar-ring for me. To see you changing so quickly. It was like you had this whole world of traditions and language I didn't un-derstand, and there wasn't a place in it for me."

She was still looking at Isby as she said this—face to her

face, her hands around the baby's waist—as if these words were meant for her ears alone. "I know the feeling," I said.

"Do you?"

I nodded. "Yeah. I do."

Now, she turned, looking at me. "I could not bear," she said slowly, making sure each word was clear, "to think that a choice I made in my life had somehow ruined yours. That would be unthinkable for me."

I thought of us that night on the phone, the way her voice had softened suddenly, when I'd brought up the divorce. My mother had always had her cold, hard shell, this brittle armor she put up between her and everyone else. But maybe, all along, she'd seen it differently. That I was not outside, banging to get in, but in there with her, protected and safe, giving her all the more reason to stay that way.

"You didn't ruin my life," I told her. "I just wish we'd talked more."

"About the divorce?"

"About everything."

She nodded, and for a moment, we just sat there, both of us watching Isby, who was studying her feet. Then she said, "That's never been my strong suit. The emotional talking thing."

"I know," I agreed. She looked at me. "It wasn't mine either. But I kind of got a crash course this summer."

"Really," she said.

"Yeah." I took in a breath. "It's not that hard, actually."

"Well." She swallowed. "Maybe you can teach me sometime."

I smiled at her. I'd just reached to put my hand over

hers, feeling it warm beneath mine, when I felt Heidi's phone buzz in my back pocket.

"Shoot," I said, pulling it out. "I better get this."

"Go ahead," she replied, sitting back and resetting Isby on her lap. "We're fine."

I got to my feet, then hit TALK without checking the ID. "Hello?"

"Heidi?"

The fact that my dad didn't recognize my voice said something, although I wasn't sure I wanted to think about what, exactly. I considered just hanging up, taking the coward's way out. But instead I said, "No. It's Auden."

"Oh." A pause. "Hi there."

"Hi," I said. I looked at my mom, who was watching me, then turned my back, starting into the foyer. It still seemed too close, though, so I headed upstairs. "Um, Heidi's not here. She left her phone by accident when she went to the Beach Bash."

It was very quiet on the line, so quiet that I had to wonder why there is interference or static only you really want to hear what the other person is saying. "Well," he said finally. "How are you?"

"I'm okay," I told him. "Busy."

"I figured. I've left you some messages." He cleared his throat. "I'm assuming you're angry at me."

"No," I said, going into the bedroom, where my purple dress was still lying across the bed. I picked it up, carrying it to the closet. "I've just been working some things out."

"And I, as well." He coughed again. "Look, I know you're there with Heidi, hearing her side of things—"

"Heidi wants you to come home."

"That's what I want, too," he said. "But it's just not that simple."

I pushed the dresses down the closet rod, the hangers clacking against each other, and stuffed the purple dress back in. Instead of shutting it, though, I kept moving through the line, looking at the other things there. I asked, "Then what is it?"

"What?"

I pulled another black dress out, this one with a pleated skirt, then shoved it back. "You keep saying that, how it's not simple. So tell me what it is, then."

I could feel his surprise, tangible, which I guess shouldn't have been that shocking itself. He was used to me chalking up whatever decisions he made to a peculiar kind of logic, all his own. It excused so much: it excused everything. He was a writer, he was moody, he was selfish. He needed his sleep, he needed his space, he needed his time. If he'd kept himself apart from the rest of the world, these things would have been just quirky annoyances, nothing more. But that was just the thing. He *did* involve other people. He reached out, drew them close. He made children with them, who then also could not separate themselves, whether they were babies or almost adults. You couldn't just pick and choose at will when someone depended on you, or loved you. It wasn't like a light switch, easy to shut on or off. If you were in, you were in. Out, you were out. To me, it didn't seem complicated at all. In fact, it was the simplest thing in the world.

"See," my dad said now, "this is what I meant when I said

you were angry. You've heard Heidi talking, and you've only gotten one side of the story."

"That's not why I'm upset with you," I told him, pushing more dresses aside. There was something so satisfying in the sound of the hangers clacking, all those colors blurring past. Pink, blue, red, orange, yellow. Each one like a shell, a skin, a different way to be, even if only for a day.

"Then what is it?" he asked.

Black, green, black, polka dot. "It's just," I said, "you have the opportunity for a second chance here."

"A second chance," he repeated.

"Yeah," I said. Short-sleeved, long-sleeved, narrow skirt, full. "But you won't even take it. You'd rather just quit."

He was quiet, the only sound the hangers sliding. I was almost to the end now, the choices narrowing to few, then fewer still. "Is that what you think?" he said slowly. "That I'm quitting on you?"

"Not on me," I said.

"On who, then?"

And then, suddenly, there it was. A simple black dress with tiny beads hanging from the skirt, matching those along the neckline. A dancing dress, a flapper dress. The perfect dress, the one I'd been looking for all along. And as I stared at it, I found something else as well. The answer to his question, and the reason, I realized suddenly, why this summer had brought so much of this to the surface.

"Isby," I told him.

When I said her name, I saw her face. Squawking, cooing, wailing, drooling. Sleeping, wakeful, fussy, content. The first day I'd seen her, asleep in Heidi's arms, and how she'd been only seconds ago, her eyes following me as I left the room. All these little parts of her, just the very beginning of who she would and could be. It was early yet. She had everything ahead of her, and more than anything, I hoped that she wouldn't need a lot of second chances. That maybe, unlike so many of us, she'd find a way to get it right the first time.

"Isby?" my dad repeated. "You mean the baby?"

"That's what I call her," I told him. "That's who she is to me."

He was quiet for a moment. Then he said, "Auden, I love Thisbe. I'd do anything in the world for her, or for you. You have to know that."

This was what my mother had said, too, only moments earlier, and I'd chosen to believe her. So why was this so much harder? Because my mom had come to me. Traveled all this way, taken that risk, retraced some, if not all, of her steps to get us back to a place where we could, hopefully, forge a new path together. My dad was still in the same spot, and as always, he wanted me to come to him. Like I'd done at the beginning of the summer, in this house, and at home as well. Always crossing that distance, crossing town, accommodating, making excuses.

"If that's true," I said to him, "then prove it."

He was quiet for a moment. Then he said, "How am I supposed to do that?"

Sometimes, you get things right the first time. Others, the second. But the third time, they say, is the charm. Standing there, a quitter myself, I figured I'd never know if I didn't get back on that bike, one last time. So instead of replying, I pulled the black beaded dress from the closet, draping it across the bed. "You figure it out," I told him. "There's something I have to do."

＊　＊　＊

I'd planned to drive. In fact, I'd had my keys in hand as I ran out the door, the black dress swishing around my knees. But then, I saw the bike, sitting right against the steps where I left it, and the next thing I knew, I was climbing on. I raised up on the pedals, tried to remember everything Maggie had taught me over the last few weeks, and then pushed off before I could change my mind.

It was weird, but as I started down the front walk—wobbling slightly, but upright at least so far—all I could think of was my mom. When I'd hung up the phone moments earlier, I'd pulled on the dress and found my flip-flops and bag, figuring I'd put Isby in the stroller and take her with me. But as I started to strap her in, hurriedly explaining myself to my mom, the baby started to fuss. Then cry. Then scream.

"Oh, no," I said as her face flooded with color. I knew the signs of a full-out fit when I saw one. "This is *not* good."

"She doesn't like the stroller?" asked my mom, who was standing behind me.

"Usually she loves it. I don't know what the problem is." I bent down, adjusting the straps, but Isby just yelled louder, now kicking her feet for emphasis. I glanced up at my mom. "I better just stay here. She's really unhappy."

"Nonsense." She gestured for me to move aside, then

leaned over, undoing the straps and lifting Isby up. "I'll watch her. You go have fun."

I did not mean for my expression to be so doubtful. Or shocked. But apparently it was, because she said, "Auden. I raised two children. I can be trusted with a newborn for an hour."

"Of course you can," I said quickly. "I just . . . I hate to leave you with her when she's like this."

"She's not like anything," my mom said, pulling the baby closer to her and patting her back. Weirdly enough, before, when Isby had been googly and cheerful, it was clear she was uncomfortable, but now, amid the screaming, she looked completely as ease. "She's just giving me a piece of her mind."

"Are you sure you want to do this?" I said, raising my voice to be heard above the din.

"Absolutely. Go." She put the baby over her shoulder, still patting. "That's right, that's right," she said, over the shrieking. "Tell me everything you have to say."

I just stood there, watching as she started to pace the kitchen floor, rocking Isby in her arms. As she walked, she fell into a rhythm: step, pat, step, pat. The baby, over her shoulder, looked at me, her face still red, mouth open. But as the space increased between us, she began to quiet down. And down. And down, until all I could hear was my mother's footsteps. And then something else.

"Shh, shh," she was saying. "Everything's all right."

Her voice was low. Soft. And with these last words, suddenly familiar in a way it had not been ever before. That voice I thought I'd imagined or conjured: it was her, all along. Not a dream, or a mantra, but a memory. A real one.

Everything's all right, I thought now, as I bumped over the curb and onto the street. There was no traffic in the neighborhood, and I thought of all those mornings with Maggie, feeling her hand on the back of my seat, her footsteps slapping the pavement as she raced to keep up before giving me one last push—*Go!*—and I was on my own.

I just kept riding, shooting under streetlights and past mailboxes, the tires whizzing against the pavement. As I turned out of the neighborhood, I had the road to myself, all the way to the single stoplight where it ended at the beach.

It was the light I focused on, solid green, up ahead of me, as I pedaled faster, the fastest yet, my hair blowing back, the spokes of the tires humming. I'd never gone so fast before, and it occurred to me that I should probably be scared, but I wasn't. On the other side of the light I could see the ocean, big and dark and vast, and I pictured myself hitting the sand and just keeping going, over the dunes and into the waves, the current the only thing strong enough to stop me. I was so immersed in this image, which was amazingly clear in my head, that I didn't see two things until I was right up on them: the banged-up Toyota truck sitting at the stoplight, and the curb right across from it.

I saw the truck first. Suddenly, it was just there, although I was positive there had been no traffic when I'd looked only seconds earlier. And maybe it was a good thing that I hardly had time to process that it was, in fact, Eli's truck. Because the next second, the curb presented itself, and it needed my full attention.

I was already zooming past Eli when I realized I had to make a decision: try to brake and turn and hope my crash was a small one, or keep going and try to jump the curb. If anyone else had been in that truck, I probably would have taken the first option. But it wasn't anyone else, and I knew—even in those dwindling seconds, when I could feel every bit of my blood rushing through my ears—that this was probably the best way to explain to him what I'd tried to that morning at the shop. So I jumped.

It wasn't like what I'd seen Maggie do that night at the park. Or the tons of bike videos I'd watched over the last few weeks. But it didn't matter. For me, the feeling of rising up suddenly, suddenly being airborne—the tires spinning into nothing—was amazing. It was like a dream. Or maybe, like waking up from one.

It only lasted a few seconds, and then I was coming down hard, the bike hitting the pavement with a bang beneath me, even as it kept moving forward. I felt the shock all the way from my fingertips to my elbows as I tried to control the handlebars, hanging on for dear life as the tires skidded, trying to fall over sideways. This was the point where I'd always given into the crash, squeezing my eyes shut as the garbage can or bushes came closer, closer, closer. But now, I kept them wide open and just held on, and after a spray of sand, I was somehow back upright, and moving on.

My hands were shaking as I carefully eased on my brake, feeling my pulse thudding in my temple. It was all so clear to me—the fast approach, spotting the curb, and launching up, up, up—and yet at the same time, I could not believe I'd actually done it. In fact, it didn't even seem real until I circled around, still shaking, and saw Eli, who at some point had pulled over to the curb and gotten out of his truck and was now just standing there, staring at me.

"Holy crap," he said finally. "That was *awesome*."

"Yeah?"

He nodded. "And here I thought you couldn't ride a bike."

I smiled, then pedaled back toward him. It was only as I got closer that I noticed he was not in his usual jeans and T-shirt or hoodie, but wearing nice black pants, some vintage-looking shiny dress shoes, and a long-sleeved white shirt, untucked. "I couldn't," I said, coming to a stop beside him. "Maggie taught me."

"How to jump, too?"

"Um, no," I said, feeling myself flush. "I kind of winged that part, actually."

"Really."

"You couldn't tell?"

He looked at me for a moment. "Actually," he said, "I could."

"What gave me away? The look of pure terror on my face?"

"Nope." He leaned back on his heels. "In fact, you didn't look scared at all."

"How did I look?"

"Ready," he replied.

I considered this as I looked down at my bike. "Yeah," I said. "I think I was, actually."

Maybe this should have felt strange, especially after all that had happened. But it didn't. Perhaps because it was nighttime, when things that might have felt odd in daylight instead seemed just right. Like riding a bike in a prom dress and crossing paths with only one person, and it's the only person you want to see.

If it was light out, I would have questioned more, second-guessed, started to overthink. But now, it seemed natural to turn to Eli and say, "You were right, you know."

"About what?"

"Me," I said. "How I always quit if I don't get something right the first time. It's been a big mistake."

"So you believe in second chances now," he said, clarifying.

"I believe," I said, "in however many you might need to get it right."

Eli slid his hands back in his pockets. "I'm believing in that, too, actually. Especially today."

"Really."

He nodded, then gestured to his truck behind him. "So . . . you know how I said no to you earlier. When you asked about the prom."

I felt my face flush. "I think I remember that, yeah."

"I had this competition, in Roardale. I've actually been back competing for a few weeks now."

"I know."

He looked surprised, which I had to admit I kind of liked, as it was so rare. "How?"

"I've been kind of keeping up with the standings," I said. "Online. So how'd you do?"

"I won."

I smiled. "That's great. So I guess you're back riding for real, now?"

"Nope. I'm done."

"You're quitting again?"

"Retiring," he corrected me. "As of today."

"Why?"

He leaned back on his heels, looking down the dark street. "I was planning to last year. You know, because I'd gotten into the U, and wanted to go to school. But then . . . "

I waited. Because with Eli, he was never trying to get you to finish for him. He always knew where he was going, even if it took a little while to get there.

" . . . Abe died," he said. "And everything just stopped. But it wasn't how I wanted to go out, just dropping off the map like that."

"You wanted to go out on top," I said.

"Or at least try to." He reached up, pulling a hand through his hair. "So I'm sorry, about today. I wish I'd explained better why I said no."

"I understand," I told him. "It was just something you had to do."

He looked at me, his eyes so dark. "Yeah," he said. "Exactly."

A car was driving up to the light now, its headlights moving across us. They paused, their turn signal ticking, before moving past. Then Eli looked me up and down, taking in my dress and my flip-flops. "So," he said. "Where are you going?"

"To the prom," I told him. "You?"

"Same. Better late than never, right?" he said. "Want a ride?"

I shook my head. He raised his eyebrows, opening his mouth to respond, but before he could I reached out, taking his hand, and pulled him closer to me. Then I stood on tiptoes, bringing my lips to his. The kiss was slow and sweet, and while it was happening, I had that image again of us so small, standing in the middle of Colby, under that stoplight, as the entire town and world turned around us. And in that moment, if only for that moment, we were right where we were supposed to be.

I smiled at him as I stepped back, then up on my pedals again. He turned slowly in a circle, watching me as I slowly rode around him, once, twice, three times, like casting a spell.

"So you don't want me to take you," he said.

"No," I replied. "But I'll meet you there."

nineteen

THE COFFEE IN the Defriese cafeteria was good, but not great. It was covered by my meal plan, though, and the cups were bottomless. So I'd learned to like it just fine.

I fit a travel lid onto my jumbo cup, then pushed out onto the quad, pulling my backpack over my shoulder with my free hand. Now that it was October it was getting colder, a chill to the air that made a warm drink that much more necessary. I climbed onto my bike, balancing my cup with one hand as I carefully rode back across the empty campus to my dorm, a light drizzle starting to fall just as I pulled up at the rack outside. By the time I got to my room, I could hear the rain pinging off the windows.

"Hey," Maggie said, peering down at me from the top of our loft as I came in, shaking off my windbreaker. "I thought you'd already taken off."

"Not yet," I told her. "I had a couple of last things to do."

She yawned, leaning back on her bed. "Oh, your phone was ringing," she said. "A couple of times, actually."

I sat down on my bed, putting my coffee down on the milk crate I used as a bedside table. In addition to my alarm clock, it also held a stack of books and the contents of Heidi's latest care package: two bath bombs, a lip gloss, and a brand-new pair of Pink Slingback jeans. I hadn't had use for any of them yet, but still, I appreciated the gesture.

Also on my table was my THE BEST OF TIMES picture frame Hollis had given me, all those months ago. I'd forgotten about it until the day I was packing to leave for school, when I realized that I finally had something I could actually put in it. But I couldn't decide if I should use a shot from the prom, or one of the several I'd taken with Maggie, Esther, and Leah in our last days in Colby. Maybe, I thought, I should use the one of me with Hollis and Laura, the day they officially announced their engagement. I had so many choices that in the end, I just chose to leave it empty until I was absolutely sure. Because maybe, the best of times were yet to come. You never knew.

There was one picture I did like to keep close at hand, but it wasn't of me. Instead, I preferred Isby's face to be the first one I saw when I rolled over in the morning. I'd been surprised by how hard it had been to leave her at the end of the summer. My last day, we'd sat together for over an hour, her asleep on my shoulder as we rocked in the chair in her room. Her warm skin, damp weight, that smell of milk and baby: I could still remember it so easily, as well as all the things I'd whispered in her ear about her, and me, and this world of girls and boys we were both just one small part of. Someday, she'd be able to tell me everything she knew, too. I couldn't wait.

In the meantime, I had one other thing to remind me of her. I'd seen it at the local Park Mart during one of my first trips out after coming to school, and without even thinking

I'd tossed it into my cart. I was lucky to have Maggie as a roommate for an endless number of reasons. But the fact that she could tolerate the sound of waves once in a while—especially fake ones—was at the top of the list.

Now, I picked up my phone, scrolling though my missed calls. Sure enough, there were two. One from my mom, who called regularly, presumably to discuss my studies, although we usually got onto other topics pretty quickly these days. Like Laura and Hollis's wedding, which was making her insane—although she was trying to keep an open mind, she swore—or her slowly growing relationship with Finn, the graduate student with the black-rimmed glasses. He was sweet and funny, and adored my mother. How she felt about him was harder to say. Although I'd been working with her, so that when she was ready to talk about it, she'd be able to.

The second message was from my dad. He was back at home with Heidi, giving it another shot, a decision he'd made the night of the prom, when he elected not to catch his flight but come over to watch Isby instead. Something about finding my mother walking the floor, soothing her, struck a chord with him, the very image able to convey all the things that I hadn't been able to. He'd sent my mom back to her hotel and sat with Isby until late that night, when Heidi arrived home, shoes in hand, all abuzz from the Beach Bash. While the baby slept, they talked. And talked.

He didn't come home right away. It was a slow process, with a lot of negotiations, and things had changed. Heidi was back at the store part-time, and my dad had dropped to teaching only one course, so they could each work but still have time with the baby. The days neither of them could be home, Isby stayed with either Karen, Eli's mom—who always liked a bit of baby time—or one of a few Weymar coeds who loved the extra perk of free clothes from Clementine's. My dad was still trying to sell his novel, but in the meantime, he'd started a new book, one that was about the "dark underbelly of parenthood and suburbia." He only had time to write late at night, but despite the less than nine hours, it seemed to suit him. Plus, he was always up for a chat if I was pulling an all-nighter as well.

I slid my phone into my pocket, then picked up my bag and coffee. "I'm out of here," I said to Maggie.

"See you tomorrow," she replied. "Oh, wait, I won't, actually. I'm going to Colby."

"You are?"

"Yeah. It's the grand reopening, remember? Oh, I meant to tell you, Adam sent a T-shirt for you. It's over on your bureau."

I couldn't believe I'd forgotten. Especially since whenever Adam had come to visit—at least every other weekend—it was all he could talk about. He'd taken over managing the shop in the fall, juggling it with his part-time class schedule at Weymar, and he was completely excited about how Clyde was letting him make changes, get in new stock, really spruce the place up. New signs, new specials, new everything. There had been one holdover from the previous manager though, one last thing he needed to do, which I saw when I picked up the shirt, unfolding it.

"Abe's Bikes," I read off the front. "It does have a nice ring to it."

"Don't you think?" she replied, sticking her head over the edge to look down at me again. "God, but Adam's a nervous wreck. He's freaking out that everything has to be perfect, and of course things keep going wrong. I'm afraid he's going to have a nervous breakdown if anything else screws up."

"Nah," I said. "But if it does, just tell him I said to get back on the bike."

"What?"

"He'll understand."

I waved at her, then pulled my bag over my shoulder as I made my way down the hallway, then the stairs, to my car. It was just after five, and the sun was going down. By the time I got off the interstate two hours later and pulled into the parking lot of Ray's, it had already been dark for a while.

I cut the engine, then sat there for a second, looking in at the bright lights and shiny tables. Ray's was no Washroom, but the waitresses were nice, and you could sit as long as you wanted. Which was a good thing, when it was late and you had no other options, the way I had been when I'd first discovered it. Now, I had plenty, but one big reason to be here just the same.

I found him at table four, our favorite, the one in the corner by the window. Mug in his hand, slice of pie, half-eaten, by his elbow, totally immersed in the textbook in front of him. This semester he was taking an insane number of hours at the U, playing catch-up for the year he'd missed, and it had been tough for him at first, going back to school.

Kind of new, definitely scary. But luckily, I knew all about inside things like this, and was more than happy to help him on his quest, one paper and test at a time.

I bent down, kissing his forehead, and he looked up at me and smiled. Then I slid in opposite him as the waitress approached, filling the mug beside me. As I picked it up, it was warm in my hands, and I felt his hand move onto my knee. Morning would come before we knew it. It always did. But we still had the night, and for now, we were together, so I just closed my eyes and drank it all in.

along *for the* ride

Come along with Sarah Dessen and read
more about the book—and her.

summer

I HAVE ALWAYS loved the summer. From my first book to this one, my ninth, it's been a theme and a season that I return to again and again. To me, summer has always been about potential. This was especially true when I was in high school. Those three or so months between one school year and the next always meant change. People got taller or wider or smaller. They broke up or came together, lost friends or gained them, had life experiences that you could tell had transformed them even if you didn't know what they were. In the summer, the days are long, stretching into each other. Out of school, everything was on pause and yet happening at the same time, this collection of weeks when anything was possible. As a teenager, I was always hoping to change, to become someone other than who I was. Each summer, I felt I had the chance to do that. All I had to do was wait and see what happened.

The summer also meant beach trips. My family has a house in Cape Cod, Massachusetts, where I've spent part of just about every summer of my life. We live on a strip of land packed with houses, all owned by relatives, and I grew up running barefoot up and down our dirt road with my cousins, learning to sail on the bay, and rising early to go crabbing on the river behind my house when the water was still. At night, we'd play hide-and-seek and beckon in the woods around the house my great-grandfather built seventy years earlier, calling to each other in the dark the way our parents had done before us.

Closer to home, there was the North Carolina coast. My family always went to Emerald Isle, renting a beach house with friends, where we'd eat saltwater taffy, play board games, and spend hours just bobbing in the waves. While our bay in Cape Cod always seemed to be on the chilly side, requiring some fortitude to really plunge in, down South the water was warmer, the beaches long and flat and going on for miles. In town, there were ticky-tacky surf shops where you could buy pretty much anything with shells glued on it—ashtrays, cosmetic boxes, magnets— and restaurants with hush puppies and fried shrimp that melted in your mouth. We'd spend the days in the sun and the nights around the table, eating huge meals and talking and laughing together. I'd go to sleep listening to the sound of the adults sitting out on the deck, their voices mingling with the sound of the waves crashing. As I drifted off, I could always still feel the water's rhythm tugging at me, into my dreams.

As I got older, though, our North Carolina beach trips be- came fewer and farther between. We still went to Cape Cod to visit with family, but back at home everyone seemed to ·

be too busy to pack up and drive east for a few hours just to see the ocean. There was always something else I had to do, year after year: college, teaching, writing. It was such a short distance, but the times I'd spent at Emerald Isle, so easy and relaxed, felt millions of miles away from my life as an adult. Things just get busy, and then they stay that way. It's how you know you're growing up, I guess.

Fast forward to the beginning of the summer of 2009, when I was waiting for this book, *Along for the Ride*, to be released. The publication date was June 16, ten days after my birthday, six after my wedding anniversary. (Like I said, I like summer. The more reasons to celebrate during it, the better.) My daughter, Sasha, was almost two, and somehow—I'm still not sure how, exactly—I was able to write and edit this book while juggling the whole new mom thing. Looking back, it seems crazy, but then most things about writing and motherhood are. You just kind of go with it and hope for the best.

After *Along for the Ride* was published, I embarked on a whirlwind of trips. I went to California, where I hit four cities in three days, then New York and Miami. I attended two conferences, where I talked to tons of fans and signed what felt like thousands of books. Best of all, though, I met my readers. In Huntington Beach, California, there was a girl who had a quote from *Just Listen* tattooed on her neck. In La Jolla, a ten-year-old reader named Nicole came with an armful of books and literally jumped up and down, she was so excited to meet me. I got scrapbooks from readers, and mix CDs, and cupcakes. Someone knitted my daughter a gorgeous little cap, which she wears regularly; some other readers drew up word puzzles for me to play while I was stuck in the airport, bored. And then there were the letters and notes, the dozens of snapshots people posted on my Facebook page, and all the dog-eared, coffee-stained books I signed that had been read again and again and again.

No matter where I went, I was touched and awed by how connected people were with my stories and my characters. Writing is a solitary thing. I spend probably too much time alone with my laptop, as I am now, typing away in an empty room. It's what I have to do, though, to work. The writing is just me, all by myself. But the publicity and the traveling are my chance to get out in the world and meet the people I am working for, shake their hands and smile for their cameras, and hear *their* stories. I love it and look forward to it. And when I'm done, I come back home, to this room, and get ready to do it all over again.

That was my plan for July, after I'd done about a full month of publicity for *Along for the Ride*. Things had gone really well. The book debuted at number one on the *New York Times* bestseller list (a first for me), and I'd gotten mentions in *Entertainment Weekly* and on the *Today* show. Somehow I'd also managed to squeeze in a trip to Cape Cod, where I sat with my parents and cousins as my book was featured on *Good Morning America*. When the segment was over, they all applauded, which was pretty much one of the best moments of my life.

It was all so great that of course, with my Auden-like

drive and ambition, I figured it could be better. I mean, why not? All I had to do was work a bit harder, add some extra traveling, push a bit more. I started to think about how I could sell more books, make this experience bigger, better. It kept me up at night, this drive for something I felt was just out of my reach. I had all these plans for how to make it happen—as soon as I got through this one little thing I had to do first.

The day *Along for the Ride* was released, I'd found out that I had to have surgery to deal with a weird pap smear I'd gotten in the spring. I was scared and dealt with it in what was probably not the best way: throwing myself even harder into pushing the book. The surgery was scheduled for exactly a month after the book came out, and I worked as hard as I could for those four weeks. I wasn't even really thinking about it. As far as I was concerned, it was just a little thing, a blip, and then I could get back to work.

It was supposed to be a simple forty-five minute out-patient procedure, easy in and out. When I woke up, I was being loaded into an ambulance. Something had gone wrong during the surgery, and they were taking me to the hospital, where I stayed for two days. It was scary and frustrating and probably just what I needed. Clearly, I hadn't been going to stop. Not for a vacation, not for even a moment. So the universe stopped me.

I had a lot of time to think as I sat there in my hospital bed. Like about how I couldn't remember the last time I'd been still for so long, hadn't checked my e-mail or Facebook or Twitter (or, let's be honest, Amazon rankings). I couldn't get up even if I wanted to. It was like being on a bullet train for so long you get used to the motion, then suddenly getting off at a quiet station. It was . . . quiet. And I began to realize how I'd missed that.

Once I was released, I still had to take it easy. I couldn't lift anything over ten pounds, which meant I wasn't even able to pick up my daughter. Plus, I was exhausted. So I did a lot of sleeping and thinking as I got my strength back. But even as I started to feel better, something still seemed off.

I kept thinking back on the summer, what a whirlwind it had been so far. All the trips and the readings were a mad blur. When I looked at the pictures, I had a hard time placing where I'd been when a shot was taken. I'd been rushing so quickly through the days I hadn't really allowed myself to enjoy them. I'd even spent most of my Cape Cod vacation, usually one of the high points of the year, glued to my e-mail and cell phone, fielding calls and worrying about events and more publicity opportunities. Sitting with my daughter, who loves to look at pictures, I'd be watching the slide show of our trip, and though the images were familiar, it was like I wasn't really *there*. I found myself longing to go back, have that time again.

I couldn't go back and relive that week. I knew that. But I started to think that maybe, like Auden, it wasn't too late for me to try for a different kind of do-over. One afternoon, I opened my browser and impulsively typed in "Emerald Isle, NC." One of the first hits was a local rental agency. Four days later, I loaded up my daughter and a babysitter and we headed to the coast.

It was totally spur of the moment, which is completely unlike me. I'm a person who plans all trips months in advance, with multiple checklists. I don't even go out for an afternoon without a detailed itinerary. And yet, here I was, driving east with no plan other than . . . well, having no plan. For months, I'd been telling myself and everyone else that I was so busy, that I had things to do. I still did. But they were different things, although equally important. It was Auden I thought of as we crossed the bridge, over all that blue water, and how she, too, had taken a chance on a whim, just like this. When I saw a girl riding a bike along the beach road shortly afterward, I took it as a good sign.

That week was amazing. I'd get up with my daughter— the earliest of early risers—and go out to watch the sunrise on the beach, picking up shells along the way. We'd build sand castles and walk along the surf, looking for dolphins and fishing boats on the horizon. I introduced her to all the things I had loved about the beach when I was a kid, taking her to surf shops and to eat classic North Carolina shrimpburgers. We both got tan, I never put on makeup once, and I started sleeping well again, for the first time I could remember in a while. At night, after my daughter was asleep, my babysitters and I would watch movies and eat popcorn, or sit out on the deck and talk, the water crashing below.

Every night, before I went to sleep, I'd sit alone on my deck, looking up at all those stars. The days were long and hot, the nights cooler and beautiful, and I could feel something in me loosening, letting go, after being clenched and tight for so long. Unlike Auden, I had been lucky enough to have a full and rich childhood, but I'd somehow forgotten about it. For that week, as I retraced the steps of my family beach trips with my own daughter, I began to remember again, and it brought me peace I hadn't even realized was missing.

After a week, we returned home. I put a few seashells on my desk, packed away the sunscreen, and slowly got back to my real life. But I made sure to plan a couple more beach trips. It was clear to me that something at the coast was what I needed, not just this once, but always. Just as Auden would always carry something from her summer in Colby with her, so too do I now hold a bit of my time in Emerald Isle close, and closer. When my daughter and I look at the pictures of us on the beach that week, I can remember every bit of it: how the sand felt cool beneath my feet, the spray of the surf, her warm hand in mine. These memories, as well as the pictures, are a reminder to be present and enjoy the moment, every moment. To take a chance every once in awhile, because it might pay off more than I could ever imagine.

As I write this, it is fall, almost November. The trees outside my window are brilliantly red and gold, the air is cool, and acorns keep bouncing off my tin roof. It's that time of year when we start building fires in the evenings, and I dig out my sweaters and Ugg boots, hunkering down. On the dreariest of days, though, when the light is short and my mood is dark, I make it a point to sit down at my kitchen table, where I have a small glass full of seashells that my daughter and I collected on our sunrise walks. As I take them out, one by one, I tell myself that summer will come again and bring with it more potential. Until it does, at least there are lots of good stories to tell. I hope you enjoy this one.

Chapel Hill, N.C.
Fall 2009

PLAYLIST FOR *ALONG FOR THE RIDE*

WHEN I WRITE, I don't listen to music, as I am entirely too distractible. I basically have to work facing a wall to get anything done. Away from my office, though, I find a lot of motivation from music, especially during those tougher writing days. By the time I finish a book, I always have a list of songs that inspired me, helped me get in better touch with my characters, and basically got me through the bad days, which, to be honest, are usually pretty plentiful. Here are the songs that helped me as I went along for the ride with Auden.

1. "Love Me Like the World Is Ending," Ben Lee. This song was pretty much my anthem while I was writing the book. In fact, Ben Lee's album *Ripe* could be the soundtrack, I listened to it so much. But this song in particular just really brought me back to that promise of summer. So much ahead, all that potential. Every time I hear it, I feel it again. *That's* a good song.

2. "As Cool as I Am," Dar Williams. There's a lot of stuff in the book about feeling like an outsider, and then

finding your way in. This song has always signified that to me, especially the line, "And then I go outside and join the others, I am the others." Nicely put.

3. "Stolen," Dashboard Confessional. A song about summer ending and the price we pay when it goes. Sad and mopey, perfect for those bad writing days when you feel all emo.

4. "I See Monsters," Ryan Adams. I was really sleep deprived when I was writing this book (who am I kidding, I'm still sleep deprived, but now I am just used to it), so I felt an affinity for any song about sleeping or not sleeping. Plus, I just love Ryan Adams. Even before he married Mandy Moore. That made him that much cooler, though.

5. "Let It Rain," Tracy Chapman. I think with every book, you have that moment when you are just exhausted and feel like you can't go on. It usually happens around page 200 or so. I was also dealing with all this other major stuff and feeling totally overwhelmed, and then I heard this song on the radio. The line "Give me hope that help is coming when I need it most," was just about perfect. Like the universe was listening or something, and things were going to be all right.

6. "Breakable," Ingrid Michaelson. My husband can never remember who Ingrid Michaelson is when I play her

music: he says she sounds like every other female singer-
songwriter whose songs have been on *Grey's Anatomy*.
But I love her stuff, and this song in particular just hit
a chord with me. So to speak.

7. "No One," Alicia Keyes. Again, a song that will get you
    through a tough spot. I love any song that says repeat-
    edly that everything will be all right, especially when
    you really need to hear it. Plus, this song makes me
    think of my daughter. "You and me together through
    the days and nights. . . ." Indeed.

8. "People Who Died," the Jim Carroll Band. Sometimes
    a particular song will just mesh in my mind with a
    character. It happened with "Angel from Montgomery"
    and Ruby's mom in *Lock and Key*: I just saw her when
    I heard it. And this song makes me think of Eli.

9. "No Sunlight," Death Cab for Cutie. Another song
    about the night, or at least the lack of day. Plus Death
    Cab always gets it right, in my mind.

10. "Whatever It Is," Ben Lee. I started this list with Ben
    Lee in my head, and I will end it with him as well. I
    actually heard this song a few weeks back, and it just
    summed up *so* much of what this book is about to me.
    "Awake is the new sleep." Yep. That says it better than
    I ever could.

Turn the page to read a chapter
from Sarah Dessen's next book,

what happened to *goodbye*

One

The table was sticky, there was a cloudy smudge on my water glass, and we'd been seated for ten minutes with no sign of a waitress. Still, I knew what my dad would say. By this point, it was part of the routine.

"Well, I gotta tell you. I see potential here."

He was looking around as he said this, taking in the décor. Luna Blu was described on the menu as "Contemporary Italian and old-fashioned good!" but from what I could tell from the few minutes we'd been there, the latter claim was questionable. First, it was 12:30 on a weekday, and we were one of only two tables in the place. Second, I'd just noticed a good quarter inch of dust on the plastic plant that was beside our table. But my dad had to be an optimist. It was his job.

Now, I looked across at him as he studied the menu, his brow furrowed. He needed glasses but had stopped wearing them after losing three pairs in a row, so now he just squinted a lot. On anyone else, this might have looked strange, but on my dad, it just added to his charm.

"They have calamari *and* guac," he said, reaching up to

push his hair back from his eyes. "This is a first. Guess we have to order both."

"Yum," I said, as a waitress sporting lambskin boots and a miniskirt walked past, not even giving us a glance.

My dad followed her with his eyes, then shifted his gaze to me. I could tell he was wondering, as he always did when we made our various escapes, if I was upset with him. I wasn't. Sure, it was always jarring, up and leaving everything again. But it all came down to how you looked at it. Think earth-shattering, life-ruining change, and you're done. But cast it as a do-over, a chance to reinvent and begin again, and it's all good. We were in Lakeview. It was early January. I could be anyone from here.

There was a bang, and we both looked over to the bar, where a girl with long black hair, her arms covered with tat-toos, had apparently just dropped a big cardboard box on the floor. She exhaled, clearly annoyed, and then fell to her knees, picking up paper cups as they rolled around her. Halfway through collecting them, she glanced up and saw us.

"Oh, no," she said. "You guys been waiting long?"

My dad put down his menu. "Not that long."

She gave him a look that made it clear she doubted this, then got to her feet, peering down the restaurant. "Tracey!" she called. Then she pointed at us. "You have a table. Could you please, maybe, go greet them and offer them drinks?"

I heard clomping noises, and a moment later, the wait in the boots turned the corner and came into view. She looked like she was about to deliver bad news as she pulled out her order pad. "Welcome to Luna Blu," she recited, her voice flat. "Can I get you a beverage."

"How's the calamari?" my dad asked her.

She just looked at him as if this might be a trick question. Then, finally, she said, "It's all right."

My dad smiled. "Wonderful. We'll take an order of that, and the guacamole. Oh, and a small house salad, as well."

"We only have vinaigrette today," Tracey told him.

"Perfect," my dad said. "That's exactly what we want."

She looked over her pad at him, her expression skeptical. Then she sighed and stuck her pen behind her ear and left. I was about to call after her, hoping for a Coke, when my dad's phone suddenly buzzed and jumped on the table, clanging against his fork and knife. He picked it up, squinted at the screen, put it down again, ignoring the message as he had all the others that had come since we'd left Westcott that morning. When he looked at me again, I made it a point to smile.

"I've got a good feeling about this place," I told him. "Serious potential."

He looked at me for a moment, then reached over, squeezing my shoulder. "You know what?" he said. "You are one awesome girl."

His phone buzzed again, but this time neither of us looked at it. And back in Westcott, another awesome girl sat texting or calling, wondering why on earth her boyfriend, the one who was so charming but just couldn't commit, wasn't returning her calls or messages. Maybe he was in the shower. Or forgot his phone again. Or maybe he was sitting in a restaurant in a town hundreds of miles away with his daughter, about to start their lives all over again.

A few minutes later, Tracey returned with the guacamole and salad, plunking them down between us on the table. "Calamari will be another minute," she informed us. "You guys need anything else right now?"

My dad looked across at me, and despite myself, I felt a twinge of fatigue, thinking of doing this all again. But I'd made my decision two years ago. To stay or go, to be one thing or many others. Say what you would about my dad, but life with him was never dull.

"No," he said now to Tracey, although he kept his eyes on me. Not squinting a bit, full and blue, just like my own. "We're doing just fine."

× × ×

Whenever my dad and I moved to a new town, the first thing we always did was go directly to the restaurant he'd been brought in to take over, and order a meal. We got the same appetizers each time: guacamole if it was a Mexican place, calamari for the Italian joints, and a simple green salad, regardless. My dad believed these to be the most basic of dishes, what anyplace worth its salt should do and do well, and as such they provided the baseline, the jumping-off point for whatever came next. Over time, they'd also became a gauge of how long I should expect us to be in the place we'd landed. Decent guac and somewhat crisp lettuce, I knew not to get too attached. Super rubbery squid, though, or greens edged with slimy black, and it was worth going out for a sport in

school, or maybe even joining a club or two, as we'd be staying a while.

After we ate, we'd pay our bill—tipping well, but not ex-
travagantly—before we went to find our rental place. Once
we'd unhitched the U-Haul, my dad would go back to the
restaurant to officially introduce himself, and I'd get to work
making us at home.

EAT INC, the restaurant conglomerate company my dad
worked for as a consultant, always found our houses for us. In
Westcott, the strip of a beach town in Florida we'd just left,
they'd rented us a sweet bungalow a block from the water, all
decorated in pinks and greens. There were plastic flamingos
everywhere: on the lawn, in the bathroom, strung up in tiny
lights across the mantel. Cheesy, but in an endearing way. Before that, in Petree, a suburb just outside Atlanta, we'd had
a converted loft in a high-rise inhabited mostly by bachelors
and businessmen. Everything was teak and dark, the furniture modern with sharp edges, and it was always quiet and
very cold. Maybe this had been so noticeable to me because of
our first place, in Montford Falls, a split-level on a cul-de-sac
populated entirely by families. There were bikes on every lawn
and little decorative flags flying from most porches: fat Santas
for Christmas, ruby hearts for Valentine's, raindrops and rain-
bows in spring. The cabal of moms—all in yoga pants, pushing
strollers as they power walked to meet the school bus in the
mornings and afternoons—studied us unabashedly from the
moment we arrived. They watched my dad come and go at his
weird hours and cast me sympathetic looks as I brought in our

groceries and mail. I'd known already, very well, that I was no longer part of what was considered a traditional family unit. But their stares confirmed it, just in case I'd missed the memo.

Everything was so different, that first move, that I didn't feel I had to be different as well. So the only thing I'd changed was my name, gently but firmly correcting my homeroom teacher on my first day of school. "Eliza," I told him. He glanced down at his roll sheet, then crossed out what was there and wrote this in. It was so easy. Just like that, in the hurried moments between announcements, I wrapped up and put away sixteen years of my life and was born again, all before first period even began.

I wasn't sure exactly what my dad thought of this. The first time someone called for Eliza, a few days later, he looked confused, even as I reached for the phone and he handed it over. But he never said anything. I knew he understood, in his own way. We'd both left the same town and same circumstances. He had to stay who he was, but I didn't doubt for a second that he would have changed if it had been an option.

As Eliza, I wasn't that different from who I'd been before. I'd inherited what my mother called her "corn-fed" looks—tall, strawberry blonde and blue-eyed—so I looked like the other popular girls at school. Add in the fact that I had nothing to lose, which gave me confidence, and I fell in easily with the jocks and rah-rahs, collecting friends quickly. It helped that everyone in Montford Falls had known each other forever: being new blood, even if you looked familiar, made you exotic, different. I liked this feeling so much that, when we moved to

Petree, our next place, I took it further, calling myself Lizbet and taking up with the drama mamas and dancers. I wore cut-off tights, black turtlenecks, and bright red lipstick, my hair pulled back into the tightest bun possible as I counted calories, took up cigarettes, and made everything Into A Production. It was different, for sure, but also exhausting. Which was probably why in Westcott, our most recent stop, I'd been more than happy to be Beth, student-council secretary and all-around joiner. I wrote for the school paper, served on yearbook, and tutored underachieving middle school kids. In my spare time, I organized car washes and bake sales to raise funds for the literary magazine, the debate team, the children in Honduras the Spanish club was hoping to build a rec center for. I was that girl, the one Everyone Knew, my face all over the yearbook. Which would make it that much more noticeable when I vanished from the next one.

The strangest thing about all of this was that, before, in my old life, I'd hadn't been any of these things: not a student leader or an actress or an athlete. There, I was just average, normal, unremarkable. Just Mclean.

That was my real name, my given name. Also, the name of the all-time winningest basketball coach of Defriese University, my parents' alma mater and my dad's favorite team of all time. To say he was a fan of Defriese basketball was an understatement, akin to saying the sun was simply a planet. He lived and breathed DB—as he and his fellow obsessives called it—and had since his own days of growing up just five miles outside campus. He went to Defriese basketball camp in the summer, knew stats for every team and player by heart, and wore a Defriese jersey in just about every school picture from kindergarten to senior year. The actual playing time on the team he eventually got over the course of two years of riding the bench as an alternate were the best fourteen minutes of his life, hands down.

Except, of course, he always added hurriedly, my birth. That was great, too. So great that there was really no question that I'd be named after Mclean Rich, his onetime coach and the man he most admired and respected. My mother, knowing resistance to this choice was futile, agreed only on the condition that I get a normal middle name—Elizabeth—which provided alternate options, should I decide I wanted them. I hadn't really ever expected that to be the case. But you can never predict everything.

Three years ago my parents, college sweethearts, were happily married and raising me, their only child. We lived in Tyler, the college town of which Defriese U was the epicenter, where we had a restaurant, Mariposa Grill. My dad was the head chef, my mom handled the business end and front of house, and I grew up sitting in the cramped office, coloring on invoices, or perched on a prep table in the kitchen, watching the line guys throw things into the fryer. We held DB season tickets in the nosebleed section, where my dad and I sat screaming our lungs out as the players scrambled around, antlike, way down below. I knew Defriese team stats the way other girls stored knowledge of Disney princesses: past and present players, shooting average of starters and second stringers, how many Ws Mclean Rich needed to make all time winningest. The day he did, my dad and I hugged each other, toasting with beer (him) and ginger ale (me) like proud family.

When Mclean Rich retired, we mourned, then worried over the candidates for his replacement, studying their careers and offensive strategies. We agreed that Peter Hamilton, who was young and enthusiastic with a great record, was the best choice, and attended his welcome pep rally with the highest of hopes. Hopes that seemed entirely warranted, in fact, when Peter Hamilton himself dropped into Mariposa one night and liked the food so much he wanted to use our private party room for a team banquet. My dad was in total DB heaven, with two of his greatest passions—basketball and the restaurant— finally aligned. It was great. Then my mom fell in love with Peter Hamilton, which was not.

It would have been bad enough if she'd left my dad for any-one. But to me and my dad, DB fanatics that we were, Peter Hamilton was a god. But idols fall, and sometimes they land right on you and leave you flattened. They destroy your family, shame you in the eyes of the town you love, and ruin the sport of basketball for you forever.

Even all this time later, it still seemed impossible that she'd done it, the very act and fact still capable of unexpect-edly knocking the wind out of me at random moments. In the first few shaky, strange weeks after my parents sat me down and told me they were separating, I kept combing back through the last year, trying to figure out how this could have happened. I mean, yes, the restaurant was struggling, and I knew there had been tension between them about that. And

I could vouch for the fact that my mom was always saying my dad didn't spend enough time with us, which he pointed out would be much easier once we were living in a cardboard box on the side of the road. But all families had those kinds of arguments, didn't they? It didn't mean it was okay to run off with another man. Especially the coach of your husband and daughter's favorite team.

The one person who had the answers to these questions, though, wasn't talking. At least, not as much as I wanted her to. Maybe I should have expected this, as my mom had never been the touchy-feely, super-confessional type. But the few times when I tried to broach the million-dollar question— why?—in the shaky early days of the separation and the still not-quite-stable ones that followed, she just wouldn't tell me what I wanted to hear. Instead, her party line was one sentence: "What happens in a marriage is between the two people within it. Your father and both love you very much. That will never change." The first few times, this was said to me with sadness. Then, it took on a hint of annoyance. When her tone became sharp, I stopped asking questions.

HAMILTON HOMEWRECKER! screamed the sports blogs. I'LL TAKE YOUR WIFE, PLEASE. Funny how the headlines could be so cute, when the truth was downright ugly. And how weird, for me, that this thing that had always been part of my life— where my very name had come from—was now, literally, part of my *life*. It was like loving a movie, knowing every frame, and then suddenly finding yourself right inside of it. But it's not a romance or a comedy anymore, just your worst freaking nightmare.

Of course everyone was talking. The neighbors, the sports-writers, the kids at my school. They were probably still talk-ing, three years and twin little Hamiltons later, but thankfully, I was not around to hear it. I'd left them there, with Mclean, when my dad and I hitched a U-Haul to our old Land Rover and headed to Montford Falls. And Petree. And Westcott. And now, here.

x   x   x

It was the first thing I saw when we pulled in the driveway of our new rental house. Not the crisp white paint, the cheerful green trim, or the wide welcoming porch. I didn't even notice, initially, the houses on either side, similar in size and style, one with a carefully manicured lawn, the walk lined with neat shrubs, the other with cars parked in the yard, empty red plas-tic cups scattered around them. Instead, there was just this, sitting at the very end of the drive, waiting to welcome us per-sonally.

We pulled right up to it, neither of us saying anything. Then my dad cut the engine, and we both leaned forward, looking up through the windshield as it loomed above us.

A basketball goal. Of course. Sometimes life is just hilari-ous.

For a moment, we both just stared. Then my dad dropped his hand from the ignition. "Let's get unpacked," he said, and pushed his door open. I did the same, following him back to the U-haul. But I swear it was like I could feel it watching me as I pulled out my suitcase and carried it up the steps.

The house was cute, small but really cozy, and had clearly been renovated recently. The kitchen appliances looked new, and there were no tack or nail marks on the walls. My dad headed back outside, still unloading, while I gave myself a quick tour, getting my bearings. Cable already installed, and wireless: that was good. I had my own bathroom: even better. And from the looks of it, we were an easy walking distance from downtown, which meant less transportation hassle than the last place. I was actually feeling good about things, basketball reminders aside, at least until I stepped out onto the back porch and found someone stretched out there on a stack of patio furniture cushions.

I literally shrieked, the sound high-pitched and so girly I probably would have been embarrassed if I wasn't so startled. The person on the cushions was equally surprised, though, at least judging by the way he jumped, turning around to look at me as I scrambled back through the open door behind me, grabbing for the knob so I could shut it between us. As I flipped the dead bolt, my heart still pounding, I was able to put together that it was a guy in jeans and long hair, wearing a faded flannel shirt, beat-up Adidas on his feet. He'd been reading a book, something thick, when I interrupted him.

Now, as I watched, he sat up, putting it down beside him. He brushed back his hair, messy and black and kind of curly, then picked up a jacket he'd had balled up under his head, shaking it out. It was faded corduroy, with some kind of insignia on the front, and I stood there watching as he slipped it on, calm as you please, before getting to his feet and picking up whatever he'd been reading, which I now saw was a textbook of some kind. Then he pushed his hair back with one hand

and turned, looking right at me through the glass of the door between us. *Sorry,* he mouthed. Sorry.

"Mclean," my dad yelled from the foyer, his voice echoing down the empty hall. "I've got your laptop. You want me to put it in your room?"

I just stood there, frozen, staring at the guy. His eyes were bright blue, his face winter pale but red-cheeked. I was still trying to decide if I should scream for help when he smiled at me and gave me a weird little salute, touching his fingers to his temple. Then he turned and pushed out the screen door into the yard. He ambled across the deck, under the basketball goal, and over to the fence of the house next door, which he jumped with what, to me, was a surprising amount of grace. As he walked up the side steps, the kitchen door opened. The last thing I saw was him squaring his shoulders, like he was bracing for something, before disappearing inside.

"Mclean?" my dad called again. He was coming closer now, his footsteps echoing. When he saw me, he held up my laptop case. "Know where you want this?"

I looked back at the house next door that the guy had just gone into, wondering what his story was. You didn't hang out in what you thought was an empty house when you lived right next door unless you didn't feel like being at home. And it was his home, that much was clear. You could just tell when a person belonged somewhere. That is something you can't fake, no matter how hard you try.

"Thanks," I said to my dad, turning to face him. "Just put it anywhere."

"Dessen's best since *This Lullaby* . . . it will captivate all readers."   —*VOYA*

★ "All the Dessen trademarks are here—the swoon-worthy boy next door who is not what he appears to be; and the supporting characters who force Ruby to rethink her cynical worldview."   —*Publishers Weekly*, starred review

"Dessen weaves a sometimes funny, mostly emotional, and very satisfying story."   —*VOYA*

"Characterization and dialogue are expertly done, and Owen's anger-management advice and efforts to broaden Annabel's music tastes ("Don't think, or judge. Just Listen") strengthen the theme of the story: honesty."

—*Booklist*

AN ALA BEST BOOK FOR YOUNG ADULTS

New York Times BEST-SELLING AUTHOR
Sarah Dessen

the truth about forever

"Dessen gracefully balances comedy with tragedy and introduces a complex heroine worth getting to know."
—*Publishers Weekly*

"Grief, fear, and love set the novel's pace, and Macy's crescendo from time-bomb perfection to fallible, emotional humanity is, for the right readers, as gripping as any action adventure."
—*SLJ*

AN ALA/YALSA TEEN'S TOP TEN PICK